I0643284

NO LIFE
OF THEIR OWN

NO LIFE
OF THEIR OWN
AND OTHER STORIES

The Complete Short Fiction
of Clifford D. Simak,
Volume Five

Introduction by David W. Wixon

OPEN ROAD
INTEGRATED MEDIA
NEW YORK

All rights reserved, including without limitation the right to reproduce this book or any portion thereof in any form or by any means, whether electronic or mechanical, now known or hereinafter invented, without the express written permission of the publisher.

These are works of fiction. Names, characters, places, events, and incidents either are the product of the author's imagination or are used fictitiously. Any resemblance to actual persons, living or dead, businesses, companies, events, or locales is entirely coincidental.

Copyright © 2016 the Estate of Clifford D. Simak

All stories reprinted by permission of the Estate of Clifford D. Simak.

"No Life of Their Own" © 1959 by Galaxy Publishing Corp. © 1987 by Clifford D. Simak. Originally published in Galaxy Magazine, v. 17, no. 6, August, 1959.

"Spaceship in a Flask" © 1941 by Street & Smith Publications, Inc. © 1969 by Clifford D. Simak. Originally published in Astounding Science Fiction, v. 27, no. 5, July, 1941.

"The Loot of Time" © 1938 by Better Publications, Inc. © 1966 by Clifford D. Simak. Originally published in Thrilling Wonder Stories, v. 12, no. 3, December, 1938.

"Huddling Place" © 1944 by Street & Smith Publications, Inc. © 1972 by Clifford D. Simak. Originally published in Astounding Science Fiction, v. 33, no. 5, July, 1944.

"To Walk a City's Street" © 1972 by Lancer Books, Inc. © 2000 by the Estate of Clifford D. Simak. Originally published in Infinity Three.

"Cactus Colts" © 1944 by Real Adventures Publishing Co., Inc. © 1972 by Clifford D. Simak. Originally published in Lariat Story Magazine, v. 14, no. 2, July, 1944.

"Message from Mars" © 1943 by Love Romances Publishing Co., Inc. © 1971 by Clifford D. Simak. Originally published in Planet Stories, v. 2, no. 4, Fall, 1943.

"Party Line" © 1978 by Charter Communications, Inc. Originally published in Destinies, v. 1, no. 1, Nov./Dec., 1978.

"A Hero Must Not Die" © 1943 by Columbia Publications, Inc. © 1971 by Clifford D. Simak. Originally published in Sky Raiders, v. 1, no. 4, June, 1943.

"The Space Beasts" © 1940 by Fictioneers, Inc. © 1968 by Clifford D. Simak. Originally published in Astonishing Stories, v. 1, no. 2, April, 1940.

"Contraption" © 1953 by Ballantine Books, Inc. © 1981 by Clifford D. Simak. Originally published in Star Science Fiction Stories, no. 1, ed. by Frederik Pohl.

"The Whistling Well" © 1980 by Clifford D. Simak. Originally published in Dark Forces, ed. by Kirby McCauley, Viking Press, 1980.

Introduction copyright © 2015 by David W. Wixon

Cover design by Jason Gabbert

978-1-5040-6033-2

Published in 2020 by Open Road Integrated Media, Inc.
180 Maiden Lane
New York, NY 10038
www.openroadmedia.com

CONTENTS

INTRODUCTION:
CLIFFORD SIMAK'S COUNTRY

*"A cawing crow skimmed over a distant ridge and slanted down into
the valley shadow. From far away, down the river, came the quacking
of a flock of mallards."*

—*Clifford D. Simak, in "Census"*

On numerous occasions during the last decades of his life, Clifford D. Simak was described, often with admiration but sometimes with just a tinge of disdain, by such phrases as "the pastoral voice of science fiction" or "the poet of rural space." He was not put off by such language; he interpreted it as recognition of his love for the land in which he grew up and the people who lived there and in other similar locations. He believed that he came from a special place, and he was right.

The work of some writers is so distinctive that a discerning and experienced reader can sometimes name the author even if no name is attached to a particular story, but it can be harder to pin down exactly what distinctive trait is being recognized: Is it plot, or theme, or tone? Is it something about the characters, or even the "purple"-ness, or lack thereof, of the prose?

But when you're asking questions like that about Clifford D. Simak, you'll find that most knowledgeable critics—or even many casual readers—point, immediately and without hesitation, to the settings of his stories: settings that, over the decades, caused him to be described in the phrases noted above. And many of those readers use the phrase *Simak Country* as a shorthand for these settings.

Nonetheless, many would be surprised to learn how often Cliff Simak's stories were *not* set in Simak Country. For every "Big Front Yard," for example, there was a "Limiting Factor"; for every "No Life of Their Own," a "Construction Shack."

So what exactly do we mean when we refer to "Simak Country"? When I say that Clifford D. Simak was born on a farm on the south side of the Wisconsin River, not far from where that stream meets the Mississippi, some will think that means he was raised on the flat Midwestern prairies. But that's not true.

One could attempt to figure out exactly how many of Cliff Simak's stories could be characterized as taking place in Simak Country, but that would require closely reading all of those stories and deciding what characteristics place a story into that category. For "Simak Country" is an ephemeral place, one of the mind and of attitude, and stories that never mention Wisconsin or the little town of Millville may nevertheless take place there. In fact, even stories set on other planets sometimes have a touch of "Simak Country," for example, when a character remembers growing up on a chicken farm back on Earth. That mere mention tells the reader something about the person.

"Brother" is clearly set in Simak Country: Edward Lambert's memories of his life on the family farm paint a place similar to the Simak family farm. And the mention that Lambert can see ships landing at the spaceport on the Iowa bluffs is enough to situate the Lambert's farm in extreme western Wisconsin. "The Ghost of a Model T," with its loving descriptions of country dance halls and old roads climbing the sides of ridges, fits the category. And the novel *Time Is the Simplest Thing* is also set in Simak Country. Although it starts in Mexico, the climax takes place along the Missouri River in South Dakota, where there is a little village set above the river, and a people set apart from the majority.

Consider the landscape into which Cliff was born.

Clifford Simak himself occasionally spoke of his land as a unique and special place. At one point, he described it as "an incredibly ancient land." And, indeed, his land had an unusual history, one that geologists recognize as part of a geological anomaly known as the "Driftless Area," so named because it largely lacked the "drifts" of material—ranging from gravel to gigantic boulders—generally left behind by retreating or melting glaciers. And that was because the Driftless Area—which encompasses a large chunk of southwestern and central Wisconsin as well as smaller portions of northwestern Illinois, northeastern Iowa, and southeastern Minnesota—did not get covered by ice during the most recent glaciation, even though lobes of ice almost surrounded it. (This is not to say that glaciers never covered Cliff's land, but it was spared the most recent encroachment.)

For that reason, the land largely retained the shape predating that most recent Ice Age; it was not ground down by the weight of moving ice, nor buried by mounds of gravel. Its only changes were a result of the slow actions of wind, rain, and the rivers.

Today, that terrain consists of ridges cut by the small valleys created by streams making their way to larger rivers such as the Wisconsin, and the combination creates a complex pattern of steep-sided branching valleys. Roads crossing the area often have to twist and curve, using switchbacks to make the steep climb from the deep valley bottoms to the ridge tops, only to face the choice of either following the ridge top, or descending into the next valley. For a long time, people living in those areas found it difficult to travel. Moreover, the land was thickly wooded, so that farms had to be literally chopped out of the forest. (Starting a farm on virgin prairie was not easy—the sod was difficult for the first plows to break through, which led to the term *sodbuster*—but it is at least arguable that having to cut down a small forest was worse.)

Knowing that, we can reasonably say that Simak stories set on or near the lower reaches of the Wisconsin River—or in similar rural settings, even if there's no mention of the Wisconsin—are set in "Simak Country." Look for such clues as mentions of Platteville limestone, a creek whose waters gurgle over stony shallows before swirling into a deeper pool, little hidden valleys ("hollows"), lilacs, deep ravines, narrow ridge-top roads, obscure paths vanishing among the trees . . .

And yet, having laid out for you some images to look for if you want to recognize "Simak Country," I must add that these physical things alone are not required. Cliff himself once said that his country "was not only a physical environment, but psychological as well." While any similar setting can be called "Simak Country" regardless of where it might be, the truth is that the most important trait that makes a place part of Simak Country is the character, the manners, of the people. Any country, after all, is best described through the character of its people.

The portrayal of such people was how Clifford Simak tried to make the people who populated his stories *ordinary*. Despite what he sometimes did to sell his fiction, he did not want to tell stories about heroes—once, when someone told him that his characters were often losers, his reply was simply that "I *like* losers!"

David W. Wixon

NO LIFE OF THEIR OWN

This story was, I believe, sent to Horace Gold in late November 1958, under the title "Rabbit's Feet, Inc." Originally published in the August 1959 issue of Galaxy Magazine, *this is yet another story about aliens coming to live and work on Earth—and the most fantastic element in the entire piece is that the Earthians accept them.*

I can't help thinking of the story as "Huck Finn meets the aliens."
—dww

Ma and Pa were fighting again, not really mad at one another, but arguing pretty loud. They had been at it, off and on, for weeks.

"We just can't up and *leave!*" said Ma. "We have to think it out. We can't pull up and leave a place we've lived in all our lives without *some* thinking on it!"

"I *have* thought on it!" Pa said. "I've thought on it a *lot!* All these aliens moving in. There was a brood of new ones moved onto the Pierce place just a day or two ago."

"How do you know," asked Ma, "that you'll like one of the Homestead Planets once you settle on it? It might be worse than Earth."

"We can't be any more unlucky there than we been right here! There ain't *anything* gone right. I don't mind telling you I am plumb discouraged."

And Pa sure-God was right about how unlucky we had been. The tomato crop had failed and two of the cows had died and a bear had robbed the bees and busted up the hives and the tractor had broken down and cost $78.90 to get fixed.

"Everyone has some bad luck," Ma argued. "You'd have it no matter where you go."

"Andy Carter doesn't have bad luck!" yelled Pa. "I don't know how he does it, but everything he does, it turns out to a hair. He could fall down in a puddle and come up dripping diamonds!"

"I don't know," said Ma philosophically. "We got enough to eat and clothes to cover us and a roof above our head. Maybe that's as much as anyone can expect these days."

"It ain't enough," Pa said. "A man shouldn't be content to just scrape along. I lay awake at night to figure out how I can manage better. I've laid out plans that should by rights have worked. But they never did. Like the time we tried that new adapted pea from Mars down on the bottom forty. It was sandy soil and they should have grown there. They ain't worth a damn on any land that will grow another thing. And that land was worthless; it should have been just right for those Martian peas. But I ask you, did they grow there?"

"No," said Ma, "now that I recollect, they didn't."

"And the next year, what happens? Andy Carter plants the same kind of peas just across the fence from where I tried to grow them. Same kind of land and all. And Andy gets bow-legged hauling those peas home."

What Pa said was true. He was a better farmer than Andy Carter could ever hope to be. And he was smarter, too. But let Pa try a thing and bad luck would beat him out. Let Andy try the same and it always went right.

And it wasn't Pa alone. It was the entire neighborhood. Everybody was just plain unlucky, except Andy Carter.

"I tell you," Pa swore, "just one more piece of bad luck and we'll throw in our hand and start over somewhere fresh. And the Homestead Planets seem the best to me. Why, you take . . ."

I didn't wait to hear any more. I knew it would go on the way it always had. So I snuck out without their seeing me and went down the road, and as I walked along, I worried that maybe one of these days they might make up their mind to move to one of the Homestead Planets. There had been an awful lot of our old neighbors who'd done exactly that.

It might be all right to emigrate, of course, but whenever I thought about it, I got a funny feeling at the thought of leaving Earth. Those other planets were so awful far away, one wouldn't have much chance of getting back again if he didn't like them. And all my friends were right in the neighborhood, and they were pretty good friends even if they were all aliens.

I got a little start when I thought of that. It was the first time it had occurred to me that they were all aliens. I had so much fun with them, I'd never thought of it.

It seemed a little queer to me that Ma and Pa should be talking about leaving Earth when all the farms that had been sold in our neighborhood had been bought up by aliens. The Homestead Planets weren't open to the aliens and that might be the reason they came to Earth. If they'd had a choice, maybe they would have gone to one of the Homesteads instead of settling down on Earth.

I walked past the Carter place and saw that the trees in the orchard were loaded down with fruit and I figured that some of us could sneak in and steal some of it when it got ripe. But we'd have to be careful, because Andy Carter was a stinker, and his hired man, Ozzie Burns, wasn't one bit better. I remembered the time we had been stealing watermelons and Andy had found us at it and I'd got caught in a barbed-wire fence when we ran away. Andy had walloped me, which was all right. But there'd been no call for him going to Pa and collecting seven dollars for the few melons we had stolen. Pa had paid up and then he'd walloped me again, worse than Andy did.

And after it was over, Pa had said bitterly that Andy was no great shakes of a neighbor. And Pa was right. He wasn't.

I got down to the old Adams place and Fancy Pants was out in the yard, just floating there and bouncing that old basketball of his.

We call him Fancy Pants because we can't pronounce his name. Some of these alien people have very funny names.

Fancy Pants was all dressed up as usual. He always is dressed up because he never gets the least bit dirty when he plays. Ma is always asking me why I can't keep neat and clean like Fancy Pants. I tell her it would be easy if I could float along like him and never had to walk, and if I could throw mudballs like him without touching them.

This Sunday morning he was dressed up in a sky-blue shirt that looked like silk, and red britches that looked as if they might be velvet, and he had a green bow tied around his yellow curls that floated in the breeze. At first glance, Fancy Pants looked something like a girl—but you better never say so, because he'd mop up the road with you. He did with me the first time I saw him. He didn't even lay a hand on me while he was doing it, but sat up there, cross-legged, about three feet off the ground, smiling that sweet smile of his on his ugly face, and with his yellow curls floating in the breeze. And the worst of it was that I couldn't get back at him.

But that was long ago and we were good friends now.

We played catch for a while, but it wasn't too much fun.

Then Fancy Pants' Pa came out of the house and he was glad to see me, too. He asked about the folks and wanted to know if the tractor was all right, now that we'd got it fixed. I answered him politely because I'm a little scared of Fancy Pants' Pa.

He is sort of spooky—not the way he looks, the way he does things. From the looks of him, he wasn't meant to be a farmer, but he does all right at it. He doesn't use a plow to plow a field. He just sits cross-legged in the air and floats up and down the field, and when he passes over a strip of ground, that strip of ground is plowed—and not only plowed, but raked and harrowed until it is as fine as face powder. He does all his work that way. There aren't any weeds in any of his crops, for he just sails up and down the rows and the weeds come out slick and clean, with the roots intact, to lie on the ground and wither.

It doesn't take too much imagination to see what a guy like that could do if he ever caught a kid in any sort of mischief, so all of us are thoughtful and polite whenever he's around.

So I told him how we'd got the tractor all fixed up and about the bear busting up the bee hives. Then I asked him about his time machine and he shook his head real sad.

"I don't know what's the matter, Steve," he said. "I put things into it and they disappear, and I should find them later, but I never have. If I'm moving them in time, I'm perhaps pushing them too far."

He would have told me more about his time machine, but there was an interruption.

While we had been talking, Fancy Pants' Pa and me, the Fancy Pants dog had run a cat up a maple tree. That is the normal situation for any cat and dog—unless Fancy Pants is around.

For Fancy Pants wasn't one to leave a situation normal. He reached up into the tree—well, he didn't reach up with his hands, of course, but with whatever he reaches with—and he nailed this cat and sort of bundled it up so it couldn't move and brought it down to the ground.

Then he held the dog so the dog couldn't do more than twitch and he put that bundled-up cat down in front of the twitching dog, then let them loose with split-second timing.

The two of them exploded into a blur of motion, with the weirdest uproar you ever heard. The cat made it to the tree in the fastest time and nearly took off the bark swarming up the trunk. And the dog miscalculated and failed to put on his brakes in time and banged smack into the tree spread-eagled.

The cat by this time was up in the highest branches, hanging on and screaming, while the dog walked around in circles, acting kind of stunned.

Fancy Pants' Pa broke off what he was saying to me and he looked at Fancy Pants. He didn't do or say a thing, but when he looked at Fancy Pants, Fancy Pants grew terribly pale and sort of wilted down.

"Let that teach you," said Fancy Pants' Pa, "to leave those animals alone. You don't see Steve here or Nature Boy mistreating them that way, do you?"

"No, sir," mumbled Fancy Pants.

"And now get along, the two of you. You have things to do."

I got this to say for Fancy Pants' Pa: he gives Fancy Pants his lickings, or whatever they may be, and then he forgets about it. He doesn't keep harping at it for the rest of the day.

So Fancy Pants and me went down the road, me shuffling along, kicking up the dust, and Fancy Pants floating along beside me.

We got down to Nature Boy's place and he was waiting out in front. I knew he had been hoping someone would come along. There were a couple of sparrows sitting on his shoulder and a rabbit hopping all around him and a chipmunk in the pocket of his pants, looking out at us with bright and beady eyes.

Nature Boy and I sat down underneath a tree and Fancy Pants came as close as he ever does to sitting down—floating about three inches off the ground—and we talked about what we ought to do. Trouble was, there wasn't really anything that needed any doing. So we sat there and talked and tossed pebbles and pulled stems of grass and put them in our mouths and chewed them, while Nature Boy's pet wild things gamboled all around us and didn't seem to be afraid at all. Except that they were a little leery of Fancy Pants. He is, when you come right down to it, a sort of sneaky rascal. Me they are fast friends with when I'm with Nature Boy, but let me meet them when I am alone and they keep their distance.

I can see how wild things might take to Nature Boy. He is fur all over, real sleek, glossy fur, and he wears nothing but that little pair of pants. Turn him loose without those pants and someone would be bound to take a shot at him.

So we sat there wondering what to do. Then I remembered that Pa had said a new family had moved onto the Pierce place and we decided to go down and see if they had any kids.

We went down the road to the old Pierce place and it turned out there was one just about our age. He was a sort of runty little kid, with a peaked face and big round eyes and kind of eager look about him, like a stunted hoot owl.

He told us his name and it was even worse than Nature Boy's and Fancy Pants' names, so we had a vote on it and decided we would call him Butch. That suited him just fine.

Then he called out his family and they stood in a row, like a bunch of solemn, runty owls roosting on a limb, while he introduced them. There was his Ma and Pa and a little brother and a kid sister almost as big as he was. The rest of them went back into the house, but Butch's Pa squatted down and began to talk with us.

You could see from the way he talked that he was a little scared of this farming business. He admitted he really was no farmer, but an optical worker, and explained to us that an optical worker designed lenses and ground them. But, he said, there was no future in a job like that back on his old home planet. He told us how glad he was to be on Earth and how he wanted to be a good citizen and a good neighbor, and a lot of other things like that.

When he started to run down, we got away from him. There ain't anything more embarrassing than a crazy adult who likes to talk with kids.

We decided that maybe we should show Butch around a bit and let him in on some of the things we had been doing.

So we struck off down Dark Hollow and we didn't make much time because all of these friends of Nature Boy were popping out to join him. Before very long, we were a sort of traveling menagerie—rabbits and chipmunks and a gopher or two and a couple of raccoons.

I like Nature Boy, of course, and I've had some good times with him, but he has spoiled a lot of fun as well. Before he showed up in the neighborhood, I did a lot of fishing and hunting, but that is all spoiled now. I can't shoot a squirrel or catch a fish without wondering if it is a friend of Nature Boy's.

After a while, we got down to the creek bed where we were digging out the lizard. We'd been at it all summer long and we hadn't uncovered very much of him, but we still figured that some day we might get him all dug out.

You understand that it wasn't a live lizard we were digging out, but a lizard that had turned to stone a zillion years ago.

There is a place where the stream runs down a limestone ledge and the limestone lies in layers. The lizard was between two of those layers. We'd got four or five feet of his tail uncovered. But the digging was getting harder, for we were working back into the limestone ledge and there was more of it to move.

Fancy Pants floated up above the limestone ledge and got himself set as solid as he could. Sitting there, he hit that limestone ledge a tremendous whack, being very careful not to crack the lizard. It was one of his better whacks, busting up a lot of stone, and while Fancy Pants rested up to take another one, the three of us piled in and threw out the busted rock.

But there was one big piece he had loosened up that we couldn't move.

"Hit it just a tap," I told him. "Break it up a little and we can get it out."

"I got it loose," he said. "It's up to you to get it out."

There was no sense arguing with him. So the three of us wrestled at the rock, but we couldn't budge it and Fancy Pants sat up there, fat and sassy, taking it easy and enjoying himself.

"You ought to have a crowbar," he told us. "If you had a crowbar, you could pry that rock out."

I was getting sick and tired of Fancy Pants, and so, just to get away from him for a while, I said I'd go and fetch a crowbar. And this new kid, Butch, said he'd go along with me.

So we left Nature Boy and Fancy Pants and climbed up to the road and started out for my place. We didn't hurry any. It would serve Fancy Pants right if he had to wait, and Nature Boy as well, for all his showing off with his animals.

We walked along the road and talked. Butch told me about the planet he had come from and it sure was a poor-mouth place, and I told him about the neighborhood, and we were getting to be friends.

We reached the Carter place and were walking past the orchard when Butch stopped dead in the middle of the road and went sort of stiff, like a hunting dog will go when he scents a bird.

I was walking right behind him and I bumped into him, but he just stood there with those eager eyes agleam and his entire body tense—so tense it seemed to quiver when it really didn't.

"What's going on?" I asked.

He kept on looking at something in the orchard. I took a look where he was looking and I couldn't see a thing.

Then he turned around like a flash and jumped the fence on the downhill side of the road and went lickety-split down across the field opposite the orchard. I jumped the fence and ran after him and caught him just before he reached the woods. I grabbed him by the shoulder and spun him around to face me. it wasn't hard to do, he was such a spindly kid.

"What's the matter with you?" I hollered. "Where do you think you're going?"

"Home to get my gun!"

"Your *gun?* What for?"

"There's a whole bunch of them up there! We have to clean them out!"

He must have seen I didn't understand.

"Don't tell me," he said, "that you didn't see them?"

I shook my head. "There wasn't anything there."

"They're there, all right," he said. "Maybe you can't see them. Maybe you're like old folks."

There's no one who can accuse me of a thing like that. I doubled up my fist and poked it underneath his nose. He hurried up to explain.

"They're things that only kids can see. And they bring bad luck. You can't leave them around or you'll have bad luck all the time."

I didn't believe it right away. But after all the things I'd seen done by Nature Boy and Fancy Pants, you don't ever catch me saying straight out that a thing's impossible.

And after I'd thought it over for a minute, it made a silly sort of sense. For the folks certainly had been plagued by hard luck for a long time now and it didn't stand to reason that luck should be all bad and never any good unless there was something making it that way.

And it wasn't the folks alone, but all the other neighbors—all of them, of course, except Andy Carter, and Andy Carter was too mean to be bothered by bad luck.

We were, I thought, sure a hard-luck neighborhood.

"All right," I said to Butch. "Let's go and get that gun."

And I was thinking even as I said it that it must be a funny kind of gun that would shoot a thing one couldn't even see.

We made it back to the old Pierce place in almost no time at all. Butch's Pa was sitting out underneath a tree, feeling sorry for himself. Butch came up to him and started jabbering and I couldn't understand a word.

His Pa listened to him for a while and then broke in. "You should talk this planet's language, son. It is most impolite to do otherwise. And you want to become a good citizen of this great and glorious planet, I am sure, and there's no better way to do it than to talk its language and observe its customs and try to live the way its people do."

I'll say this much for him: Butch's Pa sure knew how to fling around the words.

"Is it true, mister," I asked him, "that these things can bring bad luck?"

"Most assuredly," said Butch's Pa. "Back on our old home planet, we know them well."

"Pa," asked Butch, "should I get my gun?"

"Now I don't know," said his Pa. "It's something we have to give some study. Back on our home planet, there would be no question of it. But this is a different planet and it may have different ways. It may be that the man who has these creatures would object to your shooting them."

"But there isn't anyone really got them," I declared. "How can you have a thing when you can't even see it?"

"I was thinking about the gentleman in whose orchard they appeared."

"You mean Andy Carter. He doesn't know anything about them."

"That does not matter," said Butch's Pa, with a great deal of righteousness. "It becomes, it would seem to me, a quite deep problem in ethics. On our home planet, no man would want these things; he'd be ashamed to have them. But here it might be different. They bring good luck, you see, to the ones that they adopt."

"You mean they bring good luck to Andy?" I asked him. "But I thought you said that they brought bad luck."

"So they do," said Butch's Pa, "except to the ones that they adopt. To them they bring good luck, but bad luck to all the others. For it is an axiom that fortune for one man is misfortune for the rest. That is why we do not let them adopt any of us on our home planet."

"You think they have adopted Andy and that's why he has good luck?"

"You are most correct," said Butch's Pa. "You have admirably grasped the concept."

"Well, gee, why don't we just go in and shoot them?"

"This Carter gentleman would not object to your doing so?"

"Of course he would, but that's what you would expect of him. He'd probably run us off the place before we got the job half done, but we could sneak back again . . ."

"No," Butch's Pa said flat out.

He was an awful stickler for doing the right thing, Butch's Pa was—bound and determined he wasn't going to get caught off base doing something wrong.

"That is not the way to do," he said. "It is most unethical. You think that if this Carter knew he had these things, he would want to keep them?"

"I am sure he would. He doesn't care for anybody but himself."

Butch's Pa heaved a big sigh and crawled to his feet. "Young man, would your father be at home?"

"He most likely would."

"We'll go and talk with him," he said. "He is a native of this planet and an honest man and he will tell us what is right."

"Mister," I asked him, "what do you call these things?"

"We have a name for them, but it does not translate into your tongue with anything like ease. We call them something that is neither here nor there, something that is halfway between. Half-ling would be the word for it, if there is such a word."

"I don't know if there is or not," I said, "but it sounds right."

"Then," decided Butch's Pa, "for sheer convenience we shall call them that."

—

At first, Pa was as flabbergasted as I was, but the more he listened to Butch's Pa and the more he thought about it, the more he seemed to become convinced there might be something to it.

"There sure-God has been something causing all this hard luck of ours," he declared. "A man can't turn his hand to a thing but it goes wrong on him. And I must admit that it makes a man sore to have all these things happen to him and then look at Carter and see all the good luck he has."

"I am profoundly sorry," said Butch's Pa, "to discover halflings exist on this planet. There were many on our old home planet and on some of the neighboring worlds, but I had no idea they had spread this far."

"What I don't rightly understand," said Pa, lighting up his pipe and settling down to hash the matter over, "is how they can be here and a man not see them."

"There is a most precise scientific explanation, but I have not the language to translate it. You might say that they are off-phase of this existence, but still not quite into it. The child eye is undulled, the mind unclosed, so that they can see somewhat, a fraction, just a little, beyond reality. And that is why they can be seen by children but are invisible to adults. I, in my time, when I was a child, saw and killed my share of them. You understand, sir, that on my planet, it is an accepted childish chore to be eternally on watch for them and vigilantly keep their numbers down."

Pa asked me: "You didn't see these things?"

"No, Pa," I said, "I didn't."

"And you didn't see them, either?" Pa asked Butch's Pa.

"I lost my ability to see them many years ago," said Butch's Pa. "So far as your boy is concerned, it may be that only the children of certain races—"

"But they must see us," Pa insisted. "Otherwise, how would they be able to bring good luck or bad?"

"They do see us. In that, all are agreed. I assure you that the scientists of my planet have devoted many long and arduous years to the study of these beings."

"And another thing. What is their purpose in adopting people? What do they get out of it? Why should they show all this favoritism?"

"We are not sure," said Butch's Pa. "There are several theories. One is that they have no life of their own, but must have a pattern in order to live. If they did not have a pattern, they would have no form nor senses and probably no perception. They are, it would seem, like parasites in many ways."

But Pa interrupted him. Pa was all wound up and had a lot of thinking that he had to do out loud.

"I don't suppose," he said, "that they are doing it just for the hell of it. There must be a solid reason—there is to everything. It seems reasonable to me that everything is planned, that there's nothing without purpose. There's nothing, when you get right down to it, that basically is bad. Maybe these things, with the bad luck that they bring, are part of a plan to make folks face up to adversity and develop character."

I swear it was the first time I had ever heard Pa sound like a preacher, but he sure did then.

"You may be right," said Butch's Pa. "There is no agreement entirely on the reason for their being."

"They might," suggested Pa, "be a sort of gypsy tribe, just wandering around. They might up and move away."

Butch's Pa sadly shook his head. "It almost never happens, sir, that they move away."

"When I was a kid, I once went to the city with my Ma. I don't remember much about it, but I do remember standing in front of a great big window that was filled with toys and knowing that I could never have any one of them, and wishing hard that some day I might have just one of them. Maybe that's the way it is with these folks. Maybe they're just outside the window looking in on us."

"Your analogy is exceedingly picturesque," said Butch's Pa with forthright admiration.

"But here I am running on," Pa said, "as if I took for gospel every word of it. I don't wish for the world to doubt you or what you told us . . ."

"But you do and I cannot find it in my breast to blame you. Would you, perhaps, believe more readily if your son could tell you that he saw them?"

"Why, yes," Pa said thoughtfully. "I surely would."

"Before I came to Earth, I was a worker in the field of optics, and it may be possible that I can grind a set of lenses that would allow your son to see halflings. I am not sure he could, of course, but it is a chance worth taking. He is of the age to have still that ability to peer beyond reality. It may be that all his vision needs is a slight correction."

"If you could do that, if Steve here could really see these things, then I would believe you without the slightest question."

"I'll get on with it immediately," said Butch's Pa. "Later on, we can discuss the ethics of the situation."

Pa sat watching Butch and his Pa going down the road, and he sort of shuddered. "Some of these aliens sure-God come up with queer ideas. A man has got to watch himself or he might swallow some of them."

"These ones are all right," I told him.

Pa sat there thinking and I could almost see the wheels whirring in his brain. "I don't know too much about it, but the more one thinks about it, the more sense it makes. It seems reasonable to me that there might be just so much good luck and so much bad luck, and ordinarily both the good and the bad would be handed out in somewhat equal parts. But suppose something came along and corralled all the good luck for one particular man, then there ain't anything but bad luck left for the rest."

I wished that I could see it as clear as Pa. But the more I thought, the more like Greek it seemed.

"Maybe," said Pa, "when you get to the root of it, it's nothing more than simple competition. What is good luck for one man is bad luck for another. Say there is a job that everybody wants. One man gets it and that's good luck for him, but bad luck for the others. And say that this bear back in the woods just had to raid a hive. It would be bad luck for the man whose hive was raided, but good luck—or at least not bad luck—for the man whose hive the bear passed up. And say again that someone's tractor had to get busted . . ."

Pa went on like that for quite a while, but I don't think he even fooled himself. Both of us knew, I guess, that there would have to be more to it than that.

Fancy Pants and Nature Boy were sore at me for not coming back with the crowbar. They said I stood them up and I had to explain to them I hadn't and I had to tell them exactly what had happened before they would believe me. I suppose it might have been better if I had kept my mouth shut, but in the end I don't believe it made much difference.

Anyhow, we got to be friends again and we all liked Butch, so we had good times together. The other two kidded Butch a lot about the halflings at first, but Butch didn't seem to mind, so they gave it up.

We certainly had a good time that summer. There was the lizard and a lot of other things as well, including the family of skunks that fell in love with Nature Boy and followed him around. And there was the time Fancy Pants hauled all of Carter's machinery out into the back forty, with Andy hunting for it like lost cows and madder by the minute.

At home, and elsewhere in the neighborhood, there was still bad luck. The day the barn caved in, Pa was ready to admit flat out that there was something to what Butch's Pa had said. It was all Ma could do to keep him from going up the road to see Andy Carter and talk to him by hand.

I had another birthday and the folks gave me a live-it set and that was something I had not expected. I had wanted one, of course, but I knew they cost a lot and with all the bad luck they had been having, the folks were short of money.

You know what a live-it is, of course. It's something like TV, only better. TV you only watch and with a live-it set you live it.

It's a viewer that you clamp onto your head and you look into it and you pick your channel and turn it on, then settle back and live the things you see.

It doesn't take any imagination to live it, because it all is there—the action and the sound and smell and even, to some extent, the actual feel of it.

My set was just a kid's set and I could only get the kid channels. But that was all right with me. I wouldn't have wanted to live through all that mushy stuff.

All morning I spent with my live-it. There was one thing called "Survey Incident" and it was all about what happened when a human survey team put down on an alien planet. Another one was about a hunting trip on a jungle world and a third was "Robin Hood." I think, of the three of them, I liked "Robin Hood" the best.

I was all puffed up with pleasure and pride and I wanted to show the kids what the folks had given me. So I took the live-it and went down to Fancy Pants' place. But I never got a chance to show the live-it to him.

Just before I got to the gate, I saw Fancy Pants floating along, silent and sneaky—and floating along beside him, not more than a yard away, was that poor, beat-up, bedraggled cat that Fancy

Pants was always pestering. He had the cat all wrapped up in a tight bundle and it couldn't move a muscle, but I could see its eyes were wide with fright. If you ask me, that cat had a right to be afraid. There was scarcely anything in the book Fancy Pants hadn't done to it.

"Hi, Fancy Pants!" I yelled.

He put a finger to his lips and crooked another finger to let me know I could join him in whatever he was doing. So I jumped the fence and Fancy Pants floated lower until he was about my level.

"What's going on?" I asked him.

"He went away and forgot to close the padlock," whispered Fancy Pants.

"Who went away?"

"My Pa. He forgot to lock the door to the old machine shed."

"But that's where—"

"Sure," said Fancy Pants. "That's where he's got the time machine."

"Fancy Pants, you don't intend to put that cat in there!"

"Why not? Pa ain't ever tried a living thing in it and I want to see what happens."

I didn't like it and yet I wanted awful bad to see that time machine. I wondered what one looked like. No one had seen the time machine except Fancy Pants' Pa.

"What's the matter with you?" asked Fancy Pants. "Are you going chicken on me?"

"But the cat!"

"For the love of Mike, it's nothing but a cat."

And that was right, of course. It was nothing but a cat.

So I went along with him and we sneaked into the shed and pulled the door behind us. And there was the time machine in the middle of the floor.

It didn't look like much. It was a kind of hopper, and a bunch of things like coils ran around the throat where the hopper narrowed down, and that was all except for a crude control board that was nailed onto a post and hooked up to the hopper with a lot of wires.

The hopper came up to my chest and I put my live-it down on the edge of it and craned my neck to look into the throat to see what I could see.

At just that moment, Fancy Pants threw the switch that turned it on. I jerked away. For it was a scary business when you turned that hopper on.

When I sneaked back to have another look, it looked for all the world as if it were a whirlpool of cream, sort of thick and rich and shiny—and it was alive. You could see the liveness in it. And there was a feeling in it that maybe you should just jump in head first and I had to grip the edges of the hopper hard not to.

I *might* have dived in, if the cat at that very moment hadn't somehow wiggled free from Fancy Pants.

I don't know how that cat did it. Fancy Pants had it all rolled into a ball and really buttoned up. Maybe Fancy Pants got careless or maybe the cat had finally figured out an angle. But, anyhow, Fancy Pants had the cat poised above the hopper and was about to let it fall. The cat didn't get loose in part—it got loose entirely—and there it was, yowling and screaming, tail fluffed out, clawing at thin air to keep from falling down into the hopper. It managed to throw itself to one side as it fell and the claws of one paw hooked onto the hopper's edge while the other hooked into my live-it set.

I let out a yell and made a grab to try to save the live-it, but I was too late. The cat dragged it off balance and it slid down into that creamy whirlpool and was gone.

The cat shimmied up a post and up into the rafters and hung there, screaming and wailing

Just then the door came open and there floated Fancy Pants' Pa and we were caught red-handed.

I figured Fancy Pants' Pa would give me the works right then and there.

But he didn't do a thing. He just floated there for a moment looking at the two of us.

Then he looked at me alone and said: "Steve, please leave."

I went out that door as fast as I could go, with just a fast glance back over my shoulder at Fancy Pants. He was pale and already beginning to appear a little shriveled. He knew what he had coming to him, and even while I realized that he deserved every bit of it, I still felt sorry for him.

But staying wouldn't help him and I was glad enough to get off scot-free.

Except that it wasn't scot-free.

I don't know what was the matter with me—just scared stiff, I guess. Anyhow, I went straight home and told Pa right out about it and he took down the strap from behind the door and let me have a few.

But it seemed to me that he didn't have his heart in it. He was getting a little uneasy about all these alien goings-on.

For several days, I didn't go off the place. To have gone anywhere, I would have had to walk past Fancy Pants' house and I didn't want to see him—not for a while, at least.

Then one day Butch and his Pa showed up and they had the glasses.

"I don't know if they'll fit," said Butch's Pa. "I had to guess the fitting."

They looked just like any other glasses except that the lenses had funny lines running every which way, as if someone had taken the glass and twisted it until it was all crinkled out of shape.

I put them on and they were a bit loose and things looked different through them, but not a great deal different. I was looking at the barnyard when I put them on. The barnyard was still there, but it appeared strange and a little weird, although it was hard to put a finger on what was wrong with it. It was a bright, hot August day and the sun was shining hard, but when I put the glasses on, it seemed suddenly to get cloudy and a little cold. And that was some of the difference, but not all of it.

There was a feeling of strangeness that sent a shiver through me, and the light was wrong, and worst of all was the sense that I didn't belong. But there was nothing you could say flat out was absolutely wrong.

"Is it any different, son?" asked Pa.

"Some different," I answered.

"Let me see."

He took the glasses off me and put them on himself.

"I can't see a thing," he said. "Just a lot of color."

"I told you," said Butch's Pa, "that only the young can see. You and I are too fixed in reality."

Pa took the glasses off and let them dangle in his hand.

"Did you see any halflings?" he asked me.

I shook my head.

"There are no halflings here," said Butch.

"To see the halflings," Butch's Pa put in, "we must journey to the Carter place."

"Well, then," said Pa, "what are we waiting for?"

So the four of us went up the road to the Carter place.

There didn't seem to be anyone at home and that was rather queer, for either Carter himself or Mrs. Carter or Ozzie Burns, the hired man, always stayed at home if the others had to go to town or anywhere.

We stood in the road and Butch had himself a good look. There weren't any halflings around the buildings and there weren't any in the orchard or in any of the fields, so far as Butch could see. Pa was getting impatient. I knew what he was thinking—that he had been made a fool of by a bunch of aliens.

Then Butch said excitedly that he thought he saw a halfling down in one corner of the pasture, just at the edge of the big Dark

Hollow woods, where Andy had a hay barn, but it was so far away that he could not be sure.

"Give your boy the glasses," said Butch's Pa, "and let him have a look."

Pa handed me the glasses and I put them on. I had a hard time getting familiar landmarks sorted out, but finally I did, and sure enough, down in the corner of the pasture, there were things moving around that looked like human beings, but mighty funny human beings. They had a sort of smoky look about them, as if you could blow them away.

"Well, what do you see?" asked Pa.

I told him what I saw and he stood there considering, rubbing his hand back and forth across his chin, with the whiskers grating.

"There doesn't seem to be a soul around," he said. "I don't suppose it would hurt if we went down there. If the things are there, I want Steve to have a good, hard look at them."

"You think it is all right?" asked Butch's Pa, worried. "It's not unethical?"

"Well, sure," said Pa, "I suppose it is. But if we are quick about it and get out right away, Andy never need know."

So we crawled underneath the fence and went over the pasture and crossed into the woods so we could sneak up on the place where we had seen the halflings.

The going was a little rough, for in places the brush was rather heavy, and there were thick blackberry patches with the bushes loaded with black and shiny fruit.

But we sneaked along as quietly as we could and we finally reached a point opposite the place where we had seen the half-lings.

Butch nudged me and whispered fiercely: "There they are!"

I put the glasses on and there they were, by golly.

Up at the edge of the hayfield, just beyond the woods, stood Andy's hay barn, really just a roof set on poles to cover the hay that Andy didn't have the room to get into his regular barn.

It was a rundown, dilapidated thing, and there was Andy standing up there on the roof, and some packs of shingles sat on the roof beside him, while climbing up a ladder with a bunch of shingles on his shoulder was Ozzie Burns, the hired man. Andy was reaching down to get the shingles that Ozzie was carrying up the ladder, and at the foot of the ladder, hanging onto it so it wouldn't tip, was Mrs. Burns. And that was the reason none of them had been around—they were all down here, fixing to patch up the shingles on the barn.

And there were the halflings, a good two dozen of them. A bunch of them were up on the roof with Andy and a couple on the ladder with the hired man and a couple more of them helping to hold up the ladder. They looked busy and energetic and efficient, and every single one of them was the spitting image of Andy Carter.

Not that they really resembled Andy, for they didn't. They were actually wraithlike things that seemed to have but little substance to them. They were little more than a smoky outline, but those smoky outlines—every single one of them—was the squat, bulldog outline of Andy Carter. And they walked like him, with a belligerent swagger, and all their motions were like his, and you could sense the meanness in them.

In the time that I was gaping at them, Ozzie Burns had handed the shingles up to Andy and clambered up on the roof beside him and Mrs. Burns had stepped away from the ladder, not needing to hold it any longer, since Ozzie was safe up on the roof. I saw the ladder was standing on uneven ground and that was why she'd had to hold it.

Andy had been crouched down to lay the pack of shingles on the roof. Now he straightened up and looked toward the woods and he saw us standing there.

"What are you doing here?" he roared at us, and started down the ladder.

And now comes the funny part of it. I'll have to take it slow and try to tell it straight.

To me, it seemed the ladder separated and became two ladders. One was standing there against the hay barn and the other left it, and the top of this second ladder began to slide along the roof and was about to fall and carry Andy with it to the ground, just as sure as shooting.

I was about to shout for Andy to look out, although I don't know why I should have. If he fell and broke his neck, it'd have been all right with me.

But just as I was about to yell, two halflings moved fast and this second ladder disappeared. It had been sliding along the roof and was about to fall, with a second Andy clinging to it and beginning to look scared—and then suddenly there was just one ladder and one Andy instead of two.

I stood there, shaking, and I knew what I had seen, but at the moment I wouldn't admit it, not even to myself.

It was, I told myself, as if I had been looking at two separate times—at a time when the ladder should have fallen and at another time when it had not fallen because the halflings hadn't let it. I had seen good luck in actual operation. Or the averting of bad luck. Whichever it might be, it all came out the same.

And now Andy was almost at the ladder's foot and the halflings were coming down from off the roof in a helter-skelter fashion—some of them jumping off and others dropping off, and if they had been human instead of what they were, there would have been a flock of broken legs and necks.

Pa stepped out of the woods into the field and I stepped along with him. We knew we were walking into trouble, but we weren't ones to run. And trailing along behind us were Butch and his Pa, but both of them looked scared and you could see they had no heart for it.

Then Andy was down off the ladder and walking straight toward us and he sure was on the warpath. And walking along beside him, in a line on either side of him, were all those halflings, and they kept in step with him and swung their arms like him and looked as mean as he did.

"Now, Andy," said Pa, trying to be conciliatory, "let us be reasonable." But it was quite an effort, I can tell you, for Pa to speak that way. He hated Andy Carter clear up from the ground and he sure-God had his reasons. Andy had been a rotten neighbor for an awful lot of years.

"Don't you tell me to be reasonable!" yelled Andy. "I been hearing all this talk about how you are blaming me for what you call hard luck. And I tell you to your face it ain't hard luck at all. It's plain downright shiftlessness and bad management. And if you think you're going to get anywhere with all this talk of yours, you are just plain crazy. You been taken in by a lot of alien nonsense. If I had my way, I'd run all those stinking aliens right the hell off the planet."

Pa took a quick step forward and I thought he was about to clobber Andy. But Butch's Pa jumped forward and grabbed him by the arm.

"No! No!" he shouted. "There's no need to fight him! Let us go away!"

Pa stood there with Butch's Pa hanging to his arm and I wondered for a minute which one he would clobber, Butch's Pa or Andy.

"I never liked you," Andy said to Pa, "from the first day I saw you. I had you figured for a bum and that is what you are. And this taking up with aliens is the lowest thing any human ever did. You ain't no better than they are. Now get off this place and don't you ever dare set foot on it again."

Pa jerked his arm and sent Butch's Pa staggering to one side. Then he brought it up and back. I saw Andy's head start moving to one side, dropping over toward his shoulder, and for a second it looked like he had the beginning of two heads. And I knew that I was watching another accident beginning to unhappen, although it was no accident, for Pa sure meant to paste him.

But they weren't fast enough to get Andy's head tilted out of danger. They weren't dealing this time with a slowly sliding ladder.

There was a solid crack like someone had hit a tree with an axe on a frosty morning, and Andy's head jerked back and his feet came off the ground and he went tincup over teakettle, flat on his back.

And there were all those silly halflings standing in a row, with shocked looks upon their faces, as if they couldn't quite believe it. You could have bought the lot of them for no more than half a buck.

Pa turned around and held out his hand to me and said: "Come on, Steve. Let's go."

He said it in a quiet voice that was clear and level, and there was, I thought, a note of pride in it. And we turned around, the two of us, and we walked away from there, not hurrying any and not even looking back.

"I swear to God," said Pa, "I've meant to do that ever since I laid eyes on him fifteen years ago."

I hadn't noticed what had happened to Butch or to his Pa and I wondered where they might have gone to, for there wasn't hide nor hair of them. But I didn't say anything to Pa about it, for I had a hunch he might not be harboring exactly friendly feelings toward Butch's Pa.

But I needn't have worried about them, for when we got out to the road they were waiting for us, breathing kind of hard and considerably scratched up. The way they'd gone through that brush and all those blackberry patches must have been a caution.

"I am glad to see," said Butch's Pa, "that you got back safely."

"Don't mention it," Pa told him coldly, and went on down the road, hanging tight onto my hand so that I had to trot along.

We got back home and went into the kitchen to get a drink of water.

Pa said to me, "Steve, have you got those glasses?"

I dug them out of my pocket and handed them to him. He put them on the shelf above the washstand.

"Leave them there," he said. "Don't touch them again—not ever. Do you understand me?"

"Yes, sir," I replied.

To tell the truth, I would have liked it better if he'd gone ranting up and down. I was afraid that what had happened out there in the woods had made him decide to go to one of the Homestead Planets. I told myself he maybe already had made up his mind and didn't need to rant.

But he never said a word about the fight with Andy nor about the Homestead Planets and he wasn't sore at me. He kept on being quiet and I knew that he still was mad clean through and I figured that he was mostly sore at Butch and Butch's Pa for their having made a complete fool of him.

I did a lot of wondering about what I'd seen down there in Andy's hayfield. And the more I thought about it, the more I was convinced that I had grasped the secret of how the halflings operated.

For I must have been seeing in two different times when I'd been looking at the ladder. I must have looked into the future and seen the ladder slip. Except it never slipped, for the halflings, seeing that it would slip, had made one leg of it settle in the ground. And then, with the ladder sitting solid, it never slipped, of course. The halflings had done no more than look ahead a bit and then righted something that was about to happen before it had a chance to happen.

And that, I told myself, was the basis of good luck and bad. The halflings could spot disaster coming and try to head it off.

Except they couldn't always make it. They had tried to protect Andy when Pa took a lick at him and they had failed. So I figured that they weren't infallible and that made me feel some better.

For if they could make good luck for Andy, it stood to reason they could make bad luck for the rest of us. All they had to do, if they had a mind to, was to see good luck heading for us and change it into bad.

It might even be possible, I told myself, that the halflings lived ahead of us, by a few seconds or so, and that the only thing which separated us from them was this matter of a different time.

But there was something else that troubled me a lot. Why had I been able to see two different times? It was clear to me that Butch and his people couldn't, for if they could, they'd have more answers to the halfling situation. They'd been studying it for years, and so far as I could figure, they didn't know for certain about this two-time business.

It seemed to me, when I thought about it, that Butch's Pa might have ground better than he knew when he made my glasses. He might have put in something or taken out something or done something he didn't know about at all.

Or it might be that the human race had a different kind of vision, or maybe just a little different, and when you added the correction for Butch's kind of vision to our kind of vision, you brought out a thing you couldn't even guess at.

I tried and tried to get it clear within my mind, but I couldn't do it. I just went around in circles.

I stayed close to home for several days because I had a feeling that I should be ignoring Butch to uphold the family honor and that is how I missed the big hassle between Fancy Pants and Nature Boy.

It seems that Nature Boy got sick and tired of how Fancy Pants was mistreating that poor, bedraggled cat. So he took one member of the skunk family that had fallen in love with him and he clipped and dyed that skunk to look exactly like the cat. And one day he sneaked over to Fancy Pants' place and switched the skunk for the cat without anyone seeing him.

The skunk didn't want to be Fancy Pants' skunk; he belonged to Nature Boy. So he started beating it back home as fast as he could go, which wasn't very fast.

Just then Fancy Pants floated out of the door and he saw the skunk going through the gate. He thought the cat was trying to sneak away from him, so he reached out and grabbed it up and rolled it into a ball and tossed it pretty high into the air, sort of careless like, to teach that cat a lesson.

It went up in the air and came down smack-dab on top of Fancy Pants, who was floating out there in the yard a few feet off the ground.

The skunk was scared witless. As soon as it got its claws fastened into Fancy Pants and had some leverage, it retaliated with enthusiasm. And for the first time in his life, Fancy Pants thumped down to the ground and, among other things, he got his clothes as dirty as any other kid.

I would give a zillion dollars to have seen it.

For a while, they figured that they might have to take Fancy Pants out somewhere and bury him for a week or two to make him presentable again. But they finally got him to a point where one could come near him.

Fancy Pants' Pa went storming down to talk with Nature Boy's Pa and the two of them put on a ruckus that had the neighborhood chuckling for a week.

And now I was really strapped for playmates. I was still cold-shouldering Butch and I knew better than to take up again with either Nature Boy or Fancy Pants. They both were mean cusses when they set their mind to it. I was sure we hadn't heard the last of this feud of theirs and I didn't want to get tangled up in it by being friends with either one of them.

It was plenty tough, let me tell you. Here I was with vacation almost ended and no one to pal around with and my live-it gone. I watched the days slip past and regretted every minute of it.

Then one day the sheriff drove up to the house.

Pa and I were out in the barnyard trying to tinker up a corn binder that was all tied together with haywire and other makeshift odds and ends. Pa had been threatening to buy one for a long time now, but with all the tough luck we'd been having, there wasn't any money.

"Good morning, Henry," the sheriff said to Pa.

Pa said good morning back.

"I hear you been having a little trouble with your neighbors," said the sheriff.

"Not what you would call real trouble," Pa told him. "I busted one in the snoot the other day is all."

"Right on his own farm, too."

Pa quit working on the binder and squatted back on his heels to look up at the sheriff. "Andy been around complaining?"

"He was in the other day. Said you had swallowed some fool story that this new alien family started. About some sort of bad-luck critters he'd been harboring on his farm."

"And you talked him out of it?"

"Well, now," said the sheriff, "I am a peaceable man and I hate to see two neighbors fighting. Andy wanted to put you under peace bond, but I said I'd come over and have a talk with you."

"All right," invited Pa. "Go ahead and talk."

"Now look here, Henry. You know the story about them hard-luck critters is so much poppycock. I'm surprised you took any stock in it."

Pa got up slowly. He had a hard look on his face and I thought for a minute he was about to bust the sheriff. I was scared, I tell you, for that is something no one should ever do—up and bust a sheriff.

—

I don't know what he might have done or what he might have said, for at that moment Nature Boy's Pa came tearing down the road in his old jalopy and pulled in behind the sheriff's car, intending to park there. But he miscalculated some and he smacked into the sheriff's car hard enough to skid it ahead six feet or so with the brakes all set.

The sheriff broke into a run. "By God!" he said. "It isn't even safe to drive out into this corner of the county!"

The two of us ran along behind him. I was running just because there was some excitement, but I figure maybe Pa was running so he could help Nature Boy's Pa if the sheriff should take it into his head to get feisty with him.

And the funny thing about it was that Nature Boy's Pa, instead of sitting there and waiting for the sheriff, had jumped out of his car and was running up the slope to meet us.

"They told me I'd find you here," he panted to the sheriff.

"You found me, all right." said the sheriff, practically breathing fire. "Now I'm going to—"

"My boy is gone!" yelled Nature Boy's Pa. "He wasn't home last night . . ."

The sheriff grabbed him and said to him: "Now let's take this easy. Tell me exactly what happened."

"He went off yesterday, early in the morning, and he didn't show up for meals, but we didn't think too much of it—he often goes off for an entire day. He has a lot of friends out there in the woods."

"And he didn't come home last night?"

Nature Boy's Pa shook his head. "Along about dusk, we got worried. I went out and hunted for him and I didn't find him. I hunted all night long, but there wasn't any sign of him. I thought maybe he'd just holed up for the night with one of his friends in the woods. I thought maybe he'd show up when it got light, but he never did."

"Well, all right," said the sheriff, "you leave it to me. We'll rouse out all the neighbors and organize a hunt. We'll find him."

He said to me: "You know the lad? You did some playing with him?"

"All the time," I answered.

"Lead us to all the places where you played. We'll look there first."

Pa said: "I'll start phoning the neighbors. I'll get them here right away."

He ran up the hill toward the house.

In an hour or less, there were a hundred people gathered and the sheriff took them all in hand. He divided them into posses and appointed captains for each posse and told them where to hunt.

It was the most excitement we've ever had in the neighborhood.

The sheriff took me with the posse he headed up and we went down Dark Hollow. I took them to the place where we were digging out the lizard and the place where we had started to dig ourselves a cave and the hole in the creek where Nature Boy had made friends with some whopping trout, and some other places, too. We found some old tracks of Nature Boy's, but there was no fresh sign, although we hunted up and down the hollow clear to where it flowed into the river, and we trailed back come night, and I was tuckered out.

And a little scared as well.

For an awful suspicion had come to me.

And no matter how hard I tried to keep from thinking of it, I couldn't help myself, for all the time I was trying to remember if the hopper in that time machine had been big enough to take a kid the size of Nature Boy.

Ma fed me and sent me up to bed and later she came up and tucked me in and kissed me. She hadn't done that in years. She knew I was too big to be tucked in and kissed, but she did it anyhow.

And then she went downstairs and I lay there listening to some men who still were out there in the yard, talking among themselves. Some of the others still were hunting and I knew that I should be out there hunting with them, but I knew Ma wouldn't let me go and I was glad of it. For I was tired all through and the woods at night can be a scary place.

I should by rights have gone straight to sleep. Any other night I would have. But I lay there thinking about that hopper in the time machine and I wondered how long it would take before someone told the sheriff about the ruckus between Fancy Pants and Nature Boy, and I thought perhaps they already had. And if so, the sheriff probably was looking into it right now, for the sheriff was nobody's fool.

I wondered if I should tell him myself if no one else had. But that was one fight I didn't have any hankering to get tangled up in.

Finally I went to sleep and it seemed to me I hadn't been asleep any time at all when something woke me up. It still was dark, but there was a red glow shining through the window. I sat up quick, with my hair standing half on end.

I thought at first it might be our barn or the machine shed, but then I saw it wasn't that close. I skinned out of bed and over to the window. That fire was a big one and it wasn't too far up the road.

It looked as if it was on the Carter place, but I knew that must be wrong, for if bad luck like that struck anyone, it wouldn't be Andy Carter. Unless, of course, he was loaded with insurance.

I went downstairs in my bare feet and Ma was standing at the door, looking up the road toward the blaze.

"What is it, Ma?" I asked.

"It's the barn on the Carter place," she said. "They phoned the neighborhood for help, but all the men are out hunting Nature Boy."

We stood there, Ma and me, and watched until the blaze almost died out, and then Ma hiked me off to bed.

I crawled underneath the covers, weak with this new excitement. I wondered why we should tag along for months with nothing happening, and then all at once have it busting out all over.

I lay there and thought about Andy Carter's barn and there was something wrong about it. Andy had been the luckiest man in seven counties and now, without any warning, he was having bad luck just like the rest of us.

I wondered if the halflings might have gone off and left him, and if that was the case, I wondered why they had. Maybe, I told myself, they had gotten plain disgusted with Andy's meanness.

It was broad daylight when I woke again and I jumped straight out of bed and climbed into my clothes. I rushed downstairs to see if there was any word of Nature Boy.

Ma said there wasn't, that the men were still out hunting. She had breakfast ready for me and insisted I eat it and warned me about wandering off or trying to join one of the searching parties. She said it wasn't safe for me to be out in the woods with so many bears about. And that was funny, for she had never worried about the bears before.

But she made me promise I wouldn't.

As soon as I got out, I zipped down the road as fast as I could go. I had to see the place where the Carter barn had burned down and I just had to talk with someone. And Butch was the only one left that I could talk to.

There wasn't much to see at the Carter place, just burned and blackened timbers that still were smoking some. I stood out in the road a while and then I saw Andy come out of the house and he stood there for a minute looking straight at me. So I got out of there.

I went past Fancy Pants' place real fast, hoping I wouldn't see him. At the moment, I didn't want a thing to do with Fancy Pants.

When I got to Butch's place, his Ma told me he was sick in bed. She didn't think it was catching, she said, so I went up to see him.

Butch sure looked terrible lying there—more like a runty hoot owl than he ever had before—but he was glad to see me. I asked him how he was and he said he felt better. He made me promise I wouldn't tell his Ma, then told me that he'd got sick from eating some green apples he'd pinched off the Carter orchard.

He'd heard about Nature Boy and I told him in a whisper the suspicions I had.

He lay there looking at me solemnly and finally he said to me: "Steve, I should have told you this before. That is no time machine."

"No time machine? How do you know?"

"Because I saw the stuff that Fancy Pants' Pa put through it. It didn't go anywhere. It still is lying there."

"You saw . . ." And then I had it. "You mean it went to where the halflings are?"

"That's what I mean," said Butch.

Sitting there on edge of the bed. I tried to think it through, but there were so many questions bubbling up in me that I couldn't do it.

"Butch," I asked, "where is this place that the halflings are?"

"I don't know," said Butch. "It's close to us, almost in the world, but not really."

And I remembered something Pa had said several weeks before. "You mean it's like a place behind a plate-glass window that's between our world and theirs?"

"Something like that."

"And if Nature Boy is there, what would happen to him?"

Butch shuddered. "I don't know."

"Would he be all right? Could he breathe in there?"

"I suppose he could," said Butch. "I think the halflings do."

I got up from the bed and started for the door. Then I turned back again.

"Butch, what are the halflings doing? What are they hanging around for?"

"No one's sure," said Butch. "There are a lot of ideas about what they are after. One is that they have to be near something that is living before they can live themselves. They can't live a life themselves; they've got to have a life to—well, like imitate, only that's not the word."

"They need a pattern," I said, remembering what Butch's Pa had said that day, before Pa choked him off with his own rambling about what the halflings might be after.

"I guess you could call it that," said Butch.

And I stood there thinking what a lousy life the halflings must have led, using Andy Carter as their pattern.

But that wasn't so, for the halflings, that time I had seen them, had sure-God been happy. They'd been running around up there on the roof and keeping themselves busy and enjoying themselves.

And they had, every one of them, looked like Andy Carter. And of course they would, with Andy as their pattern.

Thinking about it, I could see how someone like Andy, with his kind of disposition, might enjoy being mean as dirt and ornery with his neighbors. He'd have a sense of independence and the feel of every hand being raised against him and him standing there like a mighty warrior, defying all of them. And from that he'd get a sense of strength and domination. All in all, I supposed, Andy, for a man like him, might be living a pretty darned satisfactory life.

I started for the door, and Butch called after me, "Where are you going, Steve?"

"I'm going to find Nature Boy," I said.

"I'll go with you."

"No, you stay in bed. Your Ma will skin both of us if you don't."

I got out of the house and headed fast for home, and as I ran, I kept on thinking about how the halflings had no life of their own, but had to find another life and pattern themselves on it.

Sometimes they'd be mighty lucky and fasten onto someone who'd give them a good and exciting life, or maybe a good and contented life, but other times they'd get a mighty poor one. But you had to say this for them—they gave all the help they could to the one they'd picked out as a pattern, and they kept working at it.

And I wondered how many persons who had been great successes might have been watched over by the halflings. What an awful letdown it would be if they were to learn that they had not become great or rich or famous through any particular effort or brilliance of their own, but by the grace of a bunch of things that helped them from outside.

I got home and went into the kitchen and over to the sink.

"Is that you, Steve?" Ma called from the living room.

"I'm getting a drink," I told her.

"Where you been?"

"Just around."

"Now don't you go running off," she warned.

"No, ma'am, I won't."

And all the time I was talking to her, I was climbing on a chair so I could reach those glasses where Pa had put them on the shelf and told me not to touch them again—not ever.

Then I had them in my pocket and was climbing off the chair.

I heard Ma heading for the kitchen and I hurried out as quietly as I could.

I didn't put the glasses on until I got to where the Carter farm cornered on the road. I went along the road, watching carefully, and finally I found a bunch of halflings down in a fence corner just beyond the orchard. They were standing there and squabbling over something and they didn't seem to notice me until I got real close.

Then they all swung around and stood facing me. They seemed to be talking among themselves and pointed at me.

And there on the head of one of them, pushed up on his forehead, was the live-it set I had lost down the time machine.

When I saw that, I realized Butch actually had seen the stuff that Fancy Pants' Pa had put through the time machine.

At first I don't think they realized that I could see them, but after I stood there for a while, staring at them, they began to move up closer to me.

I could feel the hair rearing right up on my head. There was nothing I wanted to do more than turn around and run. But I told myself they couldn't reach me and there was nothing to be scared of, so I stood on my ground.

They reminded me of a bunch of crows. They must have seen I didn't have a gun, or maybe this particular bunch didn't know about the guns Butch's people had. And they crowded up real close to me, like a flock of crows is not afraid of an empty-handed man, but will keep their distance when he has a gun.

I could see their mouths moving at me, but naturally I couldn't hear a thing, and they kept pointing at the one that had my live-it on his head.

To tell the honest truth, I didn't pay too close attention to what they might have been doing at the start of it. I was too busy looking at them and trying to figure out what might have happened to them. There was one thing certain—this either was a different bunch than I had seen down in Andy Carter's hay field or they had changed a lot. There was still some of Andy in them, although not as much of him as someone else, as if Andy and someone else had gotten sort of scrambled together.

Finally I made out that they were pointing at the one with the live-it on his head and then tapping their own heads, and I figured out that each of them was asking for a live-it too.

I didn't know what I would have said to them or how I would have said it, if I had had the chance, only I never had the chance. They suddenly parted, as if someone from behind had pushed them to one side, and there was Nature Boy, standing face to face with me.

We stood there and looked at one another for a good long time, not saying anything, not making any motion. Then he stepped forward and I stepped forward until we were almost nose to nose. I was afraid there, for a moment, we'd walk right through each other. What would have happened then? Probably nothing much.

"You O.K.?" I asked him, thinking maybe he could read my lips even if he couldn't hear me, but he shook his head. So I asked him once again, talking slowly and forming my words as distinctly as I could. But he shook his head again.

Then I thought of something else.

I lifted up my hand and stuck out my finger and pretended I was writing on the imaginary window that separated us.

"YOU O.K.?" I wrote, taking it slow, because he'd have to read it backwards.

He didn't get it right away and I did it once again and this time he understood.

"O.K.," he wrote. And then he wrote real slow: "GET ME OUT!"

I stood there looking at him and it was horrible, for there he was and here I was, as so far as I could see, there was no way to get him out.

He must have sensed what I was thinking, because all at once his mouth trembled and that was the first time I'd ever seen Nature Boy even close to crying. Not even that time when we were digging out the lizard and a big rock fell on his toe.

I thought how bad it must have been for him, trapped in that place and able to see out, but knowing that no one could see in. He might even have followed some of the searching parties, hoping that someone might accidentally glimpse him, but knowing they couldn't. Maybe he had trailed along behind his Pa, as close as he could get to him, and his Pa not knowing it. And maybe he'd gone back home and watched his family and been all the lonelier for their not knowing he was there. And undoubtedly he'd hunted around for Butch, who he knew could see him, only Butch had been sick in bed.

And while I was thinking all of this, I got a faint idea. I told myself that it probably wouldn't work, but the more I thought about it, the more it seemed it might.

So I reached up with my finger and I wrote: "MEET ME AT FANCY PANTS."

I pocketed my glasses and hurried along home. I circled around the house because I didn't want to take the chance of Ma seeing me and not letting me go. I went into the machine shed and found a length of rope and hunted up a hacksaw.

Lugging these, I made my way back to Fancy Pants' place. The machine shed was back of the barn, so no one from the house could see me, and anyhow no one seemed to be around. I knew that Fancy Pants' Pa, and maybe Fancy Pants himself, would be out with the searchers, floating around over places where it would be impossible for the men on foot to go.

I laid down the rope and hacksaw and put on my glasses and Nature Boy was there, right beside the machine shed door. He had some of the halflings with him, including the one who still had the live-it perched up on his forehead. And scattered all around the place, just like Butch had said, were tea cups and pie plates and children's blocks and a lot of other junk—the stuff that Fancy Pants' Pa had fed into the time machine.

I looked at the halflings again and all at once I knew what was different about them. They were still some of Andy, but they were Nature Boy as well. And then I knew why Andy's barn had burned. These halflings of his had been so busy tagging around Nature Boy that they had not been able to give Andy their attention.

It seemed only natural, of course. A halfling would get a lot more good out of a real live human inside that world of theirs than they would someone they could only see from behind a plate-glass window.

I took the glasses off and put them in my pocket and got to work. It was no easy job to saw through that padlock. The steel was awfully hard and the blade was dull and I was afraid it might break before I got through the steel. I cussed myself for not thinking to bring along an extra blade or two.

The sawing made an awful racket because I had forgotten to bring along some oil to squirt into the cut. But nobody heard the sawing.

Finally I got through.

I opened the door and stepped into the shed and the time machine was there, just the way I remembered it. I laid down the rope and went over to the control board and studied it, but it wasn't very complicated.

I got it turned on and the creamy whirlpool was sliding in the hopper's throat.

I picked up the rope and put my glasses on and got an awful fright. The machine shed was built on a gentle slope and the floor I was standing on was four or five feet above the ground and there I was, standing in the air, or so it seemed to me.

I had a sense, not of falling, but that by rights I should be falling, that any minute now I would begin to fall. I knew I wouldn't, naturally—I was standing on a transparent but solid floor. But knowing that didn't help much. That horrible, dreamlike feeling that I was about to tumble to the ground still kept hold of me.

And to make it even worse, there was Nature Boy, standing underneath me, with his head about level with my feet, looking up at me. His face was hopeful and he was motioning me to get busy with the rope.

Moving cautiously, even if there was no need of caution, I took one end of the rope and tossed it down the hopper and felt the suck and tug of the creamy whirlpool pulling down the rope. Down underneath the hopper, I could see the rope coming out, dangling into that place where Nature Boy was trapped. He moved over quickly and grabbed hold of the rope and I could feel the weight of the pull he put on it.

Nature Boy was about my size, perhaps a little smaller, and I knew I'd have to pull as hard as ever I could to get him out of there. I even wound a hitch around my hand to make sure it wouldn't slip. I pulled with all my might. And that rope didn't budge. It felt as if I were pulling against a house. I couldn't gain an inch.

So I quit pulling and knelt down, still hanging to the rope, peering at the base of the time machine.

It was a funny thing. The rope went to the bottom of the hopper's throat and then it skipped a foot or two. There was a foot or so of sidewise space where there wasn't any rope, and then the rope took up again, dangling down into that other place where Nature Boy had hold of it.

It didn't make sense. That rope should have gone into that other world in a straight and simple line. But the fact was that it didn't. It went off somewhere else before it fell into the other world.

And that, I figured, was the reason I couldn't pull it out.

You could put a thing through the time machine, but you couldn't pull it back.

I looked down at Nature Boy and he looked back at me. I knew he'd seen it and knew as well as I did exactly what it meant. He looked pretty pitiful and I don't suppose I looked any better.

Just then the machine shed door screeched open.

I jumped up, still hanging to the rope, and there was Fancy Pants' Pa.

He was all burned up and I couldn't blame him. Not after seeing how I had sawed the padlock to break into the place.

"Steve," he said, and you could hear him fighting to keep his voice level, "I thought I told you to keep out of here."

"Yes, sir," I said, "but Nature Boy's in there."

"Nature Boy!" he shouted. Then his voice dropped. "You don't know what you're talking about. How could he get in?"

"I don't know," I said, though I could have told him.

"Those glasses you are wearing," asked Fancy Pants' Pa. "Are those the ones that were made for you by Butch's father?"

I nodded.

"Then you can see?"

"I can see Nature Boy," I said. "Just as plain as day."

I let go of the rope to take my glasses off and the rope slid down that hopper slicker than a whistle.

"It's all right, I guess," I said. "I couldn't pull him out."

"Steve," said Fancy Pants' Pa, "I want you to tell me the truth. You're not just thinking up a story? You are not pretending?"

He was awful pale and I saw what he was thinking—if Nature Boy had gone down that hopper, the entire neighborhood would be down on him like a ton of bricks.

I crossed my heart. "And hope to die," I added.

That seemed good enough for him.

He shut off the time machine, then went outdoors. I followed him.

"Now," he said, "you stay right here. I'll be back immediately."

He floated off in somewhat of a hurry, zooming away above the pasture woods. He was out of sight in no time.

I sat down with my back against the machine shed and I was feeling pretty low. I knew I should put on my glasses, but I kept them in my pocket. I couldn't have stood the sight of Nature Boy looking out at me.

It was done and over with, I knew. There was no way in the world for me or anyone to rescue Nature Boy. He was gone for good and all. He was worse than gone.

And sitting there, I thought up some pretty dreadful things to do to Fancy Pants. For there was no doubt in my mind that Fancy Pants had got into the shed and had grabbed Nature Boy, just like he did the cat, and dumped him down the hopper.

He was pretty sore, I knew, about the trick that Nature Boy had played on him with that skunk disguised as a cat. There was nothing he would have stopped at to get even.

I was sitting there and thinking when Fancy Pants' Pa came floating up the road, and panting along behind him were Pa and the sheriff and Butch's Pa and Nature Boy's Pa and some other neighbors.

The sheriff came straight for me and he grabbed me by the shoulders and gave me a good, sharp shake.

"Now," he bellowed, "what is this foolishness? I warn you, boy, it will go hard with you if you've been pulling our leg."

I tried to break away from him, but he wouldn't let me go. Then Pa stepped up and flung out his arm so that it caught the sheriff straight across the chest and sent him staggering back.

"You keep your hands off him," Pa said to the sheriff.

"But that story," blustered the sheriff. "You surely don't believe—"

"I do," said Pa. "I believe every word of it. My boy doesn't lie."

I'll say this for Pa: He may storm around and yell and he may take the strap to you for a lot of trifling things, but when it comes down to the pinch, he's standing there beside you.

"I'll remind you, Henry," said the sheriff, bristling, "that you're not entirely in the clear yourself. There's that business of the breach of peace I talked Andy Carter out of."

"Andy Carter," said Pa, speaking more slowly than one would expect him to. "He's the man who lives just down the road, if I recall correctly. Has there been any of you who have seen him lately?"

He looked around the crowd and it seemed that no one had.

"Last time I talked to Andy," said Pa, "was when I called him on the phone and told him we needed help. He said he was too busy to go hunting any alien whelp. He said it would be good riddance if all of them got lost."

He looked around the crowd and no one spoke a word. I don't suppose it was quite polite of Pa to say what he had, with Nature Boy's Pa and Butch's Pa and all the rest of those alien people standing there before us. But it sure-God was the truth, and they needed it right then, and Pa was the one who was not afraid to give it to them right between the eyes.

Then someone spoke up from the crowd and there were so many of them I couldn't be sure exactly who it was. But whoever it was said: "I tell you, folks, it was nothing but plain justice when Andy's barn burned down."

The sheriff bristled up. "If I thought one of you had a hand in that, I would—"

"You wouldn't do a thing," said Pa. He turned to me. "All right, Steve, tell us what you have to tell. I promise you that everyone will listen and there won't be any interruptions."

He looked straight at the sheriff when he was saying it.

"Just a second, sir," said Butch's Pa. "I want to voice one important point. I know this boy can see the halflings, for I myself am the one who made the glasses for him. I know it is immodest of me to say a thing like this, but if I am nothing else, I am one fine optician."

"Thank you, sir," Pa said. "And now, Steve, go ahead."

But I never got a chance to say a single word, for Butch came stumbling around the barn and he had the gun with him. Or at least I took it for the gun, although it didn't look like one. It was a sticklike thing and it glittered in the sunlight from all sorts of prisms and mirrors set into it at all kinds of crazy angles.

"Pa," yelled Butch, "I heard about it and I brought the gun. I hope I'm not too late."

He ran up to his Pa and his Pa took the gun away from him and held it with everyone looking at him.

"Thank you, son," said Butch's Pa. "It was good of you, but we won't need a gun. We aren't shooting anything today."

Then Butch cried out: "There he is, Pa! There's Nature Boy!"

I am not too sure that all of them believed I had found Nature Boy. Some might have had their reservations, and kept quiet about it because they didn't want to tangle with my Pa. But Butch was a different matter. He could see these things without any silly glasses. And he was an alien, and everyone expected aliens to do these sort of crazy things.

"All right," admitted the sheriff, "so I guess he must be there. Now what do we do?"

"There doesn't seem to be much to go on," said Pa, "but we can't leave the boy in there." He looked at Nature Boy's Pa. "Don't you worry. We'll figure a way to get him out."

But he spoke with so much confidence that I knew he was only talking so that Nature Boy's Pa would know we weren't giving up.

Personally, I could see no hope. If you couldn't get him out the way he had gotten in, there didn't seem to be any other way. There were no doors into that other place.

"Gentlemen," said Butch's Pa, "I have a small idea."

We all turned and waited.

"This gun," he said, "is used to keep down the number of halflings. It ruptures the wall between the two worlds sufficiently to let a bullet through. There might be an adaptation made of it, and we can do that later, or have someone do it for us, if that be necessary. But it seems possible to me we could use the gun itself."

"But we don't want to shoot the boy," the sheriff protested. "What we want to do is get him out."

"I have no intention, sir, of shooting him. There will be no bullet in the gun. All we'll use is the device to rupture the curtain or whatever it may be that lies between the worlds. And I can— what is the word?—tinker, I believe. I can tinker up the gun so that rupture will be greater."

He sat down on the ground and began working on the gun, shifting prisms here and there and adjusting tiny mirrors.

"There is just one thing," he said. "The rupture will last for but a moment. The boy must be immediate to take advantage of it. He must leap outward instantly the rupture should appear."

He turned to me. "Steve, can you communicate with him?"

"Communicate?"

"Talk to him. With signs, perhaps? Or the reading of the lips? Or some other way?"

"Sure, I can do that."

"Please, would you do it then?"

So I put on my glasses and looked around until I found Nature Boy. I had quite a time making him understand what we planned to do. It wasn't any easier to talk with him with all those crazy halflings standing all around him and making motions at me and pointing at the live-it, then tapping their own heads.

I was sweating plenty, for I was afraid that I had not got it all across to him, but I knew that any more of it would do no more than confuse him.

So I told Butch's Pa that we were all set, and Butch's Pa handed Butch the gun, and the rest stepped back a ways, and there was Butch with the gun and me standing right behind him. And there was Nature Boy standing in that other place, and a bunch of those silly halflings clustered all about him, and they sure didn't know about the alien gun or they'd not have been standing there. And Nature Boy looked like someone who'd been stood against a wall and was being executed without even any blindfold.

Out of the tail of my eye, I saw Fancy Pants floating off to one side of us, and he was the saddest-looking sack you ever saw.

Suddenly there was a strange white flash of brilliance as all the prisms and the mirrors moved on the gun that Butch was holding. He had pulled a trigger, or whatever it was.

For a second, straight in front of us, a funny sort of hole seemed to open up in the place that should not have been there at all—a jagged, ragged hole that appeared in nothingness. And I caught sight of Nature Boy jumping through the hole the second it stayed open.

And there he was, staggering a bit from the jump that he had made—only he was not alone. He had one of the halflings with him!

He had him by the wrist in a good tight grip and it was plain to see that he had jerked him through with him, for the halfling did not seem at all happy about what had happened to him. I saw at once that it was the halfling who had the live-it on his head.

Butch pushed the halfling toward me and he said: "Here, Steve. It was the only way I could get your live-it back."

I saw that Butch was letting go of the halfling and I grabbed quick by the other wrist and was somewhat surprised to find that he was solid. I would not have been astonished if my hand had gone right through him, for he still had that swirl-smoky look about him, although it seemed to me he might be hardening up a bit and becoming more substantial.

Pa moved over close beside me, saying, "You be careful, Steve!"

"Aw, he's all right," I said. "He's not even trying to get away from me."

Someone raised a shout and I whirled around and stared.

A half-dozen of the halflings had grabbed hold of the edges of that door into the other world, and they were tugging for dear life so it would stay open, and pouring out of it was that entire herd of halflings! They were shoving and pushing and scrambling to get through, and there were a lot more of them, it seemed to me, than I had thought there were.

We just stood there and watched them until they all were through. We didn't do a thing because there was not a thing we could do. And they stood there in a bunch, packed tight together, staring back at us.

The sheriff came alongside Pa. He pushed back his hat until it roosted on his neck. You could see that the sheriff was flabbergasted and I enjoyed it, for it had been apparent from the very first that the sheriff hadn't believed a word he'd heard about the halflings.

I don't know, maybe he still was thinking that it might be nothing but some sort of alien joke. You could see, without half trying, that the sheriff didn't cotton to any aliens.

"How come," he asked suspiciously, "that this one here has got a live-it on?"

So I told him and he blinked at me, dazed and dumfounded, but he said nothing back. I sure had shut him up.

Fancy Pants' Pa had floated up while I was telling it and he said I told the truth, for he'd been there and seen it.

Everyone began to talk at once, but Fancy Pants' Pa floated up a little higher and held up his hand to command attention.

"Just a moment, if you please," he said. "Before we get down to more serious business, I have something you must hear. As you may suspect, knowing the episode of the skunk, my family undoubtedly has a great deal to answer for in this incident."

A human saying things like that would sound silly and pompous, but Fancy Pants' Pa could get away with it.

"So," said Fancy Pants' Pa, "I now announce to you that my malefactor son, for the forthcoming thirty days, must walk upon his feet. He must not float an inch. If the punishment does not seem sufficient—"

"It's enough," Pa cut in. "The boy has to learn his lesson, but there is no use being harsh with him."

"Now, sir," said Nature Boy's Pa, being very formal, "it is not necessary—"

"I insist," Fancy Pants' Pa said. "I really must insist. It can be no other way."

"Say," bawled the sheriff, "will someone explain to me what this is all about?"

"Sheriff," Pa said to him, "your understanding of this matter is of no great importance and it would take too long to explain. We have more important business we should be attending to." He turned around a bit so he faced the crowd. "Well, gentlemen, what do we do next? It appears to me that we have some guests. And remembering that these critters are bearers of good luck, it would seem to me we should treat them as kindly as we can."

"Pa," I said, tugging at his coat sleeve, "I know how we can get them over on our side. Every one of them wants a live-it set."

"That's right," spoke up Nature Boy. "All the time I was in there, they pestered me and pestered me about how to get the sets. All the time they squabbled over who would get to use Steve's set next."

"You mean," the sheriff asked, in a weak voice, "that these things can talk?"

"Why, sure they can," said Nature Boy. "They learn a lot more back in that world of theirs than you could ever guess."

"Well, now," Pa said with a lot of satisfaction, "if that is all they want, it's not too great a price for us to pay to get us some good luck. We'll just buy a lot of live-it sets. We can probably get them wholesale—"

"But if we get the live-its," objected Butch's Pa, "they'll just lie around and use them and be of no help to us at all. They won't need us any more. They'll have all these patterns they need from the live-it sets."

"Well, anyhow," said Pa, "even if that should be true, we'll get them off our necks. They won't pester us with this bad luck they commit."

"It won't do us any good however you look at it," declared Butch's Pa, who had a mighty low opinion of the halflings. "They all live together. That's the way it's always been. They never helped an entire neighborhood, but just one man or family in the neighborhood. A whole tribe of them comes in and they give one family all the benefit. You couldn't get them to split up and work for all of us."

"If you jerks would listen," said the halfling with the live-it on his head, "I can get you straightened out."

It was a shock, I tell you, to hear him speak at all. He was the kind of thing you'd figure shouldn't speak at all—just a sort of dummy. And the way he spoke and the tone he used made it even worse. It was the way Andy Carter always talked—either wild and blustering, or out of the corner of his mouth, sarcastic. After listening to Andy all these years, that poor halfling didn't know any different.

Everyone just stood there, staring at the halfling who had spoken, while all the other halflings were nodding their heads in such mad agreement with him that I thought they'd snap their necks.

Pa was the first one to get his feet back under him.

"Go ahead," he said to the halfling. "We all are listening."

"We'll make a deal with you," said the halfling, using ornery words but speaking most respectful, "but you'll have to level with us, see? We'll work hard for you and guard against mishap, but we got to have the live-its and no mistake about it. One for each of us—and if I was you, mister, I wouldn't try to chisel."

"Well, now," said Pa, "that sounds fair enough. But you mean all of us?"

"All of you," the live-it halfling said.

"You mean you will split up?" asked Pa. "Each of us will have at least one of you? You won't all live together any more?"

"I think, sir," said Fancy Pants' Pa, "that we can depend on that. I believe I understand what this gentleman is thinking. It is something that happened with the human race on Earth."

"What happened here on Earth?" asked Pa, sort of flabbergasted.

"Why," said Fancy Pants' Pa, "the elimination of the need for social clustering. There was a time when the human race found it necessary to congregate in families and tribes for companionship and entertainment. Then the race got the record player and the radio and TV and there was less need for get-togethers. A man had entertainment of his own in his home. He need not move beyond his living room to be entertained. So the spectator and group sports simply petered out."

"And you think," asked Pa, "that the same thing will happen with the halflings if we gave them live-its?"

"Certainly," said Fancy Pants' Pa. "We supply them, as it were, entertainment for the home, personal entertainment. There will be no further need for tribal living."

"You said it, pal!" the halfling said enthusiastically.

All the rest of them were nodding in agreement.

"But it's still no good," yelped Butch's Pa, getting real riled. "They're in this world now, and how do you get them back? And while they're here, can they do anything for us?"

"You can stop shooting off your mouth right now," the halfling said to Butch's Pa with utmost respect. "We can't do anything here for you, that's sure. In this world of yours, we can't see ahead. And to do you any good, we have to see ahead."

"You mean that if we give you live-its, you'll go back home again?" asked Pa.

"Sure," said the halfling. "Back there is our home. Just try to keep us from it."

"We won't even try," Pa said. "We might even push you back. We'll give you the live-its and you get back there and start to work for us."

"We'll work for you hard," said the halfling, "but not all the time. We take out some time for looking at the live-it. That all right with you?"

"Sure," Pa agreed. "Sure, that's O.K. with us."

"All right," said the halfling, "get us back where we belong."

I turned around and walked out of the crowd, out to the edge of it. For it was all settled now and I had a belly full of it. It would be all right with me if we never had any more excitement in the neighborhood.

Up by the barn I saw Fancy Pants limping along on the ground. He was having a tough time walking. But I didn't feel the least bit sorry for him. He had it coming.

I figured in just a little while I'd go up around the barn and clobber him for that time he mopped up the road with me.

It should be an easy job, I told myself, with him grounded by his Pa for thirty days.

SPACESHIP IN A FLASK

"Spaceship in a Flask" was purchased by Astounding Science Fiction *early in 1941; they paid Cliff seventy-five dollars and published the story in July 1941. It is one of the many Simak stories that features a newspaperman protagonist, and it displays a bit of the culture of the era, which often included, among other things, crusty, streetwise reporters who lived in uneasy truces with mobsters—for a while.*

—dww

Old Eli was plastered when I found him in the Sun Spot, one of the many disreputable dives situated against the walls of the domed city of New Chicago on the Twilight Belt of Mercury.

I had been afraid of that. As soon as I had heard the old Sunwarder was in town, I had set out to track him down by checking all the joints. The Sun Spot was the thirty-third.

Eli always was good for a story—the kind of a story the Solar Press ate up. No one in New Chicago believed a word he said, especially that yarn about being a couple of hundred years old. Some of the stuff he told about the Sunward side might be true, for few men ventured there, but the story about his age was just too much to swallow.

Most of his tales were alcoholic. He had to have a bit of glow to do much talking. But this time I saw he was pretty far gone.

He regarded me across the table with bleary eyes.

"I was a-comin' to see you, son," he cackled. "Kept thinkin' all the time, 'I gotta go see Sherm.'" He shoved the bottle at me. "Grab yourself a snort, son."

I shook my head. "Can't. Doctor's orders. Got a lousy stomach."

He guffawed in minor key and pounded the table in drunken mirth.

"I remember now. Doggone if I don't. Always taking pills or something, ain't you?"

"Capsules," I said, icily. I can't appreciate jokes about my stomach.

"Don't need water nor nothin' to wash them down," he went on. "Just pop them into your mouth and swallow. Funniest danged thing I ever see. Me, I never took a pill without a heap of gaggin'."

He hoisted the bottle and let it gurgle.

"What did you do this trip?" I asked.

"Not much of nothin'," said Eli. "Couldn't find a thing. This danged planet is getting too crowded. Too many prospectors runnin' around. Bumped into a feller out there, I did. First time that has ever happened. Don't like it. Have to go out to Pluto where a man's got elbow room."

He wrestled the bottle again and wiped his whiskers.

"Wouldn't have come in at all 'cept I had to bring Doc some of them salts of his."

"What salts are those?" I asked.

"What! Ain't I ever told you about them salts. Doc buys them off of me. Danged if I know why. Don't seem to be good for nothin'."

He reached into a bulging coat pocket, pulled forth a canvas bag and slung it on the table.

"Take a look," he urged. "Maybe you can tell me what it is. Doc pays me good for it. Takes good care of me, too. Caught the fever out on Venus, long time ago. He gives me injections to fight it off."

Eli stumbled a little over 'injections' but finally made it.

"Who is this Doc?" I asked quietly, afraid I'd scare him into silence. "One of the doctors here in town?"

"Nope. The big doc. The feller out at the sanitarium."

"Dr. Vincent?"

"That's the one," said Eli. "Used to sell them to Dr. Anderson and Dr. Brown, too."

I let that pass. It was just another one of old Eli's tales. Both Anderson and Brown had been dead these many years, Anderson before Eli was born.

I opened the bag and poured part of its contents into one hand. Tiny, shining crystals winked, reflecting the lights above the bar.

"Took some to a chemist once," said Eli, "but he said it wasn't nothin'. Not valuable at least. Some peculiar combin . . . combi—"

"Combination."

"That's it. I didn't tell him about Doc. Didn't tell him nothin'. Thought maybe I'd made a find and could cash in on it. Thought maybe Doc was takin' me for a ride. But the chemist said it wasn't worth a thing. Offered to sell him some but he didn't want any. Out of his line, he said."

"Maybe you'd let me have some. Just a sample," I suggested, still afraid of scaring him off. For I sensed, even then, that he was telling me something he shouldn't tell.

He waved a generous hand.

"Take some. Take a lot. Take all you want."

I felt in my pockets.

"I haven't anything to put it in," I said.

He cackled at me, hoisting the bottle.

"Fill up a couple of them pills of yours. Dump out the stuff that's in them. Won't do you any good. Likker's the only thing for a touchy stomach."

"Good idea," I said, grinning at him.

I pulled three of the capsules apart, spilled out the powders, refilled them with the salts and carefully placed them in my vest pocket. The bag I shoved back across the table.

"Where do you find this stuff?" I asked.

Eli wagged a shaky finger.

"Secret," he whispered, huskily.

His eyes, I saw, were blearier than ever. He wobbled even as he sat. But his hand snaked out with what amounted to instinct to cuddle the bottle.

"Good drinkin' likker," he mumbled. "Good for the stomach—"

His head drooped and rested on the table. The bottle tipped and the little remaining liquor splashed onto the floor.

"Well, I'll be damned," I said to the man behind the bar.

"Soon as he sobers up," the man told me, "he'll light out for Sunward. Been going there for years. Queer old duck. Figure there's anything to him claiming he's a couple hundred years old?"

"Not a chance," I told him.

He held a glass up to the light, blew on it, polished it with a cloth until it shone.

"A bunch of the boys had him yarning good just before you came in. Marty Berg was setting them up."

"About this time Marty always sets them up," I told him. "Election day is getting close."

I started to go and then turned back and laid a coin on the bar.

"When he wakes up give him a drink on me," I said. "He'll need one then. I'll try to catch him again before he hits for Sunward."

But I didn't catch him again.

Twenty-four hours later they found old Eli's body in the badlands just west of the city's port. He had been killed by three vicious knife thrusts. The police said he had been dead twelve or eighteen hours.

Marty Berg was one of those men who can't go back to Earth. Just what the trouble was no one knew and no one cared to ask. It might have been any number of things, for Marty's talents are varied.

As a ward heeler in the North Wall precinct, he always delivered the vote. The methods he used were never questioned. What he got out of it no one really cared, for New Chicago had not as yet developed civic consciousness.

When he came into my office I gave him the glad hand, for he was a news source. More than once he'd tipped me off on political shenanigans.

"What's the news on Eli?" he asked.

"None at all," I told him. "The police are baffled."

Marty wagged his head. "Too bad. I hope they catch the guy."

"What can I do for you, Marty?"

"Just a little favor," said Marty. "I hear you're going to Earth for a bit of vacation—"

"In a day or two," I said. "It'll be good to see Earth again. A man sort of misses—"

And there I stopped, remembering about Marty not being able to go back.

But he didn't seem to notice.

"You remember Chesty Lewis? The bird they hooked for forgery?"

"Sure, I met him a couple of times. The cops back in New York used to run him in every now and then."

"He's out again," said Marty, "and I'd like to send him a little gift. Just a remembrance from an old pal. I thought maybe you'd take it along and hand it to him. I'd mail it but the mail rates—"

I could understand that. The mail rates *were* high.

Marty hauled a package from his pocket and set it on the desk.

I picked it up and shook it. "Listen, Marty, you wouldn't be getting me into trouble, would you?"

He spread his hands. "Why should I be getting a friend of mine into any trouble? It's just to save the mailing costs I'm doing this. I'll tell you what it is. Just one of those sand flasks with different colored sands made into a pretty picture. A picture of a spaceship, this one is. A white ship out in space, with red sand like blasts shooting from the rockets—"

"Forget it, Marty," I said. "I just wondered. Sure, I'll take it."

"Chesty will be nuts about it," said Marty. "He always did like pretty things."

Floyd Duncan, veteran chief of the New Chicago office of the Solar Bureau of Investigation, was the first to find the clue in old Eli's murder and when he found it he didn't believe it.

He growled at me when I came into his hangout, but I kidded him along and pretty soon he softened up.

"This case has got me down," he growled.

"No clues?" I asked.

"Hell, yes," he said. "I got a clue but it's worse than not having one because it can't be right."

"What's wrong with it?"

"About one hundred years," he said, rustling papers on his desk and trying to act ferocious.

"You're all haywire," I said. "Years haven't anything to do with clues."

"You ever heard of Dr. Jennings Anderson?" he asked me.

"The chap who built the sanitarium out on Sunward?"

"That's the fellow. Built it one hundred fifty years ago. Doc was all of fifty then, himself. Put every dime he had in it. Thought he could cure the space dopes. For that matter the sanitarium is still trying to cure them, but not getting very far."

I nodded, remembering Anderson's story. The sanitarium out on the Sunward side still stood as a monument to his hopes and humanitarianism. Recognizing the space disease, which regularly struck down the men who roamed the trails between the planets, as a challenge to his knowledge and his love of humankind, he had constructed the sanitarium, had tried to cure the stricken spacemen by use of the radiations which slashed out from the Sun.

Duncan rattled some more papers and then went on. "Anderson died over one hundred years ago. He's buried out there at the sanitarium. Folks back on Earth subscribed a pile of money to put up the shaft over his grave. Had to use zero metal. Only thing that will stand up in the radiations."

I watched Duncan narrowly, wondering what he was getting at. He was right about Doc Anderson being dead, for I had seen the shaft myself, with his name inscribed on it.

"We found a brand-new dollar bill on old Eli," said Duncan. "We checked for fingerprints. Found a lot of them. Money picks prints up fast, you know. We checked all the prints and they all check out to nothing—all except one."

He ran blunt fingers through his iron-gray hair.

"That one print," he told me, "Is that of old Doc Anderson!"

"But, look," I blurted, "that can't be right!"

"Of course it can't be right," he said. "That's what worries me."

Back in my apartment I opened up the package Marty had given me and got the surprise of my life. For once, Marty had told the truth. The thing in the package really was a sand flask, one of those things the gift shops sell to tourists. Made of brilliant Mercutian sands, some of them are really bits of art.

The one I took out of the package wasn't any piece of art, but it was a fair enough piece of work. I put it on a table and looked at it, wondering why Marty would be sending something like that to an egg like Chesty.

And the more I looked at it, the stronger grew the hunch that there was something wrong. Somewhere something didn't tie together. This business of sending a sand flask to Chesty Lewis somehow didn't click.

So I wrapped it up again and hid it in my dresser drawer. Then I went out and hunted through the shops until I found one just like it. I bought that one and wrapped it up and put it in the mails, addressing it to Chesty in care of a boardinghouse that I knew could get in touch with him.

Why I did a thing like that I can't explain, even to this day. It was just a hunch, one of those unaccountable sixth senses that newsmen sometimes acquire. The whole deal had a phony ring, had put me on my guard.

Back in the apartment once again, I closed the blinds, turned off the lights and tried to go to sleep.

I was dog-tired, but I had a lot of trouble dropping off. My mind kept buzzing round.

I thought about old Eli and the new dollar bill with the one-hundred-year-old fingerprints upon it. I thought about Marty Berg sending a sand flask to Chesty Lewis and wondered if what I had just done would make any difference. I wondered about Doc Anderson, dead these hundred years or more, resting under the stele of zero metal.

Finally I did go to sleep, only to be wakened a short time later with severe stomach pains. Groping blindly on the bedside table I found a couple of capsules, swallowed them and waited for the pain to ease.

It was hours later when I finally awoke.

All sign of stomach distress was gone. I felt a good ten years younger, I told myself, lying there, reluctant to get up. It's wonderful what a good long sleep will do.

Squaring off in front of the mirror after plugging in my razor, I noticed something funny about the face that stared back at me.

I leaned closer to the glass, trying to figure out what could be wrong. The image that stared back at me was me all right, but it had a different look. There weren't nearly so many wrinkles and the baggy cheeks had filled up a little bit, and there was a slight flush of color in them.

But that wasn't all.

The streak of gray on the left side of my head was gone! The hair was coal-black!

Alarmed, I rumpled my hair, searching for gray ones. There weren't any.

It wasn't until then I remembered the capsules.

A frantic search of the vest pocket where I had placed the ones filled with old Eli's salts failed to locate them.

There was just one explanation. Absent-mindedly I had fished them out of the pocket, put them with the others on the bedside table.

Could it be that I had taken one of them when I had awakened? And if I had, would that account for the filled out cheeks, the disappearance of the gray streak?

I sat down, flabbergasted.

I remembered old Eli had told me he sold those salts to Dr. Vincent out at the Sunward sanitarium.

Back at my shaving once again, I knew there was just one thing to do. I had to see Dr. Vincent right away.

And when I went to see him I would carry a short steel bar. One that would fit my coat pocket. There would be a use for it.

Seeing Dr. Vincent was easier said than done. Few people saw him. Both he and his predecessor, Dr. Brown, were noted for their reluctance to appear in public. Too engrossed in their work, they had always said.

Anderson, Brown and Vincent, three strange men. Anderson under the stele that rose before the sanitarium entrance. Brown, undoubtedly dead, but with his later life, after he had left the sanitarium, shrouded in mystery. Vincent, present head of the institution, practically unknown to the medical profession except by reputation.

Three men who had dedicated their lives to finding a cure for the space sickness. Men who, so far, had failed. To them, from all the far corners of the Solar System came the space dopes, the men stricken by the dread disease which even now spelled the swift doom of all on whom it fastened. Not so swiftly now, perhaps, but nevertheless certain.

For the sanitarium had made some progress. By its treatment with radiations it could ease the pain, could slow up the ravages, give each victim a few more months to live, an easier death. But that was all. The space sickness still was fatal. There was no cure.

I had visited the sanitarium only once before—when I first had come to New Chicago. The New York office had wanted a feature story about the place and I had gotten it, but not from Dr. Vincent. I had not, in fact, seen Dr. Vincent. The soft-voiced robot secretary had told me he was very busy. An equally soft-voiced robot attendant had taken me in tow, had shown me the building, explained its workings, discussed learnedly the work of Dr. Vincent. It was a good story.

Practically all the attendants, I knew, were robots.

"We do not make mistakes," the soft-voiced metal-man had told me. "Here, where mistakes are fatal, we are better than a human being."

Which sounded like a good explanation, but left one sort of hanging in the air.

This time, as the time before, I had no trouble getting to the secretary who guarded Vincent's office. And this time, as the time before, I got the same answer.

"Dr. Vincent is very busy. What is it you want?"

I leaned closer, across the desk, cutting off access to the row of call buttons.

"It's a matter of life and death," I said and even as I spoke I yanked the short steel bar out of my pocket and struck.

I put everything I had into that blow and I knew just where to hit, right between the robot's gleaming eyes.

The one blow was enough. It dented in the heavy metal, smashed the delicate mechanism. The robot slid off the chair, clanged onto the floor.

For long seconds I stood there, hoping against that the walls were soundproofed. They must have been, for there was no scurry of feet outside, no sound from Vincent's inner office.

Walking softly, thanking my stars the doors did not boast newfangled locks but the simple latches of the day when the sanitarium had been built, I locked the outer door, then strode across the room and twisted the knob to Vincent's office. It turned in my hand and I stepped inside.

A man sat at a desk directly opposite the door. A man well past middle age, with snow-white hair. He was busy and did not look up when I came in. If he had heard me at all, he probably thought I was the secretary.

"Dr. Anderson?" I asked.

"Why, yes. What can I—"

And then he jerked his head up and stared at me.

I laughed at him softly.

"I thought so," I said.

Muscles jerked around his jaws, as if he were trying to keep his teeth from chattering.

"Who are you?" he asked hoarsely.

"A friend of old Eli's," I told him.

"He sent you?"

"No, he didn't send me. Eli is dead."

He started out of his chair at that. "What's that you say? Old Eli is dead? Are you certain?"

"The news," I told him, "has been in the papers. The radio carried it."

"I get no papers," he said. "I have no time to read them. The radio over there," he jerked his head toward an old set in the corner, "hasn't been turned on for months."

"It is the truth," I said. "Murdered. And the salts were stolen."

The man behind the desk went pale.

"The salts stolen!"

"Someone," I said, "who guessed what they were."

He sat down slowly, as if every ounce of strength had drained from his body. Huddled behind his desk he looked an old, old man.

"You've been afraid of this for years," I said.

He nodded dumbly.

Silence hung between us, a long and empty silence and looking at the man, I felt sorry for him.

"Afraid of it," he said, "for two reasons. But I guess it doesn't matter any more. I've failed. There is no cure. There was just one hope left and that has failed—"

I paced swiftly across the room.

"Look," I shot at him, "are you actually admitting that you are Dr. Anderson?"

He looked at me. "Why not?"

I stammered a little. "I thought you would put up a fight."

"There's no use of fighting any more," he said. "Two hundred years is too long for any man to live. Especially when he fails year after year at the goal he had set himself."

"Dr. Anderson," I said, half speaking to myself, half to him. "Dr. Brown and now Dr. Vincent."

He smiled faintly. "All three of them. It was easily arranged. I built the sanitarium, I owned it. I was accountable to no one. I named my successor and my successor named his successor. Why should the world wonder? The men who were named were men from the laboratory in this place. Obscure men, of course, but men familiar with the work."

He smiled wanly at me. "Clever?"

"But the staff?" I asked.

"Except at first, there has been none. Just myself and the patients and the robots. The robots don't talk, the patients die."

He drummed his fingers on the desk. "And who are you?"

I took a long breath. "Sherm Marshall of the Solar Press."

"And you want a story?"

I nodded, fearful of what would happen next.

And the thing that happened was the last thing I expected.

"Sit down," he said. "Since you are here, you may as well know what has been going on."

"That's swell of you, Doctor," I said, waiting for the lightning to strike.

No lightning struck.

"Have you ever kept a thing bottled up inside yourself so long you wanted to shriek?" he asked. "Have you ever ached to tell something that you knew and still you couldn't tell it?"

I nodded.

"That's me," said Dr. Anderson.

He sat silent so long I thought he had forgotten me, but finally he went on.

"I came here with a theory that the radiations thrown out by the Sun, properly screened for selectivity, would have a curative effect upon the victims of space sickness. It worked, to an extent. It alleviated the malady, but it was not a cure. It didn't go far enough. It gave a few added months, in some cases a few added years, of life, but that was all. I knew that I had failed.

"It was about the time I came to this realization that old Eli stumbled in. His car had broken down, his spacesuit was down to the last half-hour of oxygen. With him he had some peculiar salts—a queer earth such as he had never seen before. He had only a sample. I offered to analyze it for him and he left it. Quite by accident I discovered its properties.

"At about the time a very close friend of mine was brought here with the sickness. It was then that the full force of my failure was brought home to me. I knew my friend would die despite all that I could do. But he had hopes that I could save him—and that only made it worse."

He stopped and stared at something on the opposite wall, but there was nothing there.

So I reminded him: "These salts of Eli's? They prolonged life?"

It was as if something had struck him with a whip. He started and then settled back.

"Yes, they do," he said. "The extent of their possibilities I cannot say. I can tell you roughly what they do, but I don't understand just how—

"Perhaps we had better start at the beginning.

"If one is to accept the hypothesis that death is the result of the final hydrolysis of the proteins in the protoplasm, then it would seem reasonable that anything which would arrest hydrolysis or would catalyze resynthesis of the proteins would hold death at bay.

"The salts apparently do this, but whether they merely arrest the process of hydrolysis, preventing one from growing older, or whether they completely resynthesize a portion of the original proteins contained in the protoplasm I cannot even guess.

"If resynthesis actually does occur, then one might speculate upon the possibility that a larger dosage, by resynthesizing all or nearly all of the proteins would cause a man to grow younger instead of merely stopping him from growing older."

He smiled. "I never experimented. I was satisfied with arresting old age."

I didn't say a thing. I almost held my breath. It seemed incredible the man could be sitting there, telling me that story. There was something wrong. Either he was wacky or I was batty—or maybe both.

I wanted to pinch myself to make sure it wasn't all a dream, because, if it wasn't, here was the biggest story the world had ever read.

Here was the sort of thing Ponce de Leon, the old Earth explorer, had dreamed about. Here, in hard truth, was an age-old myth that had echoed down the world for ages.

He was quiet so long that I finally spoke. "So you took some of the salts. Possibly so you could continue your work?"

"That's it," he said. "I talked it over with my friend, the one who expected me to help him—the one I knew I couldn't help.

"He understood and agreed to do his part. I was to prolong my life so I could continue with my work. He was to continue his so I could use him as a subject for experiments. It wasn't an easy decision for him to make, for it meant years of torturing illness. The salts seemed to help him to some extent, perhaps repairing some of the ravages of the disease and for a while we thought they might be the cure. But they failed us, too. He lived—it's true—but he wasn't cured."

"But why was it necessary to continue his life?" I asked. "Necessary for the experiments, I mean. Certainly you had plenty of other patients to experiment upon."

"They died too fast," said Anderson. "A few months, a few years at the most. I needed long range observation."

He matched fingertips, speaking slowly, as if choosing his words with care.

"Perhaps you wonder why I did not pass my work along, why I did not select someone else and train them so they could pick up where I left off. Maybe that would have been the best. I've often blamed myself for not doing it instead of this. But my research had become an obsession. It wasn't all pride or scientific ardor. There was the human angle to it, too. No man could have seen those poor devils, doomed, without a single chance, and not wanted to do something for them. They weren't just patients. They were human beings, crying for someone to do something—and no one had. I tried to—God knows how I tried.

"I was afraid, you see, that someone else, no matter how carefully selected, might not be able to carry on with the singleness of purpose that seemed necessary—that somewhere along the way they might falter, might get sick of the job. That couldn't be, that was the one thing that simply could not happen. Someone at least had to keep on trying to help those men for whom there was no help."

"So you killed yourself off," I said. "You let yourself be buried. You saw the stele erected in your honor. You became Dr. Brown and later Dr. Vincent. And yet, when I called you Dr. Anderson you answered."

"I've always been Anderson," he said. "The robots, of course, call me by the name I go by at the moment, but my friend who has stood by me all these years always calls me Anderson."

He grimaced. "He never could get used to my other names."

"And Eli?"

"Eli was easy to manage. I made him believe he had a malignant ailment, cautioned him he must come here at regular intervals for injections. The injections, of course, were his own salts. They have to be taken at intervals. After a time the hydrolysis would reach a point where it was necessary to set the catalytic action back to work again."

He rose from the desk and paced up and down the room.

"But now Eli is dead. And I have failed. And someone else knows about the salts."

He stopped in front of me.

"Do you realize what the knowledge of the salts will do to the Solar System?" he demanded. "Can you see what I have feared all these years?"

"What are you talking about?" I asked. "The salts would be the greatest blessing the world has ever known—"

He stared at me.

"Greatest blessing, did you say?" he whispered.

His fists clenched and unclenched by his side.

"They would be the greatest curse that could fall on mankind. Can you see what men would do to get them? No crime too foul, no treachery too great. Can you imagine what those in power would charge for them? Charge in money and service and power? The man who had them would rule the Solar System, for he could hold forth or withdraw the hope of eternal youth, of eternal life.

"Can you even remotely imagine the economic consequences? Men beggaring themselves for a few more years of life. Life insurance companies crashing as the people grabbed at the hope of living forever. For if a man is to live forever why bother with insurance? And when the insurance companies crashed they would drag others with them—companies that hold their paper—and other companies that—But why go on. Surely you must see.

"Envision the wars that might result. The mad hunt for the magic salts—"

"Wait a minute," I shouted at him. "You're forgetting that the man who killed Eli probably didn't find out where Eli got the salts. He stole the salts that Eli had, but he probably doesn't know—"

"That makes no difference," said Anderson. "No difference at all. Once the System knows such salts exist all hell will break wide open. Mercury will be swamped with men looking for them—"

He stopped his tirade, walked around the desk and sat down.

"I hope you've enjoyed my story, Mr. Marshall."

I gulped at that one. "Enjoyed it! Why, it's the greatest story the System's ever known. They'll give it headlines two feet high. They'll spread it—"

I stopped because I didn't like the look that had crept into his eyes.

"You realize, of course, Mr. Marshall, that you shall never print it."

"Never print it," I yelped. "What did you tell it to me for?"

"I took advantage of you," said Anderson. "I had to tell it to someone. I've had it corked up in me too long. And I needed time."

I gulped again. "Time—"

He nodded. "Time for the robots to take certain measures. By this time they have discovered something is wrong. They are quick at things like that."

He seemed to be laughing at me.

"You'll never leave this place alive," he said.

—

We sat there looking at one another. He was smiling. I don't know how I looked. I was mad and plenty scared.

"Don't misunderstand me," he said. "We mustn't be dramatic. I don't mean I am going to kill you. I mean that you will never leave this place. If you try you'll most assuredly be killed. You see, I can't let you go. Not knowing what you know."

"You dirty—" but he stopped me.

"You asked for it," he said.

A door back of the desk opened softly and a ray of light slashed into the room. Through the door I caught the glimpse of a laboratory.

A tall, gaunt man stood in the doorway. His face was pallid above the black lounging robe he wore.

"Anderson—" he began excitedly.

"Why, Ernie," said Anderson. "I didn't expect to see you. We have a guest. Mr. Sherman Marshall. He's staying for a while"—he cast me a sidelong look—"for quite a while," he finished.

"I am glad to know you," Ernie said to me. "Do you, by chance, play whist? Anderson is no good at it. Claims it is old-fashioned—absolutely primitive."

"I don't know a thing about it," I said, "but I'm handy with cards."

"Of course," said Anderson to me, "you must have guessed that Ernie is my partner in crime. Not quite as old as I am but almost. Ernie Hitchcock. Once one of the best captains that ever flew in space."

"I came to tell you," said Hitchcock, speaking to Anderson with the old urgency in his voice, "that there has been a reaction. The kind we were hoping for. I made sure before—"

Anderson's hands grasped at the table.

"A reaction—" he choked. "You mean it . . . really . . . what we were looking for?"

Hitchcock nodded.

Anderson turned to me. "You will excuse us?"

I nodded, not knowing what to say. I was trying to make head and tail or what had happened. What did the tall, gaunt man mean by reaction? Could it mean that a cure had been found, after all these years, for the space sickness? Did it mean that Dr. Anderson, at the moment all seemed lost, had triumphed in this search that had stretched over three lifetimes?

The two went out the door, into the laboratory and I watched them go. Minutes dragged by. I got up and paced around the room. I stared at the books in the shelves, but there was nothing to interest me, mostly medical works.

Knowing it wouldn't do me any good, I went to the door leading into the room where I'd bashed the robot on the head. I opened it and there squarely in front of it, stood a robot with his arms folded across his chest. He looked as if he were just waiting for me to make a break. He said nothing and I said nothing. I simply shut the door.

The radio caught my attention and I wondered if it would work. Anderson had said it hadn't been tuned in for months. Radio reception usually is almost impossible here, but with the new broadcast units put in at New Chicago in the last few months it should be halfway decent, I thought.

I turned it on and the set lighted up and hummed. Swiftly I spun the dial to the New Chicago wave length and the voice of Jimmy Doyle, newscaster, blared out, somewhat disrupted by static, but still intelligible.

Jimmy was just starting his broadcast and what he had to say held me rooted to the spot —

"—still searching for Sherman Marshall, wanted for the murder of Eli Lawrence. A warrant was issued for Marshall's arrest ten hours ago when a canvas bag belonging to the murdered man was found in an alley near the North Wall. Marshall's fingerprints, the police say, were found upon it. A bartender at the Sun Spot, a night club—"

There was a lot more to it, and I listened, but it didn't mean much. The things that mattered were my fingerprints upon the canvas bag in which old Eli had carried his salts and the story the bartender at the Sun Spot had told the police.

Back at New Chicago the cops were in full cry. Intent to hang the murder on someone. Anxious to make a showing because election was near.

And with those fingerprints and the bartender's story it wouldn't be so hard to hang it on me.

Numbly I reached out and snapped off the radio. Covering trials, both in New Chicago and back on Earth, I often had tried to put myself in the defendant's place, had tried to imagine what he was thinking, how he felt.

And now I knew!

I was safe, I knew, for a while, for no one would think of looking for me here. Perhaps even if they did come looking they wouldn't find me, for Anderson would want to keep me hidden. It would be to his interest to keep me where I couldn't talk.

I thought back over the events immediately preceding and following Eli's death—and I suddenly remembered the sand flask hidden in my dresser drawer. The sand flask with the white spaceship!

The door to the laboratory opened and Anderson entered the room. He was all smiles and he almost beamed at me.

"I have been thinking," he said. "Perhaps I can let you go."

"What's that?" I yelped.

"I said I was thinking I needn't keep you here."

"But, Doc," I protested, "I really want to stay. I think—"

And then I saw it wasn't any good. If he was ready to let me leave, he would be no protection if I stayed.

"But why this sudden switch?" I demanded. "If you let me go, I'll publish the story. Sure as hell, I will."

"I don't think you will," he said. "Because I am trading you another story for it. A bigger story—"

"The cure? You've found the cure?"

He nodded. "There had seemed just one thing left to do. A very dangerous thing and with slight chance of success. If that failed, we feared that we were done. We had then explored every possibility. We had come to the end.

"We tried and failed—or so it seemed. But what had seemed failure was really success. The reaction was slower than we thought, took longer to manifest itself. We know now that we can cure the space sickness."

He was staring at the wall again and there still was nothing there—

"It will take some time," he finally said. "A little time to perfect the method. But I still have a little time . . . a little time . . . enough—"

"But, Doctor," I yelled at him, "you must have some salts. You certainly didn't use all that Eli brought you. There is no need to talk of time."

He turned tired eyes to me.

"Yes, I have some salts," he said. "Let me show you—"

He rose and went through the laboratory. I followed him.

From a cabinet above a sink he lifted down a box and opened it. Inside I saw the crystals.

"Look," said Anderson.

He upended the box, dumped the salts into the sink, reached out and turned the tap. In silence we watched the water wash them down the drain.

"Try and tell that story now," he said. "You'll be laughed out of your profession. There is no evidence. I am the only evidence and I will soon be dead.

"I've waited for this day—for the day when I could pour them down the drain. I've done what I set out to do. I've taken the terror out of space. I've answered the prayers I have seen in the eyes of dying men. No one, even if they knew, and believed, my story, could say now that I had been wrong in doing what I did."

"You forget just one thing, Doctor."

"What is that?"

"There still is evidence. Someone stole some salts from Eli."

He blanched at that. I knew he would. In the triumph of the moment he had forgotten it. His hand shook as he put back the box, turned off the water.

And in that instant, I think, I realized what he stood for. I could envision those long lonely years. Facing failure every year, despairing of ever doing what need be done. Keeping within his brain a knowledge that would have brought him greater glory than any man had ever had and yet keeping silent because he knew what his secret would do to the people of the System.

"Look, Doctor," I said.

"Yes?"

"About those salts that Eli had. You needn't worry. I know where they are."

"You know where they are?"

"Yes, but I didn't until a minute ago."

He didn't ask the question, but I answered it.

"I'll do what's necessary," I said.

Silently he held out his hand to me.

I knew where those salts were, all right. But the problem was to reach them.

I knew, too, who had murdered Eli. But there was no way to prove it. The salts would have furnished the proof, but it was doubtful if any court, any jury would have believed my story. And using them as evidence would have told the world, would have broken faith with Dr. Jennings Anderson.

My first job was to get them.

How I did it I still don't clearly remember. I remember that I came into the west port of the city with a jam of other cars, gambling on the belief the police would be watching outgoing cars, would pay little attention to incoming ones.

Once inside I ran the car into a side street, ducked it into an alley and abandoned it. I remember dodging up alleys, hiding in recessed doorways to avoid passers-by, working nearer and nearer to my apartment house.

Getting into the house was simpler than I thought.

Plain-clothes men were watching the place, but their watch had eased up a bit. After all, what murderer would be crazy enough to come back to a place he knew was being watched?

I waited my chance and took it. I met one man in the hall, but turned to one of the doors, fumbling in my pocket as if for a key, shielding my face from him until he was past.

My own room was unguarded. Probably they figured that it was impossible for me to slip into the building, so why guard the room?

The place had been ransacked, but nothing, apparently, had been taken.

Swiftly I went to the dresser in the bedroom, pulled out the drawer, lifted out the sand flask. With trembling fingers I pried out the cork, shook out the contents.

There was no mistaking the appearance of the white sand. It wasn't white sand—it was the crystals Eli had shown me at the Sun Spot.

What was it Anderson had said—"*if resynthesis actually does occur a man would grow younger*—"

I hesitated for a moment, but only for a moment. Then I scooped up some of the crystals, put them in my mouth and swallowed. They went down hard—like sand. But they went down. I took some more, just to make sure. I had no way of knowing how many I should take. Then I washed the rest down the bathroom drain.

After that I sat down to wait. I knew it was a dangerous thing to do, but probably it was as safe there in my room as any other place.

Four hours later I walked out of the apartment house, through the lobby, right past Floyd Duncan, SBI chief. He didn't know me. For that matter I hardly knew myself. To all appearances, I was a youth of no more than twenty years.

The newsboys began screaming an extra as I neared the Martian Times building in Sandebar. I stopped to listen to their shouts.

"Extra!" they bellowed. "Marty Berg Guilty. Marty Berg Guilty of Eli Lawrence Murder."

I shrugged my shoulders. It had taken Duncan plenty of time to crack that one. I grinned as I remembered him sitting in the apartment lobby, never blinking an eyelash as I sauntered past.

In the newsroom I walked up to the city editor's desk.

"What do you want?" a hard-boiled guy barked at me.

"I thought you might need a man."

"Can you write?"

I nodded.

"Experience?"

I rattled off the story I had fixed up.

"What the hell are you doing on Mars?" he demanded. "This isn't any fit place for a man to live."

"Bumming around," I told him. "Seeing the System."

He made doodles on a sheet of paper.

"I'll try you out," he said. "I like your looks. Remind me of someone. Someone I met." He shook his head. "Can't place him."

But I had placed him. He was Herb North. I'd met him once, years before, at a press convention. We'd gone on a bat together.

"Ever hear of a guy named Chesty Lewis?" he asked.

"Read about him. New York gangster, isn't he?"

"He used to be in New York," said North, "but he lammed out here a few months ago. He's coming up for trial this morning. That will be your first job. Funny case. Seems he took an old bird for about a billion bucks. Told the old sucker he had some stuff that would make him young again. But it didn't and so—we have a trial."

I nodded. I knew all about it.

Chesty Lewis had sold Andrew J. Rasmussen, Mars utility magnate, a small bottle of white sand—the kind that comes in those picture flasks they sell to tourists out on Mercury.

THE LOOT OF TIME

Clifford D. Simak has always shown an interest in ancient humans. Not only in this story—which was published in the December 1938 issue of Wonder Stories—*but in several later stories, his characters evoked their caveman ancestors. (Cliff also wrote a sequel to "The Loot of Time," called "The Legend of Time"—which went unpublished—and a nonfiction book titled* Prehistoric Man.) *Keep in mind that when archaeological evidence was found indicating that people had lived in Minnesota in ancient times, Cliff Simak was the journalist assigned to investigate and report on it.*

—dww

Chapter I
The Time Tractor

Hugh Cameron rose from his knees and dusted his hands. He looked at Jack Cabot and Conrad Yancey and the two of them stared back at him, questioningly.

"We're ready to go," Cameron announced. "I've checked everything."

"You give me the willies," Yancey spoke flatly. "Checking and rechecking."

"Got to make sure," Cameron told him. "Can't take any chances, not on a trip like this."

Cabot shoved up his hat and scratched his head.

"Are you sure that the theory and the mechanism are all right, Hugh?" he asked anxiously. "I still have a feeling we're all crazy."

Cameron nodded.

"Near as I can make out, Jack, it will work. I've gone over it step by step. Pascal has something here that's unique. A theory that has no precedent. Treating time as something abstract, but using that very basis for time-travel."

"It would take a guy who got kicked out of Oxford for saying Einstein's relativity theory was all haywire to make something like this," observed Yancey.

Cameron pointed at a crystal globe atop a mass of intricate machinery.

"The whole answer is in that time-brain," he said. "That's the one thing I can't figure out. How he made it I don't know. But it works. I have proof of that. The rest all checks out.

"Pascal has taken the position that time is purely subjective. That it has no existence in fact. That it is only a mental concept, but something that is entirely necessary for orientation."

"That's the part I can't get my teeth into," protested Cabot. "It seems to me that if a man were going to travel in time there'd have to be existent time to travel in. Time would have to be an actual factor. Otherwise it would not obey mechanical rules. There'd be no theater for mechanical operation. In other words, just how in hell are we going to travel through something that doesn't exist?"

Cameron lit a cigarette and tried to explain.

"Your mind sticks on the mechanical part," he said. "Pascal's theory isn't all mechanics or all mathematics, although there're plenty of both. There're a lot of psychological concepts and that's one place where they come in. He figures that even if time is nonexistent, even if it has no factual identity, that the human brain has a well-developed time-sense. Time seems entirely natural to us. Viewed from the commonplace point of view, there is absolutely no mystery about it. It is firmly embedded in the human consciousness.

"Pascal figured that if you constructed a mechanical brain you could construct it in such a manner that its time-sense would be enormously magnified. Maybe ten thousand times that of a human mind. Maybe more. There's no way to tell. So Pascal not only constructed the mechanical counterpart of a human brain, but he constructed it with an exaggerated time-sense. That brain over there knows more about time right now than the human race will ever know. Nobody else on Earth could have done it. No twentieth-century man. Pascal's a wizard. That's what he is."

"Listen, Hugh," said Cabot, "I want to be sure. I sent over to America, had you come out to London because I knew that if any man could tell me anything about this pipe-dream it would be you. I want you to feel absolutely certain. I can't understand it myself. I figure you can. If you have any doubt, say so now. I don't want to get stuck halfway back in time."

Cameron puffed away at his smoke.

"It isn't a pipe-dream, Jack. It's the goods. The time-sense in the brain is developed to a point where it has an ability to assume mastery over time. It can move through time. What's more, it can move the time-tractor through time—with all of us inside the tractor. Not hypnotism, because in hypnotism you only think you're some place or doing something that isn't so.

"The brain actually can move back and forth in time and it can move us back and forth in time. It develops some sort of a force. Not electricity. Pascal thought it was that at first. But it isn't, although it's related to electricity. For want of a better term we might call it a time-force. That describes it well enough. It develops this force in sufficient amount to operate the control mechanism that guides the brain's movement through time."

He flipped his hands helplessly.

"That's all I can tell you. The rest of it is mathematics that would be pure Greek to you and mechanics that you'd have to take eight years of college to understand."

He looked at Cabot.

"You have to take my word for it, Jack, that the damn thing will run."

Cabot smiled.

"That's good enough for me, Hugh," he said.

A shadow blotted out the sunlight on the floor. The three looked toward the door.

Dr. Thomas Pascal stood there, a white-haired man with a face that was almost childish in its simplicity. He was one of 1940's scientific wizards.

"All ready to start?" he asked cheerfully.

Cameron nodded.

"Everything seems all right, Doctor," he said. "I've checked every cable, every cog, every contact. They're all in perfect order."

"All right, then," growled Yancey. "What are we waiting for. I'm all set to slaughter me a saber-tooth."

"You'll find plenty of them," Pascal told him. "I told you I'd take you to a virgin game field. A place where a rifle shot had never been fired. That's what I'm going to do."

Cameron laughed.

"Doctor," he asked, "how did you ever get the idea of selling these two mad hunters on this proposition? A hunting trip back into time. That's one for the records."

"I needed money to finish the tractor," Pascal told him, "so I cast around for someone who might be interested, but interested in such a way that my invention would not be used for base ends. Then I heard of Mr. Cabot and Mr. Yancey. Plenty of money. Famous hunters. What could be more appealing to them than a hunting trip back into the past? But they weren't easy to convince. They listened only when I consented to let you check the entire machine."

Cabot shook his head stubbornly.

"Doctor, you still have to show me those game fields back in the Riss-Wurm interglacial period. It's fifty thousand years or more back there. A long ways to go."

"You'll eat mammoth steak for dinner tonight," Pascal told him.

"If you're going to make good on that promise," Cameron suggested, "we had better get started. All our supplies are stored, the machinery is checked. We're ready."

"All right," agreed Pascal. "Will someone shut the door and make sure the ports are closed?"

Yancey walked to the doorway, reached out to pull the door shut and lock it. For a moment he stood still, staring out over the green hills. There, only a few miles away, lay the village of Aylesford. And beyond lay the valley of the Thames. A country steeped in legend and history. In a few minutes they would be moving back, through and beyond the days which had given rise to that legend and history. Two American hunters on the maddest hunting trip the world had ever known.

Yancey closed the door, chuckling.

"Wonder how much lead it takes to stop a saber-tooth?" he mused.

Turning back to the interior of the great tractor, he saw that the time-brain was glowing greenly. Dr. Pascal, standing before it, seemed like a tiny, misshapen gnome, working before a fiery furnace.

"Door closed and locked," Yancey reported.

"Ports all tight," said Cabot.

"Okay," replied Pascal.

Machinery hummed faintly, nothing more than a whisper of a sound.

There was nothing to indicate they had left the present, were moving backward through time, but when Yancey looked through a port, he choked back an exclamation.

There was nothing outside the port. Just a blank, flat, gray plane of nothingness, with now and then shadows that flitted and were gone.

Pascal sucked in his breath as the tractor rocked and bumped. The gray outside the port became less dense. Objects became faintly discernible.

"We're going too fast," Pascal explained. "Ground seems to be rising. Have to take it slower. We might hit something. Most things wouldn't stop us, but there's no use taking chances."

"Sure the ground is rising," Cameron told him. "Maybe by this time there isn't any English channel. Back in the Riss-Wurm period the British Isles were connected with the continent. The Thames flowed north through the North Sea basin to reach the North Sea."

The gray outside the ports thinned even more. The tractor rocked like a boat in a gentle swell. Then the grayness turned to white, a dazzling white that blinded Yancey. The tractor moved sharply upward, seemed to be riding a huge wave, then dropped, but more slowly.

"We just passed the Wurm glacier," Pascal told them. "We're in the Riss-Wurm now."

"Take it just a little easier," Cameron warned him. "That last bump busted a tube in the field radio. We can fix that, but we may need that radio. We don't want to smash it entirely."

Outside the port now Yancey could make out objects. A tree became clearer, was sharply defined and beyond it Yancey saw solid landscape, bathed in a rising sun.

He heard Pascal's voice.

"Seventy thousand years, approximately," he said. "We should be where we intended to go."

But Yancey was intent on the scene outside. The tractor stood on the top of a high knoll. Below unfolded a panorama of wild beauty. Rolling hills fell away to a wide valley, green with lush grass, while in the distance a stream caught the sunlight of early dawn and glinted like a ribbon of silver. And on the hills and in the valley below were black dots, feeding game herds, some so close he could make out individual animals. Others mere black spots.

Yancey whistled soundlessly.

He wheeled from the port.

"Jack," he began breathlessly, "there are thousands of herds out there—"

But Cabot, he saw, had already unlocked the door.

The four of them stood grouped in the doorway and stared out. Pascal smiled.

"You see," he reminded them, "that I told you the truth."

Cabot drew in his breath sharply.

"You sure did," he admitted. "I doubt if Africa in its prime was better than this."

"An overlapping of fauna," said Pascal. "The old Stone Age merging with the modern. One type dying out, another coming in. The most diversified and plentiful game herds that ever existed on the face of the earth before or since. The cave bear, the saber-tooth, the cave hyena, the mammoth and woolly rhinoceros living coincidentally with vast herds of wild ox, reindeer, Irish elk and other animals of more recent times."

"Some hunting!" said Yancey.

Cabot nodded in agreement. He stepped down from the door onto the ground.

"Let's stretch our legs," he suggested.

"Can't right now," said Cameron. "Have to check the machinery over. I want to be sure everything's all right."

Yancey jumped to the ground.

"You fellows had better take your rifles," warned Cameron.

Cabot laughed.

"We have our revolvers," he said. "We aren't going far away."

The two hunters walked slowly, wonderingly, away from the tractor. The ground beneath their feet was soft to the tread with thick grass. Head-high thickets spotted the hillsides that sloped away toward the river. On some of the hills reared great, grotesque rock formations. And everywhere was game.

Yancey halted and lifted a pair of binoculars to his eyes. For several minutes he stood, studying the landscape. Then he lowered the glasses and slipped the thong from his neck. He handed them to Cabot.

"Take a look, Jack," he invited. "You won't believe it until you see it with your own eyes. There's a herd of mammoth down by the river. That dark spot just this side of the big grove. And there's another big bunch up the river a bit. I picked up a few woolly rhinos. And bison, something like the old American buffalo."

"*Bos priscus,*" said Cabot. "I read up some on Stone Age animals the last few weeks. Primitive form of bison. Maybe we'll be able to get a few *Bos latifrons.* Big brutes with a horn spread of ten feet. But maybe they're extinct. They're the grandpappies of those fellows out there."

"What's that big bunch across the river?" Yancey asked.

Cabot trained the glasses in the direction of Yancey's pointing finger.

"Irish elk," he pronounced.

A coughing roar brought the two men halfway around. What they saw held them petrified for a moment.

Less than a hundred feet away, at the edge of a thicket, through which he must have come without a sound, stood a massive bear. A huge beast, six feet at the shoulders. He was dark brown in color and he was angry. He rocked gently from side to side and champed his jaws. From his chest rumbled a growl that seemed to shake the earth.

"For God's sake," hissed Cabot, "don't move fast! Edge over toward the tractor easy. That boy is ready to charge!"

Yancey's hand dropped to his gun butt. Out of the tail of his eye Cabot caught the motion.

"Yancey, you damn fool," he whispered huskily, "keep your hand away from that. A forty-five slug wouldn't more than tickle him."

Slowly the two men backed away from the bear, back toward the towering gray form of the time-tractor, their eyes never leaving the monstrous beast that stood swaying before them. The bear was working himself into a rage. His chest rumbling was almost continuous now, like a train crossing a long trestle. He snarled and the snarl was a sound of raw fury that sent cold shivers up Cabot's spine.

Tensely they paced their slow backward march. Yancey's heel caught in a root and he stumbled, but righted himself quickly. The bear growled thunderously and shook his head. Foam from his drooling jaws flecked the massive brown shoulders.

Then the bear charged. With no apparent preliminary move he launched into full motion, with the speed of an avalanche.

"Run," shrieked Cabot, but his cry was drowned out by a blasting report. The charging bear lurched forward, struck head and shoulders on the ground and somersaulted.

Cabot, racing toward the time-tractor, saw Cameron and Pascal framed in the doorway, heavy elephant guns at their shoulders.

"Wait," roared Cabot. "Make that second shot count!"

In three leaps he was beside the tractor door.

Pascal shoved the gun at him.

"Never shot one before in my life," he told Cabot.

Cabot spun about, gun in hand.

The bear was on its feet, swaying heavily from side to side. Its small pig eyes gleamed balefully and red foam flecked its jaws and shoulders.

Deliberately Cabot brought the gun-barrel up, centered the sights squarely between the two eyes and squeezed the trigger. The bear coughed gently and rolled over.

Yancey wiped his brow with the back of his hand.

"Closest shave I've ever had," he confessed.

"Cave bear," said Pascal. "Just one of the big life-forms you will find here."

Cameron stepped down from the tractor.

"You'll find out these animals aren't the gun-shy brutes you two have been hunting," he stated. "These babies don't fear man. They figure man isn't dangerous, if in fact they've ever seen a man. The Neanderthalers that are living somewhere in this country right now are no match for a brute like that."

Yancey wiped his brow again.

"This is the damnest place I ever saw," he declared. "Jack and me just step out for a smoke and a look-around. We aren't gone five minutes and a bear jumps us."

Cameron guffawed.

"Picked you out for breakfast," he said.

Yancey grimaced, but made no reply.

Suddenly Cabot hunched forward, finger pointing to a patch of tall grass beyond the dead bear.

"There's something in there!" he whispered harshly.

A tawny shape raced from the grass, landed on top of the bear's brown body. With glinting claws and powerful teeth it laid back the hide on the great shoulder. Then, seeing the men, it backed away, its face twisted into a blood stained snarl.

Yancey's .45 leaped out of its holster and exploded almost as it cleared. One explosion blending with another, the gun set up a roll of thunder that beat against the ears of the four men.

Still snarling, the tawny beast jerked to the impact of the heavy slugs. Then it sprawled and tumbled as Yancey's gun clicked on an empty cartridge.

But it was not dead. Snarling and spitting, it regained its feet, slunk low in a deadly slouch, razor-sharp, foot-long fangs bared in a murderous sneer.

Cabot whipped out his revolver as Yancey rapidly clicked new cartridges into the cylinder. Cameron snapped the elephant gun to his shoulder. The rifle bellowed and the cat rolled over. Cabot slid his gun back into the holster.

"Saber-tooth," said Pascal coolly.

"He sure carries lead," Yancey commented, breathing hard.

Cameron cradled the rifle in his arm and stared at the two animals.

"Hunting," he said. "Hell, this isn't hunting. This is an eternal Custer's last stand—a continuous battle in self-defense."

"Those critters sure are blood-thirsty," agreed Yancey.

"And," he added, "not afraid of us."

Cameron blew smoke through the gun barrel.

"Wonder how cave bear steaks taste," he mused.

Yancey looked the huge animal over.

"Probably tougher than hell," he said appraisingly.

Chapter II
The Centaurians

From the office of Time Travel, Inc., on the 600th story of the Berkley stratosphere building, New York lay stretched below, a fairy city. Under the soft glow of millions of lights it took on an unearthly beauty. It was a city of slender pinnacles of pure white beauty, looping arches of rainbow hues, formal gardens and parks, gleaming towers of argent, black domes.

Steve Clark liked the view. He often came here at night to sit and talk with his friend, Andy Smith, one of the ace pilots of the Time Travel service.

Smith was reading the last edition of the *Daily Rocket*. Steve Clark had brought it in only a moment before, fresh from the press, and thrown it on the desk. Smith had it spread in the white circle thrown by the lone light. The rest of the office was in darkness. Beyond the desk lockers, other desks and record files loomed darkly. The time-machines themselves were in an adjoining room, ready for launching from the face of the building.

"How's business?" asked Clark, with his feet fixed firmly on top of the desk.

Andy Smith grunted.

"Not so good. It's the fifty-sixth century, time-travel isn't a novelty any more and our rates are too high. Didn't have more than a dozen or two trips all week." He jabbed his finger at the purple headlines. "Times seem to be all right for you newspaper fellows," he said. "Lots of big news this afternoon."

"Yeah," Steve Clark agreed. "The Centaurians again. They're always good for a banner-line any day. Made a real haul this time."

"I should say so," Smith said. "Martian bongo stones, eh? Fourteen of them. Largest and most perfect collection in the entire Solar System."

"That's it," said Clark. "The old man almost busted a blood vessel when that story came in an hour ago. Wanted to scoop the city."

Clark chuckled.

"We did," he said.

Andy Smith folded the paper carefully.

"Steve," he said, "what are the Centaurians? Nobody seems to know."

"They're super-crooks for one thing," Clark said, "and when you've said that, you've said about all that anyone knows about them for sure. They've laughed at the best brains in the police business for the last five hundred years. And I figure they'll still be laughing five hundred years from now if they live that long and there's no reason to think they won't. Unless they're keeping it a secret, the flatfeet don't even know where their hideout is located. They've made monkeys out of everyone. Hell, didn't they steal a gold shipment out from under the nose of the Interplanetary Police, and keep it, too, in spite of the fact that every damn IP man in the System was turned loose on the case?"

"You figure, then," asked Smith, "that the Centaurians are real? That they are something that isn't human. A super-gang of unearthly bandits?"

"You know," Clark replied, "a newspaperman doesn't take to fables very easy. He breaks more myths than any other kind of critter I know. But, as a newspaper man, I'm telling you that these Centaurians aren't human. Probably a lot of jobs have been blamed on them that they never had a thing to do with. But there are cases on record of eye-witnesses who saw them. Only two or three such instances in the last five hundred years, but they check up well.

"All agree on vital points. They got tails and they're covered with scales and instead of feet they have hoofs. Whatever they are, they don't go in for penny-ante stuff. When they make a haul, it's one that's worthwhile. Those bongo stones. They were worth ten billion if they were worth a dime. And the shipload of IP gold."

Smith whistled.

"Then you figure they came from Alpha Centauri?" he asked.

"Either Alpha Centauri or some other place outside the System. Nothing like them have been found on any of the planets here. I always sort of figured they were fugitives from their own System. Maybe things got too hot for them, wherever they were, and they had to take it on the lam. Whatever they are or wherever they come from they sure have easy pickings here. They walk off with just about whatever they want to and nobody's even come close to catching up with them.

"I read some place, long time ago, that it is believed they came to Earth in some sort of a crazy space ship. Wrecked when it struck. The ship was smashed up and two or three of its occupants were killed—but I guess they never did find out much about them from that. The ship was all in pieces and the things in it were crushed to pulp. Maybe it was something or somebody else, not the Centaurians at all."

Steve Clark lighted a Venus-weed cigar and puffed.

"Whatever they are," he said, "they make damn good news copy."

Smith glanced at this watch.

"I'll be off in a few minutes," he said. "What say we hop over to Paris and buy us a round of drinks?"

"Sounds all right," agreed Clark.

Smith rose from his chair, stuffing the paper into his pocket. And standing there, beside the desk, he froze in astonishment.

The office door was open and inside it stood a group of black-shrouded figures that seemed to blend with the darkness. Something gleamed in the light reflected from the polished table-top.

A voice spoke out of the darkness, a voice that spoke the English tongue with slurred accent.

"You will please resume your seat," it suggested.

Smith sat down again and Clark, dropping his feet from the desk, jerked his chair around.

"You also, sir," said the voice.

Clark obeyed. There was some metallic menace in those short, clipped, incredibly accented words which held a definite note of threat.

Slowly, majestically, one of the black-shrouded figures strode forward, leaving his companions by the door. He stopped before the desk, still in the darkness, but better defined now in the reflections from the desk-top. The man wore dark glasses and he was shrouded in a dark cape, the edge of which trailed to the floor, covering his feet. A black cowl, a part of the cape, covered his head and draped over his face, hiding most of his features.

Steve Clark felt the hair crawl at the back of his neck as he studied the visitor.

Smith made his voice pleasant.

"Anything I can do for you?" he asked.

"Yes, there is," said the strange, black-draped figure, and in the faint light Smith saw the quick, smooth flash of white teeth in the shadowed face. He couldn't make out the face. Couldn't see anything, in fact, except the flash of teeth when he spoke and the occasional dull shine of reflected light from the man's eyes.

The teeth flashed again.

"I want a time-condensor," he said.

Andy Smith managed to choke back a gasp of astonishment, but his face was blank when he answered.

"We don't sell parts," he said.

"No," said the black-robed one, and the single word sounded more like a challenge than a question.

"There is no call for them," Smith explained. "Time Travel has the only time-machines in existence. They operate under strict governmental supervision. No one else owns a time-machine. Naturally, the only ones who would have use for spare parts would be our own company."

"But you have an extra condensor?"

"Several of them," Smith admitted. "We have need of replacements frequently. It's dangerous to go into time with a faulty condensor."

"I know that," the other replied. "Contrary to what you may believe, there is at least one time machine in existence other than the ones you own. I have one."

Something like a chuckle sounded from his lips.

"Strangely enough I obtained it from your company. Many years ago. I came here to get a condensor," said the man. The ugly muzzle of some sort of a weapon poked from the folds of his cape. "I can take it by force if need be. I would prefer not to. On the other hand, if you would cooperate, I would be willing to pay."

He leaned closer to the desk. A hand flashed out of the cape, was visible for only an instant and then disappeared inside the cape again. But the hand had tossed several small round objects on the desk-top, objects that seemed to spin in a blaze of color under the lamp-light.

"Bongo stones," said the white teeth. "Not the ones stolen this afternoon. No way to identify them. But bongo stones. Worth a fortune."

Steve Clark stared at the stones, his mind spinning.

Bongo stones! He counted them. Ten of them! In a flash he knew who this visitor was, knew that the myth of the Centaurians was true. For he had glimpsed that hand during the swift instant it had tossed the stones on the desk-top. A scaly hand, like the paw of a reptile. And the clicking of the thing's feet when it walked was like the sound of cloven hoofs.

Through his buzzing mind came the voice.

"And now suppose I take a condensor under my arm and walk out. Leaving the stones behind."

Smith hesitated.

The muzzle of the weapon gestured imperiously, impatiently.

"Otherwise," said the cold voice, "I shall kill you and take the condensor in any event."

Smith rose and walked mechanically to a locker. Steve Clark heard the rasp of a key as his friend opened the door to take out a condensor.

But he still stared at the bongo stones.

Now he knew why the police had never found the Centaurians' hiding place. They had no hiding place! They were bandits in time! The whole scope of space and time for their operations! They could sack the Queen of Sheba's mines one day and the next day move on to snatch treasures out of the remote future, treasures yet undreamed of!

"Clever," he said. "Damn clever."

Andy Smith was standing beside him, looking at the stones. They were alone in the room.

"You gave them the condensor?" Clark asked.

Smith nodded, dry-lipped.

"There wasn't anything else I could do, Steve."

Clark motioned toward the stones.

"What about these, Andy?"

"I was thinking," Smith said. "We couldn't sell them here—or anywhere else. They'd ask us how we got them. They'd lock us up. Probably before they got through with it, they'd prove we stole them and send us to the Moon-mines."

"There's a way," Clark suggested. He nodded toward the hangar where the time-machines were ranged.

Smith wet his lips.

"I thought of that," he said. "After all, those fellows stole a time-machine from the company once. Probably the company never reported the loss. Afraid of what the government might do."

Silence hung like a breathing menace over the room.

"Those were the Centaurians, weren't they?" Andy Smith asked.

Clark nodded. Then waited.

"The company will throw me out for this," said Smith bitterly. "After ten years of working with them."

Pounding feet sounded in the corridor outside.

Clark's hand shot out and scooped up the stones.

"Can't let anyone find us with these on us," he whispered huskily. "Let's duck into the hangar."

Swiftly the two leaped through the doorway into the darkened room. Crouched under the wing of one of the time-fliers, they saw figures come into the room they had just quitted. Figures in police uniforms.

The police stood stock-still in the center of the room, staring.

"What's going on here?" shouted one of them.

Silence fell more heavily.

"What do you think that fellow meant, telling us he saw some funny looking birds coming out of here?" one of them asked the other two.

"Let's look in the hangar," one of the policemen said. He leveled a flash and a spear of light cut the deep gloom, just missing the two men crouched under the wing of the time-flier.

Clark felt Smith tugging at him.

"We got to get out of here," Smith hissed in his ear.

Clark nodded in the darkness. And he knew there was only one way to get out of there.

Together they tumbled through the door of the time-flier.

"Here we go," said Smith. "We're criminals now, Steve."

The machine lurched out through the suddenly opened lock.

The time mechanism hummed and two men, one with ten bongo stones in his pocket, fled through time.

Chapter III
Anachronic Treasure

Old One-Eye was fighting his last battle. His great stone-ax lay out of reach, its handle broken, swept from his hand by a blow aimed at him by the mighty cat. His body was mauled and across one shoulder was a deep wound from which a stream of crimson trickled down his hairy chest.

To flee was useless. One-Eye knew that he could not outdistance Saber-Tooth. There was only one thing to do—stand and fight. So with shoulders hunched, with his hands poised and ready for action, with his one eye gleaming balefully, the Neanderthal man faced the cat.

The animal snarled and spat, its tail twitching, crouched for a leap. Its long, curved fangs slashed angrily at the air.

One-Eye had no delusions about what was going to happen. He had killed many saber-tooths in his life. In company with others of his kind, he had faced the charge of the great cave-bear. He had trailed and brought down the mighty mammoth. In his day One-Eye had been a great hunter, an invincible warrior. But now he had reached the end of life. A man's two hands were no weapon against the tooth and claw of a saber-toothed tiger. One-Eye knew he was going to be killed.

Dry brush crackled back of the cat and the saber-tooth pivoted swiftly at this threat of new danger from the rear. One-Eye straightened and froze in his tracks.

Conrad Yancey, standing at the edge of the brush, slowly raised his rifle.

"I reckon this has gone about far enough," he said. "A man's got to stick by his own kind."

Startled, the great cat's snarls rose into a siren of hate and fear.

Yancey lined the sights on the ugly head and squeezed the trigger. The saber-tooth leaped into the air, screaming in rage and terror. Again the rifle blazed and the cat straightened, reared on its hind legs, fell backward to the ground, coughing great streams of blood.

Across the body of the beast One-Eye and Yancey exchanged glances.

"You put up a swell battle," Yancey told the Neanderthaler. "I watched you for quite a spell. Glad I was around to help."

Petrified by terror, One-Eye stood stock-still, staring. His nostrils twitched as he sniffed the strange smells which had come with the stranger and his shining spear. The spear, when it spoke in a voice of thunder, had a smell all its own, a smell that stung One-Eye's sensitive nostrils and his throat and made him want to cough.

Yancey took a slow, tentative step toward the Neanderthaler. But when the sub-man stirred as if to flee, he stopped short and stood almost breathless.

Yancey saw that the Neanderthaler's left eye at some time had been scooped out of his head by the vicious blow of a cruelly taloned paw. Deep scratches and a tortuous malformation of the region above the cheek-bone told a story of some terrible battle of the wilderness.

Short of stature and slightly stooping of posture, the Neanderthaler was a model of awkward power. His head was thrust forward at an angle between his shoulders. His neck was thick as a tree boll. The long arms hung almost to the knees of the bowed legs and the body was completely covered with hair. The heavy bristle of hair on his enormously projecting eyebrows was snowy white and throughout the heavy coat of hair which covered the man were other streaks and sprinklings of gray and white.

"An old buck," said Yancey, half to himself. "Slowing down. Someday he won't move quite fast enough and a cat will have him."

Conrad Yancey took another slow step forward and this time the Neanderthaler, bristling with terror, wheeled about with a strange, strangled cry of fear and ran, shuffling awkwardly, down the hill to plunge straight into a dense thicket.

Back at the time-tractor camp Yancey told the story of the battle between the caveman and the cat, of how he watched and had finally stepped in to save the man's life.

But the others had stories, too. Cabot and Cameron, hunting together a few miles to the east, had been charged by an angry mammoth bull, had stopped him only after they had placed four well aimed heavy-caliber bullets into him. Pascal, remaining at the tractor, had scared off a cave bear and reported that a pack of five vicious, slinking wolves had patrolled the camp throughout the afternoon. He had shot two of them and then the rest had scattered.

For here was a land that was teeming with game; a land where the law of claw and fang ruled and was the only law; where big animals preyed on smaller animals and in turn were preyed upon by still bigger ones. Here was a land without human habitation, with the few Neanderthalers who did live here hiding in dark, dank caves. Here was a land that had no human tenets, no softening hand of civilization.

But here, in this primeval wilderness of what later was to become the British Isles, was the greatest hunting ground Cabot and Yancey had ever seen. They shot in self-defense as often as they shot to bring down marked game. They found that a cave bear would carry more lead than an elephant, that the saber-tooth was not so hard to kill as might be thought, that only superb marksmanship and the heaviest bullets would bring the mammoth to his knees.

The flickering campfire, lighting up the gray, shadowy bulk of the time-tractor, was the only evidence of civilized life upon the darkening world as a blood-red moon climbed over the eastern horizon and lighted a land that growled and snarled, shivered and whimpered, hunted and was hunted.

Yancey saw Old One-Eye lurking on the edge of the camp when he arose in the morning. He had just a glimpse of the old fellow, squatting in a clump of bushes, looking over the camp with his one good eye. He disappeared so quickly, so soundlessly that Yancey blinked and rubbed his eyes, hardly believing he had left.

In the field that day Yancey and Cabot caught sight of him several times, lurking in their wake, spying upon them.

"Maybe," Cabot suggested, "he is trying to get up enough courage to thank you for saving his life."

Yancey grunted.

"Hell, I had to do that, Jack," he said. "He isn't more than an animal, but he's still a man. We got to play along with our own kind in a place like this. He was such a brave old cuss. Standing there, ready to go to bat with that cat with his bare hands."

Back at the camp, Pascal looked at it in a scientific light.

"Just natural curiosity," he said. "The first glimmering of intelligence. Trying to figure things out. With what limited brain power he has that old fellow is doing some heavy thinking right now."

"Maybe he recognizes you as one of his descendants. Great-grandson to the hundredth generation, maybe," Cameron jibed at Yancey.

"The Neanderthal race is not the ancestor of man," Pascal protested. "They died out or were killed off by the Cro-Magnons, who'll be moving in within another ten or twenty thousand years. The Neanderthaloids were just a sort of blind alley. An experiment that didn't go quite right."

"Seems damn human, though," protested Yancey.

One-Eye became a camp fixture. He lurked around the tractor, trailed Yancey when he went afield. Degree by degree he became bolder. Meat was left where he could find it and he carried it off into the brush. Later he didn't bother to drag it off. In plain view of the hunters he squatted on his haunches, ripping and rending it, snarling softly, gulping great, bloody mouthfuls of raw flesh.

He haunted the campfire like a dog, apparently pleased with the easy living he had found. He came farther away from the encircling brush, squatted and jabbered just outside the circle of firelight, waiting for the bits of food tossed to him.

At last, seemingly convinced he had nothing to fear from these strange creatures, he joined the campfire circle, sat with the men, blinking at the campfire, jabbering away excitedly.

"Maybe he has a language," said Pascal, "but if he has it's very primitive. Not more than a dozen words at most."

He liked to have his back scratched, grunting like a contented hog. He begged for cubes of sugar.

"Makes a nice pet," Cameron declared.

But Yancey shook his head.

"Something more than a pet, Hugh," he said.

For between Yancey and the old Neanderthaler something akin to comradeship had developed. It was by Yancey that the old one-eyed savage sat when he came into the ring of firelight. It was at Yancey that he directed his chatter. During the day he haunted Yancey's footsteps like a shadow, at times coming out openly to join him, ambling along with his awkward gait.

One night Yancey gave him a knife, half wondering if One-Eye would know what it was. But One-Eye recognized in this wondrous piece of polished metal something akin to the fist ax that he and his people used to flay the pelts from the animals they killed.

Turning the knife over and over, One-Eye slobbered in delirious glee. He jabbered excitedly at Yancey, clawed at the man's shoulder with caressing paw. Then he leaped from his place by the campfire and slithered away into the darkness. Not so much as a breaking twig heralded his plunge into the night.

Yancey rubbed his eyes.

"I wonder what the damn old fool is up to now?" he asked.

"Went off to try his new knife," suggested Cabot. "Something like that calls for a little throat-slitting."

Yancey listened to the moaning of a saber-tooth in the brush only a short distance away, heard the bellow of a mammoth down by the river.

He shook his head dolefully.

"I sure hope he watches his step," he said. "He's slowing up. Getting old. That saber-tooth out there might get him."

But in fifteen minutes One-Eye was back again. He waddled into the circle of firelight so silently that the men did not hear his approach.

Looking over his shoulder, Yancey saw him standing back of him. One-Eye was holding out a clenched fist, but within the fist was something that glinted in the flare of the campfire.

Pascal caught his breath.

"He's brought you something," he told Yancey. "Something in exchange for the knife. I would never have believed it. The barter principle."

Yancey rose and held out his hand. One-Eye dropped the shiny thing into it. Living flame lanced from it, striking Yancey's eyeballs.

It was a stone. Yancey rotated it slowly with his fingers and saw that within its center dwelt a heart of icy blue flame, while from its many facets swarmed arcing colors of breath-taking beauty.

Cabot was at his elbow, staring.

"What is it, Yancey?" he gasped.

Yancey almost sobbed.

"It's a diamond," he said. "A diamond as big as my fist!"

"But it's cut," protested Cabot. "That's not a stone out of the rough. A master jeweler cut that stone!"

Yancey nodded.

"Just what would a cut diamond be doing in the old Stone Age?" he asked.

Chapter IV
The Broadcast in Time

One-Eye pointed down into the throat of a cave and jabbered violently at Yancey. The hunter patted the hoary shoulders and One-Eye danced with glee.

"This must be it," Yancey said.

"I hope so," said Cameron. "It's taken plenty of time to make him understand what we wanted. I still can't understand how we did it."

Cabot wagged his head.

"I can't understand any of it," he confessed. "A Neanderthaler lugging around cut diamonds. Diamonds as big as a man's fist."

"Well, let's go down and see for ourselves," suggested Yancey.

One-Eye led the way down the steep, slippery mouth of the cave and into a dimly lit cavern, filled with a sort of half-light that filtered in from the mouth of the cave on the ground above.

Cabot switched on a flashlight and cried out excitedly.

In cascading piles upon the floor of the cavern, stacked high against its rocky sides, were piles of jewels that flashed and glittered, scintillating in the beams of the torch.

"This is it!" yelled Cameron.

Pascal, down on his knees in front of a pile of jewels, dipped his hands into them, lifted a fistful and let them trickle back. They filled the cavern with little murmurings as they fell.

Cabot swept the cave with the light. They saw piles of jewels; neat stacks of gold ingots, apparently freshly smelted; bars of silver-white iridium; of argent platinum; chests of hammered bronze and copper; buckskin bags spilling native golden nuggets.

Yancey reached out a hand and leaned weakly against the wall.

"My God," he stammered. "The price of empires!"

"But," said Pascal, slowly, calmly, although his face, as Cabot's torch suddenly lighted it, was twisted in an agony of disbelief, "how did this all come here? This is a primitive world. The art of the goldsmith and the jewel-cutter is unknown here."

Cameron's voice cut coolly out of the darkness.

"There must be an explanation. Some reason. Some previous civilization. A treasure cache of that civilization."

"No," Pascal told him, "not that. Look at those gold bars. New. Freshly smelted. No sign of age. And platinum—that's a comparatively recent discovery. Iridium even more recent."

Cabot's voice held an edge of steel command.

"We can argue about how it got here after we have it stowed away," he said. "Pascal, you and Hugh go down and bring up the tractor. Yancey and I will start carrying this stuff up to the surface right away."

Yancey toiled up the throat of the cave. Reaching the surface he slid the sack of jewels from his shoulder and wiped his brow.

"Tough work," he told Cameron.

Cameron nodded.

"But it's almost over now," he comforted. "Just a few more hours and we'll have the last of the stuff in the tractor. Then we can get out of here."

Yancey nodded.

"I don't feel too safe," he admitted. "Somebody hid all this junk in the cave. How they did it, I don't have the faintest idea. But I have a queer feeling it wouldn't go easy with us if they caught us."

Pascal stagger out of the cave and slid a gold bar from his shoulder.

He mopped his brow with a shirt sleeve.

"I'm going down to the tractor and get a drink of water before I pack that a foot farther," he announced.

Yancey stooped to pick up his gunny sack. Pascal's scream echoed.

The hillside below the tractor before had been empty of everything except a few scattered boulders and trees. Now a machine rested there, a grotesque machine of black metal, streamlined, with stubby wings, suggestive of a plane. As Yancey caught his first sight of it, it was indistinct, blurred, as if he saw it through a shimmering haze. Then it became clear, sharp-cut.

Like a slap in the face came the knowledge that here was the answer to those vague fears he had felt. Here must be the owners of the treasure cache.

His hand slapped down to his thigh and his gun whispered out of its holster.

A door in the strange machine snapped open and out of it stepped a man—but hardly a man. The creature sported a long tail, and it was covered with scales. Twin horns, three inches or so in height, sprouted from its forehead.

The newcomer carried something that looked like a gun in his hand, but no gun such as Yancey had ever seen. He saw the weapon tilt up toward him and his .45 exploded in his fist. Even as flame blossomed from his gun, he saw a .45 come up in Cameron's hand, in the second after the blast of his own gun, then heard the deadly click of a cocking hammer.

The first of the scaly men was down. But others were tumbling out of the strange mechanism.

Cameron's gun barked and once again Yancey felt the comforting kick of the .45 against the heel of his palm, hardly knowing he had squeezed the trigger.

From one of the guns carried by the scaly men whipped out a pencil of purple flame. Yancey felt its hot breath clip past his cheek.

Before the time-tractor lay Pascal, stretched out, inert, like an empty sack. Over him stood Cabot, gun flaming. Another one of those purple flames reached out, hit a boulder beside Yancey. The boulder glowed with sudden heat, started to chip and crack.

With mighty leaps, Yancey skidded down the slope, landing in a crouch beside Pascal. He grasped the old scientist by the shoulder and lifted him. As he straightened, he glanced at the strange machine in which the scaly men had come. Through the open door he could see a mass of machinery, with banks of glowing tubes.

Then the machinery erupted in a thunderous explosion. The roar seemed to blot out the world. For one split second he glanced up and saw on Cabot's face a baleful grin of triumph, knew that he had fired a shot which had wrecked the scaly men's machine.

The ground seemed to be weaving under Yancey's feet. With superhuman effort he plodded toward the door of the timetractor, dragging Pascal. Hands reached out to help him, hauling him inside.

Slowly his brain cleared. He was sitting on the floor of the tractor. Beside him lay Pascal and he saw now that the scientist was dead. His chest had been burned away by one of the pencils of purple flame.

Cabot swung down on the door-locking mechanism and stepped back into the room.

"What are they, Jack?" Yancey asked, his mind still fuzzy.

Cabot shook his head wearily.

"Don't you recognize them?" asked Cameron. "Horns, hoofs, tails. Today we've seen the devil in person. Those are the people who gave rise to the ancient legend of the devil."

Yancey got to his feet and looked down at Pascal.

"Feel bad about that," he whispered. "He was a regular guy."

Cameron nodded, stiff-lipped.

From a port Cabot spoke.

"Those devil-men are up to something," he announced. "They'll probably make it hot for us now."

He wheeled on Cameron.

"Can you get us out of here, Hugh?"

Cameron considered the question.

"Probably could," he said, "but I would rather not try it right now. I think we're safe here for a little while. That time brain is a tricky outfit. I know its principle and given time I could figure it out so I could take a try at it. If worse comes to worse, I'll do it. Take a chance."

He walked to the time-brain apparatus and snapped the switch. The brain glowed with a weird green light.

"That must be a time-machine out there," said Yancey. "Another machine would explain the treasure cache. I'll bet those birds are robbing stuff through time and bringing it back here to cache it. Damn clever."

"And they landed up ahead to cache some stuff and found some of it missing. Then they came back through time to find out what was wrong," supplied Cabot.

Cameron smote his thigh.

"Listen," he said. "It that's right it means time-travel is well established up ahead in the future. We might be able to reach help there. Those fellows out there must be outlaws. If so, we'd rate some help."

"But how will we reach the future?" demanded Cabot. "How will they know we need help?"

"It's just a chance," said Cameron. "A bare chance. If it doesn't work I can always try to get us back to the twentieth century, although the chances are nine out of ten I'll kill all of us trying it."

"But how?" persisted Cabot.

"Pascal said the 'time force' or whatever the brain generates, is similar to electricity. But with differences. It is important just what those differences are. I don't know, not enough, anyhow. The time mechanism is run by the force generated by the brain, but we have regular electricity for the tractor operation."

Cameron pondered.

"I wonder," he mused, "if the time force would be sufficiently like electricity to operate the radio?"

"What difference would that make?" snapped Yancey.

"Maybe we could broadcast in time," Cameron suggested.

"But that brain generates very little power," protested Yancey.

"We might not need much power," Cameron told him. "It's just a blind shot in the dark. A gamble—"

"Sounds plausible," Yancey asserted, "let's take a long shot."

Cameron switched off the brain mechanism and with lengths of wire connected the radio to the mechanism. Then he switched the brain back on again. The sending set hummed with power.

"Better start gambling," said Cabot. "Those boys out there are beginning to ray us. Playing that purple flame on the tractor."

Cameron's voice boomed out, speaking into the microphone.

"SOS . . . SOS . . . party of time travelers stranded in the Thames valley, near the village of Aylesford, approximately seventy thousand years before the twentieth century. Attacked by beings resembling the devils of mythology. SOS . . . SOS . . . party of time travelers stranded in the Thames valley . . ."

Cameron's voice boomed on and on.

Yancey and Cabot stared out of the ports.

The devil-men were ringed around the tractor, playing the purple beams on the machine. They stood stolidly, like statues, without a trace of emotion in their features.

The tractor was beginning to heat up. The air was becoming hot and the metal was warm to the touch.

The interior of the tractor suddenly flashed with a green burst of flame.

Yancey and Cabot wheeled about.

The brain mechanism was a mass of twisted wreckage.

"Blew up," said Cabot. "Something in the purple rays. This is the end of us now if our time-casting didn't work. We can't even operate the time-mechanism without the brain."

"Look here!" cried Cabot from a port.

Cameron and Yancey rushed to his side.

Swooping down toward the tractor was a black ship, an exact duplicate of the time machine of the devil-men.

Like an avenging meteor the black craft tore downward. From its nose flashes of green fire stabbed out viciously and living lightning bolts crashed among the devil-men.

Terrified, the devil-men tried to scurry out of reach, but the lightning bolts sought them out, caught them, burned them into cinders.

"A ship out of the future!" gasped Yancey. "Our radio worked!"

Chapter V
The Thrill-Hunters

Andy Smith spoke earnestly. "There's just one thing," he said. "We can't go back to the fifty-sixth century. Steve and I stole this time-machine. Lucky for you fellows we did, because apparently no one else caught your radio message. But if we're caught back there it means a life stretch on Mercury for us. Our machine is the second one ever stolen. The first one is over there."

He nodded toward the devil-men's machine, blasted on the hillside.

"Hell," said Yancey, "what are we blabbering around about? We have a machine that will take us through time and space. Any place we want to go. There's plenty of room for all of us.

The ship's loaded with treasure. Do we have to decide where to go? Why can't we just skip around and stop wherever things look good to us? Like those Centaurians. Me, I don't care whether I ever go back to the twentieth century. I didn't leave anybody back there."

"Just an old maid aunt," Cabot spoke for himself. "And she didn't approve of me. Figured I should have settled down and made more money—added to the family fortune. Thought hunting was silly."

The four of them looked at Cameron. He grinned.

"I'd like to find out something about what the next couple three hundred thousand years have done in the way of science," he admitted. "Maybe could pick up a few tricks. Skim the cream of the world's science. Probably lots of ideas we could incorporate in the time-flier."

"Wish we knew more about that time-brain," mourned Smith. "But I can't understand it. The fifty-sixth hasn't anything like it. Our machines are run on an entirely different basis. Warping of world lines principle."

They sat in silence for a moment. From the river came the roaring bellow of a mammoth bull.

"Say," asked Yancey, "has anyone seen anything of One-Eye?"

"No," said Cameron. "He must have hit for high timber when all the fireworks broke out."

"By the way," asked Steve Clark, "What are you going to do with Pascal's body?"

"Leave it here," suggested Yancey. "In the tractor. If we worked a million years we couldn't erect a more suitable burial site. Shut the door and leave him there. With his time brain. No one else will ever build another. It was all in Pascal's head. No notes, nothing. Just his brain. He told me he meant to write a book when he got around to it. We can't take the body back to the twentieth century and deliver it to the authorities. Because nobody would believe us. They'd throw us in the can."

"We might take it back and leave it somewhere on his premises for someone to find," Cabot suggested.

Yancey shook his head.

"That would be senseless. Just stir up a lot of fuss. An autopsy and an inquest and Scotland Yard half nuts over a new mystery. Pascal would rather be left here."

"I'm inclined to agree," said Cameron.

"That's settled then," said Smith, getting to his feet. "What do you say we get started? We got lots of places to go."

Clark laughed.

"You know," he said, sweeping a hand toward the wrecked time-flier, "I get a big kick out of the way this Centaurian business turned out. For five hundred years those long-tailed gangsters just toured all over hell, robbing everything that looked like it was worth taking. Dragging it back into prehistoric time and hiding it away. And in the end all their work was done so that five Earthmen could use it to finance a life-time of time wandering."

Andy Smith looked thoughtful.

"But," he said, "the Centaurians must have been robbing for some purpose. They must have had something in mind. They amassed billions of dollars in treasure. For what reason? Not just for the love of it, surely. Not just to look at. Not just for the thrill of taking it. What were they going to do with it?"

"There," said Cameron, "is one question that will never be answered."

Old One-Eye squatted inside the time-tractor.

It was snowing outside, but the tractor provided an excellent shelter and One-Eye was well wrapped in furs and skins. In one corner of the tractor was plenty of food.

Wrapped to his ears in a great mastodon robe, One-Eye nodded sleepily. Life was pleasant for the old Neanderthaler. Pleasant and easy. For the tribe which had wandered into the valley and found him living in the shining cave had taken him for a god. As a result they brought him food and furs, weapons and other offer-ings, gifts to appease his wrath, to court his favor. For who could doubt that anyone but a god would live in a cave that glinted in the sunshine, a cave made of hard, smooth stone, beautifully shaped, a cave that had no draughts and was secure against the attack of any wild beast.

One-Eye, dozing, dimly remembered the day when, curiously and idly jiggling at the door handle of the tractor, the handle moved in his hand and the door had swung smoothly open.

Henceforward the tractor had become One-Eye's cave. In it he had lived through many summers and many snows. In it he would live out the rest of his days.

One-Eye remembered the strange friends who had come to him in this shining cave. They had gone, long ago. And One-Eye missed them. Vaguely he was lonesome for them. Many times he wished they might come back again.

The old Neanderthaler drew in his breath with a slobbering sigh. Perhaps some day they would. In the meantime, he kept close and jealous guard and maintained the proper respect to the one of them that had stayed behind, the one whose bones lay neatly arranged in one corner of the tractor.

But they had remembered One-Eye before they left, these other friends of his. Of that One-Eye was sure. Had they not left behind them, in the tractor, for him to find, the great shining stone which he had given them so long ago in exchange for the shining, keen-edged knife?

One-Eye slobbered pleasurably now as he looked at the stone, sparkling and flashing with hidden fire as it lay in the palm of his hand. One-Eye could not know that the stone had been left in the tractor accidentally, overlooked by the 20th and 56th century men before they left on their excursion into time. Not knowing this, One-Eye held close to him the thought that these friends of his had left behind a token . . . a token that some day, perhaps, they would return and sit around a fire with him and give him bones to gnaw and scratch his back where it itched the most.

Outside the wind howled dismally and the snow slanted down in a new fury. A blizzard raged over the Thames valley.

But One-Eye, snug in his furs, comfortable in his old age, a god to his contemporaries, played with a diamond the size of a man's fist, unmindful of the weather.

HUDDLING PLACE

Originally published in the July 1944 issue of Astounding Science
Fiction, *"Huddling Place" is one of the best-known stories in the
iconic volume City. It is the seed from which all the tragedy in the
remaining stories in the series springs, and it brings to life Simak's
visions of talking dogs and robots. Simak himself felt that in creating
those stories, he became a mature and accomplished writer.*

—*dww*

The drizzle sifted from the leaden skies, like smoke drifting
through the bare-branched trees. It softened the hedges and
hazed the outlines of the buildings and blotted out the distance.
It glinted on the metallic skins of the silent robots and silvered
the shoulders of the three humans listening to the intonations of
the black-garbed man, who read from the book cupped between
his hands.

"For I am the Resurrection and the Life—"

The moss-mellowed graven figure that reared above the door
of the crypt seemed straining upward, every crystal of its yearning body reaching toward something that no one else could see.
Straining, as it had strained since that day of long ago when men
had chipped it from the granite to adorn the family tomb with a
symbolism that had pleased the first John J. Webster in the last
years he held of life.

"And whosoever liveth and believeth in Me—"

Jerome A. Webster felt his son's fingers tighten on his arm, heard the muffled sobbing of his mother, saw the lines of robots standing rigid, heads bowed in respect to the master they had served. The master who now was going home—to the final home of all.

Numbly, Jerome A. Webster wondered if they understood— if they understood life and death—if they understood what it meant that Nelson F. Webster lay there in the casket, that a man with a book intoned words above him.

Nelson F. Webster, fourth of the line of Websters who had lived on these acres, had lived and died here, scarcely leaving, and now was going to his final rest in that place the first of them had prepared for the rest of them—for that long line of shadowy descendants who would live here and cherish the things and the ways and the life that the first John J. Webster had established.

Jerome A. Webster felt his jaw muscles tighten, felt a little tremor run across his body. For a moment his eyes burned and the casket blurred in his sight and the words the man in black was saying were one with the wind that whispered in the pines standing sentinel for the dead. Within his brain remembrance marched—remembrance of a gray-haired man stalking the hills and fields, sniffing the breeze of an early morning, standing, legs braced, before the flaring fireplace with a glass of brandy in his hand.

Pride—the pride of land and life, and the humility and greatness that quiet living breeds within a man. Contentment of casual leisure and surety of purpose. Independence of assured security, comfort of familiar surroundings, freedom of broad acres.

Thomas Webster was joggling his elbow. "Father," he was whispering. "Father."

The service was over. The black-garbed man had closed his book. Six robots stepped forward, lifted the casket.

Slowly the three followed the casket into the crypt, stood silently as the robots slid it into its receptacle, closed the tiny door and affixed the plate that read:

NELSON F. WEBSTER
2034–2117

That was all. Just the name and dates. And that, Jerome A. Webster found himself thinking, was enough. There was nothing else that needed to be there. That was all those others had. The ones that called the family roll—starting with William Stevens, 1920–1999. Gramp Stevens, they had called him, Webster remembered. Father of the wife of that first John J. Webster, who was here himself—1951–2020. And after him his son, Charles F. Webster, 1980–2060. And his son, John J. II, 2004–2086. Webster could remember John J. II—a grandfather who had slept beside the fire with his pipe hanging from his mouth, eternally threatening to set his whiskers aflame.

Webster's eyes strayed to another plate. Mary Webster, the mother of the boy here at his side. And yet not a boy. He kept forgetting that Thomas was twenty now, in a week or so would be leaving for Mars, even as in his younger days he, too, had gone to Mars.

All here together, he told himself. The Websters and their wives and children. Here in death together as they had lived together, sleeping in the pride and security of bronze and marble with the pines outside and the symbolic figure above the age-greened door.

The robots were waiting, standing silently, their task fulfilled.

His mother looked at him.

"You're head of the family now, my son," she told him.

He reached out and hugged her close against his side. Head of the family—what was left of it. Just the three of them now. His mother and his son. And his son would be leaving soon, going out to Mars. But he would come back. Come back with a wife, perhaps, and the family would go on. The family wouldn't stay at three. Most of the big house wouldn't stay closed off, as it now was closed off. There had been a time when it had rung with the life of a dozen units of the family, living in their separate apartments under one big roof. That time, he knew, would come again.

The three of them turned and left the crypt, took the path back to the house, looming like a huge gray shadow in the mist.

A fire blazed in the hearth and the book lay upon his desk. Jerome A. Webster reached out and picked it up, read the title once again:

"Martian Physiology, With Especial Reference to the Brain" by Jerome A. Webster, M.D.

Thick and authoritative—the work of a lifetime. Standing almost alone in its field. Based upon the data gathered during those five plague years on Mars—years when he had labored almost day and night with his fellow colleagues of the World Committee's medical commission, dispatched on an errand of mercy to the neighboring planet.

A tap sounded on the door.

"Come in," he called.

The door opened and a robot glided in.

"Your whiskey, sir."

"Thank you, Jenkins," Webster said.

"The minister, sir," said Jenkins, "has left."

"Oh, yes. I presume that you took care of him."

"I did, sir. Gave him the usual fee and offered him a drink. He refused the drink."

"That was a social error," Webster told him. "Ministers don't drink."

"I'm sorry, sir. I didn't know. He asked me to ask you to come to church sometime."

"Eh?"

"I told him, sir, that you never went anywhere."

"That was quite right, Jenkins," said Webster. "None of us ever go anywhere."

Jenkins headed for the door, stopped before he got there, turned around. "If I may say so, sir, that was a touching service at the crypt. Your father was a fine human, the finest ever was. The robots were saying the service was very fitting. Dignified like, sir. He would have liked it had he known."

"My father," said Webster, "would be even more pleased to hear you say that, Jenkins."

"Thank you, sir," said Jenkins, and went out.

Webster sat with the whiskey and the book and fire—felt the comfort of the well-known room close in about him, felt the refuge that was in it.

This was home. It had been home for the Websters since that day when the first John J. had come here and built the first unit of the sprawling house. John J. had chosen it because it had a trout stream, or so he always said. But it was something more than that. It must have been, Webster told himself, something more than that.

Or perhaps, at first, it had only been the trout stream. The trout stream and the trees and meadows, the rocky ridge where the mist drifted in each morning from the river. Maybe the rest of it had grown, grown gradually through the years, through years of family association until the very soil was soaked with something that approached, but wasn't quite, tradition. Something that made each tree, each rock, each foot of soil a Webster tree or rock or piece of soil. It all belonged.

John J., the first John J., had come after the breakup of the cities, after men had forsaken, once and for all, the twentieth century huddling places, had broken free of the tribal instinct to stick together in one cave or in one clearing against a common foe or a common fear. An instinct that had become outmoded, for there were no fears or foes. Man revolting against the herd instinct economic and social conditions had impressed upon him in ages past. A new security and a new sufficiency had made it possible to break away.

The trend had started back in the twentieth century, more than two hundred years before, when men moved to country homes to get fresh air and elbow room and a graciousness in life that communal existence, in its strictest sense, never had given them.

And here was the end result. A quiet living. A peace that could only come with good things. The sort of life that men had yearned for years to have. A manorial existence, based on old family homes and leisurely acres, with atomics supplying power and robots in place of serfs.

Webster smiled at the fireplace with its blazing wood. That was an anachronism, but a good one—something that Man had brought forward from the caves. Useless, because atomic heating was better—but more pleasant. One couldn't sit and watch atomics and dream and build castles in the flames.

Even the crypt out there, where they had put his father that afternoon. That was family, too. All of a piece with the rest of it. The somber pride and leisured life and peace. In the old days the dead were buried in vast plots all together, stranger cheek by jowl with stranger—

He never goes anywhere.

That is what Jenkins had told the minister.

And that was right. For what need was there to go anywhere? It all was here. By simply twirling a dial one could talk face to face with anyone one wished, could go, by sense, if not in body, anywhere one wished. Could attend the theater or hear a concert or browse in a library halfway around the world. Could transact any business one might need to transact without rising from one's chair.

Webster reached out his hand and drank the whiskey, then swung to the dialed machine beside his desk.

He spun dials from memory without resorting to the log. He knew where he was going.

His finger flipped a toggle and the room melted away—or seemed to melt. There was left the chair within which he sat, part of the desk, part of the machine itself and that was all.

The chair was on a hillside swept with golden grass and dotted with scraggly, wind-twisted trees, a hillside that straggled down to a lake nestling in the grip of purple mountain spurs. The spurs, darkened in long streaks with the bluish-green of distant pine, climbed in staggering stairs, melting into the blue-tinged snow-capped peaks that reared beyond and above them in jagged saw-toothed outline.

The wind talked harshly in the crouching trees and ripped the long grass in sudden gusts. The last rays of the sun struck fire from the distant peaks.

Solitude and grandeur, the long sweep of tumbled land, the cuddled lake, the knifelike shadows on the far-off ranges.

Webster sat easily in his chair, eyes squinting at the peaks.

A voice said almost at his shoulder: "May I come in?"

A soft, sibilant voice, wholly unhuman. But one that Webster knew.

He nodded his head. "By all means, Juwain."

He turned slightly and saw the elaborate crouching pedestal, the furry, soft-eyed figure of the Martian squatting on it. Other alien furniture loomed indistinctly beyond the pedestal, half guessed furniture from that dwelling out on Mars.

The Martian flipped a furry hand toward the mountain range.

"You love this," he said. "You can understand it. And I can understand how you understand it, but to me there is more terror than beauty in it. It is something we could never have on Mars."

Webster reached out a hand, but the Martian stopped him.

"Leave it on," he said. "I know why you came here. I would not have come at a time like this except I thought perhaps an old friend—"

"It is kind of you," said Webster. "I am glad that you have come."

"Your father," said Juwain, "was a great man. I remember how you used to talk to me of him, those years you spent on Mars. You said then you would come back sometime. Why is it you've never come?"

"Why," said Webster, "I just never—"

"Do not tell me," said the Martian. "I already know."

"My son," said Webster, "is going to Mars in a few days. I shall have him call on you."

"That would be a pleasure," said Juwain. "I shall be expecting him."

He stirred uneasily on the crouching pedestal. "Perhaps he carries on tradition."

"No," said Webster. "He is studying engineering. He never cared for surgery."

"He has a right," observed the Martian, "to follow the life that he has chosen. Still, one might be permitted to wish."

"One could," Webster agreed. "But that is over and done with. Perhaps he will be a great engineer. Space structure. Talks of ships out to the stars."

"Perhaps," suggested Juwain, "your family has done enough for medical science. You and your father—"

"And his father," said Webster, "before him."

"Your book," declared Juwain, "has put Mars in debt to you. It may focus more attention on Martian specialization. My people do not make good doctors. They have no background for it. Queer how the minds of races run. Queer that Mars never thought of medicine—literally never thought of it. Replaced it with a cult of fatalism. While even in your early history, when men still lived in caves—"

"There are many things," said Webster, "that you thought of and we didn't. Things we wonder now how we ever missed. Abilities that you developed and we do not have. Take your own specialty, philosophy. But different than ours. A science, while ours never was more than fumbling. An orderly, logical development of philosophy, workable, practical, applicable, an actual tool."

Juwain started to speak, hesitated, then went ahead. "I am near to something, something that may be new and startling. Something that will be a tool for you humans as well as for the Martians. I've worked on it for years, starting with certain mental concepts that first were suggested to me with arrival of the Earthmen. I have said nothing, for I could not be sure."

"And now," suggested Webster, "you are sure."

"Not quite," said Juwain. "Not positive. But almost."

They sat in silence, watching the mountains and the lake. A bird came and sat in one of the scraggly trees and sang. Dark clouds piled up behind the mountain ranges and the snow-tipped peaks stood out like graven stone. The sun sank in a welter of crimson, hushed finally to the glow of a fire burned low.

A tap sounded from a door and Webster stirred in his chair, suddenly brought back to the reality of the study, of the chair beneath him.

Juwain was gone. The old philosopher had come and sat an hour of contemplation with his friend and then had quietly slipped away.

The rap came again.

Webster leaned forward, snapped the toggle and the mountains vanished; the room became a room again. Dusk filtered through the high windows and the fire was a rosy flicker in the ashes.

"Come in," said Webster.

Jenkins opened the door. "Dinner is served, sir," he said.

"Thank you," said Webster. He rose slowly from the chair.

"Your place, sir," said Jenkins, "is laid at the head of the table."

"Ah, yes," said Webster. "Thank you, Jenkins. Thank you very much, for reminding me."

Webster stood on the broad ramp of the space field and watched the shape that dwindled in the sky, dwindled with faint flickering points of red lancing through the wintry sunlight.

For long minutes after the shape was gone he stood there, hands gripping the railing in front of him, eyes still staring up into the steel-like blue.

His lips moved and they said: "Good-by, son"; but there was no sound.

Slowly he came alive to his surroundings. Knew that people moved about the ramp, saw that the landing field seemed to stretch interminably to the far horizon, dotted here and there with hump-backed things that were waiting spaceships. Scooting tractors worked near one hangar, clearing away the last of the snowfall of the night before.

Webster shivered and thought that it was queer, for the noonday sun was warm. And shivered again.

Slowly he turned away from the railing and headed for the administration building. And for one brain-wrenching moment he felt a sudden fear—an unreasonable and embarrassing fear of that stretch of concrete that formed the ramp. A fear that left him shaking mentally as he drove his feet toward the waiting door.

A man walked toward him, briefcase swinging in his hand and Webster, eyeing him, wished fervently that the man would not speak to him.

The man did not speak, passed him with scarcely a glance and Webster felt relief.

If he were back home, Webster told himself, he would have finished lunch, would now be ready to lie down for his midday nap. The fire would be blazing on the hearth and the flicker of the flames would be reflected from the andirons. Jenkins would bring him a liqueur and would say a word or two—inconsequential conversation.

He hurried toward the door, quickening his step, anxious to get away from the bare-cold expanse of the massive ramp.

Funny how he had felt about Thomas. Natural, of course, that he should have hated to see him go. But entirely unnatural that he should, in those last few minutes, find such horror welling up within him. Horror of the trip through space, horror of the alien land of Mars—although Mars was scarcely alien any longer. For more than a century now Earthmen had known it, had fought it, lived with it; some of them had even grown to love it.

But it had only been utter will power that had prevented him, in those last few seconds before the ship had taken off, from running out into the field, shrieking for Thomas to come back, shrieking for him not to go.

And that, of course, never would have done. It would have been exhibitionism, disgraceful and humiliating—the sort of a thing a Webster could not do.

After all, he told himself, a trip to Mars was no great adventure, not any longer. There had been a day when it had been, but that day was gone forever. He, himself, in his earlier days had a made a trip to Mars, had stayed there for five long years. That had been—he gasped when he thought of it—that had been almost thirty years ago.

The babble and hum of the lobby hit him in the face as the robot attendant opened the door for him, and in that babble ran a vein of something that was almost terror. For a moment he hesitated, then stepped inside. The door closed softly behind him.

He stayed close to the one wall to keep out of people's way, headed for a chair in one corner. He sat down and huddled back, forcing his body deep into the cushions, watching the milling humanity that seethed out in the room.

Shrill people, hurrying people, people with strange, unneighborly faces. Strangers—every one of them. Not a face he knew. People going places. Heading out for the planets. Anxious to be off. Worried about last details. Rushing here and there.

Out of the crowd loomed a familiar face. Webster hunched forward.

"Jenkins!" he shouted, and then was sorry for the shout, although no one seemed to notice.

The robot moved toward him, stood before him.

"Tell Raymond," said Webster, "that I must return immediately. Tell him to bring the 'copter in front at once."

"I am sorry, sir," said Jenkins, "but we cannot leave at once. The mechanics found a flaw in the atomics chamber. They are installing a new one. It will take several hours."

"Surely," said Webster, impatiently, "that could wait until some other time."

"The mechanic said not, sir," Jenkins told him. "It might go at any minute. The entire charge of power—"

"Yes, yes," agreed Webster, "I suppose so."

He fidgeted with his hat. "I just remembered," he said, "something I must do. Something that must be done at once. I must get home. I can't wait several hours."

He hitched forward to the edge of the chair, eyes staring at the milling crowd.

Faces—faces—

"Perhaps you could televise," suggested Jenkins. "One of the robots might be able to do it. There is a booth—"

"Wait, Jenkins," said Webster. He hesitated a moment. "There is nothing to do back home. Nothing at all. But I must get there. I can't stay here. If I have to, I'll go crazy. I was frightened out there on the ramp. I'm bewildered and confused here. I have a feeling—a strange, terrible feeling. Jenkins, I—"

"I understand, sir," said Jenkins. "Your father had it, too."

Webster gasped. "My father?"

"Yes, sir, that is why he never went anywhere. He was about your age, sir, when he found it out. He tried to make a trip to Europe and he couldn't. He got halfway there and turned back. He had a name for it."

Webster sat in stricken silence.

"A name for it," he finally said. "Of course there's a name for it. My father had it. My grandfather—did he have it, too?"

"I wouldn't know that, sir," said Jenkins. "I wasn't created until after your grandfather was an elderly man. But he may have. He never went anywhere, either."

"You understand, then," said Webster. "You know how it is. I feel like I'm going to be sick—physically ill. See if you can charter a 'copter—anything, just so we get home."

"Yes, sir," said Jenkins.

He started off and Webster called him back.

"Jenkins, does anyone else know about this? Anyone—"

"No, sir," said Jenkins. "Your father never mentioned it and I felt, somehow, that he wouldn't wish me to."

"Thank you, Jenkins," said Webster.

Webster huddled back into his chair again, felt desolate and alone and misplaced. Alone in a humming lobby that pulsed with life—a loneliness that tore at him, that left him limp and weak.

Homesickness. Downright, shameful homesickness, he told himself. Something that boys are supposed to feel when they first leave home, when they first go out to meet the world.

There was a fancy word for it—agoraphobia, the morbid dread of being in the midst of open spaces—from the Greek root for the fear—literally, of the market place.

If he crossed the room to the television booth, he could put in a call, talk with his mother or one of the robots—or better yet, just sit and look at the place until Jenkins came for him.

He started to rise, then sank back in the chair again. It was no dice. Just talking to someone or looking in on the place wasn't being there. He couldn't smell the pines in the wintry air, or hear familiar snow crunch on the walk beneath his feet or reach out a hand and touch one of the massive oaks that grew along the path. He couldn't feel the heat of the fire or sense the sure, deft touch of belonging, of being one with a tract of ground and the things upon it.

And yet—perhaps it would help. Not much, maybe, but some. He started to rise from the chair again and froze. The few short steps to the booth held terror, a terrible, overwhelming terror. If he crossed them, he would have to run. Run to escape the watching eyes, the unfamiliar sounds, the agonizing nearness of strange faces.

Abruptly he sat down.

A woman's shrill voice cut across the lobby and he shrank away from it. He felt terrible. He felt like hell. He wished Jenkins would hurry up.

The first breath of spring came through the window, filled the study with the promise of melting snows, of coming leaves and flowers, of north-bound wedges of waterfowl streaming through the blue, of trout that lurked in pools waiting for the fly.

Webster lifted his eyes from the sheaf of papers on his desk, sniffed the breeze, felt the cool whisper of it on his cheek. His hand reached out for the brandy glass and found it empty, put it back.

He bent back above the papers once again, picked up a pencil and crossed out a word.

Critically, he read the final paragraphs:

The fact that of the two hundred fifty men who were invited to visit me, presumably on missions of more than ordinary importance, only three were able to come, does not necessarily prove that all but those three are victims of agoraphobia. Some may have had legitimate reasons for being unable to accept my invitation. But it does indicate a growing unwillingness of men living under the mode of Earth existence set up following the break up of the cities to move from familiar places, a deepening instinct to stay among the scenes and possessions which in their mind have become associated with contentment and graciousness of life.

What the result of such a trend will be, no one can clearly indicate since it applies to only a small portion of Earth's population. Among the larger families economic pressure forces some of the sons to seek their fortunes either in other parts of the Earth or on one of the other planets. Many others deliberately seek adventure and opportunity in space while still others become associated with professions or trades which make a sedentary existence impossible.

He flipped the page over, went on to the last one.

It was a good paper, he knew, but it could not be published, not just yet. Perhaps after he had died. No one, so far as he could determine, had ever so much as realized the trend, had taken as matter of course the fact that men seldom left their homes. Why, after all, should they leave their homes?

Certain dangers may be recognized in—

—

The televisor muttered at his elbow and he reached out to flip the toggle.

The room faded and he was face to face with a man who sat behind a desk, almost as if he sat on the opposite side of Webster's desk. A gray-haired man with sad eyes behind heavy lenses, eyes that were filled with the sadness and humility of having looked on death and misery, compassionate eyes.

For a moment Webster stared, memory tugging at him.

"Could it be—" he asked and the man smiled gravely.

"I have changed," he said. "So have you. My name is Clayborne. Remember? The Martian medical commission—"

"Clayborne! I'd often thought of you. You stayed on Mars."

Clayborne nodded. "I've read your book, doctor. It is a real contribution. I've often thought one should be written, wanted to myself but I didn't have the time. Just as well I didn't. You did a better job. Especially on the brain."

"The Martian brain," Webster told him, "always intrigued me. Certain peculiarities. I'm afraid I spent more of those five years taking notes on it than I should have. There was other work to do."

"A good thing you did," said Clayborne. "That's why I'm calling you now. I have a patient—a brain operation. Only you can handle it."

Webster gasped, his hands trembling. "You'll bring him here?"

Clayborne shook his head. "He cannot be moved. You know him, I believe. Juwain, the philosopher."

"Juwain!" said Webster. "He's one of my best friends. We talked together just a couple of days ago."

"The attack was sudden," said Clayborne. "He's been asking for you."

Webster was silent and cold—cold with a chill that crept upon him from some unguessed place. Cold that sent perspiration out upon his forehead, that knotted his fists.

"If you start immediately," said Clayborne, "you can be here on time. I've already arranged with the World Committee to have a ship at your disposal instantly. The utmost speed is necessary."

"But," said Webster, "but . . . I cannot come."

"You can't come!"

"It's impossible," said Webster. "I doubt in any case that I am needed. Surely, you yourself—"

"I can't," said Clayborne. "No one can but you. No one else has the knowledge. You hold Juwain's life in your hands. If you come, he lives. If you don't, he dies."

"I can't go into space," said Webster.

"Anyone can go into space," snapped Clayborne. "It's not like it used to be. Conditioning of any sort desired is available."

"But you don't understand," pleaded Webster. "You—"

"No, I don't," said Clayborne. "Frankly, I don't. That anyone should refuse to save the life of his friend—"

The two men stared at one another for a long moment, neither speaking.

"I shall tell the committee to send the ship straight to your home," said Clayborne finally. "I hope by that time you will see your way clear to come."

Clayborne faded and the wall came into view again—the wall and books, the fireplace and the paintings, the well-loved furniture, the promise of spring that came through the window.

Webster sat frozen in his chair, staring at the wall in front of him.

Juwain, the furry, wrinkled face, the sibilant whisper, the friendliness and understanding that was his. Juwain, grasping the stuff that dreams are made of and shaping them into logic, into rules of life and conduct. Juwain using philosophy as a tool, as a science, as a stepping stone to better living.

Webster dropped his face into his hands and fought the agony that welled up within him.

Clayborne had not understood. One could not expect him to understand since there was no way for him to know. And even knowing, would he understand? Even he, Webster, would not have understood it in someone else until he had discovered it in himself—the terrible fear of leaving his own fire, his own land, his own possessions, the little symbolisms that he had erected. And yet, not he, himself, alone, but those other Websters as well. Starting with the first John J. Men and women who had set up a cult of life, a tradition of behavior.

He, Jerome A. Webster, had gone to Mars when he was a young man, and had not felt or suspected the psychological poison that ran through his veins. Even as Thomas a few months ago had gone to Mars. But twenty-five years of quiet life here in the retreat that the Websters called a home had brought it forth, had developed it without him even knowing it. There had, in fact, been no opportunity to know it.

It was clear how it had developed—clear as crystal now. Habit and mental pattern and a happiness association with certain things—things that had no actual value in themselves, but had been assigned a value, a definite, concrete value by one family through five generations.

No wonder other places seemed alien, no wonder other horizons held a hint of horror in their sweep.

And there was nothing one could do about it—nothing, that is, unless one cut down every tree and burned the house and changed the course of waterways. Even that might not do it—even that—

The televisor purred and Webster lifted his head from his hands, reached out and thumbed the tumbler.

The room became a flare of white, but there was no image. A voice said: "Secret call. Secret call."

Webster slid back a panel in the machine, spun a pair of dials, heard the hum of power surge into a screen that blocked out the room.

"Secrecy established," he said.

The white flare snapped out and a man sat across the desk from him. A man he had seen many times before in televised addresses, in his daily paper.

Henderson, president of the World Committee.

"I have had a call from Clayborne," said Henderson.

Webster nodded without speaking.

"He tells me you refuse to go to Mars."

"I have not refused," said Webster. "When Clayborne cut off the question was left open. I had told him it was impossible for me to go, but he had rejected that, did not seem to understand."

"Webster, you must go," snapped Henderson. "You are the only man with the necessary knowledge of the Martian brain to perform this operation. If it were a simple operation, perhaps someone else could do it. But not one such as this."

"That may be true," said Webster, "but—"

"It's not just a question of saving a life," said Henderson. "Even the life of so distinguished a personage as Juwain. It involves even more than that. Juwain is a friend of yours. Perhaps he hinted of something he has found."

"Yes," said Webster. "Yes, he did. A new concept of philosophy."

"A concept," declared Henderson, "that we cannot do without. A concept that will remake the solar system, that will put mankind ahead a hundred thousand years in the space of two generations. A new direction of purpose that will aim toward a goal we heretofore had not suspected, had not even known existed. A brand new truth, you see. One that never before had occurred to anyone."

Webster's hands gripped the edge of the desk until his knuckles stood out white.

"If Juwain dies," said Henderson, "that concept dies with him. May be lost forever."

"I'll try," said Webster. "I'll try—"

Henderson's eyes were hard. "Is that the best that you can do?"

"That is the best," said Webster.

"But, man, you must have a reason! Some explanation."

"None," said Webster, "that I would care to give."

Deliberately he reached out and flipped up the switch.

Webster sat at the desk and held his hands in front of him, staring at them. Hands that had skill, held knowledge. Hands that could save a life if he could get them to Mars. Hands that could save for the solar system, for mankind, for the Martians an idea—a new idea—that would advance them a hundred thousand years in the next two generations.

But hands chained by a phobia that grew out of this quiet life. Decadence—a strangely beautiful—and deadly—decadence.

Man had forsaken the teeming cities, the huddling places, two hundred years ago. He had done with the old foes and the ancient fears that kept him around the common campfire, had left behind the hobgoblins that had walked with him from the caves.

And yet—and yet—

Here was another huddling place. Not a huddling place for one's body, but one's mind. A psychological campfire that still held a man within the circle of its light.

Still, Webster knew, he must leave that fire. As the men had done with the cities two centuries before, he must walk off and leave it. And he must not look back.

He had to go to Mars—or at least start for Mars. There was no question there, at all. He had to go.

Whether he would survive the trip, whether he could perform the operation once he had arrived, he did not know. He wondered vaguely, whether agoraphobia could be fatal. In its most exaggerated form, he supposed it could.

He reached out a hand to ring, then hesitated. No use having Jenkins pack. He would do it himself—something to keep him busy until the ship arrived.

From the top shelf of the wardrobe in the bedroom, he took down a bag and saw that it was dusty. He blew on it, but the dust still clung. It had been there for too many years.

As he packed, the room argued with him, talked in that mute tongue with which inanimate but familiar things may converse with a man.

"You can't go," said the room. "You can't go off and leave me."

And Webster argued back, half pleading, half explanatory. "I have to go. Can't you understand? It's a friend, an old friend. I will be coming back."

Packing done, Webster returned to the study, slumped into his chair.

He must go and yet he couldn't go. But when the ship arrived, when the time had come, he knew that he would walk out of the house and toward the waiting ship.

He steeled his mind to that, tried to set it in a rigid pattern, tried to blank out everything but the thought that he was leaving.

Things in the room intruded on his brain, as if they were part of a conspiracy to keep him there. Things that he saw as if he were seeing them for the first time. Old, remembered things that suddenly were new. The chronometer that showed both Earthian and Martian time, the days of the month, the phases of the moon. The picture of his dead wife on the desk. The trophy he had won at prep school. The framed short snorter bill that had cost him ten bucks on his trip to Mars.

He stared at them, half unwilling at first, then eagerly, storing up the memory of them in his brain. Seeing them as separate components of a room he had accepted all these years as a finished whole, never realizing what a multitude of things went to make it up.

Dusk was falling, the dusk of early spring, a dusk that smelled of early pussy willows.

The ship should have arrived long ago. He caught himself listening for it, even as he realized that he would not hear it. A ship, driven by atomic motors, was silent except when it gathered speed. Landing and taking off, it floated like thistledown, with not a murmur in it.

It would be here soon. It would have to be here soon or he could never go. Much longer to wait, he knew, and his high-keyed resolution would crumble like a mound of dust in beating rain. Not much longer could he hold his purpose against the pleading of the room, against the flicker of the fire, against the murmur of the land where five generations of Websters had lived and died.

He shut his eyes and fought down the chill that crept across his body. He couldn't let it get him now, he told himself. He had to stick it out. When the ship arrived he still must be able to get up and walk out the door to the waiting port.

A tap came on the door.

"Come in," Webster called.

It was Jenkins, the light from the fireplace flickering on his shining metal hide.

"Had you called earlier, sir?" he asked.

Webster shook his head.

"I was afraid you might have," Jenkins explained, "and wondered why I didn't come. There was a most extraordinary occurrence, sir. Two men came with a ship and said they wanted you to go to Mars."

"They are here," said Webster. "Why didn't you call me?"

He struggled to his feet.

"I didn't think, sir," said Jenkins, "that you would want to be bothered. It was so preposterous."

Webster stiffened, felt chill fear gripping at his heart. Hands groping for the edge of the desk, he sat down in the chair, sensed the walls of the room closing in about him, a trap that would never let him go.

"I had a rather strenuous time, sir," said Jenkins. "They were so insistent that finally, much as I disliked it, I resorted to force. But I finally persuaded them you never went anywhere."

TO WALK A CITY'S STREET

"To Walk a City's Street" was originally written for the anthology Infinity Three, *which was published in 1972 by Lancer Books. For some reason, the story has not appeared in print very often. Its greatest implausibility involves members of Congress not seeking control of Ernie's mutant powers. Too bad.*

—*dww*

Joe stopped the car.

"You know what to do," he said.

"I walk down the street," said Ernie. "I don't do nothing. I walk until someone tells me it is time to stop. You got the other fellows out there?"

"We have the fellows out there."

"Why couldn't I just go alone?"

"You'd run away," said Joe. "We tried you once before."

"I wouldn't run away again."

"The hell you wouldn't."

"I don't like this job," said Ernie.

"It's a good job. You don't have to do anything. You just walk down the street."

"But you say which street. I don't get a pick of streets."

"What difference does it make what streets you walk?"

"I can't do anything I want, that's the difference that it makes. I can't even walk where I want to walk."

"Where would you want to walk?"

"I don't know," said Ernie. "Any place you weren't watching me. It used to be different. I could do what I wanted."

"You're eating regular now," said Joe. "Drinking regular, too. You have a place to sleep each night. You got money in your pocket. You have money in the bank."

"It don't seem right," said Ernie.

"Look, what's the matter with you? Don't you want to help people?"

"I ain't got no beef against helping people. But how do I know I help them? I only got your say-so. You and that fellow back in Washington."

"He explained it to you."

"A lot of words. I don't understand what he tells me. I'm not sure I believe what he tells me."

"I don't understand it, either," said Joe, "but I have seen the figures."

"I wouldn't know even if I seen the figures."

"Are you going to get started? Do I have to push you out?"

"No, I'll get out by myself. How far you want I should walk?"

"We'll tell you when to stop."

"And you'll be watching me."

"You're damned right we will," said Joe.

"This ain't a nice part of town. Why do I always have to walk the crummy parts of all these crummy towns?"

"It's your part of town. It's the kind of place you lived before we found you. You wouldn't be happy in any other part of town."

"But I had friends back there where you found me. There was Susie and Jake and Joseph, the Baboon and all the other people. Why can't I ever go back and see my friends?"

"Because you'd talk. You'd shoot off your mouth."

"You don't trust me."

"Should we trust you, Ernie?"

"No, I guess not," said Ernie.

He got out of the car.

"But I was happy, see?" he said.

"Sure, sure," said Joe. "I know."

There was one man sitting at the bar and two sitting at a table in the back. The place reminded Ernie of the place where he and Susie and Joseph, the Baboon, and sometimes Jake and Harry used to spend an evening drinking beer. He climbed up on a stool. He felt comfortable and almost as if he were back in the good old days again.

"Give me a shot," he said to the bartender.

"You got money, friend?"

"Sure, I got money." Ernie laid a dollar on the bar. The bartender got a bottle and poured a drink. Ernie gulped it down. "Another one," he said. The man poured another one.

"You're a new one," the bartender said.

"I ain't been around before," said Ernie.

He got a third drink and sat quietly, sipping it instead of throwing it right down.

"You know what I do?" he asked the bartender.

"Naw, I don't know what you do. You do like all the rest of them. You don't do nothing."

"I cure people."

"Is that so?"

"I walk around and I cure people when I walk."

"Well, great," said the bartender. "I got the beginning of a cold. So cure me."

"You're already cured," said Ernie.

"I don't feel no different than when you walked in here."

"Tomorrow. You'll be all right tomorrow. It takes a little time."

"I ain't going to pay you," said the bartender.

"I don't expect no pay. Other people pay me."

"What other people?"

"Just other people. I don't know who they are."

"They must be nuts."

"They won't let me go home," said Ernie.

"Well, now, ain't that too bad."

"I had a lot of friends. I had Susie and Joseph, the Baboon—"

"Everyone got friends," the bartender said.

"I got an aura. That is what they think."

"You got a what?"

"An aura. That is what they call it."

"Never heard of it. You want another drink?"

"Yeah, give me another one. Then I got to go."

Charley was standing on the sidewalk outside the joint, looking in at him. He didn't want Charley walking in and saying something to him, like get going. It would be embarrassing.

He saw the sign in an upstairs window and darted up the stairs. Jack was across the street and Al just a block or so ahead. They would see him and come running, but maybe he could get to the office before they caught up with him.

The sign on the door said: Lawson & Cramer, Attorneys-at-Law. He moved in fast.

"I got to see a lawyer," he told the receptionist.

"Have you an appointment, sir?"

"No, I ain't got no appointment. But I need a lawyer quick. And I got money, see."

He brought out a handful of crumpled bills.

"Mr. Cramer is busy."

"What about the other one? Is he busy, too?"

"There isn't any other lawyer. There used to be—"

"Look, lady, I can't fool around."

The door to the inner office came open and a man stood in it.

"What's going on out here?"

"This gentleman—"

"I ain't no gentleman," said Ernie. "But I need a lawyer."

"All right," said the man. "Come in."

"You're Cramer?"

"Yes, I am."

"You'll help me?"

"I'll try."

The man closed the door and went around the desk and sat down.

"Have a chair," he said. "What is your name?"

"Ernie Foss."

The man wrote on a yellow pad.

"Ernie. That would be Ernest, would it?"

"Yeah, that's right."

"Your address, Mr. Foss."

"I ain't got no address. I just travel around. Once I had an address. I had friends. Susie and Joseph, the Baboon, and—"

"What seems to be the trouble, Mr. Foss?"

"They're holding me."

"Who's holding you?"

"The government. They won't let me go home and they watch me all the time."

"Why do you think they're watching you? What have you done?"

"I ain't done nothing. I got this thing, you see."

"What thing? What have you got?"

"I cure people."

"You can't mean you're a doctor."

"No doctor. I just cure people. I walk around and cure them. I got an aura."

"You have what?"

"An aura."

"I don't understand."

"It's something in me. Something I put out. You got a cold or something?"

"No, I haven't a cold."

"If you had, I'd cure you."

"I tell you what, Mr. Foss. Why don't you go out into the outer office and have a seat. I'll be back with you right away."

As he went out the door, Ernie saw the man reaching for the phone. He didn't wait. He went out the door and into the hall as fast as he could manage. Jack and Al were waiting for him there.

"That was a stupid thing you did," Joe said to Ernie.

"He didn't believe me," Ernie said. "He was reaching for the phone. He would have called the cops."

"Maybe he did. We thought he might. That's why we got out of there."

"He acted as if he thought maybe I was crazy."

"Why did you do it?"

"I got my rights," said Ernie. "Civil rights. Ain't you ever heard of them?"

"Of course we have. You have your legal rights. It was all explained to you. You're employed. You're a civil servant. You agreed to certain conditions of employment. You're being paid. It's all legal."

"But I don't like it."

"What don't you like about it? Your pay is good. Your work is light. You just do some walking. There aren't many people who are paid for walking."

"If I am paid so good, why do we always stay in crummy hotels like this one?"

"You aren't paying for your room and food," said Joe. "You're on an expense account. We take care of it for you. And we don't stay in good hotels because we aren't dressed for it. We'd look funny in a good hotel. We'd attract attention."

"You guys dress like me," said Ernie. "Why do you dress like me? You even talk like me."

"It's the way we work."

"Yeah, I know. The crummy part of town. And that's all right with me. I never was nowhere but the crummy part of town. But you guys, I can tell. You're used to dressing in white shirts and ties and suits. Suits all cleaned and pressed. And when you aren't with me, you talk different, too. I bet."

"Jack," said Joe, "why don't you and Al go out with Ernie and have a bite to eat. Charley and me will go later on."

"That's another thing," said Ernie. "You never go into any place or out of any place together. You make it look as if you aren't all together. Would that be so we aren't noticed, too?"

"Oh," said Joe, disgusted, "what difference does it make?"

The three of them left.

"He's getting hard to handle," Charley said.

"Wouldn't you know," said Joe. "There is only one of him and he has to be a moron. Or damn close to one."

"There is no sign of any other?"

Joe shook his head. "Not the last time I talked with Washington. Yesterday, that was. They're doing all they can, of course, but how do you go about it? A statistical approach is the only way. Try to spot an area where there is no disease and once you find it, if you ever find it, try to spot the one who's responsible for it."

"Another one like Ernie."

"Yes, another one like Ernie. You know what? I don't think there is another one like him. He's a freak."

"There might be another freak."

"The odds, I'd think, would be very much against it. And even if there were, what are the chances they'll find him? It was just dumb, blind luck that Ernie was located."

"We're going at this wrong."

"Of course we're going at it wrong. The right way, the scientific way is to find out what makes him the way he is. They tried that, remember? For damn near a year they tried. All sorts of tests and him bitching every minute. Wanting to go back to Susie and Joseph, the Baboon."

"They might have quit just at the time when they might have found . . ."

Joe shook his head. "I don't think so, Charley. I talked with Rosenmeir. He said it was hopeless. A thing has to get real bad for a man like Rosy to admit that it is hopeless. It took a lot of soul searching to decide to do what we are doing. He couldn't be kept in Washington for further study when there was so little chance of learning anything. They had him. The next logical step was to make some use of him."

"But the country is so big. There are so many cities. So many ghettos. So many pestholes. So much misery. We walk him down a few miles of street each day. We parade him past hospitals and old folks' homes and . . ."

"And don't forget. For every step he takes there may be a dozen people who are made well, another dozen people who won't contract the ailments they would have gotten if it hadn't been for him."

"I don't see how he can help but realize that. We've told him often enough. He should be glad of it, of a chance to help."

Joe said, "I told you. The man's a moron. A little selfish moron."

"You have to see it his way, too, I suppose," said Charley. "We jerked him away from home."

"He never had a home. Sleeping in alleys and flophouses. Panhandling. Doing a little stealing when he had the chance. Shacking up with his Susie when he had a chance. Getting a free meal now and then from some soup kitchen. Raiding garbage cans."

"Maybe he liked it that way."

"Maybe he did. No responsibility. Living day to day, like an animal. But now he has a responsibility—perhaps as great a responsibility, as great an opportunity as any man ever did. There is such a thing as accepting a responsibility."

"In your world, perhaps. In mine. Maybe not in his."

"Damned if I know," said Joe. "He has me beat. He's a complete phony. This talk of his about a home is all phony, too. He was only there for four or five years."

"Maybe if we let him stay in one place and brought people to him, on one pretext or another. Let him sit in a chair, without being noticeable, and parade them past him. Or take him to big meetings and conventions. Let him live it up a little. He might like it better."

"This was all hashed out," said Joe. "We can't be noticed; we can't stand publicity. Christ, can you imagine what might happen if this became public knowledge? He brags about it, of course. He probably was telling them all about it in that dive he stopped off at this afternoon. They paid no attention to him. The lawyer thought that he was crazy. He could stand on a rooftop and yell it to all the world and no one would pay attention. But let one hint come out of Washington . . ."

"I know," said Charley. "I know."

"It's being done," said Joe, "the only way it can be done. We're exposing people to good health, just the way they are exposed to disease. And we're doing it where the need of it is greatest."

"I have a funny feeling, Joe."

"What's that?"

"We may be doing wrong. It sometimes doesn't seem quite right to me."

"You mean going blind. Doing something and not knowing what we are doing. Without understanding it."

"I guess that's it. I don't know. I am all confused. I guess we're helping people."

"Ourselves included. The exposure we are getting to this guy, we should live forever."

"Yes, there's that," said Charley.

They sat silent for a moment. Finally Charley asked, "You got any idea, Joe, when they'll end this tour? It's been going for a month. That's the longest so far. The kids won't know me when I get home if it isn't soon."

"I know," said Joe. "It's tough on a family man like you. Me, it doesn't matter. And I guess it's the same with Al. How's it with Jack? I don't know him well. He's a man who never talks. Not about himself."

"I guess he's got a family somewhere. I don't know anything about it, just that he has. Look, Joe, would you go for a drink? I have a bottle in my bag. I could go and get it."

"A drink," said Joe, "is not a bad idea."

The telephone rang and Charley, who had started for the door, stopped and turned around.

"It might be for me," he said. "I called home a while ago. Myrt wasn't there. I asked little Charley to have her call. I gave both room numbers, just in case I was here."

Joe picked up the phone and spoke into it. He shook his head at Charley. "It's not Myrt. It's Rosy."

Charley started for the door.

Joe said, "Just a minute, Charley."

He went on listening.

"Rosy," he finally said, "you are sure of this?"

He listened some more. Then he said, "Thanks, Rosy. Thanks an awful lot. You stuck out your neck calling us."

He hung up the phone and sat, staring at the wall.

"What's the matter, Joe? What did Rosy want?"

"He called to warn us. There is a mistake. I don't know how or why. A mistake is all."

"What did we do wrong?"

"Not us. It's Washington."

"You mean about Ernie. His civil rights or something."

"Not his civil rights. Charley, he isn't curing people. He is killing them. He's a carrier."

"We know he is a carrier. Other people carry a disease, but he carries—"

"He carries a disease, too. They don't know what it is."

"But back there in his old neighborhood, he made all the people well. Everywhere he went. That is how they found him. They knew there must be someone or something. They hunted till they—"

"Charley, shut up. Let me tell you. Back in his old neighborhood they're dying like flies. They started a couple of days ago and they still are dying. Healthy people dying. Nothing wrong with them, but they're dying just the same. A whole neighborhood is dying."

"Christ, it can't be, Joe. There must be some mistake . . ."

"No mistake. It's the very people he made well who are dying now."

"But it doesn't make sense."

"Rosy thinks maybe it's a new kind of virus. It kills all the rest of them, all the viruses and bacteria that make people sick. No competition, see? It kills off the competition, so it has each body to itself. Then it settles down to grow and the body is all right, because it doesn't intentionally harm the body, but there comes a time . . ."

"Rosy is just guessing."

"Sure Rosy is just guessing. But it makes sense to hear him tell it."

"If it's true," said Charley, "think of all the people, the millions of people . . ."

"That's what I'm thinking of," said Joe. "Rosy took a chance in calling us. They'll crucify him if they find out about the call."

"They'll find out. There'll be a record of it."

"Maybe none that can be traced to him. He called from a phone booth out in Maryland somewhere. Rosy's scared. He is in it up to his neck, the same as us. He spent as much time with Ernie as we did. He knows as much as we do, maybe more than we do."

"He thinks, spending all that time with Ernie, we might be carriers, too?"

"No, I guess not that. But we know. We might talk. And no one can talk about this. No one will be allowed to talk about this. Can you imagine what would happen, the public reaction . . ."

"Joe, how long did you say Ernie spent in that neighborhood of his?"

"Four or five years."

"That's it, then. That's the time we have. You and I and all the rest of us, maybe have four years, probably less."

"That's right. And if they pick us up, we'll spend those years where there won't be any chance of us talking to anyone at all. Someone probably is headed here right now. They have our itinerary."

"Then let's get going, Joe. I know a place. Up north. I can take the family. No one will ever think of looking."

"What if you're a carrier?"

"If I'm a carrier, my family has it now. If I'm not, I want to spend those years—"

"And other people . . ."

"Where I'm headed there aren't many people. We'll be by ourselves."

"Here," said Joe. He took the car keys out of his jacket pocket and tossed them across the room. Charley caught them.

"What about you, Joe?"

"I have to warn the others. And, Charley . . ."

"Yeah?"

"Ditch that car before morning. They'll be looking for you. And when they miss you here, they'll watch your family and your home. Be careful."

"I know. And you, Joe?"

"I'll take care of myself. As soon as I let the others know."

"And Ernie? We can't let him—"

"I'll take care of Ernie, too," said Joe.

CACTUS COLTS

*Cliff Simak's journals do not mention a story named "Cactus Colts."
I suspect that it is the one named "Boothill Brothers Talk with Bullets"—an ugly title, but that kind of thing was common in the pulp
westerns of those days. But I am not too confident of that conclusion
due to a discrepancy in dates. At any rate, "Cactus Colts," which first
appeared in* Lariat Story Magazine's *July 1944 issue, is shorter than
most of Cliff's westerns, meaning that it's a terse, taut creation.*

—dww

Jeff Jones stumbled when a loose board on the steps in front
of the Silver Dollar buckled beneath him. Snarling huskily, he
reached out and grabbed a porch post to save himself from falling. Savagely, he wrenched his foot free of the broken board and
glanced around, waiting for the yell of laughter that would greet
his stumble.

There was no laughter. There was no one to laugh. This Cactus City street drowsed dustily in the silent afternoon. The air was
heavy with the heat, and the sunlight was something that came
pouring from the molten bowl of sky, so brilliant it hurt one's
eyes. Jeff's pony stood with drooping head beside the hitching
post, the only living thing in sight.

Beyond the town marched the glassy plains, tan with sun-
scorched grass.

Jeff strode across the narrow porch and through the batwing doors. For a moment he stopped, blinking in the shade that seemed almost like darkness after the sun-washed street.

A bartender, flour sack for an apron, mopped moodily. Three men were lined against the bar. At one of the tables a bearded drunk was sleeping. His battered hat had fallen from his head and lay canted on its brim.

Jeff moved to the bar and flipped a dollar down. The bar-keeper set a bottle out and Jeff poured a drink. The liquor slashed down his throat, cutting the dust. His left cheek, the one with the scar, twitched nervously. He poured another drink.

A savage voice snarled behind him.

"Jones!"

Jeff spun around, hand to gun.

One of the men at the other end of the bar had stepped out into the room, stood spraddle-legged, hands above his butts.

Eyes still unadjusted from the blaze of sun outside, Jeff could not see the other's face. It was no more than a smudgy blue of white. But there was no mistaking the meaning of the hands above those guns.

There was no time for thought, no space for wondering. Jeff's mind clicked blank with sudden concentration, every-thing else wiped out but that spraddle-legged figure set for a double draw.

Chill silence had seeped into the room. The two men at the bar were rigid. The drunk was awake, clutching for his hat.

Jeff felt the breath rasping in his throat, wished for one wild moment that the light was better. Then the other man's hands were moving and his guns were coming out.

With a swift flip of his wrist, Jeff brought his own gun free.

Twin eyes of red twinkled for a moment almost straight into Jeff's face and he felt his own gun kicking against his arm, its muzzle drooling fire. Behind him glass crashed and tinkled like little silver bells.

The white smudge face twisted in sudden pain and the two guns clattered on the floor.

Jeff flipped his gun toward the silent figures at the bar.

"Anyone else?" he asked and his voice was so brittle he hardly knew it for his own.

One of the men stirred. "It ain't our fight, stranger."

The man out in the center of the room had made no move to pick up the fallen guns. He was bent over, like someone with the stomach ache, moaning softly, left hand clutching right wrist.

The man who had spoken stepped away from the bar and paced slowly forward.

"I'm Owen," he said.

Jeff stabbed the gun at him. "Your name," he said, "don't mean a thing to me."

Owen stopped short. He was a big man, a bear of a man, a sleek bear with shiny black coat and a black cravat in which a stickpin gleamed.

"I own the place," he said. "Can't imagine what got into Jim. One minute he was there talking with us. Next minute he was out there calling you."

The wounded man straightened up. "He's Peaceful Jones," he screamed. "I'd know him anywhere by that scar across his face."

Jeff slid the gun back into its holster. "Meaning which?" he asked.

"You know damn well what I mean," yelled Jim. "Back in Texas..."

"Shut up," snapped Owen. "By rights, you should be buzzard bait."

"I don't kill no man without he has his guns," said Jeff.

"You, Buck, pick up them guns," said Owen, "and put them on the bar. Jim, you better hightail it for the doc and get that wrist fixed up."

The wounded man mumbled, started for the door, still holding his wrist, fingers stained with red. Buck picked up the guns, grinned wolfishly at Jeff.

"So you're Peaceful Jones," said Owen.

Jeff hesitated. His name was Jones, all right, but he wasn't Peaceful Jones. Leastwise, he'd never been called that anywhere before.

"I been waiting for you," Owen told him. He eyed Jeff speculatively. "Thought maybe we could talk some business."

"I'm sort of busy," Jeff declared. "Looking for someone."

"Sure," said Owen. "I know all about that. Come out in the back and kill a bottle with me."

He reached out and took the bottle the bartender had set out for Jeff.

For a moment, Jeff hesitated. He wasn't Peaceful Jones and maybe he'd save himself a heap of trouble by up and saying so. But he'd come to Cactus City looking for trouble and now that he'd found it . . .

"Guess I can spare some time," he said slowly.

The drunk, he saw, had fallen asleep once more. His hat had fallen off again and lay on the floor.

The back room was a bare affair. An empty bottle, a few glasses and a deck of greasy cards littered the table.

Jeff slid into a chair while Owen poured liquor into two glasses.

"So Banker Slemp hired you," Owen fired at Jim.

Jeff picked up a glass, twirled it between his hands. Owen stared at him.

"Lay down your cards," said Jeff. "Face up."

"You're making it tough to deal with you," Owen complained.

"Me," said Jeff. "I got a job."

"With Slemp," said Owen.

Jeff nodded.

"That way you're bucking me," Owen told him flatly.

"I don't know about that," said Jeff. "Slemp has a job for me. That's all I know about it."

Owen drained his glass, thumped it on the table.

"Likely figuring on cheating you out of half your money," he declared. "Same as he's cheated all the ranchers."

"What you figuring on doing about it?" demanded Jeff.

Owen hiked his chair forward, leaned across the table. "What if the bank happened to get robbed and Slemp got killed?"

Jeff stifled his gasp. He bent his head, staring at the glass, brain racing. Trying to figure it out, trying to find the answer.

"Slemp wouldn't be underfoot any more," he said.

"You catch on quick," said Owen. "Quick on the trigger, quick on the savvy. That's the way I like it."

"Bank robbing," Jeff pointed out, "is sometimes downright risky."

Owen chuckled thickly. "Not the way we'd do it. With you inside and us outside it would be a cinch. Some night when Slemp was working on the books. And it would be blamed on the Hills gang."

He chuckled again. "No one would even think of us."

Jeff tilted the glass and swallowed the whisky, put the glass back on the table. He rose and hitched up his gunbelt.

"There'd be something in it for me?" he asked.

Owen guffawed. "Plenty. You needn't worry. I ain't interested in the money. Just Slemp."

"I'll be in to see you," Jeff said.

"We'll be watching you," warned Owen.

"Just be careful," said Jeff, "that you don't crowd me none."

On the street in front of the Silver Dollar, Jeff stood for a moment, looking down the street. One sign said RESTAURANT. Another said SADDLES. The third one said BANK.

The pony still stood with hanging head, switching lazily. A dog had come from somewhere and lay curled in the shadows at the corner of a building.

Jeff headed down the street. Little puffs of dust spatted around his boots. The dog watched him with sad, half interested eyes.

The bank was one room, divided in half by a counter topped by a black iron netting that formed a cage. There was one window. A man writing at a desk got up.

"You Slemp?" asked Jeff.

The banker nodded.

"I'm Jones," said Jeff.

What passed for a smile glinted beneath the weedy mustache.

"You must have made good time, Mr. Jones. I hadn't expected you for a day or two."

"When I travel," said Jeff, "I travel."

"I'll let you in, Mr. Jones," said Slemp.

"The name," said Jeff, "is Peaceful."

"I'll lock up," said Slemp. "It's almost closing time anyhow. Not much business these days."

He pulled a chain from his pocket, selected a key and walked to the front door.

Jeff heard a lock click and Slemp was back again, holding open the door that led behind the cage.

"Have a chair," he invited.

Jeff hooked a chair from under the desk with the toe of his boot and sat down.

"What's on your mind?" he asked.

Slemp motioned. "Those guns? You handy with them?"

"Might say I was," admitted Jeff.

"You may have occasion to use them," declared Slemp.

"What's the trouble, Slemp? Some of the ranchers on the prod?"

"What do you mean?" rasped Slemp.

Jeff grinned. "Some bankers ain't too popular. Just a mite particular about foreclosure laws."

"I've never had any trouble that way," Slemp declared. "Whatever I've done was strictly legal. Any foreclosures I might have made were only carried out to protect the loan."

"Naturally," said Jeff.

"The man you have to watch," said Slemp, leaning closer, lowering his voice, "is a man named Owen. Owns the Silver Dollar."

"Yeah," said Jeff, "I know. I stopped there for a drink."

Slemp frowned. "Didn't meet Owen, did you?"

"Me and him," said Jeff, "had a drink together."

"Know who you were?"

"Guess he did," admitted Jeff. "Hombre in there recognized me. Came gunning for me. Claimed I'd crossed him down in Texas."

"You killed him?"

"Nope, Just gun-whipped him some."

Slemp shook his head. "Don't like that, Jones. You should have come straight here."

Jeff's hand shot out and grasped Slemp by the shirt front, pulling the fabric tight with a vicious twist, dragging the man close to him.

"Don't start telling me what I should of done," he snarled. "Don't start figuring you can treat me like a hired hand. Tell me what the layout is and tell me quick. Quit beating around the bush and tell it straight."

"It's Owen," gasped Slemp. "I'm getting afraid of him. He's planning something. I got ways of finding out."

"Spies?"

The banker's face twisted. "Yes, you might call them that. Men in Owen's gang that tell me things I need to know. I pay them for it."

"Why are you afraid of Owen?" rapped Jeff. "What's he got against you?"

Slemp hesitated. Jeff shook him roughly.

"We were in some deals together," Slemp said, eyes showing white with fear.

"And you double-crossed him?"

"No. No, Jones, it isn't that. Between us we run this country. But Owen isn't satisfied with that. He wants it all himself. I'm afraid . . ."

Jeff released his hold upon the shirt.

"You got a damn good right to be," he said.

The banker reached out a hand for a chair, sat down in it carefully.

"So I'm supposed to save your hide," said Jeff. "What do you want me to do? Just some plain and fancy guarding or gunsmoke Owen and his gang plumb out of town?"

Slemp gulped. "Just guarding," he said. "Just a month or two. I'm fixing up a deal to run Owen out myself. Vigilante committee or a law and order association or something like that."

Jeff spat in disgust. "You can do it, too. A solid citizen like you."

"You bet I can," the banker said.

"Figure all those ranchers you robbed are going to back you up, heh?"

Slemp flared. "I didn't rob anyone, Jones. The boys all knew when they got their loans they had to have the payments here on time. I told them so before they got the money. Ain't my fault they couldn't make it."

"Have it your own way," said Jeff. "I'll start work tomorrow."

"You've already started," declared Slemp. "From now on you stay with me. Eat with me. Sleep at my place. Stay . . ."

"Nope," insisted Jeff. "Tomorrow. Me, I'm likkering up tonight. Never drink while I'm on the job and my throat is dusty."

"I don't like it," protested Slemp.

"I don't give a damn if you do or not," said Jeff. "Haul out that key of yours and let me out of here."

The sun was setting in the bloody welter of the west, throwing powdery blue shadows across the dusty street. A dog trotted between a couple of buildings. Several ponies were tied to the rack in front of the Silver Dollar. A man down the street called out a greeting.

Cactus City was coming to life.

At the hitching rail, Jeff untied the pony and headed down the street toward the livery barn.

There was no one at the barn, but Jeff led the pony in, chose a stall and unsaddled. From the bin he took a measure of oats and poured them in the box, set to work rubbing down his mount.

A shadow fell across the stall and Jeff looked up. A man stood there, staring at him. A man with a bandaged right hand.

Jeff straightened, dropped the brush into the straw.

The man grinned. "No need of reaching for your irons, stranger," he said. "I made a fool mistake. It was that scar, I guess."

"You didn't give me no chance to set you right," Jeff declared. "There wasn't nothing left to do but smoke it out."

"You do look some like Peaceful," said the man. "But you ain't. If you had been I'd be stone cold by now."

He thrust out his good left hand. "I'd be plumb honored to shake," he said.

They shook.

"Name is Churchill," said the man. "Jim Churchill. I own this here barn. Got everything you want?"

"Everything," said Jeff. "Found the oats. There's just one thing you can do. I sure would appreciate it if you didn't let on I wasn't Peaceful Jones. For a while, at least."

"Any way you want it," Churchill said.

"Name really is Jones," Jeff explained. "Jeff Jones. But I never heard of this Peaceful jasper. Looking for my brother, Dan. Use to have a ranch out east a ways."

"Dan Jones," said Churchill. "Yeah, I heard of him. Up and disappeared couple, three months ago. Slemp took over his ranch."

"I know," Jeff told him. "Rode past the place coming in. Feller there said he was minding it for Slemp. Seems Dan had a mortgage on it."

"Lots of fellows around here losing their spreads to Slemp," said Churchill. "Downright uncanny how it happens sometimes. Some of them get killed and some of them are robbed and some just naturally come up missing. Seems almost as if Slemp has luck plumb on his side. Ain't a one of those places but is worth a sight more than the money owing on them."

"Who did the killing?" asked Jeff.

"Bunch of riders out in the hills, I guess," said Churchill. "Leastwise, that's what we always figured. Hills gang, they're called. Got the lawmen of ten counties fit to be tied."

The layout was loaded with sudden death. There could be no doubt of that.

Maybe, Jeff told himself, he should get out before the shooting started. After all, he had deliberately stuck out his neck without proper thought. Had accepted the identity of Peaceful Jones, had listened to Owen's cold-blooded proposition of robbery and murder, had gone to Slemp pretending he was the man that Slemp had sent for.

That he would be in the middle when the shooting started, Jeff knew all too well.

Both Owen and Slemp, he realized, were ruthless men. Owen was planning to wipe out Slemp who, with his planted spies, knew he was planning it. And neither one, Jeff felt, could be trusted for a fraction of a second.

Hunched above his plate of ham and eggs, Jeff stared out the window of the restaurant to the evening-softened street. A few men were riding in, probably heading for the Silver Dollar.

We had some deals together, Slemp had said in describing why he was afraid of Owen. It wasn't too hard to imagine what sort of deals they might have been . . . not hard to understand why men who owed Slemp money were killed or robbed or simply disappeared.

Dan had had the money to pay Slemp. Jeff knew that, for he, himself, had sent part of it to him, had planned on coming out later on and going in with Dan. That, he remembered, had been something they had talked about for years . . . the day when they could own a spread together.

Jeff's fingers tightened on the fork and it shook so that the piece of ham fell off.

Dan, most likely, was dead. That was a thing he had to face. A fact he must accept. Somewhere out here, Dan Jones, his brother, had been shot down, probably from ambush, with not a single chance of fighting back.

Jeff finished the ham, mopping up the egg yolk with the last few pieces, and drained the coffee mug.

Outside night had fallen and the dusky copper of lamplight had bloomed along the street. The stars were a faint, powdery drift in the black vault of the sky and a lonesome wind drummed above Cactus City with a hollow sound.

Jeff stumped up the street toward the bank. Slemp, he knew, must be at work, for the two windows glowed orange with light.

Opposite the bank, Jeff started to cross the street and then drew back into the shadows of the buildings. Someone was inside with Slemp.

Jeff glanced up and down the street. There was no one nearby. Down by the Silver Dollar a few horses were hitched to the rail and a couple of men lounged in front of the livery barn.

Swiftly Jeff strode across the street toward the bank. Through the window he could see Slemp and the other man, standing beside the open back door, talking together. Then the second man stepped out and Slemp closed the door, shot the heavy bolt.

But Jeff had recognized the other man. Tall, haggard, wolfish, there could be no mistake. The man was Buck . . . the one who had been in the Silver Dollar that afternoon, the one who had picked up the guns that Churchill dropped.

Jeff waited for ten minutes, propped against the building, whistling soundlessly. Then he rapped on the window and pressed his face against the pane. Slemp looked up from his books, peered over the caged-in counter like a startled rabbit. Jeff rapped again.

Slowly, uncertainly, Slemp came from behind the cage and moved toward the window. Then, seeing who it was, he motioned toward the door.

The door opened and Jeff stepped in.

Slemp rubbed his hands together. "So you decided to start the job right away," he said.

"Get your hat," said Jeff. "You're coming with me."

"My hat?"

"Sure, your hat. We're going down to the Silver Dollar."

Jeff stepped close and lifted the six gun from the banker's holster.

"You won't be needing this," he said. He ran his hand over Slemp's coat, making sure he had no shoulder gun.

The banker tried to speak, but the words dried up in his mouth and he only sputtered. Jeff reached up, took Slemp's hat from the nail beside the door and socked it on his head.

"But the Silver Dollar," yelled Slemp. "Owen . . ."

"That's just what I thought," said Jeff. "You and Owen will want a little talk."

He drilled the gun muzzle into the banker's stomach and motioned at the door.

"Out you go," he said. "Walk ahead of me. Not too fast, not too slow. As natural as you can. If you try to get away I'll fill you full of holes."

"You can't do this," sputtered the banker. "I hired you to protect me. I'm the one . . ."

"You hired Peaceful Jones to protect you," snapped Jeff, "and he ain't got here yet. Me, I'm another Jones, no relative of his."

"You aren't Peaceful Jones!"

"Naw, I'm Jeff Jones. Had a brother name of Dan. Maybe you remember him. He had a mortgage with you."

"But listen, Jones, all I did . . ."

"Yeah, I know. You didn't do a thing except foreclose all legal like. He didn't show up with the money, so you took his land. We're going to find out what Owen knows about it."

"You'll be sorry for this," stormed Slemp. "You're way out on a limb."

"Maybe so," admitted Jeff. "We're finding out."

He prodded Slemp's belly with the gun barrel. "Out the door and remember what I said."

Slemp sidled out the door and Jeff followed.

From the Silver Dollar came the sound of voices, the clink of glasses on the bar, the tinkling music of a tinny piano.

Jeff grinned grimly. This was the payoff. If it failed, if it didn't click, he had his neck way out and no time to pull it back.

Slemp marched ahead, not looking to left or right, his shoulders hunched as if at any moment he expected the impact of a bullet. At the steps to the saloon he turned and climbed to the porch. Jeff followed.

He stumbled, his foot tripping on the broken board.

In the dark beyond the porch a sixgun hammered and red flames splashed angrily. Jeff went to his knees, hands outflung, the bullet an angry drone above his head. The sixgun roared again and white splinters flew from the porch floor just in front of him.

Savagely, Jeff ripped out a gun, fired at the place from which the shots had come. The hidden Colt barked again and someone was running down the street.

Twisting around, Jeff lined his sights between the porch railing posts and fired. The runner staggered drunkenly, came to his knees in a slashing path of lamplight that spewed from the restaurant.

The ponies were snorting, rearing and jerking at their ties. The Silver Dollar's batwing doors crashed open under the weight of rushing men. The piano stopped abruptly.

Jeff wrenched his foot free of the broken step, the step that had broken under him that afternoon. A broken step, he knew, that probably had saved his life. For it he hadn't stumbled when he did, the killer's bullet would have found him.

———

The man on his knees in front of the restaurant was leveling his gun. It bellowed and the slug raked across Jeff's ribs with a blow that numbed his side.

Behind Jeff a sixgun crashed and the kneeling man tipped over, arms outflung, body bent at an awkward angle.

Jeff whirled, grabbed the arm that held the smoking gun and twisted hard. The weapon dropped.

"Someone swiped my shooting iron," wailed a voice. "Snatched it plumb away from me. Just wait until I get my hands . . ."

"It's on the ground," Jeff said tersely. "Pick it up."

He spoke to the man he held. "Right nice of you to save my life."

Slemp squirmed in his grasp, terror on his face. "So you fixed it up," said Jeff. "You had him planted here. I might have known when I saw him in there with you. One of your spies. Afraid of me, so you decided to scratch me out."

Slemp tried to speak, but Jeff snarled at him.

"Shut up!"

Three men came back from the restaurant, carrying the limp body.

"It's Buck," said one of them. "He's deader than a door nail."

They laid him on the porch and someone brought a blanket to throw over him.

Jeff looked up and saw Owen standing on the porch, staring down at him and Slemp.

"I see," said Owen, "that you're taking your new job right serious."

"I aim to," Jeff told him. He nodded at the blanket covered form. "One of your men, wasn't he?"

Owen shook his head. "Must be something wrong, Jones. Buck never would have climbed you."

"He did, though."

"And," said Owen, callously, "he got what was coming to him."

Owen turned away and headed for the doors. "Drinks on the house," he called.

The men trooped in to line up against the bar.

"Get going," Jeff told Slemp.

Together they climbed the steps and went through the doors, stopped just inside of them.

Everyone else was at the bar . . . except one man. The drunk still slept at the table, hat still canted on its brim. He snored and the snore made his whiskers flutter as if there were a wind.

"Owen," said Jeff and his voice, edged with steel, cut through the voices at the bar, brought every man around, clapped the place in silence.

For a long minute the silence held, then Owen stepped out of the line.

"Yes, Jones, what is it?"

Jeff twisted his arm and sent the banker spinning into the center of the room. Off balance, Slemp tried to right himself, skidded and slipped, sat down hard and slid.

"Slemp here wants to ask you about some money," said Jeff. "The mortgage money that never got to him."

"He's crazy," screamed the sitting Slemp. "He don't know what he's talking about."

"I had a brother Dan," said Jeff. "He started for Cactus City to pay up his mortgage. He never got here. He . . ."

At the bar a man moved swiftly, his arms a blur of motion, his gun a streaking thing that glinted in the light.

Jeff's hands pistoned for his Colts, but he knew he'd be too late. The play had failed . . . it never had a chance . . . .

A crashing gun bark jarred the room and the man at the bar huddled forward, twisting, fighting to keep his feet. He staggered out into the room, his guns dropped from his hand and he sat down limply, one shoulder oozing red.

The drunk, drunk no longer, crouched behind his table, two guns out. One of them smoking.

The crowd at the bar surged forward, but Jeff swept the gun barrels at them.

"Stay where you are," he yelled. "And reach for the sky."

They halted, retreated until their backs were against the bar. Slowly their hands came up.

"Some of you hombres are all right," said Jeff, "and some of you ain't. I ain't got no way of knowing. The ones that move, I'll figure that they ain't."

The drunk spoke slowly, almost conversationally. "You take them from that side, kid, and I'll take them from the other."

"Dan!" yelled Jeff.

"Yeah, it's me, all right. But keep your eyes peeled. That buckaroo on the floor must be one of them that dry gulched me that day. Can't explain what he did no other way."

The blood drummed through Jeff's head, but he kept his eyes straight ahead. Dan was alive . . . alive and in this room with him. The two of them putting down the chips against Slemp and Owen.

The tableau held. The line of men against the bar were still and silent, hands high in the air. Slemp still on the floor, Owen standing just a few feet out in the room. The wounded man slumped on the floor, head hanging, hand clawing at his shoulder.

But it would have to break. It couldn't last, Jeff knew.

He stared at the faces staring at him. Jim Churchill was the only one he knew. But there must be others here who were ready to fight Slemp and Owen.

The wounded man was babbling. "I was sure I got him. It was dark, but I was sure. His horse ran and it was dark. The money was in the saddle bags and I didn't go back to look. I was . . ."

"Shut up, you fool," yelled Owen.

"So," snarled Jeff, "you don't want him to talk."

"Men," yelled Owen, "are you going to stand for this? Are you going to let this hombre get away with it?"

A few of those at the bar stirred uneasily, but no one went for his guns.

Churchill, arms still high, moved out.

"Better explain yourself, Jones," he snapped.

"Simple," said Jeff. "Owen and his gang here has been killing off the ranchers when they're coming in to pay their loans. Owen gets the money and Slemp gets the land."

"I never had a thing to do with it," yelled Slemp. "It was Owen thought it up . . ."

The line at the bar exploded. A gun roared and a bullet thudded into the door post behind Jeff's head.

Owen was charging and Jeff brought up a gun, pressed the trigger. But the big man came on.

Shots were hammering and a lamp crashed, spraying oil across the floor.

Jeff leaped to meet Owen's charge, but his foot slipped in the pool of oil and his hands slid off Owen's body. The batwings flapped as if hit by a sudden wind and the man was gone.

A bullet thudded into the floor and flying splinters stabbed at Jeff's face. A gun crashed directly above him. One of his own guns was lost, but he still had the other. With a heave he gained his feet and plunged for the door.

Owen was on his hands and knees in the dust of the street, like a trapped animal, with one foot fast in the broken bottom step.

With a yell, Jeff launched himself in a flying tackle even as Owen's foot came free.

Warned by the yell, Owen twisted to meet him, flung up an arm that broke the swing of Jeff's gun. Thudding into the man, Jeff felt his arm go numb, felt the gun fly from suddenly limp fingers.

A fist caught him in the jaw, rocked him back against the porch. In front of him, Owen was scrambling to his feet, hands reaching for the guns that dangled from his hips.

Desperately, Jeff leaped, good arm swinging. The blow caught Owen in the side of the head and staggered him. Jeff followed, left fist punching as Owen clawed for steel.

One of Owen's guns was out and coming up. Jeff swung again, stepping in fast, putting every ounce of power into the blow. It connected with a thud that snapped Owen's head back between his shoulders, sent him rocking on his heels against the hitching rail. A gun blasted and Jeff felt a sharp snarl of pain slash across his leg.

Owen was against the rail, groggy, weaving. Jeff stepped forward and his leg screamed with agony. The gun came up again, shaky, uncertain.

Jeff's fist lashed out, straight to the chin. Owen slumped like a sack, gun tumbling from his hand.

Hanging onto the railing, Jeff stooped and picked it up, straightened up again, still clutching the rail. He couldn't move, he knew. He had to hang to that rail.

He lifted his head, stared dully at the Silver Dollar. The place was a hum of voices, but there was no shooting. Light still spilled from the windows.

His head spun and he fought to keep his grip. But the railing seemed to writhe and twist and his hand slipped off. He knew that he was plunging to the street, flat on his face.

He awoke choking and coughing, clawing at his throat. Through bleary eyes he saw a glass half full of whisky in a fist before his face.

He fought his way to a sitting posture and looked around. Men were standing in a circle, among them a man with a bearded face.

"How about it, Dan?" he asked, his voice raspy.

"It's all right, kid," said Dan. "Slemp coughed up his guts. We got enough evidence to hang them all."

"But you," asked Jeff. "How did you get away with it?"

Dan laughed. "Slemp was the only one that ever saw me close. I was too busy on the ranch to spend much time in town. And then the beard fooled them, would have fooled even Slemp. And no one pays much attention to a floating drunk. I figured what the setup was and I meant to get the evidence. But you almost upset my plans. When you came barging in this afternoon, I nearly came dealing myself a hand when Churchill jumped you . . ."

"Lucky thing for me," said Churchill, "that you didn't."

"Only thing," said Dan, "I wasn't even sure, myself. That scar of yours."

Jeff's hand went to his cheek, "Got it the week after you left home," he said. "Bronc bucked me off into a barbed wire fence."

MESSAGE FROM MARS

Originally named "Martian Lilies," this story, which was apparently written in late 1939 or early 1940, was rejected by Amazing Stories, Astounding Science Fiction, *and another magazine not named in Cliff's journals before being accepted by* Planet Stories *late in 1942. The magazine paid Cliff a hundred dollars, and the story appeared its fall 1943 issue. In a way, readers can view this story as a reversal of the plot of H. G. Wells's* War of the Worlds, *as well as an extension of the idea underlying the Superman comic books (I know Cliff read Wells, but there's no evidence that he ever read the Superman comics). But the most important thing about "Message from Mars" is that it contains, appropriately, the seeds of the later Simak novel* All Flesh Is Grass.

—dww

I

"You're crazy, man," snapped Steven Alexander, "you can't take off for Mars alone!"

Scott Nixon thumped the desk in sudden irritation.

"Why not?" he shouted. "One man can run a rocket. Jack Riley's sick and there are no other pilots here. The rocket blasts in fifteen minutes and we can't wait. This is the last chance. The only chance we'll have for months."

Jerry Palmer, sitting in front of the massive radio, reached for a bottle of Scotch and slopped a drink into the tumbler at his elbow.

"Hell, Doc," he said, "let him go. It won't make any difference. He won't reach Mars. He's just going out in space to die like all the rest of them."

Alexander snapped savagely at him. "You don't know what you're saying. You drink too much."

"Forget it, Doc," said Scott. "He's telling the truth. I won't get to Mars, of course. You know what they're saying down in the base camp, don't you? About the bridge of bones. Walking to Mars over a bridge of bones."

The old man stared at him. "You have lost faith? You don't think you'll go to Mars?"

Scott shook his head. "I haven't lost my faith. Someone will get there . . . sometime. But it's too soon yet. Look at that tablet, will you!"

He waved his hand at a bronze plate set into the wall.

"The roll of honor," said Scott, bitterly. "Look at the names. You'll have to buy another soon. There won't be room enough."

One Nixon already was on that scroll of bronze. Hugh Nixon, fifty-fourth from the top. And under that the name of Harry Decker, the man who had gone out with him.

The radio blurted suddenly at them, jabbering, squealing, howling in anguish.

Scott stiffened, ears tensed as the code sputtered across millions of miles. But it was the same old routine. The same old message, repeated over and over again . . . the same old warning hurled out from the ruddy planet.

"No. No. No come. Danger."

Scott turned toward the window, stared up into the sky at the crimson eye of Mars.

What was the use of keeping hope alive? Hope that Hugh might have reached Mars, that someday the Martian code would bring some word of him.

Hugh had died . . . like all the rest of them. Like those whose names were graven in the bronze there on the wall. The maw of space had swallowed him. He had flown into the face of silence and the silence was unbroken.

The door of the office creaked open, letting in a gust of chilly air. Jimmy Baldwin shut the door behind him and looked at them vacantly.

"Nice night to go to Mars," he said.

"You shouldn't be up here, Jimmy," said Alexander gently. "You should be down at the base, tending to your flowers."

"There're lots of flowers on Mars," said Jimmy. "Maybe some-day I'll go to Mars and see."

"Wait until somebody else goes first," said Palmer bitterly.

Jimmy turned about, hesitantly, like a man who had a purpose but had forgotten what it was. He moved slowly toward the door and opened it.

"I got to go," he said.

The door closed heavily but the chill did not vanish from the room. For it wasn't the chill of the mountain's peak, but another kind of chill . . . a chill that had walked in with Jimmy Baldwin and now refused to leave.

Palmer tipped the bottle, sloshed the whiskey in the glass.

"The greatest pilot that ever lived," he said. "Now look at him!"

"He still holds the record," Alexander reminded the radio operator. "Eight times to the Moon and still alive."

The accident had happened as Jimmy's ship was approaching Earth on that eighth return trip. A tiny meteor had struck the hull, drilling a sharp-cut hole. It had struck Andy Mason, Jimmy's best friend, squarely between the eyes.

The cabin had been filled with the scream of escaping air, had turned cold with the deadly breath of space and frost crystals had danced in front of Jimmy's eyes.

Somehow Jimmy had patched the hole in the hull, had reached Earth in a smashing rocket drive, knowing he had little air, that every minute was a borrowed eternity.

Most pilots would have killed themselves or blown up their ships in that reckless race for Earth, but Jimmy, ace of all the space-men of his day, had made it.

But he had walked from the ship with a blank face and babbling lips. He still lived at the rocket camp because it was home to him. He puttered among his flowers. He watched the rockets come and go without a flutter of expression. And everyone was kind to him, for in his face they read a fate that might be theirs.

"All of us are crazy," said Scott. "Every one of us. Myself included. That's why I'm blasting off alone."

"I refuse to let you go," said Alexander firmly.

Scott rested his knuckles on the desk. "You can't stop me. I have my orders to make the trip. Whether I go alone or with an assistant pilot makes no difference. That rocket blasts on time, and I'm in it when it goes."

"But it's foolishness," protested Alexander. "You'll go space-mad. Think of the loneliness!"

"Think of the coordinates," snapped Scott. "Delay the blast-off and you have to work out a set of new ones. Days of work and then it'll be too late. Mars will be too far away."

Alexander spread his hands. "All right then. I hope you make it."

Scott turned away but Alexander called him back.

"You're sure of the routine?"

Scott nodded. He knew the routine by heart. So many hours out to the Moon, landing on the Moon to take on extra fuel, taking off for Mars at an exact angle at a certain minute.

"I'll come out and see you off," said Alexander. He heaved himself up and slid into a heavy coat.

Palmer shouted after Scott. "So long, big boy. It was nice knowing you."

Scott shrugged. Palmer was a little drunk and very bitter. He'd watched them go too long. His nerves were wearing out.

Stars shone like hard, bright jewels in the African sky. A sharp wind blew over the summit of Mt. Kenya, a wind that whined among the ice-bound rocks and bit deep into the flesh. Far below blazed the lights of the base camp, hundreds of feet down the slope from the main rocket camp here atop the mountain set squarely on the Earth's equator.

The rasping voice of a radio newscaster came from the open door of the machine shop.

"New York," shrieked the announcer. "Austin Gordon, famous African explorer, announced this afternoon he will leave soon for the Congo valley, where he will investigate reports of a strange metallic city deep in the interior. Natives, bringing reports of the discovery out of the jungle, claim the city is inhabited by strange metallic insects."

Someone slammed the door and the voice was cut off.

Scott hunched into the wind to light a cigarette.

"The explorers are going crazy, too," he said.

Probably, later on in the program the announcer would have mentioned Scott Nixon and Jack Riley would blast off in a few minutes in another attempt to reach Mars. But it would be well along in the program and it wouldn't take much time. Ten years ago Mars had been big news. Today it rated small heads in the press, slight mention on the air.

But the newscaster would have been wrong about Jack Riley. Jack Riley lay in the base camp hospital with an attack of ptomaine. Only an hour before Jack had clasped Scott's hand and grinned at him and wished him luck.

He needed luck. For in this business a man didn't have even an inside chance.

Scott walked toward the tilted rocket. He could hear the crunch of Alexander's feet as the man moved with him.

"It won't be new to you," Alexander was saying, "you've been to the Moon before."

Yes, he had been to the Moon three times and he was still alive. But, then, he had been lucky. Your luck just simply didn't hold forever. There was too much to gamble on in space. Fuel, for one thing. Men had experimented with fuel for ten years now and still the only thing they had was a combination of liquid oxygen and gasoline. They had tried liquid hydrogen but that had proved too cold, too difficult to confine, treacherous to handle, too bulky because of its low density. Liquid oxygen could be put under pressure, condensed into little space. It was safe to handle, safe until it combined with gasoline and then it was sheer death to anything that got within its reach.

Of course, there had been some improvements. Better handling of the fuel, for instance. Combustion chambers stood up better now because they were designed better. Feed lines didn't freeze so readily now as when the first coffins took to space. Rocket motors were more efficient, but still cranky.

But there were other things. Meteors, for one, and you couldn't do much about them. Not until someone designed a screen, and no one had. Radiations were another. Space was full of radiations and, despite the insulating jacket of ozone some of them seeped through.

Scott climbed through the rocket valve and turned to close it. He hesitated for a moment, drinking in the smell and sight of Earth. There wasn't much that one could see. The anxious face of Alexander, the huddled shadows that were watching men, the twinkling base camp lights.

With a curse at his own weakness, Scott slammed the valve lock, twirled it home.

Fitting himself into the shock absorbent chair, he fastened the straps that held him. His right foot reached out and found the trip that would fire the rockets. Then he lifted his wrist in front of his eyes and watched the second hand of the watch.

Ten seconds. Eight. Now five. The hand was creeping up, ticking off the time. It rested on the zero mark and he slammed down his foot. Cruel weight smashed down upon him, driving his body back into the padded chair. His lungs were flattened, the air driven from them. His heart thumped. Nausea seized him, and black mists swam before his eyes. He seemed to be slipping into a midnight chasm and he cried out weakly. His body went limp, sagging in the chair. Twin streams of blood trickled from his nose and down his lip.

He was far out in space when he struggled back to consciousness. For a time he did not stir. Lying in the chair, it took long minutes to realize where he was. Gradually his brain cleared and his eyes focused and made impressions on his senses. Slowly he became aware of the lighted instrument board, of the rectangle of quartz that formed the vision panel. His ears registered the silence that steeped the ship, the weird, deathly silence of outer space.

Weakly he stirred and sat upright, his eyes automatically studying the panel. The fuel pressure was all right, atmospheric pressure was holding, speed was satisfactory.

He leaned back in the chair and waited, resting, storing his strength. Automatically his hand reached up and wiped the blood from his lips and chin.

II

He was in space. Headed for the Moon and from there for Mars. But even the realization of this failed to rouse him from the lethargy of battered body and tortured brain.

Taking off in a rocket was punishment. Severe, terrible punishment. Only men who were perfect physical specimens could attempt it. An imperfect heart would simply stop under the jarring impact of the blast-off.

Someday rockets would be perfected. Someday rockets would rise gently from the Earth, shaking off Earth's gravity by gradual application of power rather than by tremendous thrusts that kicked steel and glass and men out into space.

But not yet, not for many years. Perhaps not for many generations. For many years men would risk their lives in blasting projectiles that ripped loose from the Earth by the sheer savagery of exploding oxygen and gasoline.

A moan came from the rear of the ship, a stifled pitiful moan that brought Scott upright in the chair, tearing with nervous hands at the buckles of his belt.

With belt loosened, body tensed, he waited for a second, hardly believing he had heard the sound. It came again, a piteous human cry.

Scott leaped to his feet, staggered under the lack of gravitation. The rocket was coasting on momentum now and, while its forward motion gave it a simulation of gravity, enough so a man could orient himself, there was in actuality no positive gravity center in the shell.

A bundle of heavy blankets lay in a corner formed by a lashed down pile of boxes . . . and the bundle was moving feebly. With a cry in his throat, Scott leaped forward and tore the blankets aside. Under them lay a battered man, crumpled, with a pool of blood soaking into a blanket that lay beneath him. Scott lifted the body. The head flopped over and he stared down into the vacant, blood-streaked face of Jimmy Baldwin.

Jimmy's eyes fluttered open, then closed again. Scott squatted on his heels, wild thoughts hammering in his head. Jimmy's eyes opened again and regarded the pilot. He raised a feeble hand in greeting. The lips moved, but Jimmy's voice was faint.

"Hello, Scott."

"What are you doing here?" Scott demanded fiercely.

"I don't know," said Jimmy weakly. "I don't know. I meant to do something, but I forgot."

Scott rose and took a bottle of water from a case. Wetting his handkerchief, he bathed the bloodied face. His hands ran over Jimmy's body but found no broken bones. It was a wonder the man hadn't been killed outright. Some more Baldwin luck!

"Where are we, Scott?" Jimmy asked.

"We're in space," said Scott. "We're going out to Mars." No use of telling him anything but the truth.

"Space," said Jimmy. "I use to go out in space. Then something happened." He shook his head wearily. Mercifully, the memory of that *something* had been wiped from his brain.

Half dragging, half carrying, Scott got him to the assistant pilot's seat, strapped him in, gave him a drink of water. Jimmy's eyes closed and he sank back into the cushions. Scott resumed his chair, leaned forward to look out into space.

There was little to see. Space, viewed from any angle, unless one was near a large body, looked pretty much the same. The Moon was still out of his range of vision. It would be hours before it would move upward to intersect the path of the rocket's flight.

Scott leaned back and looked at Jimmy. Apparently the man had sneaked aboard just before the take-off. No one paid much attention to him. Everyone was kind to him and he was allowed to do as he pleased. For he was not insane. The tragedy of those few minutes years before had merely wiped out his memory, given him the outlook of a child.

Perhaps when he had gotten into the ship he had held some reason for his action, but now even that purpose had escaped him. Once again Jimmy Baldwin was a bewildered child's brain in the body of a man.

"Anyway," said Scott, half speaking to himself, half to the silent form, "you're the first rocket stowaway."

They would miss Jimmy back at the camp, would wonder what had happened to him. Perhaps they'd organize a posse and search for him. The possibility was they would never know what happened, for there was slight chance, Scott told himself, that he or Jimmy or the ship would ever get back to Earth again.

Someone else would have to tend Jimmy's flowers now, but probably no one would, for his flowers were the Martian lilies. And Martian lilies no longer were a novelty.

It had been the lilies that started the whole thing, this crazy parade of men who went into space and died.

Slightly over twelve years ago, Dr. Steven Alexander reported that, from his observatory on Mt. Kenya, he had communicated with Mars by ultrashort wave radio. It had been a long and arduous process. First the signals from Earth, repeated in definite series, at definite intervals. And then, finally, the answer from the Red Planet. After months of labor slow understanding came.

"We send you," signaled the Martians. *"We send you."* Over and over again. A meaningless phrase. What were they sending? Slowly Alexander untangled the simple skein of thought. Mars finally messaged: *"We send you token!"* That word "token" had been hard. It represented thought, an abstract thought.

The world waited breathlessly for the token. Finally it came, a rocket winging its way across space, a rocket that flashed and glinted in the depth of space as it neared Earth. Kept informed of its location by the Martians, Earth's telescopes watched it come. It landed near Mt. Kenya, a roaring, screaming streak of light that flashed across the midnight sky.

Dug up, it yielded an inner container, well-insulated against heat and cold, against radiation and shock. Opened, it was found to contain seeds. Planted, jealously guarded, carefully tended, the seeds grew, were the Martian lilies. They multiplied rapidly, spread quickly over the Earth.

Back on Earth today the Martian lilies grew in every hamlet, clogged the fence rows of every farm. Relieved of whatever natural enemies and checks they might have had on their native planet, they flourished and spread, became a weed that every farmer cursed whole-heartedly.

Their root structure probed deep into the soil. Drought could not kill them. They grew rapidly, springing to full growth almost overnight. They went to unkillable seed. Which was what might have been expected of any plant nurtured on the stubborn soil of Mars. Earth, to the Martian lilies, was a paradise of air and water and sunlight.

And, as if that first token-load had not been enough, the Martians kept on sending rocket loads of seeds. At each opposition the rockets came, each announced by the messages from the Martian transmitter. And each of them landed almost precisely on the spot where the first had landed.

That took mathematics! Mathematics and a superb knowledge of rocketry. The rockets apparently were automatic. There was no intelligence to guide them once they were shot into space. Their courses must have been plotted to the finest detail, with every factor determined in advance. For the Martian rockets were not aimed at Earth as one broad target but at a certain spot on Earth and so far every one of them had hit that mark!

At the rocket camp each Martian rocket was awaited anxiously, with the hope it would bring some new pay load. But the rockets never brought anything but seeds . . . more Martian lily seeds.

Jimmy stirred restlessly, opened his eyes and looked out the vision plate. But there was no terror in his eyes, no surprise nor regret.

"Space?" he asked.

Scott nodded.

"We're going to the Moon?"

"To the Moon first," said Scott. "From there we go to Mars."

Jimmy lapsed into silence. There was no change upon his face. There never was any change upon his face.

I hope he doesn't make any trouble, Scott told himself. It was bad enough just to have him along. Bad enough to have this added responsibility.

For space flight was a dangerous job. Ever since the International Mars Communication Center had been formed, with Alexander in charge, space had flung men aside. Ship after ship, pilot after pilot. The task, alone, of reaching the Moon had taken terrible toll.

Men had died. Some had died before they reached the Moon, some had died on the Moon but mostly they had died heading back for Earth. For landing on Earth, jockeying a rocket through Earth's dense atmosphere, is a tricky job. Others had died en route to Mars, ships flaring in space or simply disappearing, going on and on, never coming back. That was the way it had been with Hugh.

And now his brother, Scott, was following the trail that Hugh had blazed, the trail to the Moon and out beyond. Following in a bomb of potential death, with a blank-faced stowaway in the chair beside him.

Half way to Mars and the ship was still intact. Running true to course, running on schedule, flashing through space under the thrust of momentum built up during the blast-off from the Moon.

Half way to Mars and still alive! But too early yet to hope. Perhaps other men had gotten as far as this and then something had happened.

Scott watched the depths of space, the leering, jeering emptiness of star-studded velvet that stretched on and on.

There had been days of waiting and of watching. More days of waiting and of watching loomed ahead.

Waiting for that warning flicker on the instrument panel, that split second warning before red ruin struck as cranky fuel went haywire.

Waiting for the "tick" of a tiny meteor against the ship's steel wall . . . the tiny, ringing sound that would be the prelude to disaster.

Waiting for something else . . . for that unknown factor of accident that would spatter the ship and the two men in it through many empty miles.

Endless hours of watching and of waiting, hastily snatched cat-naps in the chair, hastily snatched meals. Listening to the babbling Jimmy Baldwin who wondered how his flowers were getting on, speculated on what the boys were doing back in the rocket camp on Earth.

One thing hammered at Scott Nixon's brain . . . the message of the Martian radio, the message that had been coming now for many years. *"No. No. No come. Danger."* Always that and little else. No explanation of what the danger was. No suggestion for circumventing or correcting that danger. No helpfulness in Earthmen's struggle to cross the miles of space between two neighboring planets.

Almost as if the Martians didn't want Earthmen to come. Almost as if they were trying to discourage space travel. But that would hardly be the case, for the Martians had readily cooperated in establishing communications, had exhibited real intelligence and earnestness in working out the code that flashed words and thoughts across millions of miles.

Without a doubt, had they wished, the Martians could have helped. For it was with seemingly little effort that they sent their own rockets to earth.

And why had each Martian rocket carried the same load each time? Could there be some significance in those Martian lily seeds? Some hidden meaning the Earth had failed to grasp? Some meaning that the things from Mars hope would be read with each new rocket-load?

Why hadn't the Martians come themselves? If they could shoot automatic rockets across the miles of space, certainly they could navigate rockets carrying themselves.

The Martian rockets had been closely studied back on Earth but had yielded no secrets. The fuel always was exhausted. More than likely the Martians knew, to the last drop, how much was needed. The construction was not unlike Earth rockets, but fashioned of a steel that was hardened and toughened beyond anything Earth could produce.

So for ten years Earthmen had worked unaided to cross the bridge of space, launching ships from the Earth's most favored take-off point, from the top of Mt. Kenya, heading out eastward into space, taking advantage of the mountain's three mile height, the Earth's rotation speed of 500 yards per second at the equator.

Scott reviewed his flight, checked the clocklike routine he had followed. Blast-off from Earth. Landing in the drear, desolate Mare Serenitatis on the Moon, refueling the ship from the buried storage tanks, using the caterpillar tractor from the underground garage to haul the rocket onto the great turn-table cradle. Setting the cradle at the correct angle and direction, blasting off again at the precise second, carrying a full load of fuel, something impossible to do and still take off from Earth. Taking advantage of the Moon's lower gravity, its lack of atmosphere. Using the Moon as a stepping stone to outer space.

Now he was headed for Mars. If he landed there safely, he could spend two days, no more, no less, before he blasted off for Earth again.

But probably he wouldn't reach Mars. Probably he and Jimmy Baldwin, in the end, would be just a few more bones to pave the road to Mars.

III

A gigantic building, rising to several hundred feet in height, domed, without door or window, stood lonely in the vastness of the red plain that stretched to the far-off black horizon.

The building and nothing more. No other single sign of habitation. No other evidence of intelligent life.

The Martian lilies were everywhere, great fields of them, bright scarlet against the redness of the sand. But in its native soil the Martian lily was a sorry thing, a poor apology for the kind of flower that grew on Earth. Stunted, low-growing, with smaller and less brilliant flowers.

The sand gritted under Scott's boots as he took a slow step forward.

So this was Mars! Here, at the North pole . . . the single building . . . the only evidence of intelligence on the entire planet. As the ship had circled the planet, cutting down its tremendous speed, he had studied the surface in the telescopic glass and this building had been the only habitation he had seen.

It stood there, made of shimmering metal, glinting in the pale sunlight.

"Bugs," said Jimmy, at Scott's elbow.

"What do you mean, bugs?" asked Scott.

"Bugs in the air," said Jimmy. "Flying bugs."

Scott saw them then. Things that looked like streaks of light in the feeble sunshine. Swarms of them hovered about the great building and others darted busily about.

"Bees," suggested Jimmy.

But Scott shook his head. They weren't bees. They glinted and flashed when the sun's light struck them and they seemed more mechanical than life-like.

"Where are the Martians?" Jimmy demanded.

"I don't know, Jimmy," declared Scott. "Damned if I do."

He had envisioned the first Earthmen reaching Mars as receiving thunderous ovation, a mighty welcome from the Martians. But there weren't any Martians. Nothing stirred except the shining bugs and the lilies that nodded in a thin, cold breeze.

There was no sound, no movement. Like a quiet summer afternoon back on Earth, with a veil of quietness drawn over the flaming desert and the shimmering building.

He took another step, walking toward the great building. The sand grated protestingly beneath his boot-heels.

Slowly he approached the building, alert, watching, ready for some evidence that he and Jimmy had been seen. But no sign came. The bugs droned overhead, the lilies nodded sleepily. That was all.

Scott looked at the thermometer strapped to the wrist of his oxygen suit. The needle registered 10 above, Centigrade. Warm enough, but the suits were necessary, for the air was far too thin for human consumption.

Deep shadow lay at the base of the building and as he neared it, Scott made out something that gleamed whitely in the shadow. Something that struck a chord of remembrance in his brain, something he had seen back on Earth.

As he hurried forward he saw it was a cross. A white cross thrust into the sand.

With a cry he broke into a run.

Before the cross he dropped to his knees and read the crudely carved inscription on the wood. Just two words. The name of a man, carven with a jack-knife:

HARRY DECKER

Harry Decker! Scott felt his brain swimming crazily.

Harry Decker here! Harry Decker under the red sand of Mars! But that couldn't be. Harry Decker's name couldn't be here. It was back on Earth, graven on that scroll of bronze. Graven there directly beneath the name of Hugh Nixon.

He staggered to his feet and stood swaying for a moment.

From somewhere far away he heard a shout and swinging around, ran toward the corner of the building.

Rounding it, he stopped in amazement.

There, in the shelter of the building, lay a rusted space ship and running across the sand toward him was a space-suited figure, a figure that yelled as it ran and carried a bag over its shoulder, the bag bouncing at every leap.

"Hugh!" yelled Scott.

And the grotesque figure bellowed back.

"Scott, you old devil! I knew you'd do it! I knew it was you the minute I heard the rocket blasts!"

"It's nice and warm here now," said Hugh, "but you'd ought to spend a winter here. An Arctic blizzard is a gentle breeze compared with the Martian pole in winter time. You don't see the Sun for almost ten months and the mercury goes down to 100 below, Centigrade. Hoar frost piles up three and four feet thick and a man can't stir out of the ship."

He gestured at the bag

"I was getting ready for another winter. Just like a squirrel. My supplies got low before this spring and I had to find something to store up against another season. I found a half dozen different kinds of bulbs and roots and some berries. I've been gathering them all summer, storing them away."

"But the Martians?" protested Scott. "Wouldn't the Martians help you?"

His brother looked at him curiously.

"The Martians?" he asked.

"Yes, the Martians."

"Scott," Hugh said, "I haven't found the Martians."

Scott stared at him. "Let's get this straight now. You mean you don't know who the Martians are?"

Hugh nodded. "That's exactly it. I tried to find them hard enough. I did all sorts of screwy things to contact that intelligence which talked with the Earth and sent the rockets full of seed, but I've gotten exactly nowhere. I've finally given up."

"Those bugs," suggested Scott. "The shining bugs."

Hugh shook his head. "No soap. I got the same idea and managed to bat down a couple of them. But they're mechanical. That's all. Just machines. Operated by radium.

"It almost drove me nuts at first. Those bugs flying around and the building standing there and the Martian lilies all around, but no signs of any intelligence. I tried to get into the building but there aren't any doors or windows. Just little holes the bugs fly in and out of.

"I couldn't understand a thing. Nothing seemed right. No purpose to any of it. No apparent reason. Only one thing I could understand. Over on the other side of the building I found the cradle that is used to shoot the rockets to Earth. I've watched that done."

"But what happened?" asked Scott. "Why didn't you come back? What happened to the ship?"

"We had no fuel," said Hugh.

Scott nodded his head.

"A meteor in space."

"Not that," Hugh told him. "Harry simply turned the petcocks, let our gasoline run into the sand."

"Good Lord! Was he crazy?"

"That's exactly what he was," Hugh declared. "Batty as a bedbug. Touch of space madness. I felt sorry for him. He cowered like a mad animal, beaten by the sense of loneliness and space. He was afraid of shadows. He got so he didn't act like a man. I was glad for him when he died."

"But even a crazy man would want to get back to Earth!" protested Scott.

"It wasn't Harry," Hugh explained. "It was the Martians, I am sure. Whatever or wherever they are, they probably have intelligences greater than ours. It would be no feat for them, perhaps, to gain control of the brain of a demented man. They might not be able to dominate us, but a man whose thought processes were all tangled up by space madness would be an easy mark for them. They could make him do and think whatever they wanted him to think or do. It wasn't Harry who opened those petcocks, Scott. It was the Martians."

He leaned against the pitted side of the ship and stared up at the massive building.

"I was plenty sore at him when I caught him at it," he said. "I gave him one hell of a beating. I've always been sorry for that."

"What finally happened to him?" asked Scott.

"He ran out of the airlock without his suit," Hugh explained. "It took me half an hour to run him down and bring him back. He took pneumonia. You have to be careful here. Exposure to the Martian atmosphere plays hell with a man's lung tissues. You can breathe it all right . . . might even be able to live in it for a few hours, but it's deadly just the same."

"Well, it's all over now," declared Scott. "We'll get my ship squared around and we'll blast off for Earth. We made it here and we can make it back. And you'll be the first man who ever set his foot on Mars."

Hugh grinned. "That will be something, won't it, Scott? But somehow I'm not satisfied. I haven't accomplished a thing. I haven't even found the Martians. I know they're here. An intelligence that's at least capable of thinking along parallel lines with us although its thought processes may not be parallel with ours."

"We'll talk it over later," said Scott. "After we get a cup of coffee into you. I bet you haven't had one in weeks."

"Weeks," jeered Hugh. "Man, it's been ten months."

"Okay, then," said Scott. "Let's round up Jimmy. He must be around here somewhere. I don't like to let him get out of my sight too much."

The silence of the dreaming red deserts was shattered by a smashing report that drummed with a mighty clap against the sky above. A gush of red flame spouted over the domed top of the mighty building and metal shards hammered spitefully against the sides, setting up a metallic undertone to the ear-shattering explosion.

Sick with dread, Scott plunged to the corner of the building and felt the sick dread deepen.

Where his space ship had lain a mighty hole was blasted in the sand. The ship was gone. No part of it was left. It had been torn into tiny fragments and hurled across the desert. Wisps of smoke crept slowly from the pit in the sand, twisting in the air currents that still swirled from the blast.

Scott knew what had happened. There was no need to guess. Only one thing could have happened. The liquid oxygen had united with the gasoline, making an explosive that was sheer death itself. A single tremor, a thrown stone, a vibration . . . anything would set it off.

Across the space between himself and the ship came the tattered figure of a man. A man whose clothes were torn. A man covered with blood, weaving, head down, feet dragging.

"Jimmy!" yelled Scott.

He sprinted forward but before he could reach his side, Jimmy had collapsed.

Kneeling beside him, Scott lifted the man's head.

The eyes rolled open and the lips twitched. Slow, tortured words oozed out.

"I'm sorry . . . Scott. I don't know why . . ."

The eyes closed but opened again, a faint flutter, and more words bubbled from the bloody lips.

"I wonder why I did it!"

Scott looked up and saw his brother standing in front of him.

Hugh nodded. "The Martians again, Scott. They could use Jimmy's mind. They could get hold of him. That blasted brain of his . . ."

Scott looked down at the man in his arms. The head had fallen back, the eyes were staring, blood was dripping on the sand.

"Hugh," he whispered, "Jimmy's dead."

Hugh stared across the sand at the little glimmer of white in the shadow of the building.

"We'll make another cross," he said.

IV

The Martians hadn't wanted them to come. That much, at least, was clear. But having gotten here, the Martians had no intention of letting them return to Earth again. They didn't want them to carry back the word that it was possible to navigate across space to the outer planet.

Maybe the Martians were committed to a policy of isolation. Maybe there was a "Hands Off" sign set up on Mars. Maybe a "No trespassing" sign.

But if that had been the case, why had the Martians answered the radio calls from Earth. Why had they co-operated with Dr. Alexander in working out the code that made communication possible? And why did they continue sending messages and rockets to the Earth? Why didn't they sever the diplomatic relationship entirely, retire into their isolation?

If they didn't want Earthmen to come to Mars why hadn't they trained guns on the two ships as they came down to the scarlet sand, wiped them out without compunction? Why did they resort to the expedient of forcing Earthmen to bring about their own destruction? And why, now that Harry Decker and Jimmy Baldwin were dead, didn't the Martians wipe out the remaining two of the unwanted race?

Perhaps the Martians were merely efficient, not vindictive. Maybe they realized that the remaining two Earthmen constituted no menace? And maybe, on the other hand, the Martians had no weapons. Perhaps they never had a need for weapons. It might be they had never had to fight for self preservation.

And above and beyond all . . . what and where were the Martians? In that huge building? Invisible? In caverns beneath the surface? At some point far away?

Maybe . . . perhaps . . . why? Speculation and wonderment.

But there was no answer. Not even the slightest hint. Just the building shimmering in the unsetting Sun, the metallic bugs buzzing in the air, the lilies nodding in the breeze that blew across the desert.

Scott Nixon reached the rim of the plateau and lowered the bag of roots from his shoulder, resting and waiting for Hugh to toil up the remaining few yards of the slope.

Before him, slightly over four miles across the plain, loomed the Martian building. Squatting at its base was the battered, pitted space ship. There was too much ozone in the atmosphere here for the steel in the ship to stand up. Before many years had passed it would fall to pieces, would rust away. But that made little difference, for by that time they probably wouldn't need it. By that time another ship would have arrived or they would be dead.

Scott grinned grimly. A hard way to look at things. But the only way. One had to be realistic here. Hard-headed planning was the only thing that would carry them through. The food supply was short and while they'd probably be able to gather enough for the coming winter, there was always the possibility that the next season would find them short.

But there was hope to cling to. Always hope. Hope that the summer would bring another ship winging out of space . . . that this time, armed by past experience, they could prevent its destruction.

Hugh came up with Scott, slid the bag of roots to the ground and sat upon it.

He nodded at the building across the desert.

"That's the nerve center of the whole business," he declared. "If we could get into it . . ." His voice trailed away.

"But we can't," Scott reminded him. "We've tried and we can't. There are no doors. No openings. Just those little holes the bugs fly in and out of."

"There's a door somewhere," said Hugh. "A hidden door. The bugs use it to bring out machines to do the work when they shoot a rocket out for Earth. I've seen the machines. Screwy looking things. Work units pure and simple but so efficient you'd swear they possessed intelligence. I've tried to find the door but I never could and the bugs always waited until I wasn't around before they moved the machines in or out of the building."

He chuckled, scrubbing his bearded face with a horny hand.

"That rocket business saved my life," he said. "If the power lead running out of the building to the cradle hadn't been there I'd been sunk. But there it was, full of good, old electricity. So I just tapped the thing and that gave me plenty of power . . . power for heat, for electrolysis, for atmospheric condensation."

Scott sank down heavily on his sack.

"It's enough to drive a man nuts," he declared. "We can reach out and touch the building with our hand. Just a few feet away from the explanation of all this screwiness. Inside that building we'd find things we'd be able to use. Machines, tools . . ."

Hugh hummed under his breath.

"Maybe," he said, "maybe not. Maybe we couldn't recognize the machines, fathom the tools. Mechanical and technical development here probably wasn't any more parallel to ours than intelligence development."

"There's the rocket cradle," retorted Scott. "Same principle as we use on Earth. And they must have a radio in there. And a telescope. We'd be able to figure them out. Might even be able to send Doc Alexander a message."

"Yeah," agreed Hugh, "I thought of that, too. But we can't get in the building and that settles it."

"The bugs get under my skin," Scott complained. "Always buzzing around. Always busy. But busy at what? Like a bunch of hornets."

"They're the straw bosses of the outfit," declared Hugh. "Carrying out the orders of the Martians. The Martians' hands and eyes, you might say."

He dug at the sand with the toe of his space boot.

"Another swarm of them took off just before we started out on this trip," he said. "While you were in the ship. I watched them until they disappeared. Straight up and out until you couldn't see them. Just like they were taking off for space."

He kicked savagely at the sand.

"I sure as hell would like to know where they go," he said.

"There've been quite a few of them leaving lately," said Scott. "As if the building were a hive and they were new swarms of bees. Maybe they're going out to start new living centers. Maybe they're going to build more buildings . . ."

He stopped and stared straight ahead of him, his eyes unseeing. Going out to start new living centers! Going out to build new buildings! Shining metallic buildings!

Like a cold wind from the past it came to him, a picture of that last night on Earth. He head the whining wind on Mt. Kenya once again, the blaring of the radio from the machine shop door, the voice of the newscaster.

"Austin Gordon . . . Congo Valley . . . strange metallic city . . . inhabited by strange metallic insects!"

The memory shook him from head to foot, left him cold and shivery with his knowledge.

"Hugh!" he croaked. "Hugh, I know what it's all about!"

His brother stared at him: "Take it easy, kid. Don't let it get you. Stick with me, kid. We're going to make it all right."

"But, Hugh," Scott yelled, "there's nothing wrong with me. Don't you see, I know the answer to all this Martian business now. The lilies are the Martians! Those bugs are migrating to Earth. They're machines. Don't you see . . . they could cross space and the lilies would be there to direct them."

He jumped to his feet.

"They're already building cities in the Congo!" he yelled. "Lord knows how many other places. They're taking over the Earth! The Martians are invading the Earth, but Earth doesn't know it!"

"Hold on," Hugh yelled back at him. "How could flowers build cities?"

"They can't," said Scott breathlessly. "But the bugs can. Back on Earth they are wondering why the Martians don't use their rockets to come to Earth. And that's exactly what the Martians are doing. Those rockets full of seeds aren't tokens at all. They're colonization parties!"

"Wait a minute. Slow down," Hugh pleaded. "Tell me this. If the lilies are the Martians and they sent seeds to Earth twelve years ago, why hadn't they sent them before?"

"Because before that it would have been useless," Scott told him. "They had to have someone to open the rockets and plant the seeds for them. We did that. They tricked us into it.

"They may have sent rockets of seeds before but if they did, nothing came of it. For the seeds would have been useless if they weren't taken from the rocket. The rocket probably would have weathered away in time, releasing the seeds but by that time the seeds would have lost their germinating power."

Hugh shook his head.

"It seems impossible," he declared. "Impossible that plants could have real intelligence . . . that flowers could hold the mastery of a planet. I'm ready to accept almost any theory but that one . . ."

"Your mind sticks on parallel evolution," Scott argued. "There's no premise for it. On Earth animals took the spotlight, pushing the plants into a subordinate position. Animals got the head start, jumped the gun on the plants. But there's absolutely no reason why plants should not develop along precisely the same lines here that animals developed on Earth."

"But the Martian lily lives only one season . . . ten months . . . and then it dies," Hugh protested. "The next season's growth comes from seed. How could plants build intelligence? Each new crop would have to start all over again."

"Not necessarily," declared Scott. "Animals are born with instinct, which is nothing more or less than inherited intelligence. In mankind there are strange evidences of racial memory. Why couldn't the plants do the same thing with their seed . . . progress even a step further? Why couldn't the seed carry, along with its other attributes, all the intelligence and knowledge of the preceding generation? That way the new plant wouldn't have to start from scratch, but would start with all the accumulated knowledge of its immediate ancestor . . . and would add to that knowledge and pass the sum total on to the generation that was to follow."

Hugh kicked absent-mindedly at the sand.

"There would be advantages in that sort of development," he agreed. "It might even be the logical course of survival on a planet like Mars. Some old Martian race, for all we know, might deliberately have shaped their development toward a plant existence when they realized the conditions toward which the planet was headed."

"A plant society would be a strange one," said Scott. "A sort of totalitarian society. Not the kind of a society animals would build . . . for an animal is an individual and a plant is not. In a plant race individuality would count for nothing, the race would count for everything. The driving force would be the preservation and advancement of the race as a whole. That would make a difference."

Hugh glanced up sharply.

"You're damned right that would make a difference," he said. "They would be a deadly race. Once they got started, noting could stop that singleness of purpose."

His face seemed to blanch under the tan.

"Do you realize what's happening?" he shouted. "For millions of years these plants have fought for bare existence on Mars. Every ounce of their effort has been toward race preservation. Every fall the bugs carefully gather all the seeds and carry them inside the building, bring them out and plant them in the spring. It if hadn't been for some arrangement like that they probably would have died out years ago. Only a few scattered patches of them left now . . ."

"But on Earth . . . ," said Scott.

And the two of them, white-faced, stared at one another. On Earth the Martian lilies would not have to carry on a desperate fight for their very existence. On Earth they had plenty of water, plenty of sunlight, plenty of good, rich soil. On Earth they grew larger and stronger and straighter. Under such conditions what would be the limit of their alien powers?

With the lilies multiplying each year, growing in every fence row, every garden, crowding out the farmers' crops, lining every stream, clogging every forest . . . with swarm after swarm of the metallic bugs driving out into space, heading for the Earth . . . what would happen?

How long would the lilies wait? How would they attack? Would they simply crowd out every other living thing, conquering by a sort of population pressure? Or would they develop more fully those powers of forcing animal minds to do their bidding? Or did they have, perhaps, even stronger weapons?

"Hugh," Scott rasped, "we have to warn Earth. Somehow we have to let them know."

"Yes," Hugh agreed, "but how?"

Together, limned against the harsh horizon, they stood, looking across the desert toward the Martian building.

Tiny figures, dimmed by distance, scurried about the building.

Scott squinted his eyes against the desert glare.

"What are those?" he asked.

Hugh seemed to jerk out of a trance.

"The machines again," he said wearily. "They're getting ready to shoot another rocket out to Earth. It'll be the last one of the season. Earth is drawing away again."

"More seeds," said Scott.

Hugh nodded. "More seeds. And more bugs going out. And the worst of it is that Earth doesn't know. No man in his right mind on Earth could even dimly speculate upon the possibility of high intelligence in plant life. There's no reason to. No precedent upon which to base such a speculation. Earth plants have never had intelligence."

"A message is all we need," declared Scott. "Just get word to the Earth. They'd root up every plant on the face of the entire globe. They'd . . ."

He stopped abruptly and stared out across the desert.

"The rocket," he whispered. "The rocket is going to Earth!"

Hugh swung on him fiercely.

"What are you . . ."

"We could send a message by the rocket!" yelled Scott. "They always watch for them . . . always hoping each one will carry something new. Some new thing from Mars. It's the only way we can get a message back to Earth."

"But they won't let us near," protested Hugh. "I've tried to get up close to the cradle when they were launching one and those machines always drove me away. Didn't hurt me . . . but threatened."

"We have guns," said Scott.

"Guns," said Hugh, "wouldn't be worth a damn against them. The bullets would just glance off. Even explosive bullets wouldn't harm them."

"Sledges then," said Scott. "We'll make junk out of the damn things. We've got a couple of sledges in the ship."

Hugh looked at him levelly.

"Okay, kid, let's get going."

V

The machines paid them no attention. No higher than a man's waist, they curiously resembled grotesque spiders. Gangling rods and arms sprouted out all over them and from their trunks sprouted waving, steel antennae.

Overhead hung a swarm of the metallic bugs, evidently directing the work of making the rocket ready.

"It takes just three minutes or thereabouts from the time they finally have her ready until she blasts," said Hugh. "Whatever we are going to do has to be done in those three minutes. And we've got to hold them off until the rocket blasts. They'll suspect there's something wrong and will try to stop it but if we can hold them off . . ."

"They must already have radioed Earth the rocket is coming," said Scott. "We always got word days in advance. Probably they won't follow up with their location messages but Doc will be watching for it anyhow."

They stood tensed, waiting, each grasping a heavy hammer.

The space about the cradle was a scene of intense, but efficient activity. Last minute adjustments were made. Readings and settings were checked. Each machine seemed to act by rote, while overhead hung the cloud of humming bugs.

"We know what we're to do," said Hugh. "We've simply got to do it."

Scott nodded.

Hugh shot a glance at him.

"Think you can hold them off, kid? It'll take a while to unscrew the inner and outer caps and we have got to get that message inside the inner container or it'll burn when the rocket hits atmosphere."

"You just get that message in and the caps back on," said Scott. "I'll hold them off for you."

Suddenly the machines scurried back from the cradle, leaving a clear space of several yards around it.

"Now!" Hugh shouted and the two men charged.

The attack was a surprise. Their rush carried the line of machines between them and the cradle.

One machine barred Scott's way and he smashed at it savagely with the heavy hammer. The blow flung it aside, crippled, dented, half-smashed.

Hugh was already at the cradle, clambering up the superstructure.

A machine rushed at Scott, steel arms flailing. Ducking a murderous swipe, the Earthman brought his sledge into play. It sheared through the arms, smashed into the body of the machine. The stricken mechanism seemed to reel, staggered erratically, then collapsed upon the sand.

In two leaps Scott gained the superstructure, scaled it and straddled the cradle. His sledge smashed savagely upon a climbing mechanism, flung it to the ground. But others were swarming up the steel lattice work. Tentacles snaked out, seeking to entrap him. A wicked blow on the leg almost brought him down.

His sledge worked steadily and at the foot of the cradle broken mechanisms bore testimony to its execution.

Out of the corner of his eye he saw that Hugh had inserted the envelope carrying the message in the inner container with the seeds, was tightening the screwcap. All that remained was to screw on the larger, heavier outer cap.

But only seconds must remain, precious seconds before the rocket blasted. And before that happened they had to be away from the cradle, for the back-lash of flames would burn them to a cinder.

Scott felt perspiration streaming over his body, running off his eyelids, blearing his sight, trickling down his nose. He heard the rasp of metal as Hugh drove home the cap with savage thrusts of the wrench.

A machine rushed up the lattice at him and he smashed at it with unreasoning fury. The head of the sledge bit deep into the metal body.

A tentacle wrapped about his leg and jerked. He felt himself losing his balance, tumbling off the cradle into the melee of threshing metal things beneath him.

Then he was on the ground, buffeted and pounded by the maddened metal creatures. He fought savagely, blindly staggering forward. The shatterproof glass in his vision plate had been "broken," its texture smashed into a million tiny criss-cross lines, until it was like frosted glass.

He heard the tough fabric of his suit rip with a screeching sound. The bugs still were hammering against him.

The thin, acrid atmosphere of Mars burned into his nose and his lungs labored.

Unseeingly, he swung his sledge in swath-like circles. Shrieking like a wild Indian, he felt it smash and slam into the bodies of his metallic opponents.

Then the world was blotted out by a resounding roar, a Niagara of sound that beat in waves against one's body.

That was the rocket leaving.

"Hugh!" he yelled insanely. "Hugh, we did it!"

The attack had fallen away and he stood unsteadily on his feet, panting, stiff from punishment, but filled with exultation.

They had won. He and Hugh had sent the message. Earth would be warned and Mars would lose its hope of conquering a new and younger world. Whatever dreams of conquest this old red planet may have nurtured would never come to be.

He put his hands up and ripped the helmet from his head, flinging it on the ground.

The metallic machines were ringed around him, motionless, almost as if they were looking at him. Almost as if they were waiting for his next move.

Wildly he whooped at them. "Start something, damn you! Just start something!"

But the line in front of him parted and he saw the blackened thing that lay upon the sand. The twisted, blasted, crumpled thing that huddled there.

Scott dropped his sledge and a sob rose in his throat. His hands clenched at his side and he tottered slowly forward.

He stood above the body of his brother, flung there on the sand by the searing back-lash of the rocket blast.

"Hugh!" he cried, "Hugh!"

But the blackened bundle didn't stir. Hugh Nixon was dead.

Eyes bleared, Scott stared around at the machines. They were breaking up, scattering, moving away.

"Damn you," he screamed, "don't you even care?"

But even as he spoke, he knew they didn't care. The plant civilization of Mars was an unemotional society. It knew no love, no triumph, no defeat, no revenge. It was mechanistic, cold, logical. It did only those things which aimed at a definite end. So long as there was a chance of protecting the rocket, so long as there was hope of halting its flight after it had been tampered with, that civilization would act. But now that it was in space, now that it could not be recalled, the incident was over. There would be no further action.

Scott looked down at the man at his feet.

Harry Decker and Jimmy Baldwin and now Hugh Nixon. Three men had died here on Mars. He was the only one left. And he probably would die, too, for no man could for long breathe that Martian air and live.

What was it Hugh had said that first day?

"It plays hell with the tissues of your lungs."

He stared around him, saw the interminable red deserts and the scarlet patches of Martian lilies, nodding in the breeze. Saw the humming bugs flashing in the pale sunlight. Saw the shimmer of the mighty building that had no doors or windows.

His lungs were aching now and his throat was raw. It was harder and harder to breathe.

He knelt in the sand and lifted the blackened body. Cradling it in his arms, he staggered along.

"I have to make another cross," he said.

Far overhead, in the depths of space, twinkled the blue planet whose life would never know the slavery of the emotionless race of a dying world.

PARTY LINE

Even the title of this story speaks a little of the way Clifford D. Simak wrote: he took an old country institution and used it for a story about an ultra-futuristic idea. "Party Line" was originally published in the November/December 1978 issue of Destinies—*the very first issue of the paperback-size magazine experiment by Baen Books. And it features a theme Cliff utilized more and more frequently in the latter part of his career: how members of a disparate group talk among themselves a lot, conversing and learning from, and with, one another. I wonder whether that might not have been Cliff's idea of heaven?*

—dww

I

Einstein did not come in. That was unusual. Very seldom was Einstein late or absent. Usually he was waiting, ready to take up again the patient teaching that had been going on for months.

Jay Martin tried again.

—Einstein. Einstein. Are you there?

Einstein was not there.

The console in front of Martin hummed and the sensor lights were flickering. The cubicle was quiet, an engineered quietness, insulated against all distraction. Martin reached up and adjusted the helmet more firmly on his head.

—Einstein. Einstein. Where are you?

A faint sense of beginning panic flicked across Martin's mind. Had Einstein finally given it all up as a bad job? Had he (or she, or it, or them?) simply slipped away, dropping him, finally despairing of making so ignorant a student understand what he had to say?

Something out there stirred, a thin whistle of distant emptiness. Strange, thought Martin, how it always came that way— the haunting sense of distant emptiness. When there was, in fact, no distance nor no emptiness involved. The carrier waves were immune to any of the limitations of the electromagnetic spectrum. Instantaneous, no lag, as if distance, matter, time did not exist.

—Einstein? he asked, convinced that it wasn't Einstein. It didn't feel like Einstein, although he would have been hard pressed if he had been called upon to tell how Einstein felt.

The thin whistle came again.

—Yes, said Martin, I'm here. Who are you?

And the voice (the thought? the pulse? the intelligence?) spoke.

—The turning point, it said.

—Unclear, said Martin. What turning point?

—The universe. The universe has reached its turning point. Universal death has started. The universe has reached its farthest point. It now is running down. Entropy has been accomplished.

—That, said Martin, is a strange way to say it.

—The universe always strove toward entropy.

—Not here, said Martin. No entropy here. The stars still burn.

—At the edge. The outer fringe. The universe at the edge has reached the point of entropy. Heat death. No more energy. And now is falling back. It is retreating.

The distance whistled. The emptiness keened.

—You are at the edge?

—Near the rim. That is how we know. Our measurement . . .

The distance howled, drowning out the words.

—How long? asked Martin. How long till the end?

—Equal to the time since the beginning. Our calculations—

—Fifteen billion years, said Martin.

—We do not grasp your measurement.

—Never mind, said Martin. It makes no difference. I should not have said it.

—The pity of it! The irony!

—What pity? What irony?

—We have tried so long. Everyone has tried so long. To understand the universe and now we have no time.

—We have lots of time. Another fifteen billion years.

—You may have. We haven't. We're too close to the rim. We are in the dying zone.

A cry for help, thought Martin. The moaning of self pity. And was shaken. For there'd never been a cry for help before.

The other caught his thought.

—No cry for help, it said. There is no help. This is warning only.

The pulse, the thought cut off. Distance and emptiness whistled for a moment and then it, too, cut off.

Martin sat huddled in his cubicle, the weight of all that distance, all that emptiness crashing down upon him.

2

The day began badly for Paul Thomas.

The desk communicator chirped at him.

"Yes," he said.

His secretary's voice said, "Mr. Russell is here to see you."

Thomas grimaced. "Show him in," he said.

Russell was prissy and precise. He came into the office and sat down in a chair across the desk from Thomas.

"What can I do for R&D this morning?" Thomas asked, ignoring all conversational preliminaries. Russell was a man who was impatient with social amenities.

"A lot more than you're doing," Russell said. "Goddammit, Paul, I know that you are hip-deep in data. It's piling up on you. We haven't had a thing from you in the last six months. I know the rules, of course, but aren't you giving them too strict an interpretation?"

"What are you interested in?"

"The faster-than-light business for one thing. I happen to know that Martin . . ."

"Martin still is working on it."

"He must have something. Besides being a good telepath, he also happens to be a top-notch astrophysicist."

"That's true," said Thomas. "We don't often get a man like him. Mostly, it's a raw farm boy or some girl who is clerking in the five-and-dime. We're running recruiting programs all the time, but . . ."

"You're trying to throw me off the track, Paul. I've got men aching to get started on this FTL thing. We know you're getting something."

"The funny thing about it is that we aren't."

"Martin's been on it for months."

"Yeah, for months. And not understanding anything he's getting. Both he and I are beginning to believe we may have the wrong man on it."

"The wrong man on it? An astrophysicist?"

"Ben, it may not be physics at all."

"But he has equations."

"Equations, yes. But they make no sense. Equations aren't the magic thing all by themselves that people think they are.

They have to make some sense and these make no sense. Jay is beginning to think they're something entirely outside the field of physics."

"Outside the field of physics? What else could they be?"

"That's the question, Ben. You and I have been over this, again and again. You don't seem to understand. Or refuse to understand. Or are too pig-headed to allow yourself to understand. We aren't dealing with humans out there. I understand that and my people understand it. But you refuse to accept it. You think of those other people out there among the stars as simply funny-looking humans. I don't know, no one knows, what they really are. But we know they aren't humans, not even funny-looking humans. We wear ourselves out at times trying to work out what they are. Not because of any great curiosity on our part, but because we could work with them better if we knew. And we have no idea. You hear me? No idea whatsoever. Hal Rawlins is talking to someone he is convinced is a robot—a funny-looking robot, of course—but he can't even be sure of that. No one can be sure of anything at all. The point is that we don't really have to be. They accept us, we accept them. They are patient with us and we with them. They may be more patient than we are, for they know we are newcomers, new subscribers on this party line we share. None of them think like us, none of us think like them. We try to adapt ourselves to their way of thinking, they try to adapt themselves to our way of thinking. All we know for sure is that they are intelligences, all they know is that we are some outrageous kind of intelligent life form. We are, all of us, a brotherhood of intelligences, getting along the best we can, talking, gossiping, teaching, learning, trading information, laying out ideas."

"This is the kind of crap you're always talking," said Russell, wrathfully. "I don't give a damn about all your philosophizing. What I want is something to work on. The deal is that when you have something that is promising, you pass it on to us."

"But the judgment is mine," said Thomas, "and rightly so. In some of the stuff we get here, there could be certain implications . . ."

"Implications, hell!"

"What are you doing with what we have given you? We gave you the data on artificial molecules. What have you done on that?"

"We're working on it."

"Work harder, then. Quit your bellyaching and show some results on that one. You and I both know what it would mean. With it, we could build to order any material, put together any kind of structure we might wish. Could build the kind of world we want, to order. The materials we want to our own specifications—food, metal, fabrics, you name it."

"Development," Russell said, defensively, "takes time. Keep your shirt on."

"We gave you the data on cell replacement. That would defeat disease and old age. Carried to its ultimate degree, an immortal world—if we wanted an immortal world, and could control it and afford it. What are you doing with that?"

"We're working on that one, too. All these things take time."

"Mary Kay thinks she has found what may be an ideal religion. She thinks that she may even have found God. At times, she says, she feels she's face to face with God. How about that one? We'll hand it over to you anytime you say."

"You keep that one. What we want is FTL."

"You can't have FTL. Not until we know more. As you say, we have mountains of data on it . . ."

"Give me that data. Let my boys get to work on it."

"Not yet. Not until we have a better feel of it. To tell you the truth, Ben, there's something scary about it."

"What do you mean, scary?"

"Something wrong. Something not quite right. You have to trust our judgment."

"Look, Paul, we've gone out to Centauri. Crawled out there. Took years to get there, years to get back. And nothing there. Not a goddamn thing. Just those three suns. We might just as well not have gone. That killed star travel. The public wouldn't stand still for another one like that. We have to have FTL, or we'll never go to the stars. Now we know it can be done. You guys have it at your fingertips and you won't let us in on it."

"As soon as we have something even remotely possible, we'll hand it over to you."

"Couldn't we just have a look at it? If it's as bad, as screwed up as you say it is, we'll hand it back."

Thomas shook his head. "Not a chance," he said.

3

There were no words, although there was the sense of unspoken words. No music, but the sense of music. No landscape, but a feel of tall slender trees, graceful in the wind; of park-like lawns surrounding stately houses; of a running brook glistening in an unseen sun, babbling over stones; of a lake with whitecaps racing in to shore. No actuality, but a compounded belief that a shattering actuality lurked just around the corner, waiting to burst out.

Mary Kay sank into it and let all of it enfold her. This time, she had thought, this time, please God, there will be something that I can understand. But once she had sunk into it, she no longer prayed there would be something to take back. This, in itself, was quite enough. This was all that anyone might want, or need. What was here filled the soul and wiped out the mind.

A stray, human thought intruded, but only momentarily: *Some day I'll have it; some day there will be data. Some day there'll be an inkling.*

And then the thought snapped off. For there was no need to know. Being here was all.

She was no longer human. She was not anything at all. She simply existed. She was stripped of everything but the inner core of consciousness. She had no body and no mind. The intellectuality took in only the wonder and the breath-catching happiness, the innocent sensuality, the mindless well-being and the rightness of it all—the rightness of being here. Wherever here might be. She did not even wonder at the here. She simply did not care.

Duty and purpose struggled feebly with the carelessness.

—But? she cried, why show me only? Why not tell me, too? I'm an intelligence. I want to know. I have the right to know.

—Sh-h-h-h-h

A shushing, a lullaby. A compassion. A tenderness.

Then the holiness.

She surrendered herself wholly to the holiness.

4

They looked to him, thought Thomas. That was the hell of it; they all looked to him for guidance, direction and comfort and he had none of these to give. They were out there on the firing line and he was sitting safely back and it would seem there should be something he could offer. But try as he might, he knew that he had nothing. Each of them a sensitive, for if they were not sensitives, they'd not be telepaths.

It took raw courage, he thought, a special kind of courage, to reach out into the cosmos, out into that place where time and space pressed close even if time and space were cancelled out. Even knowing this, knowing that space-time had been brushed aside, the consciousness of it must be always there, the fear of it always there, the fear of being snared and left and lost within the deepest gulf of it. A special courage to face up to another mind that might be only a few light-years distant or millions of light-years distant, and the alienness that the light-years conjured up and magnified. And, worst of all, the never-forgotten realization that one was a newcomer in this community of intelligence, a novice, a hick, the bottom of the totem pole. A tendency to be retiring and apologetic, even when there was no reason to be apologetic. A kindergartener in a school where high school seniors and college students reared to godlike heights.

Thomas rose from his desk and walked across the room to stand before a window. The desert lay outside, aloof and noncaring, a humped plain of sand and rock, sterile and hostile. Better judgment would have been to place this installation, he thought, in a kinder land where there would be friendly trees and purling streams and forest paths to walk in. But the desert, in the administrative mind, served a better purpose. Its long distances, its discomforts and its loneliness discouraged the curious who otherwise might come flocking in to stare. No secret project, in the usual sense, but one about which not too much was said, about which as little as possible was said in the unspoken but devout hope that in time it might disappear from the public mind.

A spooky thing—too spooky to be thrown open. A shuddery business, this reaching out to other minds across the universe. Not something which the public comfortably could sleep with. And what was the matter with the public? Thomas asked himself. Did they not realize that the project was mankind's greatest hope? For thousands of years, mankind had staggered along on its own, coddling its prejudices, making its mistakes, then multiplying rather than correcting them, slipping into a too-human groove that had brought, in its turn, untold misery and injustice. New blood was needed, a new mentality, and the one place to get it was from those cultures far among the stars. A cross-pollination process that could improve the texture and might revise the purpose of mankind's stumbling destiny.

The box on his desk chirped at him. He strode from the window and snapped down the toggle.

"What is it, Evelyn?"

"Senator Brown is on the phone."

"Thank you," said Thomas.

There was no one he wanted to talk with less than the senator.

He leaned back in his chair and pressed the button to activate the visor. The visor lighted to reveal the hatchet-face of the senator—ascetic, thin, wrinkled, but with a tightness to the wrinkles.

"Senator," he said, "how kind of you to call."

"I thought to pass the time of day," said the senator. "It has been a long time since we have had a chat."

"Yes, it has."

"As you may know," said the senator, "the budget for your project is coming up before committee in the next few weeks. I can get nothing out of these jackasses who are your superiors in Washington. They talk about knowledge being the most precious commodity. They say no market value can be placed upon it. I wonder if you would concur."

"I think I would," said Thomas, "although, if that is all they say, it's a fairly general statement. There is so much spinoff. I suppose they told you that."

"They did," said the senator. "They dwelt most lovingly upon it."

"Then what is it you want of me?"

"Realism. Some old-fashioned realism. A hard-headed assessment."

"I'm fairly close to the operation. It's hard for me to step back those few necessary paces to take a good objective look at it."

"Well, do the best you can. This is off-the-record. Just between the two of us. If necessary, we'll have you in to testify. To start with, maybe, how good are the chances for FTL?"

"We are working on it, senator. I have a feeling we still have a long way to go. We're beginning to have a feeling that it may not be a simple matter of physical laws."

"What could it be, then?"

"Emphasizing the fact that we do not really know, I'd be willing to hazard a guess that it might be something we have never heard of. A procedure, or a technique, maybe even a state of mind, that is outside all human experience."

"Now you're going mystic on me. I don't like this mystic stuff."

"In no way mystic, senator. Just a willingness to admit mankind's limitations. It stands to reason that one race on one planet is not going to come up with everything there is."

"Have you anything to back that up?"

"'Senator, I think I have. For the last several months, one of our operators has been trying to explain to his opposite number some of the fundamentals of our economic system. It has been and still is a trying task. Even the simplest fundamentals—things like buying and selling, supply and demand—have been hard to put across. Those folks out there, whoever they are, have never even thought of our brand of economics, if, in fact, any kind of economics. What makes it even harder is that they appear to stand in absolute horror of some of the things we tell them. As if the very ideas were obscene."

"Why bother with them, then?"

"Because they still maintain an interest. Perhaps the ideas are so horrible that they have a morbid fascination for them. As long as they maintain that interest, we'll keep on working with them."

"Our idea in starting this project was to help ourselves, not a lot of other folks."

"It's a two-way street," said Thomas. "They help us, we help them. They teach us, we teach them. It's a free interchange of information. And we're not being as altruistic as you think. It is our hope that as we go along with this economic business, we'll pick up some hints."

"What do you mean, some hints?"

"Perhaps some indications of how we may be able to revise or modify our economic system."

"Thomas, we have spent five or six thousand years or more in working out that economic system."

"Which doesn't mean, senator, that it is letter perfect. We made mistakes along the way."

The senator grunted. "This, I take it, will be another long-term project?"

"All of our work, or the most of it, is long-term. Most of what we get is not readily or easily adapted to our use."

"I don't like the sound of it," growled the senator. "I don't much like anything I hear. I asked you for specifics."

"I've given you specifics. I could spend the rest of the day giving you specifics."

"You've been at this business for twenty-five years?"

"On a job like this, twenty-five years is a short time."

"You tell me you're getting nowhere on FTL. You're piddling away your time teaching an economics course to some stupid jerks who are having a hard time knowing what you are talking about."

"We do what we can," said Thomas.

"It's not enough," said the senator. "The people are getting tired of seeing their taxes go into the project. They were never very much for it to start with. They were afraid of it. You could slip, you know, and give away our location."

"No one has ever asked for our location."

"They might have ways of getting it, anyhow."

"Senator, that's an old bugaboo that should long ago have been laid to rest. No one is going to attack us. No one is going to invade us. By and large, these are intelligent, and I would suspect, honorable gentlemen with whom we're dealing. Even if they're not, what we have here would not be worth their time and effort. What we are dealing in is information. They want it from us, we want it from them. It's worth more than any other commodity that any of us may have."

"Now we're back to that again."

"But, dammit, senator, that's what it's all about."

"I hope you're not letting us be taken in by some sort of slicker out there."

"That's a chance we have to take, but I doubt it very much. As director of this branch of the project, I've had the opportunity . . ."

The senator cut him off. "I'll talk with you some other time."

"Any time," said Thomas, as affably as he was able. "I'll look forward to it."

5

They had gathered in the lounge, as was their daily custom, for a round of drinks before dinner.

Jay Martin was telling about what had happened earlier in the day.

"It shook me," he said. "Here was this voice, from far away . . ."

"How did you know it was far away?" asked Thomas. "Before they told you, that is."

"I can tell," said Martin. "You get so you can tell. There is a certain smell to distance."

He bent over quickly, reaching for a handkerchief, barely getting it up in time to muffle the explosive sneeze. Straightening, he mopped his face, wiped his streaming eyes.

"Your allergy again," said Mary Kay.

"I'm sorry," he said. "How in hell can a man pick up pollen out here in this desert? Nothing but sage and cactus.'"

"Maybe it's not pollen," said Mary Kay. "It could be mold. Or dandruff. Has anyone here got dandruff?"

"You can't be allergic to human dandruff. It has to be cat dandruff," said Jennie Sherman.

"We haven't any cats here," said Mary Kay, "so it couldn't be cat dandruff. Are you sure about human dandruff, Jennie?"

"I'm sure," said Jennie. "I read it somewhere."

"Ever see a physician about it?" asked Thomas.

Martin shook his head, still mopping at his eyes.

"You should," said Thomas. "You could be given allergy tests. A battery of tests until they find what you're allergic to."

"Go ahead and tell us more," said Richard Garner, "about this guy who said the world was about to end."

"Not the world," said Martin. "The universe. He was just spreading the word. In a hurry to spread the word. As if they'd just found out. Like Chicken Little, yelling that the sky was falling. Talking for just a minute, then dropping out. I suppose going on to someone else. Trying to catch everyone he could. Sounded a little frantic. As if there was little time."

"Maybe it was a joke," suggested Jennie.

"I don't think so. It didn't sound like a joke. I don't think any of the people out there joke. If so, I've never heard of it. Maybe we're the only ones who have a sense of humor. Anyone here ever hear anything that sounded like a joke?"

They shook their heads.

"The rest of you are halfway laughing at it," said Mary Kay. "I don't think it's funny at all. Here are these people out on the rim, trying all these years, for no one knows how many centuries, to understand the universe, then up pops someone and tells them the universe has run down and they, out at the edge of it, will be the first to go. Maybe they were very close to understanding. Maybe they needed only a few more years and now they haven't got the years."

"Would that be the way it would happen?" asked Hal Rawlins. "Jay, you're the physicist. You'd be the one to know."

"I can't be certain, Hal. We don't know enough about the structure of the universe. There might be certain conditions that we are not aware of. Entropy presupposes a spreading out, so that the total energy of a thermodynamic system is so evenly distributed that there is no energy available for work. That's not the case here, of course. Out at the rim of the universe, maybe. The energy and matter out there would be old, have had more time. Or would it? God, I don't know. I'm talking about something no one knows about."

"But you finally contacted Einstein," said Thomas.

"Yes, he came in a little later."

"Anything?"

"No, the same as ever. We both got tired after a time, I guess. And talked about something else."

"Is that the way it often goes?"

"Every now and then. Today we talked about houses. Or I think it was houses. Near as I can make out, they live in some sort of bubble. Got the impression of huge webs with bubbles scattered through them. Do you suppose Einstein could be some sort of spider?"

"Could be," said Thomas.

"What beats the hell out of me," said Martin, "is why Einstein sticks with me. He beats his brains out trying to tell me about FTL and I beat my brains out trying to understand what he's telling me and never getting it. I swear I'm not a great deal closer than I was to start with, but he doesn't give up on me. He just keeps boring in. What I can't figure is what he's getting out of it."

"Every once in a while I get the funny feeling," said Garner, "that maybe these aren't different people who are talking to us. Not a lot of different cultures, but a lot of different individuals, maybe different specialists, from the same society."

"I doubt that's true," said Jennie Sherman. "Mine has a personality. A real personality. And different, very different, from the personalities the rest of you talk about. This one of mine is obsessed with death . . ."

"What a doleful subject," said Rawlins. "But I guess you've told us about him before. Talking about death all this time . . ."

"It was depressing to start with," said Jennie, "but it's not any more. He's made a philosophy out of it. At times, he makes death sound almost beautiful."

"A decadent race," said Garner.

"It's not that at all. I thought so at first. But he's so joyful about it, so happy."

"Death, Jennie, is not a joyful or happy subject," said Thomas. "We've talked about this, you and I. Maybe you should put an end to it. Pick up someone else."

"I will if you say so, Paul. But I have a feeling that something will come out of it. Some new kind of understanding, a new philosophy, a new principle. You haven't looked at the data, have you?"

Thomas shook his head.

"I can't tell why I feel this way," she said. "But deep down, at the bottom of me, I do."

"For the moment," said Thomas, "that's good enough for me."

Rawlins said, "Jay spoke of something that bugs me, too. What are they getting out of it? What are any of them getting out of it? We're giving them nothing."

"That's your guilt talking," said Thomas. "Perhaps it's something all of us are feeling. We must get rid of it. Wipe it from our minds. We feel intensely that we are beginners, that we're the new kid in the neighborhood. We are takers, not givers, although that's not entirely true. Dick has spent weeks trying to explain economics to his people."

Garner made a wry face. "Trying is all I do. I try to reduce the basics to the lowest common denominator. Thoughts of one syllable. Each syllable said slowly. Printed in big type. And they don't seem to get it. As if the very idea of economics was completely alien to them. As if hearing it were somehow distasteful. How in the world could a civilization develop and have any continuity without an economic system? I can't envision it. With us, economics is our life blood. We'd be nothing without an economic system. We'd be in chaos."

"Maybe that's what they're in," said Rawlins. "Maybe chaos is a way of life for them. No rules, no regulations, nothing. Although even as I say it, that doesn't sound quite right. Such a situation would be beyond our understanding, as repugnant to us as our economics seem to be to them."

"We all have our blind spots," said Thomas. "We're beginning to find that out."

"It would help though, it would help a lot," said Martin, "if we could feel we'd done something for one or two of them. It would give us a feeling of status, of having paid our dues."

"We're new at it," said Thomas. "The time will come. How are you getting along with your robot, Hal?"

"Damned if I know," said Rawlins. "I can't pin him down to anything. I can't get in a word. This robot, if it is a robot, if it's some sort of computer system—and for the life of me, I can't tell you why I think it is. But, anyhow, it is a non-stop talker. Information, most of it trivial, I suspect, just flows out of it. Never sticks to one thing. Talks about one thing, then goes chattering off to something entirely unrelated. As if it has a memory bank filled to the brim with data and is trying, as rapidly as possible, to spew out all that information. When I pick up something that seems to have some promise to it, something that could be of more than usual interest, I try to break in to talk at greater length about it, to ask some questions. Most often I can't break in, occasionally there are times I can. But when I do, he is impatient with me. He cuts off the discussion and goes back to his chatter. There are times when I get the impression that he's not talking to me alone, but to a lot of other people. I have the idea that when I am able to break in, he uses one circuit to talk with me directly while he goes on talking to all those others through other circuits."

Thomas put his empty glass on the table beside him, rose to his feet. "The others are starting in for dinner," he said. "Shall we join them."

6

Robert Allen, the project psychiatrist, rotated the brandy snifter between his palms.

"You sent word you wanted to see me, Paul. Has something come up?"

"I don't think so," Thomas said. "Not anything I can put a finger on. Maybe just a bad day, that's all. Ben Russell was in to raise hell with me. Said we were holding back on him."

"He's always saying that."

"I know. He's probably catching heat himself. When he catches heat, he turns it back on me. A feedback mechanism. A defensive gesture. He was upset that we'd not passed FTL data on to him."

"Have we got anything to pass?"

"Just a lot of nothing. Some meaningless equations. I don't see how Jay stands up under it. He picked up that allergy of his again."

"Tension," said Allen. "Frustration. That could bring it on."

"Later in the day," said Thomas, "Brown phoned."

"The senator?"

"The senator. It was FTL again. He was all over me. The budget's coming up again."

"Faster-than-light is something that the administrative mind can understand," said Allen. "Hardware."

"Bob, I'm not too sure it's hardware. It could be something else. Jay's an astrophysicist. If it was plain physics, he would have it pegged."

"Maybe there are many kinds of physics."

"I don't think so. Physics should be basic. The same through-out the universe."

"You can be sure of that?"

"No, I can't be sure of that. But my logic rejects . . ."

"Paul, you're over-reacting. If I were you, I'd disregard this sudden flurry over FTL. It's something that comes periodically and then dies down again."

"I can't disregard it," said Thomas. "Not this time. Brown's out to get us. His power base is slipping and he needs a new issue. We would make a good issue. Here we are, here we've been for a quarter century, gobbling up tax money that could be used for something else. That's the kind of issue the people would accept. They definitely are not with us; they have a feeling that we were crammed down their throats. They were never with us. Not only do we cost a lot, but we pose threats. What if we gave away our location, so that some barbaric, bloodthirsty alien horde could come crashing in on us? What if we find out something that would upset the apple-cart, wrecking a lot of our time-honored, comfortable concepts?"

"You mean he'd destroy us just to get elected?"

"Bob, you don't know politics. I am sure he would. Even if he believed in us, he might. I have a feeling that he doesn't believe in us. If he destroyed us, he'd be a public hero. We have to do something, come up with something in the next few months or he'll have a go at us."

"We have support," said Allen. "There are people in authority, in positions of power, who are committed to the project. Good people, reasonable people."

"Good and reasonable people don't have too much chance when they come up against a demagogue. The only way to beat Brown, if he decides to make us an issue, is to pile up some points we can make with the public."

"How can I help you, Paul?"

"Honestly, I don't know. A psychiatrist as a political adviser? No, I guess not. I suppose I only wanted to unload on you."

"Paul, you didn't ask me in to talk about FTL. That's an administrative matter. You can handle it. Nor about the politics of the project. You know I'm a child in politics. There is something else."

Thomas frowned. "It's hard to tell you. Hard to put into words. I'm beginning to sense something that disturbs me. Nothing concrete. Fuzzy, in fact. Tonight Jennie—you know Jennie?"

"Yes, the little car-hop we picked up a few years ago. Nice girl. Smart."

Tonight Jennie was talking about her people. They talk about death, she said. I knew it, of course. She'd been in a couple of times to talk with me about it. Depressed. Perhaps even frightened. After all, death can be a grisly subject. She had wanted to drop these people, try to pick up someone else. I urged her to hang in there a little longer. Never can tell what will happen, I told her. Tonight, when I suggested that she should drop it, she opposed me. Let me stay a while longer, she said, some worthwhile philosophy might develop out of it. I think there was something she wasn't telling me, something she is holding back."

"Maybe the discussion has advanced beyond death," said Allen. "Maybe it's getting into what happens after death—if anything happens after death."

Thomas looked in amazement at the psychiatrist. "My thought, exactly. With one qualification. If nothing happens after death, she'd be more depressed than ever. Her interest must mean that these folks do believe something happens. They may even have proof of it. Not faith, not a religious conviction. Jennie's a hard-headed little piece. She'd not buy simple faith. It would have to be more than that."

"You could pull the data. Have a look at it."

"No, I can't. Not yet. She'd know. I'd be snooping on her private project. My operators are fiercely jealous of what they are putting into their data banks. I have to give her time. She'll let me know when it's time to have a look."

"We must always keep in mind," said Allen, "that more than words, more than thoughts and ideas, come through from the aliens. Other things are transmitted. Things the operators hear but that can't be put into the banks. Fears, hopes, perceptions, residual memories, philosophical positions, moral evaluations, hungers, sorrow . . ."

"I know," said Thomas, "and none of it gets into the banks. It would be easier in one way if it did, perhaps more confusing in another."

"Paul, I know how easy it must be for someone in your position to become overly concerned, overwhelmed with worry, perhaps, even at times doubtful of the wisdom of the project. But you must remember, we've been at it only a little more than twenty years. We've done well in that short space of time . . ."

"The project," said Thomas, "really started about a hundred years ago. With that old gentleman who was convinced he was talking with the stars. What was his name? Do you recall it?"

"George White. The last years of his life must have been a nightmare. The government took him over, ran him through all sorts of tests. They never let him be. I suspect he might have been happier if everyone had continued not believing him. They pampered him, of course. That might have, in some measure, made it up to him. We still pamper our telepaths. Giving them a luxurious residential compound, with country club overtones, and . . ."

"They have it coming to them," snapped Thomas. "They are all we have. They're our one great hope. Sure, we've made strides. Progress if you want to call it that. The world existing in a sort of loose confederation; wars a thing of the past. Colonies and industries in space. A start made on terraforming Mars and Venus. One largely abortive voyage to the nearest stars. But we have our problems. Despite expansion into space, our economy still is kicked all out of shape. We continually ride on the edge of economic disaster. Our disadvantaged are still stockpiled against that day, that probably will never come, when we will be able to do something for them. The development of synthetic molecules would give us a boost if R&D would get cracking on it instead of moaning about not having FTL. I have some hopes that Garner may get some feedback from the aliens he is trying to teach economics to, but nothing yet, maybe nothing ever. It's the only economics show we have going. I had hoped others might come up, but they haven't. The hell of it is that so much of what we have going is producing so little. Much of it is seemingly off on the wrong track. Yet you can't junk all this stuff and start grabbing out frantically for something else. Mary Kay, for example. She has found something that might be big, but she's so hooked on it that she can't look for answers. When she tries, there are no answers. No idea communications at all, apparently. Just this feeling of euphoria. Worthless as it stands, but we can't pass it by. We have to keep on trying. There may be something there that is worth waiting for."

"I think the greatest problem lies in the kind of people who turn out to be the right kind of telepaths," said Allen. "Jay is the only man trained in science that we have. The others are not equipped to handle some of the material they are getting. I still think we could try to give some of them training in certain fields."

"We tried it," said Thomas, "and it didn't work. These are a special breed of people. Sensitives. They have to be handled with kid gloves or you destroy them. And under special kinds of strain. The strange thing about it, fragile as some of their personalities may be, they stand up to these special strains. Many ordinary people would crack if they knew they were in contact with an alien mind. A few of ours have, but not many. They have stood up under it. But they occasionally need support. It's my job to try to give it to them. They come to me with their fears, their doubts, their glory and elation. They cry on my shoulder, they scream at me . . ."

"The one thing that astounds me," said Allen, "is that they still maintain their relationships with non-telepaths. They are, as you have said, a very special breed. To them, it might seem, the rest of us would be little better than cloddish animals. Yet that does not seem to be the case. They've retained their humanity. It has been my observation, as well, that they don't get chummy with the aliens they are working with. Books. I guess that's it. They treat the aliens as books they'd take down off the shelf to read for information."

"All of them except Jay. He has worked up a fairly easy relationship with this last one. Calls him Einstein. None of the others have names for their aliens."

"Jay is a good man. Wasn't he the one who came up with the synthetic molecules?"

"That's right. He was one of the first successful operators. The first, if I remember rightly, who tolerated the brain implant. Others got the implant, but they had trouble with it. Some of them a lot of trouble. Of course, by the time Jay got his, there had been some improvement."

"Paul, is the implant absolutely necessary?"

"The boys upstairs think it is. I don't know enough about it, technically that is, to be sure. First, you have to find the right kind of telepath—not just a high quality telepath, but the right kind. Then the implant is made, not to increase the range, as some people will tell you, but to re-enforce the natural ability. It also has something to do, quite a bit to do, with the storage of the information. Range, as such, probably is not really important. On the face of it, it shouldn't be, for the waves or pulses or whatever they are that enable telepaths to talk to one another are instantaneous. The time and distance factors are cancelled out entirely and the pulses are immune to the restrictions of the electromagnetic spectrum. They are a phenomenon entirely outside the spectrum."

"Key, of course, to the entire project," said Allen, "lay in the development of the capability to record and store the information that is exchanged in the telepathic communication. A development of the earlier brain-waves studies."

"You're right," said Thomas. "It would have been impossible to rely on the memories of the telepaths. Many of them, most of them, in fact, have only a marginal understanding of what they are told; they are handling information that is beyond their compre-hension. They have a general idea, probably, but they miss a lot of it. Jay is an exception, of course. And that makes it easier with him. But with the others, the ones who do not fully understand, we have a record of the communications in the memory bank."

"We need more operators," said Allen. "We're barely touch-ing all the sources out there. And we can't go skipping around a lot because if we did, we might be passing up some fairly solid material. We do our recruiting and we uncover a lot of incipient telepaths, of course, but very few of the kind we are looking for."

"At no time," said Thomas, "are there ever too many of them to find."

"We got off what we were talking about," said Allen. "Mary Kay and Jennie, wasn't it?"

"I guess it was. They're the question marks. Jay either will pin down the matter of FTL or he'll not be able to. Dick will keep on with the economics and will either get some worth-while feed-back or he won't. Those are the kinds of odds we have to play. Hal will go on talking with his alien computer and we eventually may get something out of it. One of these days, we'll jerk the memory banks on that one and see what we have. I'd guess there might be some nebulous ideas we could play around with. But Mary Kay and Jennie—Christ, they're into something that is beyond any-thing we ever bargained for. Mary Kay a simulation—or maybe even the actuality—of a heavenly existence, a sort of Paradise, and Jennie with overtones of an existence beyond the grave. These are the kinds of things that people have been yearning for since the world began. This is what made billions of people, over the ages, tolerate religions. It poses a problem—both of them pose problems."

"If something came of either of them," said Allen, "what would we do with it?"

"That's right. Yet, you can't go chicken on it. You can't just turn it off because you're afraid of it."

"You're afraid of it, Paul?"

"I guess I am. Not personally. Personally, like everyone else, I would like to know. But can you imagine what would happen if we dumped it on the world?"

"I think I can. A sweep of unrealistic euphoria. New cults rising and we have more cults than we can handle now. A disruptive, perhaps a destructive impact on society."

"So what do we do? It's something we may have to face."

"We play it by ear," said Allen. "We make a decision when we have to. As project manager, you can control what comes out of here. Which may make Ben Russell unhappy, but something like this business of Mary Kay and Jennie is precisely why the director was given that kind of authority."

"Sit on it?" asked Thomas.

"That's right. Sit on it. Watch it. Keep close tabs on it. But don't fret about it. Not now at least. Fretting time may be some distance down the road."

"I don't know why I bothered you," said Thomas. "That's exactly what I intended all along."

"You bothered me," said Allen, "because you wanted someone in to help you finish up that bottle."

Thomas reached for the bottle. "Let's be about it, then."

7

"If you had to invent a universe," asked Mary Kay, "if you really had to, I mean; if it was your job and you had to do it, what kind of universe would you invent?"

"A universe that went on and on," said Martin. "A universe with no beginning and no end. Hoyle's kind of universe. Where there'd be the time and space for everything that possibly could happen, to happen."

"That entropy thing really got to you, didn't it. A voice out of the void saying it was all coming to an end."

Martin crinkled his forehead. "More now than it did to start with. Now that I've had time to think it over. Christ, think of it. We've been sitting here, us and all the people before us, thinking that there was no end, ever. Telling ourselves we had all the time there is. Not considering our own mortality, that is. Thinking racially, not of ourselves alone. Not ourselves, but all the people who come after us. An expanding universe, we told ourselves. And maybe now it isn't. Maybe, right this minute, it is a contracting universe. Rushing back, all the old dead matter, all the played-out energy."

"It has no real bearing on us," said Mary Kay. "No physical effect. We won't be caught in the crunch, not right away at least. Our agony is intellectual. It does violence to our concept of the universe. That's what hurts. That a thing so big, so beautiful—the only thing we really know—is coming to an end."

"They could have been wrong," he said. "They might have miscalculated. Their observations might have been faulty. And it might not really be the end. There might still be another universe. Once everything retreated back as far as it could go, there might be another cosmic explosion and another universe."

"But it wouldn't be the same," she said. "It would be a different universe. Not our universe. It would give rise to different kinds of life, new kinds of intellect. Or maybe no life or intellect at all. Just the matter and the energy. Stars burning for themselves. No one to see them and to wonder. That, Jay, is what has made our universe so wonderful. Little blobs of life that held the capacity to wonder."

"Not only the wonder," Jay told her, "but the audacity to probe beyond the wonder. The grief in that warning was not that the universe was coming to an end, but that it was doing so before someone could find out what it was."

"Jay, I've been wondering . . ."

"You're always wondering. What is it this time?"

"It's silly. All my wondering is silly. But, do you suppose that we can experience things in time, reach things in time as well as in space?"

"I don't know. I've never thought of it."

"You know this place I've found. So quiet. So wonderful. So happy and so holy. Have you any idea of what it might be?"

"Let's not get into that right now," said Jay. "You'll just upset yourself. Everyone else has left. Maybe we should be leaving, too."

He looked around the empty lounge, made a motion to get up. She reached for his arm and held him there.

"I've been thinking about it," she said. "I've been wondering if this place of mine is what is left after everything is gone. When the universe is gone. The few good things left over, the worthwhile things left over. The things we have never valued enough. We or any of the others out there. The peace, the love, the holiness. These are the things, I think, that will survive."

"I don't know, Mary. God, how could I know."

"I hope it is," she said. "I so hope it is. I have a feeling that it is. I go so much on feeling. In the place I found, you have to depend on what you feel. There is nothing else. Just the feeling. Do you ever depend on feeling, Jay?"

"No, I don't," he told her. He got to his feet, put out a hand to help her up. "Do you know," he said, "that you are beautiful and crazy."

Suddenly he bent double, getting the handkerchief to his face barely in time to catch the sneeze.

"Poor Jay," she said. "You still have your allergy."

8

Martin settled himself before the console, shoved the helmet more comfortably into place. The helmet was a nuisance, but he had to wear it, for it was the mechanism that fed the information into the data banks.

—Einstein, are you there? he asked.

—I am here, said Einstein, ready to begin. You have your allergy again. Are you ingesting chemicals?

—Yes. And they don't help a lot.

—We sorrow for you greatly.

—I thank you very much, said Martin.

—When last we quit, we were discussing . . .

—A moment, Einstein. I have a question.

—Ask.

—It has nothing to do with what we were discussing. It's a question I long have wanted to ask and never had the courage.

—Ask.

—For a long time, we have been talking about faster-than-light and I am not understanding. You've been patient with me. You overlook my stupidity. Still willing to keep on, when at times it must seem hopeless to you. I want to ask you why. Why are you willing to keep on?

—Simple, Einstein said. You help us. We help you.

—But I haven't helped you.

—Yes, you have. You recall occasion first we took notice of your allergy?

—That was a long time ago.

—We asked you can you do anything to help it. And you say a term at the time we do not know.

—Medicine?

—That was it. We asked you, medicine? And you explain. Chemicals you say. Chemicals we know.

—Yes, I guess I did say that.

—Medicine-chemicals entirely new to us. Never heard of them. Never thought of them.

—You mean you had no idea of medicine?

—Correct. Affirmative. Had no idea, ever.

—But, you never asked me about it. I would have been willing to tell you.

—We did ask. Now and then we asked. Very briefly, very carefully. So you would not know.

—Why? Why briefly? Why carefully?

—So great a thing. Too big to share with others. Now I see we misjudge you. I am very sorry.

—You should be, Martin said. I thought you were my friend.

—Friend, of course, but even among friends . . .

—You were willing to tell of faster-than-light.

—No great thing. Many others have it. Very simple, once you catch it.

—I'm glad to hear you say so. How are you doing on medicine?

—Slowly, but some progress. Things we need to know.

—So go ahead and ask, said Martin.

9

Thomas looked questioningly across the desk at Martin.

"You mean to tell me, Jay, that Einstein's people had never thought of medicine. That they know chemistry and had never thought of medicine?"

"Well, it's not quite that simple," said Martin. "They have a hang-up. Their bodies are sacred. Temples of their souls. Einstein didn't actually say that; it is my interpretation of what he said. But, anyhow, their bodies are sacred and they don't tamper with them."

"In that case, they'll have a hell of a time selling medicine to their public."

"I suppose so. But with Einstein and some of his fellows, that's different. An elite clique, I gather, standing above the general public, perhaps a bit contemptuous of the public, not sharing all the superstitions the general public holds. Willing, even anxious, to pick up what might be considered iconoclastic ideas. Willing, at least, to have a try at them. With the forces of the old beliefs and prejudices bearing on them, however, it's not to be wondered at that they never thought of medicine."

"They're willing to let you tell them about it?"

"Anxious. Strangely excited about it—a sort of nervous excitement. As if they know they're doing wrong, but are going to do it anyhow. All I can give them, of course, is the basic thinking on medicine. They'll have to work out the details themselves, adapting them to their situation. I gave them what I could today. I'll have to bone up on the theory of medicine to give them much more. There should be material in the library."

"I'm sure there is," said Thomas.

"I thought for a while I'd lost Einstein. I told him that to develop medicine they'd have to know about their bodies . . ."

"And since their bodies are sacred . . ."

Martin nodded. "That's the idea, exactly. Einstein asked how they'd get to know about their bodies and I said dissection. I told him what dissection was and that was when I thought I'd blown it. He was getting more than he asked for, more than he really wanted, and a lot of it he didn't like. But he was a man about it; he gulped and gagged somewhat and finally came to terms with it. It appears he is a devoted soul. Once he gets his teeth into something, he hangs onto it."

"You think he and the rest of his clique will go ahead with it?"

"I'm not sure, Paul. I think so. He tended to wax a bit philosophical about it. Trying to talk himself more firmly into the idea of going ahead with it. And while he was doing this, I was wondering how many similar hang-ups we may have that makes it hard or impossible to use some of the ideas we may get. Here is this advanced culture, a forward-looking society, and yet an old obsession that probably dates back to primordial times has made it impossible for them to come up with the concept of medicine."

"Our own history of medicine," said Thomas, "is not too dissimilar. We had to sweep away a lot of superstition and wrong thinking before we could get even a decent start in the healing art."

"I suppose so," said Martin. "But, dammit, the whole thing makes me feel good. If Einstein goes ahead with it, and I think he will, it means we've been of some use. Like I said last night, we may be beginning to pay our dues. We aren't just Cub Scouts any longer. I had no idea, you see, of what was going on. The sneaky son-of-a-bitch was trying to steal the idea of medicine from me, bit by tiny bit."

"I'd suspect we may be doing much the same thing on our part," said Thomas. "We're handling some of those jokers out there far too gently, more than likely, than there is any need to. Going easy on them, afraid of doing something wrong and scaring them off. I would suspect this is because of our inferiority complex, brought about by the kind of company we're keeping. Get a few more deals like your medicine show under our belts and we'll no longer have it. We'll be right up there with the rest of them."

"I hesitated to ask him," said Martin, "about why he was sticking with me. Like you say, I probably was afraid of scaring him off. But it bugged me, it had bugged me for a long time. So I thought, why not? why not be honest with him? And once I was honest with him, he decided to be honest with me. It does beat hell how things sometimes turn out."

"I don't suppose you had much time to talk about FTL today. That's all right. Maybe a few days off may help. And now you'll feel less guilty at the time Einstein spends on it. You can bear down a little harder on him."

"No time on FTL today at all," said Martin. "But you may be right. I've been doing some thinking about it. I talked with Mary

Kay last night and she asked me if I stuck to hard fact all the time or if I paid some attention to my feelings, how I felt about it. I suppose she was trying to say hunches and not quite making it. I told her my feelings played no part in it. I've never let them play a part. I've tried to stick to the pure science of it—if, in fact, there is any science in it. This afternoon I got to thinking about it and maybe I was wrong . . ."

"And?"

"You know, Paul, I may finally have a handle on this FTL business. Not for certain, but maybe. A new way to go. For the last several weeks, I've been telling myself time could be the key factor and that I should be paying more attention to it. Has this project ever held any talk with some of our aliens about time?"

"I think so. Ten or fifteen years ago. We still have the record. It was fairly inconclusive, but we have stacks of data."

"Except in a superficial way," said Martin, "time can't play too much of a part in any equation, although in many problems it can be a fairly critical factor. If we knew more about time, I told myself, not as a physical, but as a mental factor in FTL, we might turn the trick. Tying a mental concept of time into the equation . . ."

"You think it might work?"

"Not now. Not any more. I have a hunch that time may be a variable, that it runs differently in different sectors of the universe, or differently in the minds of different intelligences. But there is something that would be a constant. Eternity would be a constant factor. It wouldn't vary; it would be the same everywhere."

"My God, Jay, you aren't talking about . . ."

"Not about arriving at an understanding of it, but I think we might work out a way it could be used as a constant. I'm going to take a shot at it. With it in mind, some of the other factors may come clear."

"But eternity, Jay. This business about the universe coming to an end."

"Mary Kay told me something else last night. Her hunch of what might be left when the universe is gone."

"I know. She was in just a while ago. She spilled it all on me."

"And what did you say?"

"Christ, Jay, what could I say? I patted her on the shoulder and told her to stay in there pitching."

"But if she's right, there'd be something beyond the end of the universe. There'd still be eternity. Maybe still infinity. Two constants. And room for something else to happen."

"You're getting me in beyond my depth, Jay."

"Maybe I'm beyond my depth, too. But it's a new approach. Maybe it can be handled. Tell Russell and Brown, when they start hassling you again, that we're going at it from a fresh angle."

Thomas sat a long time at the desk after Martin had left.

Last night, he thought, Allen had been no help when he'd talked with him. All the same old platitudes: don't worry, sit on it, hang in there tight, make a decision only when you have to. And this afternoon he, himself, had been no help when Jay and Mary Kay had sat across the desk from him. Stay in there pitching, he'd told Mary Kay.

These are special people, he had told Allen. He had been right, of course. They were special, but how special? How far beyond the ordinary run of mankind? Dime store clerks and car hops and raw farm boys. But what happened to them when they ventured out among the stars and made contacts with the intelligences who dwelt on planets orbiting distant suns? Allen had said, or had it been he? That all that came through from the star-flung party line was not recorded in the memory banks—the pain, the sorrow, the doubt, the hope, the fear, the prejudices, the biases, and what else? Something beyond all human experience? Something that was soaked up, that was absorbed into the fiber and the fabric of the human telepaths who listened, who chatted and gossiped with their neighbors strung across the galaxies. A factor, or factors, that made them slightly more than human or, perhaps, a great deal more than human.

Mary Kay, with her talk of a place that would still persist after the universe was gone, quite naturally was crazy. Jay, with his talk of using eternity as a constant factor, was insane as well. But crazy and insane, of course, only by human standards. And these people, these telepaths of his (perhaps, almost certainly, undeniably) had gone far beyond humanity.

A special people, a new breed, their humanity cross pollinated by the subtle intricacies of alien contact, the hope of humankind?

Ambassadors to the universe? Industrial spies? Snoopers into places where man had little right to go? Explorers of the infinite?

Dammit, he thought, it made a man proud to be a member of the human race. Even if this special breed should finally become a race apart, they still stemmed from the same origins as all the other humans.

Might it be, he wondered, that in time some of the specialness would rub off on others such as he?

And, suddenly, without any thinking on it, without due consideration, without mulling it over, without using the slow, intricate, involved process of human thought, he arrived at faith. And was convinced, as well, that his faith was justified.

Time to go for broke, he told himself.

He reached over and punched the button for Evelyn.

"Get me Senator Brown," he told her. "No, I don't know where he is. Track him down, wherever he may be. I want to tell the old bastard that we're finally on the track for FTL."

A HERO MUST NOT DIE

This story of World War II air combat appeared in the June 1943 issue of Sky Raiders. *It features members of Great Britain's Royal Air Force, probably because it was written before the United States entered that war. The story was sent out to* American Eagle *in November 1941, and while I find the name of that magazine somewhat incongruous, I have concluded that the magazine may have tried to feature stories of Americans who joined the English or Canadian forces even before the United States entered the war. The protagonist of Cliff's story seems to be such an American, although the story does not say so. At any rate,* American Eagle *and two other magazines had previously rejected the story.* Sky Raiders *took it, but they did not, however, send Cliff the twenty-five dollars he was promised until he wrote to complain. Perhaps that was to be expected from a magazine that cost just ten cents per issue.*

—dww

Even as he started his dive, Flying Officer Fred Douglas felt no apprehension. Everything, he was sure, was in control. But just to be sure he shoved the Spit's nose down and rammed the throttle up the rack.

Less than two thousand feet below, his brother, Bob Douglas, was screaming down toward the Dover cliffs, with a Messerschmitt howling on his tail.

But climbing up the sky, straight toward the diving pair, his guns hammering steel into the underside of a second Messerschmitt, was Flight Lieutenant Richard Grant.

Fred Douglas watched his air speed indicator crowd the pin as the plane settled into the downward plunge, but even then he knew there'd be no need of hm. All Grant had to do was to kick right rudder and blast the diving Jerry with his guns.

The three of them worked like a team, the two brothers and the flight lieutenant. One of them occasionally got into a jam, as Bob had now, but whenever that happened one of the others was always there with flaming guns.

Bob had saved Grant's life twice, once at Dunkerque when a Jerry got on his tail, again at Calais when three M.E.'s ganged him. Today Grant would get Bob out of a jam. And probably tomorrow Grant himself would be in a tight spot, with one of the others hurtling in to help him.

Only once had any of them failed the other. That had been the time Grant was shot down in France. But it had worked out all right, after all, for a week later a destroyer picked the flight leader up, out in the channel, trying to row a stolen boat to England.

The Merlin was a shriek of whistling sound and Fred Douglas saw he was gaining on the Messerschmitt, but knew he'd be too late to get in on the kill. It was just that he wanted to be sure . . . wanted to be there if anything went wrong, if he might be needed.

Within split seconds Grant would kick the rudder and the diving Nazi would slam head-on into a spate of steel.

Bob's ship flashed past Grant's plane and now the way was clear for the flight lieutenant.

"Take him, Grant!" Fred shrieked into the flap mike, but the flight leader's ship did not deviate from course. The Brownings spat, but not at the diving Nazi. They still were trained on the second Messerschmitt which even then was beginning to wobble.

Cold terror gripped Fred Douglas' throat as he realized Grant was not going to intervene, that he was more intent upon making sure of that second M.E. than he was of aiding Bob.

And in that second of terror, the diving Jerry was past the flight leader's ship and Fred Douglas knew the job was up to him, knew there was little chance of his getting there in time.

His hand leaped to the emergency boost and jerked out the knob. Responding, the Merlin's howl rose to a piercing scream and the bottom seemed to drop out of the sky as the British fighter literally hurled itself upon the Messerschmitt.

Finger hovering over the electric firing button, Douglas bent to the ring sight, had the Nazi centered in it . . . but the range was still too long, although the Spitfire was eating up the sky.

The blue smoke of burning cordite whipped back from the Messerschmitt and bits of tattered metal leaped from Bob's Spitfire. More metal flew at another burst and then a wing slowly crumpled.

Fingers of steel were gripping Douglas' throat and through his mind spun a string of pictures from the past. Pictures of him and Bob. Fishing on the old creek . . . their first long pants . . . their first party . . . the old car they had bought and patched up so it would run . . . the Christmases at home . . .

Bob's Spitfire was beginning to slideslip and Fred shrieked at it. "Jump, Bob! Get out of there!"

But no figure hurtled from the crippled ship. Blue smoke still streamed from the Jerry's guns. The Merlin sang its song of hate . . . and the Brownings waited.

Then Douglas squeezed the firing button, but even as he did he saw a gout of flame leap out of the sky, saw his brother's Spitfire streaking for the channel, a blazing funeral pyre.

For a single instant his brain went red with grief and anger and black with terrible hate. His finger tightened on the firing button, almost as if he could squeeze more rounds per second out of the yammering guns.

Bits of metal were flying once again, but this time German

metal. Bullets from the eight Brownings literally were chewing the Messerschmitt to bits . . . slicing off the metal skin, slamming into the fuselage, smashing into the cockpit, ripping at the engine.

And still Douglas held the button on, curses in his throat, red vengeance flaring in his brain.

One of the Jerry's wings was going now, folding up, hammered apart by the savagery of the Brownings. That bouncing thing in the cockpit was the Nazi pilot, rocked by the impact of the bullets spewing from the Spitfire's guns.

Suddenly the Messerschmitt was tumbling crazily, black smoke pouring from the cowling. The Brownings ran empty. Far below a second thinning trail of smoke drifted in the air.

Douglas eased back on the stick hauling the Spitfire out of its dive. Suddenly, now that the action was over, his body felt limp and beaten and his mind was sick . . . sick with the realization that Bob was gone. Dead in a flaming ship over the English channel. Dead because Flight Lieutenant Richard Grant had failed his unwritten pact. All he had to do was kick the rudder and slam home the firing button. Had he done that, Bob would have gone on living.

There could be no question that Grant had seen Bob and the pursuing Nazi. If there only could be . . . but there wasn't. The hard truth remained that Grant had failed his trust, had failed to aid the man who twice had saved his life.

Douglas edged the Spitfire upward. There were other Jerries up there. Jerries to be killed. Jerries to help wipe clean the score. But even as he put the ship into a climb he remembered the ammo-belts were empty.

He leveled off, swinging the ship around for home. And just then a storm of steel struck as a lurking Messerschmitt pounced upon him. In one fractional bit of time the instruments were gone as if some giant hand had smashed them. Oil sprayed into the cockpit, covering his goggles, blinding him. The Merlin stuttered and coughed and the ship slid-slipped dangerously.

Above him the Messerschmitt howled in mockery and then a silence swept upon him as the Merlin choked and died.

Instinctively, Douglas tried to roll the ship over on its back. That was the easiest way, the only practical way, to bail out of a fighter. But there was no response to the controls.

Smoke rolled from the cowling and from outside came the high, thin whistle of the atmosphere against the plunging ship.

Desperately, Douglas fought the controls. They were hopelessly jammed. For a moment panic assailed him, a panic born of the whistling shriek that told him he was dashing to his death.

Dense smoke streamed over the hatch, cutting off his vision. Some of it curled back through the broken instrument board and stung his eyes and nose. He heard the crunch of glass as his foot crushed the goggles where he had brushed them on the floor.

Flame surged back from the dead engine and bit into his flesh. The Spitfire began to spin. Furiously Douglas fought back the hatch, clawed savagely to get clear of the plane. Streamers of flame whipped at him and the lurching spin hurled him back into the pit.

Fire lashed back fiercely and the smoke turned the sunlight into night. Athrob with pain, blinded, with all sense of time and direction lost, Douglas scrambled desperately, trying to get through the hatch. The plane lurched suddenly and he was free . . . free and falling. Seared fingers found the parachute ring and jerked. He wondered dimly if the fire might not have damaged the straps, but a moment later the silk caught hold and he was dangling, floating down.

For the first time, he realized he couldn't see. His eyes seemed to be puffed shut. His hands and face were flaming balls of fire and when he tried to talk, he couldn't, for his lips were wrong and his throat was too dry to work.

—

Three months later the hospital released him as cured and perhaps the hospital knew what it was about. His hands no longer were clenched talons, held in closed-fist positions by seared muscle and flesh. His face was whole again except for a few scars that in time would disappear.

But hands and face weren't all there was to it, Douglas thought, brooding in a corner of the mess over a double brandy. Three were other things the doctors couldn't know about. For instance, the things that happened to a man's brain when he has seen his brother shot down in flames, when he himself is trapped in a blazing plane.

He hadn't slowed up. He was still bringing down the Jerries. He was still, he knew, as good a pilot as ever. But the doubt that he was as good a fighter as ever was creeping in upon him. The old dash and daring was gone. He no longer took those chances he had taken in the old days. Now he found himself fighting a grim and cautious fight, efficient and calculating . . . but cautious. Someday that caution would be the end of him. Someday when he needed to take a chance, he wouldn't take it . . .

They talked about him a little, he suspected, when he wasn't about when he was out of hearing.

The door to the briefing room swung open and Flight Lieutenant Grant came in.

"Hi, Grant," yelled one of them, "come over and have one."

"Who was that cutie you had last night?" yelled another.

"You chaps are off the beam," said Grant. "I was in quarters last night."

"You mean you weren't down to London?"

"That," Grant said, "is exactly what I mean."

Douglas grimaced. Grant was popular. Fifty-three Jerries to his credit . . . probably the actual toll was even greater, for that was only the official score. The younger men, especially, looked up to him. He was an old-timer, an ace, one of those deadly fighting men who lived a charmed life.

Douglas wiped the scene at the bar from his mind, stared into the brandy glass, his memory leaping back to the day above the channel, the day Bob's machine streaked for the cliffs of Dover. Again he felt his own ship diving, felt the terror rising in him, was reaching for the emergency boost . . .

Boots tramped across the floor and Douglas looked up. Grant, glass in hand, stood before him.

"I want to talk to you, Douglas," he said.

"I don't want to talk to you," Douglas replied, quietly. "I have to talk to you up in the air. That's quite enough."

Grant flushed but held his ground. "We once were friends."

"We aren't any more," Douglas stated flatly.

"You're eating out your heart," Grant told him. "You have to break it up."

"Is that as fight leader?" asked Douglas. "Afraid I'm endangering someone else? Hinting my flying's not so good?"

"Lord, no," said Grant. "It's merely as a friend. I hate to watch what's happening to you."

"In that case," Douglas declared, "you're concerning yourself with something that's none of your damn business."

Grant turned, but Douglas halted him.

"Did I hear you say you were in quarters last night?"

"Why, yes," said Grant, "perhaps you did."

Douglas said nothing.

"Why do you ask?"

"Impulse," Douglas explained. "Perhaps I shouldn't have. You see, I knew you weren't."

"Just why do you hate me?" Grant demanded. "I know the general reasons, of course, although I don't agree with them. But what is the basic reason?"

"You worked too hard at your career," said Douglas. "You thought too much about piling up the score. You were so busy getting that . . . twenty-eight, wasn't it? . . . Jerry, that you couldn't help a friend."

"I explained about that," protested Grant.

"You forget I saw it," Douglas snapped.

"Look, Douglas, I like you . . . in spite of all you say, the way you act. I asked that you be reassigned to the flight."

"Anytime you care to ask that I be reassigned again," said Douglas, "it'll be agreeable."

The fields of Holland were green and gold, with little canal ribbons running through them. The sweep was almost over and the R.A.F. was flying home again, leaving behind a trail of blasted ruin.

Douglas settled comfortably down to the job of piloting the Hurricane across the channel and back to base. There had been little excitement. With the Jerries busy in Russia, there was seldom much excitement these days.

Grant flew ahead and to his right was Shorty Cave. Above and behind roared the other flights that had made the sweep.

Douglas' earphones barked a single word. "Tallyhoo!" Grant's voice.

Douglas started, the shout jerking him to swift attention.

Diving at them, straight out of the sun, were the roaring shapes of M.E. 110's. How many there were, Douglas could not be sure, for there was no time to count. The Jerries had been waiting for them, lurking high up in the blue. Now they were shrieking down for a hit and run attack.

Douglas hauled back the stick, threw his ship into a climb. A black shape flickered across his line of vision and he pressed the firing button, but the Nazi was going too fast and the tracer missed. It had, at the best, been a snap shot.

Guns were hammering now as the Nazi planes slashed into the British formation. Smoke bloomed out in the sky and a ship was screaming down.

A Messerschmitt dived at him and Douglas swung his Hurricane over in a tight loop. The tracer caught his wing tip and then the Nazi was past. A second later, loop completed, Douglas was on his tail.

The M.E. was trying to pull out of the dive and Douglas found his brain clicking coolly, calculating . . . like a man sitting at a chess board, planning his attack many moves ahead.

That was the thing that terrified him at times when he sat with his brandy back at base. A smart way to fight, perhaps, but someday it would get him in a jam. No more recklessness, no more fire, no more enthusiasm. Just a grim playing of something that added up to no more than a deadly game.

He hauled back the stick deliberately to match the Messerschmitt's maneuver. The Jerry came into the ring sight, started to cross it, pulling out of the dive. Bullets slashed into the wing of the Hurricane as the Nazi rear gunner got his weapon into action.

Then the Messerschmitt hatch was in sight and Douglas opened with his guns. A short burst . . . four seconds, no more, but enough to fill the cockpit and gunnery position with screaming steel.

The Messerschmitt wobbled and skipped, heeled over, sideslipped and fell. It was always like that, Douglas thought. Take no chances, hold the guns until the correct moment, then put the bullets where they counted.

But someday. Perhaps, someday . . .

He shivered as he hauled the Hurricane around, sent it zooming into the blue. There were no more Messerschmitts in sight. The Hurricanes and Blenheims were reforming.

It had, Douglas told himself, been another typical Nazi hit-and-run affair, with the Jerries diving, hoping to gain by the element of surprise, and then streaking away before the British fighters could get in their licks.

He tilted the ship and looked over the side and as he did his heart skipped a beat. Far below a Hurricane was gliding down to earth, engine apparently dead, for Douglas could not see the slow swirl of the prop gleaming in the sun.

No parachute. That meant the pilot was taking a chance on riding the crippled ship to earth. Faster that way . . . if you lived. More time to get into hiding before a Nazi patrol swooped down.

A new sound came . . . the sound of a diving ship. Douglas stared upward, saw the Messerschmitt storming down the sky . . . straight at the gliding Hurricane. A vulture swooping on a wounded helpless victim.

With a curse of rage, Douglas slid his ship around on its wing, started a plunge that would intercept the diving M.E.

He half expected the Nazi to veer off and try to make a getaway, but the ship came on.

Once again his brain was clicking . . . like well-oiled wheels functioning mechanically. Figuring out the angle of attack, trying to anticipate what the Messerschmitt pilot would do, keeping the Hurricane aimed at that hypothetical sector of space where it would intercept the Jerry.

Like avenging meteors, the two machines bellowed down the sky, overhauling the gliding Hurricane.

Once the Jerry sees I'm going to block his play, the brain was clicking, he'll pull out and try to get me from above. So the thing to do is to anticipate him.

Douglas sucked in his breath, watched with narrowed eyes, measuring the distance, hand clutching the stick.

The Messerschmitt suddenly snapped upward and as it did, Douglas shoved the throttle to the last notch. With mere yards to spare, he sent the Hurricane hurtling under the belly of the Messerschmitt, jerked back the stick, drove his machine into a sharp climb. The Merlin screamed in rage, swishing the ship around in a tight loop. For a sickening second, the plane hung upside down and in that instant, the upward roaring Jerry climbed into the ring sight. Douglas squeezed the button and ahead of him the Messerschmitt shuddered and stalled, swung over and headed for earth with smoke streaming from the motor.

With throttle full out, Douglas slanted his ship after the gliding Hurricane.

A voice was shouting in his earphones, a voice he recognized.

"Douglas, you damn fool, go back. Thanks for what you did, but you can't do any more."

"Grant, there's a field down there," Douglas yelled. "Mush her in. I'll be right behind you. Then we're getting out of here."

"You're mad," Grant protested. "It can't be done. Get back, I tell you. It'll only mean the two of us instead of one. Go back. That's an order."

"To hell with orders. I'm coming after you. You're going home with me. Lashed to a wing . . ." He laughed. "Not dignified. But what the hell. We can't lose a man like you."

Grant was raging now. "I'll have you up for insubordination."

Douglas chuckled savagely. "Insubordination for what? For stopping you from making another grandstand play? Like the time you did before. Coming home in a boat."

Deliberately he reached out and jerked out the earphone plug.

Grant's ship just cleared the trees at the edge of the field, was pancaking toward the meadow. It struck and bounced, bounced again, threatening to nose over, then rolled to a stop.

Douglas brought his Hurricane down in a smooth landing, taxied swiftly toward the other ship.

Quickly he reached up and hauled back the hatch, leaped nimbly to the wing and hopped to the ground.

"Stay where you are!" snapped a voice and as he wheeled he saw Grant standing at the end of the wing, a Webley in his hand.

"One move," said the flight lieutenant, "and I will let you have it."

Douglas stared, wide-eyed, not understanding.

"You're crazy," he gasped. "Put that damn thing up. You're going back with me."

Grant laughed . . . a vicious laugh.

"That's where you're mistaken, Douglas. I'm not going back and neither are you."

"You aren't serious, Grant."

"Never more serious in my life, my British friend."

Silence hung between them . . . an awkward silence.

"So," Douglas said finally, "that is how it is."

Grant nodded, tight-lipped. "Clever wasn't it. And you English pigs never once suspected."

"Clever," said Douglas bitterly. "Yes, terribly clever. How many of your Nazi friends have you shot down? Over fifty, isn't it?"

"If I hadn't, someone else would have," Grant declared. "And, after all, what are a few lives more or less? Those I shot down would have gone gladly to their death had they but known."

He chuckled. "There's something else . . . something for you to think about behind the barbed wire of your prison camp. When my mission here is over, I shall go back again. As I did before. And I shall be a great English hero . . ."

"You'll go back to do it all over again?" asked Douglas calmly.

"That's right," replied Grant. "Over and over and the English will never know. For do I not shoot down the Nazis right and left?"

"That," declared Douglas, "is about the lowest form of treachery I can think of."

"Not treachery," said Grant. "I am serving the fuehrer."

The flight lieutenant motioned with the muzzle of his pistol.

"And now let us get going."

In answer, Douglas stooped and hurled himself under the wing of the plane. Grant shouted and the Webley cracked, the bullet whining viciously as it ricocheted off the ship's metal skin.

Rolling to get full protection of the wing, Douglas scrambled to his knees, hauling his Webley from the pocket of his flying togs. Another shot rang out and a bullet chugged into the ground not more than three feet from where he knelt.

Silence then . . . a long, terrifying silence. He could see nothing of Grant, not even his legs moving about. The man, he knew, must be stalking him. The short hairs rose at the nape of his neck, bristling with an atavistic fear.

If only he could see something . . . if only he could stand up and shoot it out! Anything but the sense of being trapped . . . of knowing that out there somewhere in the field a man was deliberately maneuvering himself into position to send a bullet through him.

Carefully he inched himself closer to the body of the plane, straining his eyes, listening intently. A mumbling roar came to his ears . . . the beating of a far-off motor.

So there he was, he told himself, hunkered beneath the plane, waiting for Grant to get into position . . . waiting until the one-time flight lieutenant could send a bullet through his brain. There wasn't much, he admitted, that he could do about it. The meadow was flat as the top of a table. If he showed himself, Grant would see him and start shooting. For a moment he considered a swift break, an attempt to get back into the cockpit of the Hurricane and be off, but he rejected it almost as soon as he thought of it. He preferred waiting here, waiting for the break that might never come. His fist tightened on the Webley. If he could just locate Grant!

It had been foolish to have gotten himself into such a mess. It was not, he admitted to himself, all through a desire to save Grant from falling into German hands.

That, of course, had been the first impulse . . . to save a fellow flier from capture. Funny that such a thought should have come to him unquestioningly when he knew . . . and Grant knew . . . that he hated the flight lieutenant. Hated with good cause.

But even at that, in the face of Grant's orders to turn back, he might have pulled off and continued on to England, had not the ludicrousness of bringing Grant home, lashed to the Hurricane's wing, occurred to him. The idea of spiking another possible hero-stunt like crossing the channel in a stolen boat had been too much to resist.

Such a thing, he knew, was possible, although rather tough on the wing rider. But that would have been giving Grant something that would be good for him . . . something to deflate the ego of a career-fighter.

The mumbling roar he had heard was growing louder now . . . louder and closer . . . until he knew it was a plane, the deep-voiced thrumming of a Messerschmitt. And it was coming toward the field.

He waited, crouched, wondering. Now it was above the trees at the edge of the field . . . coming in at possibly no more than a hundred feet above the ground.

Suddenly guns snickered and their first burst was followed by a scream of terror.

Leaping from under the wing, Douglas stood in astonishment. Grant was racing for the trees on the other side of the field, yelling, waving his arms, while all about him little puffs of white dust were dancing in the sunlight. With a blast of thunder the plane roared over, not more than fifty feet above the Hurricane, guns bellowing.

Frozen in his tracks, Douglas watched the tableau out there in the field. For a moment it seemed as if time stood still while the scene was etched upon his brain . . . the running man, the puffs of dust as the bullets from the Messerschmitt sprayed the ground, the tall trees looking on, the short yellow grass baking in the sun.

Then time took up again and Grant was stumbling. Stumbling while the jets of dust still flickered all around. He struck the ground, rose to his knees and crawled, then fell again and did not rise.

The Messerschmitt, with what seemed a scream of triumph, climbed over the edge of trees and howled into the sky. Circling, it swung back and roared toward the field again. Douglas quickly ducked out of sight as it skimmed over, riding on one wing, so the pilot could survey the squatting Hurricanes.

Probably, Douglas told himself, the Nazi was looking for him, for the other British pilot. For that was what Grant must have seemed . . . no more than a stranded Britisher . . . an enemy who was fair game. The man in the Messerschmitt could not possibly have known who Grant was. And after all, it added up to a sort of grim retribution. Grant, who had killed scores of his countrymen in the skies of England and along the coast, had been the quarry of his compatriot.

Douglas waited until the drone of the Messerschmitt had faded away, then ran across the field.

Grant, he saw, was dead, face downward, hands clutching at the yellow grass. Swiftly his hands felt through the pockets, found a small notebook and a sheaf of papers.

Squatting there, he leafed hurriedly through his find. The book, he saw, was filled with notes . . . closely written notes. What had seemed to a sheaf of papers was a map.

He whistled softly as he unfolded it. A map of the British Isles, showing hundreds of R.A.F. stations, a plain sign guide for an attempt to knock out the British air arm.

Studying it, he shuddered as he realized what such a map, in German hands, would mean. With that map, the Luftwaffe could deal a terrible blow to the R.A.F. That far-flung system of small bases, decentralizing the nation's aerial forces, was it best insurance against a death smash by the Nazi fleet. Without the map it would take Goering's tribe half a hundred years to hunt out and destroy, one by one, all those bases.

But with the map . . .

Douglas jerked his head up sharply. The Messerschmitt was coming back again!

The mutter rose into a hum and the hum became a roar. Stuffing the map into his pocket, Douglas sprinted for the Hurricane. Let that Messerschmitt catch him in the open and there'd be two dead men lying in the field.

Breath whistling in his throat, heart pounding furiously, he made the plane, scrambled into the cockpit and slammed the throttle up the rack. The idling prop swelled into a swirl of noise and power. The ship leaped forward and Douglas hauled back viciously on the stick.

The M.E.'s motors were a yell of hate behind him even as he cleared the treetops. He hunched his shoulders, expecting a hail of steel, almost feeling the breath of the Jerry's guns upon him.

The guns whipped out . . . too late. He felt the thud of bullets smack into his ship, but he was in a steep climb now, moving out of range. Grimly he held the Hurricane's nose almost straight up, watching the altimeter climb. Below him, he knew, the Messerschmitt must be climbing to get him. He snapped one quick look over the side, saw the Nazi ship off to his right. Giving the Hurricane the last notch on the rack, he looped and dived. With a wild yell of exultation, he snapped the ship straight at the Messerschmitt.

His finger touched the firing button and the Brownings yapped. Metal flew in showers from one of the M.E.'s wings. Trees were rushing up at him and he yanked the stick. The Hurricane groaned and whipped around just above the branches.

A storm of tracers slapped into the fuselage and he laughed wildly as he looped again and came down upon the Jerry.

There was no miss this time . . . no futile chewing of wings. He saw splintered glass flying as the Brownings raked the cockpit of the ship below him.

It wasn't until he was far above the field and headed west that he realized his brain had failed to tick. There had been no calculation, no aversion to taking chances, no grimness. It was like the old days when he and Bob and Grant had battled at Dunkerque. He had fought by pure instinct alone, had downed his plane almost in the treetops.

He touched his pockets, heard the crinkling of the map when his fingers touched it.

Intelligence would be glad to see that map and hear his story. Intelligence undoubtedly would do something about it . . . for Grant could not have been the only one, there must have been others. Probably those had been the ones Grant had been sneaking off to London to see. Maybe the girl the boys had kidded him about back in the mess might be one of them.

But Intelligence was close-mouthed and the squadron would never know. And that was best, for Grant was a hero . . . and right now Britain needed all the heroes it could get . . . alive or dead.

His own report? That wasn't hard to figure out. He could see it now:

"Flight Lieutenant Richard Grant met his death heroically, attempting to ride a crippled ship to earth."

THE END

THE SPACE-BEASTS

After being rejected by Astounding Science Fiction and Amazing Stories *in 1939,* Astonishing Science Fiction *paid Clifford Simak $42.50 for "The Flame in Space" and published it in April 1940. Cliff's journal shows that the sale was made after he sent it to Frederik Pohl, but it's not clear whether Pohl was the editor of* Astonishing *or was acting as an agent—that issue of* Astonishing *did not list an editor's name.*

This is one of a number of Simak stories that features music in space; but its spiritual element makes it seem like more than a mere space opera.

—dww

Chapter One
The Flame in Space

It wasn't possible . . . but there it was! A thing that hung in space on shimmering wings of supernal light. Wings that had about them that same elusive suggestion of life and motion as one sees in the slow crawl of a mighty river. Wings that were veined with red markings and flashed greenly in the rays of the distant Sun.

The body of the thing seemed to writhe with light and for a fleeting moment Captain Johnny Lodge caught sight of the incredible head . . . a head that was like nothing he had ever seen before. Ahead that had about it the look of unadulterated evil and primal cruelty.

He heard Karen Franklin, standing beside him, draw in her breath and hold it in her wonder.

"It's a Space Beast," said George Foster, assistant pilot. "It can't be anything else."

That was true. It couldn't be anything else. But it violated all rules of life and science. It was something that shouldn't have happened, a thing that was ruled out by the yardstick of science. Yet, there it was, straight ahead of them, pacing the *Karen,* one of the solar system's finest rocket-ships, with seeming ease.

"It just seemed to come out of nowhere," said George. "I think it must have passed the ship. Flew over us and then dipped down. I can't imagine what those wings are for, because it travels on a rocket principle. See, there it blasts again."

A wisp of whitish gas floated in space behind the winged beast and swiftly dissipated. The beast shot rapidly ahead, green wings glinting in the weak sunlight.

Karen Franklin moved closer to Captain Johnny Lodge. She looked up at him and there was something like fear in her deep blue eyes.

"That means," she said, "that those stories about the Belt are true. The stories the meteor miners tell."

Johnny nodded gravely. "They must be true," he said. "At least part of them."

He turned back to the vision port and watched the thing. A Space Beast! He had heard tales of Space Beasts, but had set them down as just one of those wild yarns which come from the far corners of the Solar System.

The Asteroid Belt was one of those far corners. Practically a No-Man's Land. Dangerous to traverse, unfriendly to life, impossible to predict. Little was known about it, for space ships shunned it for good cause. The only ones who really did know it were the asteroid miners and they were a tribe almost apart from the rest of the men who ventured through the void.

The Space Beast was real. There was no denying that. Johnny rubbed his eyes and looked again. It was still there, dead ahead.

Protoplasm couldn't live out there. It was too cold and there was no atmosphere. Protoplasm . . . that was the stumbling block. All known life was based on protoplasm, but did it necessarily follow that life must be based on protoplasm? Protoplasm, of itself, wasn't life. Life was something else, a complex phenomenon of change and motion. Life was a secret thing, hard to come at. Scientists, pushing back the barriers to their knowledge, had come very close to it and yet it always managed to elude them. They had found and defined that misty borderline one side of which was life, the other side where life had not as yet occurred. That borderline was the determining point, the little hypothetical area where life took shape and form and motion. But just because in the so-far known Solar System it had always expressed itself in protoplasm, did it necessarily mean it must always express itself in protoplasm?

He watched the metallic glitter of an asteroid off their port. It was only a few miles distant and it would pass well over them, but the sight of the thing gave him the creeps. Those barren rocks reflected little light. Hard to see, they rushed through space on erratic orbits and at smashing speeds. At times one could locate them only by the blotting out of stars.

"Karen," he said, "maybe we should turn back. It was foolish of us to try. Your Dad won't blame us. I don't like the look of things." He swept his hand out toward the soaring Space Beast.

She shook her head, obstinately. "Dad would have come himself, long ago, if it hadn't been for the accident. He'd be with us now if the doctors would let him take to space again." She looked into Johnny's face solemnly. "We mustn't let him down," she said.

"But rumors!" Johnny cried. "We've been chasing rumors. Rumors that have sent us to the far corners of the system. To Io and to Titan and even in close to the Sun seeking a mythical planet."

"Johnny," she asked, "you aren't afraid, are you?"

He was silent for a time, but finally he said: "For you and for the boys back there."

She didn't answer, but turned back to the vision plate again, staring out into the velvet black of space, watching the Space Beast and the shimmer of nearby rocks, the debris of the Belt.

He growled in his throat, watching the Beast, his brain a mad whirl of thoughts.

Metal Seven had started the whole thing. Five years ago old Jim Franklin, one of the system's most intrepid explorers and space adventurers, had found Metal Seven on Ganymede . . . just one little pocket of it, enough for half a dozen space ships. Search had failed to reveal more. Five years of hectic search throughout the system had not unearthed a single pound of the precious mineral.

Its value lay in its resistance to the radiations that poured through space. Space ships coated with a thin plating of Metal Seven acquired an effective radiation screen.

But few ships had such a screen . . . because Jim Franklin had found only enough for a few ships. The *Karen* had it, for the *Karen* was Franklin's ship, named after his only daughter. A millionaire back on Mars had paid a million dollars for enough to plate his pleasure yacht. One big passenger line had bought enough of the original find to plate two ships, but one of these had been lost and only one remained. The Terrestrial government had acquired the rest of the metal and locked it in well guarded vaults against possible need or use.

The sale of the mineral had made Jim Franklin a rich man, but a large portion of the money had been invested in the search for more extensive deposits of Metal Seven.

Two years ago Franklin, on one of his rare returns to Earth from space, had visited a rocket factory to watch some tests. A rocket tube exploded. Three men were killed . . . Jim Franklin was saved only by a miracle of surgery. But he was Earth-bound, his body twisted and broken. His physicians had warned him that he would die if he ever took to space again.

So today his daughter, Karen Franklin, carried on the Franklin tradition and the Franklin search for Metal Seven. A search that had taken the sturdy little ship far in toward the Sun, that had landed it on the surface of unexplored Titan, had driven it, creaking and protesting against the tremendous drag of Jupiter's gravity, down to little Io, until then unvisited by any rocket-ship. A search that was now taking it into the heart of the Asteroid Belt, following the trail pointed by the mad tale of a leering little man who had talked to Karen Franklin at the Martian port of Sandebar.

It might have been an accident . . . just that one little pocket of Metal Seven found on Ganymede. There might be no more in the solar system. Special conditions, some extraordinary set of circumstances might have deposited just enough for half a dozen ships.

But it didn't seem right. Somewhere in the system, on some frigid rock of space, there must be more of Metal Seven, enough to protect every ship that plowed through space. A magic metal, screening out the vicious radiations that continually streamed through space without rhyme or reason, eliminating the menace of those deadly little swarms of radioactive meteors which swooped down out of nowhere to engulf a ship and leave it a drifting hulk filled with dead and dying.

Karen's voice roused him from his thoughts, "Johnny, I

thought I saw a light. Could that be possible? Would there be any lights out here?"

Johnny started, saying nothing, staring through the vision plate.

"There it goes!" cried George. "I saw it."

"I saw it again, too," said Karen. "Like a blue streak way ahead of us."

A tremulous voice spoke from the doorway of the control room. "Is it a light you are seeing, Johnny?"

Johnny swung around and saw Old Ben Ramsey. He was clad in a bulky work suit and his twisted face and gnarled hands were grease-streaked.

"Yes, Ben," said Johnny. "There's something out ahead."

Ben wagged his head. "Strange things I've heard about the Belt. Mighty strange things. The Flame That Burns in Space and the Space Beasts and the haunts that screech and laugh and dance in glee when a rock comes whizzing down and cracks a shell wide open."

He dragged his slow way across the room, his feet scraping heartbreakingly, hunching and hobbling forward, a shamble rather than a walk.

Johnny watched him and dull pity flamed within his heart. Radiations had done that to Old Ben. The only man left alive after his ship hit a swarm of radioactive meteors. Metal Seven could have saved him . . . if there had been any Metal Seven then. Metal Seven, the wonder metal that screened out the death that moved between the planets.

"I saw it again!" yelled George. "Just a flash, like a blue light blinking."

"It's the Flame that burns in space," Old Ben said, his bright eyes glowing with excitement. "I've heard wild tales about the Flame and Space Beasts, but I never really did believe them."

"Start believing in them, then," said Johnny grimly, "because there's a Space Beast out there, too."

Old Ben's face twisted and he fumbled his greasy cap with misshapen, greasy hands. "You don't say, Johnny?"

Johnny nodded. "That's right, Ben."

The old man stood silent for a moment, shuffling his feet.

"I forgot, Johnny. I came up to report. I loaded the fuel chambers and checked everything, like you told me to. Everything is ship-shape."

"We're going deeper into the Belt," said Johnny. "Into a sector that is taboo to the miners. You couldn't hire one of them to come in here. So be sure everything is ready for prompt action."

Ben mumbled a reply, shuffling away. But at the door he stopped and turned around.

"You know that contraption I picked up at the sale in Sandebar?" he said. "That thing I bought sight unseen?"

Johnny nodded. It was one of the jokes of the ship. Old Ben had bought it in the famous Martian market, bought it because of the weird carvings on the box which enclosed it. Somehow or other, those carvings had intrigued the old man, touched some responsive chord of wonder deep in his soul. But the machine inside the box was even more weird . . . an assembly of discs and flaring pipes, an apparatus that had no conceivable purpose or function. Old Ben claimed it was a musical instrument of unknown origin and despite the friendly jibes and bickering of the other crew members he stuck to that theory.

"I was just thinking," said Old Ben. "Maybe that danged thing plays by radiations."

Johnny grinned. "Maybe it does at that."

The old man turned and shuffled out.

Chapter Two
Attack!

The ship careened and bucked as George blasted with port tubes to duck a wicked chunk of rock that suddenly loomed in their path. Johnny saw the needle-like spires as the asteroid swung below them, spires that would have sheared the ship as a knife cuts cheese.

There was no doubt now that the flash they had sighted actually was a light. They could see it, a streak of blue that arced briefly across the vision port, lending its surroundings a bluish tint.

"It's an asteroid," declared George, "and our little friend is heading right for it."

What he had said was true. The Space Beast had gained on them but was still almost directly ahead, apparently moving in toward the distant light.

The *Karen* drove on with flaming tubes. The meteoric screens flared again and again, in short flashes and long ripples, as tiny debris of the Belt struck like speeding bullets and were blasted into harmless gas.

"Johnny," asked George, "what are we going to do?"

"Keep going," said Johnny. "Head for the blue light. We want to see what it is if we can. But be ready to sheer off and give it all you've got at the first sign of danger."

He looked at Karen for confirmation of the decision. She nodded at him with a half-smile, her eyes bright . . . the kind of brightness that had shown in the eyes of old Jim Franklin when his fists knotted around the controls as his ship thundered down toward new terrain or nosed outward into unexplored space.

Hours later they were within a few miles of the asteroid. Minutes before the weird Space Beast had dived for the surface, was roosting on one of the rocky spires that hemmed in the little valley where the light flamed in blue intensity.

Speechless, Johnny stared down at the scene. The flame was not a flame at all. Not a flame in the sense that it burned. Rather it was a glowing crown that hovered over a massive pyramid.

But it was not the flame, nor the roosting Beast of Space, nor even the fact that here was an old tale come to life which held Johnny's attention. It was the pyramid. For a pyramid is something which never occurs naturally. Nature has never achieved a straight line and a pyramid is all straight lines.

"It's uncanny," he whispered.

"Johnny," came George's hoarse whisper, "look over that highest peak. Just above it."

Johnny lined his vision over the peak, saw something flash dully. A shimmering flash that looked like steel reflecting light.

He squinted his eyes, trying to force his sight just a little farther out into the black. For an instant, just a fleeting instant, he saw what it was.

"A ship!" he shouted.

George nodded, his face grim.

"There's two or three out there," he declared. "I saw them a minute ago. See, there's one of them now."

He pointed and Johnny saw the ship. For a moment it seemed to roll, catching the shine from the blue light atop the pyramid.

Johnny's lips compressed tightly. The skin seemed to stretch, like dry parchment, over his face.

"Derelicts," he said, and George nodded.

Karen had turned from the vision plate and was staring at them. For the first time there was terror on her face. Her cheeks were white and her lips bloodless. Her words were little more than a whisper: "Derelicts! That means . . ."

Johnny nodded, finishing the sentence: "Something happened."

A nameless dread reached out and struck at them. Alien fear creeping in from the mysterious reaches of the Asteroid Belt.

"Johnny," said George quietly, "we better be getting out of here."

Karen screamed even as Johnny leaped for the controls.

Through the panel he saw what had frightened her. Another Space Beast had swept across their vision . . . and another . . . and another. Suddenly the void seemed to be filled with them.

Mad thoughts hammered in his brain as he reached for the levers. Something had happened to those other ships! Something that had left them drifting hulks, derelicts that had taken up an orbit around the asteroid with its flame-topped pyramid. This was an evil place with its derelicts and its Space Beasts and its flaming stones. No wonder the miners shunned it!

His right hand shoved the lever far over and the rockets thundered. The ship was shaking, as if it was being tossed about by winds in space, as if something had it in its teeth and was worrying it.

Johnny felt the blood drain from his face. For an instant his heart seemed to stand stock still.

There was something wrong. Something was happening to the ship!

He heard the screech of shearing metal, the shriek of suddenly released atmosphere, the crunching of stubborn beams and girders.

His straining ears caught the thud of emergency bulkheads automatically slamming into place.

The rocket motors no longer responded and he snatched his eyes away from the control panel to glance through the vision plate.

The ship was falling toward the asteroid! Directly below loomed the little valley of the pyramid. From where he stood he could look straight down into the glare of the blue light.

A great wing, a wing of writhing flame, swept quarteringly across the vision plate. For a moment the cabin was lighted with a weird green and blue . . . the gleaming instruments reflecting the light from the wing and the pyramid flame. Weird shadows danced and crawled over the walls, over the whiteness of the watching faces.

The Space Beast veered off, volplaning down toward the flame. Johnny caught his breath. The Beast was monstrous! Cold shivers raced up and down his spine. His flesh crawled.

From the creature's beak hung a mass of twisted steel, bent and mangled girders ripped from the *Karen's* frame. Gripped in its talons, or what should have been its talons, was an entire rocket assembly.

The *Karen* was plunging now, streaking down toward the asteroid, headed straight for the pyramid.

In the brief second before the crash Johnny recreated what had happened. Like a swift motion picture it ran across his brain. The Beast had attacked the ship, had ripped its rear assembly apart, had torn out the rocket tubes, had plucked out braces and girders as if they had been straws. The *Karen* was falling to destruction. It would pile up down in that little valley, a useless mass of wreckage. It would mark where its crew had died. For most of the others back there must be dead already . . . and only seconds of life remained for him and the other two.

The ship struck the pyramid's side a glancing blow, metal howling against the stone. The *Karen* looped, end over end, struck its shattered tail on the rocky valley floor and toppled.

Johnny picked himself out of the corner where he had been thrown by the impact. He was dazed and blood was flowing into his eyes from a cut across his forehead. Half blinded, he groped his way across the tilted floor.

He was alive! The thought sang across his consciousness and left him weak with wonder. No man could have hoped to live through that crash, but he was still alive . . . alive and able to claw his way across the slanting floor.

He listened for the hiss of escaping air, but there was no hiss. The cabin was still air-tight.

Hands reached out and hosted him to his feet. He grasped the back of the anchored pilot's chair and hung on tightly. Through the red mist that swam before his eyes he saw George's face. The lips shaped words:

"How are you, Johnny?"

"I'm all right," Johnny mumbled. "Never mind about me. Karen!"

"She's okay," said George.

Johnny wiped his forehead and gazed around. Karen was leaning against a canted locker.

She spoke softly, almost as if she were talking to herself.

"We won't get out of here. We can't possibly. We're here to stay. And back on Earth, and on Mars and Venus, they will wonder what happened to Karen Franklin and Captain Johnny Lodge."

Johnny let go of the chair back and skated dizzily across the floor to where she leaned against the locker. He shook her roughly by the shoulder.

"Snap out of it," he urged. "We got to make a try."

Her eyes met his.

"You think we have a chance?"

He smiled, a feeble smile.

"What do you think?" he challenged.

She shook her head. "We're stuck here. We'll never leave."

"Maybe," he agreed, "but we aren't giving up before we try. Let's get into suits and go out. There are radiations out there, but we'll be safe. There's Metal Seven in those suits and Metal Seven seems to be screening it out in here all right."

Karen jerked her head toward the rear of the ship.

"The men back there," she said.

Johnny shook his head. "Not a chance," he told her.

George was opening another locker and taking out suits. He stopped now and looked at Johnny.

"You say there's radiations out there," he said. "You mean the Flame is radiation?"

"It couldn't be anything else," said Johnny. "How else could you explain it?"

"That's what happened to those other ships," declared George. "They couldn't screen out the radiation. It killed the crews and the ships took up an orbit around the asteroid. We were all right because we had the Metal Seven screen. But the Beast came along and ruined us. So here we are."

Johnny stiffened, struck by a thought.

"Those ships out there," he said, speaking slowly, his voice cold with suppressed excitement. "Some of them might be undamaged, might be made to operate."

George stared.

"Don't get your hopes up, Johnny," he cautioned. "They're probably riddled with meteors."

"We could patch them up," said Johnny. "Seal off the pilot room and stay there. We'd be safe in the suits until we got it fixed."

Chapter Three
Beasts of the Pyramid

The valley of the Pyramid was a nightmare place. A place of alien beauty, lit by the blue radiations that lapped, flame-like, around the tip of the massive monument of masonry. Weird and eerie, with a quality that set one's teeth on edge.

An outpost of hell, Johnny told himself. Lonely and forbidding, with the near horizon of jagged peaks and rocky pinnacles lancing against the black of space. A puddle of blue light holding back the emptiness and blackness of surrounding void. The rocks caught up the shine of the Flame and glowed softly, almost as if endowed with a brilliance of their own. The blue light caught and shattered into a million dancing motes against the drifts of eternally frozen gases, evidence of an ancient atmosphere which lay in the rifts and gullies that traversed the peaks hemming in the valley.

Hunched things squatted on the peaks. Imps of space. Things that resembled nothing Man had ever seen before. The Beasts, no two alike, squatting like malevolent demons keeping silent watch. Mind-shattering forms made even more horrible by the play of light and shadow, like devils circling the pit and speculating darkly upon the punishments to be meted out.

"It's pretty terrible, isn't it," said Karen Franklin and her voice was none too steady.

One of the things spread its wings and lifted from a peak. They could see the cloud of whitish vapor which shot from the "rocket tubes" and lifted it into space. It soared toward the Flame, hovered for a moment above it and then dipped down, almost into the play of bluish light.

Karen cried out and Johnny stared, unbelieving. For the thing was changing! In the shifting light of the radiations it was actually taking on new form! Old features of its appearance dropped away and new ones appeared. The face of the Beast, seen clearly in the light, seemed to vanish like a snatched-off mask. For a moment it was faceless, featureless . . . and then the new features began to form. Features that were even more horrible than the ones before. Features that had cold fury and primal evil stamped upon them. The wings shimmered and changed and the body was undergoing metamorphosis.

"Mutation," Johnny said, his voice brittle with the terror of the moment. "The Flame mutates those things. A sort of re-birth. From all regions of Space they come to get new bodies, perhaps new vitality. The Flame is the feeding grounds, the source of nourishment, the place of rejuvenation for them."

Another Beast shot down from the blackness that crowded close over the valley, skimmed lightly for a peak and came to perch.

Thoughts banged against one another in Johnny's skull.

Mutations! That meant then, the Flame was a source of life. That it held within its core a quality that could renew life . . . perhaps, a startling thought . . . even create life. Back on Earth men had experimented with radiations, had caused mutations in certain forms of life. This was the same thing, but on a greater scale.

"A solar Fountain of Youth," said George, almost echoing Johnny's thoughts.

The pyramid, then, had been built for a purpose. But who had built it? What hands had carried and carved and piled those stones? What brain had conceived the idea of planting here in space a flame that would burn through the watches of many millennia?

Surely not those things squatting on the peaks! Perhaps some strange race forgotten for a million years. Perhaps a people who were more than human beings.

And had it been built for the purpose for which it was now being used? Might it not be a beacon light placed to guide home a wandering tribe? Or a mighty monument to commemorate some deed or some event or some great personage?

"Look out!" shrieked George.

Automatically Johnny's hand swept down to his belt and cleared the blaster. He swung the weapon up and saw the Space Beast plunging at them. It seemed almost on top of them. Blindly he depressed the firing button and the blaster slammed wickedly against the heel of his hand. Swaths of red stabbed upward. George was firing too, and Johnny could hear Karen sobbing in breathless haste as she tried to clear her weapon.

Inferno raged above their heads as the beams from the weapons met the plunging horror. The body of the thing burst into glowing flame, but through the glow they still could see the darkness of its outline. The blast from the guns slowed it, so that it hung over them, caught in the cross-fire of the blazing weapons.

Suddenly it shot upward, out of the range of the guns. Shaken by the attack, they watched it flame though space, as if in mortal agony, twisting and turning, writhing against the black curtain that pressed upon the asteroid.

Another Beast was dropping from a pinnacle, shooting toward them. And another. Once again the beams lashed out and caught the things, slowed them, halted them, made them retreat, flaming entities dancing a death fandango above the blue-tipped pyramid.

"This won't do," said Johnny quietly. "They'll coop us up inside the ship. They'd attack us if we tried to take off in the emergency boat to reach one of the ships up there."

He stared around the horizon, at the roosting Beasts hunched on the jagged rim. Men, he realized, were intruders here. They were treading on forbidden ground, perhaps on sacred ground. The Beasts resented them, quite naturally. He seemed to hear the subdued rustling of wings, wings of flame sounding across countless centuries.

Wings! That was it. He knew there was something incongruous about the Beasts. And that was it . . . their wings. Wings were useless in space. They had no function and yet the Beasts spread them exactly like the winged things in Earth's atmosphere. He racked his brain. Might those wings, after all, have some definite purpose or were they mere relics of some other life, some different abode? Might not the Beasts have been driven from some place where there was an atmosphere? Had they been forced to adapt themselves to space? Or were the wings only for occasional use when the things plummeted down upon the worlds of Man and other earth-bound things?

Johnny shuddered, remembering the old dragon myths, the old tales of flying dragons, back on Earth. Had these things once visited Earth? Had they given rise to those old tales out of mankind's dim antiquity?

He jerked his mind back, with an effort, to the problem at hand. He had to take up the emergency boat and find a ship. From among all those derelicts there certainly would be several that still would operate, would take them from this hell-lit slab of rock. But with the Beasts standing guard there wasn't a chance.

Perhaps, if all of them could get into the emergency boat they could make a dash for it and trust to luck. But there was only room for one.

If there were only a way. If Old Ben were only alive. Old Ben could think of some way. Old Ben, with his shuffling walk and twisting face. He closed his eyes and a vision of Old Ben seemed to form within his brain. The twisted lips moved. *"I am here, Johnny."*

Johnny jumped, for the words had actually rung within his brain. Not spoken words, but thought even louder than the words themselves.

Chapter Four
Mutation of Old Ben

"Who said that?" asked Karen sharply.

"It's Old Ben, ma'm," said the soundless voice. "Old Ben is speaking to you."

"But Ben," protested Johnny, "it can't be you. You were back in the engine room. You're . . ."

"Sure, Johnny," said the voice. "You think I'm dead and probably I am. I must be dead."

Johnny shivered. There was something wrong here. Something terribly wrong. Dead men didn't talk.

"It was the radiations," said Old Ben. "They changed me into something else. Into something that you can't see. But I can see you. As if you were far away."

"Ben . . . ," Karen cried but the soundless words silenced her.

"It's hard to talk. I have to hurry. I haven't any mouth to talk with. Nothing like I used to have. But I'm alive . . . more alive than I have ever been. I *think* at you. And that is hard."

Johnny sensed the struggle in the thoughts that hammered at his brain. Inside the helmet perspiration dripped down his forehead and ran in trickling streams along his throat. Unconsciously he tried to help Old Ben . . . or the thing that once had been Old Ben.

"The musical instrument," said Old Ben, the thoughts unevenly spaced. "The musical instrument I brought in Sandebar. Get it and open the box."

They waited but there was nothing more.

"Ben!" cried Johnny.

"Yes, Johnny."

"Are you all right, Ben? Is there anything we can do?"

"No lad, there isn't. I'm happy. I have no mangled body to drag around. No face to keep all streaked with grease so it won't look so bad. I'm free! I can go any place I want to go. I can be everywhere at once. Any place I want to be. And there are others here. So I won't be lonesome."

"Wait a minute, Ben!" Johnny shrieked, but there was no answer. They waited and the silence of space hung like a heavy curtain all about them. The valley was a place of silence and of weird blue light that sent shadows dancing.

George was running for the shattered stern of the ship. Johnny wheeled to follow him.

He shouted at Karen:

"Get back into the lock and wait for us. You'll be safe there."

The two men climbed through the gaping hole the Beast had torn. Carefully, torturously, they made their way through the twisted girders and battered plates. The engine room was a mass of wreckage, but there were no bodies.

"The radiations," said George. "It changed all of them into the kind of things . . . well, into whatever Old Ben is."

Thoughts ran riot in Johnny's brain. Radiations that changed life. Changing Beasts into other shapes and forms. Changing men into entities that could not be seen, entities that had no bodies but could go anywhere they pleased, could be any place they wanted to, or in all places at the same time!

If the worst came to the worst there was still a way of escape! Still a way open to them. A doorway it would take courage to cross, but it was there. A doorway to another way, to another form of life, to a life that might be better than the one they had. Old Ben said he was happy . . . and that was all that mattered. Just strip off their suits and walk unprotected into the full glare of the light.

He cursed at himself, savagely. That wasn't the way to do things. If it happened and one couldn't help it . . . all right. But to do it deliberately . . . that was something else. Perhaps, if all else failed, if there was no other way . . .

They found the box containing the strange musical instrument and between them they lugged it out. Despite the lesser gravity it was heavy and hard to handle.

Outside, in front of the lock, they pried up the lid. Instantly, music filled all of space. Not music in the sense that it was sound, but a rhythmic pulse and beat that one could sense. Music that filled the heart with yearning, music that made one want to dance, music that plucked and pulled at the heartstrings with tripping, silvery fingers. Sobbing notes and clear, high notes that rang like the gladsome clanging of a bell, rippling music like wind across the water and sonorous chords like the bellowing of a drum. Music that swelled and swelled, reaching out and out, appealing to all emotions, crying for understanding.

Johnny saw the astonished oval of Karen's face through the helmet plate.

She saw him looking at her. "How lovely!" she cried.

"It's the radiations again," said George, breathlessly. "Old Ben was right. The thing plays by radiation."

"Look at the Beasts!" Johnny shouted.

The Beasts were shuffling toward them, hopping and running, sliding down from their perches on the soaring pinnacles, racing across the boulder jumbled valley floor.

George and Johnny lifted their guns from the holsters and waited. The Beasts advanced and stopped, forming a half circle in front of the wrecked ship. Every line of their gruesome bodies had assumed a pose of rapt attention. They did not even seem to see the Earthmen. Motionless, as if carven from stone, they listened to the swelling paean that swept up and out of the metal box.

Johnny let out his breath, slowly. But he still kept a tight grip upon the gun. The Beasts seemed to be hypnotized, held entranced by the music that poured from out the radiation instrument.

Johnny spoke softly to the others: "As long as the music lasts it will keep them quiet. Keep in the lock and watch. Don't take any chances."

"What are you going to do?" asked Karen, sharp anxiety in her voice.

"There's one emergency boat left," said Johnny. "All the others are smashed. I'm taking it up and see about the ships. They are our only chance."

"I'll help you," offered George.

Johnny turned to face Karen. "Please take care of yourself."

She nodded. "And you, Johnny. You take care of yourself, too."

The ship was old . . . a thousand years at least, but it seemed to be serviceable. The hull appeared in good shape. The rocket tubes were intact. A meteor had drilled a hole as big as a man's hand through the pilot cabin. But it had missed the instruments and it would not be too big a job to patch the holes. Probably there were other similar holes through the rest of the ship but they wouldn't matter unless the rocketing projectiles had smashed the machinery. The machinery in a ship of this sort was elemental. Mostly fuel tanks, combustion chamber and tubes. No niceties.

Johnny walked to the control board and grinned as he looked over the instruments and controls. Not much to them. In the days when this craft had set out to sail the void a space ship was a rocket pure and simple . . . nothing else.

But the ship was the best he had found so far. He had visited three others and all three were damaged beyond repair. The fuel tanks had been smashed in one. In another the control panel had been shattered by a tiny bit of whizzing stone and the third had one of the rockets sheared off.

Johnny walked back to the open lock and peered down at the asteroid. The valley where the pyramid was situated was just coming over the horizon and the light from the flame made it appear that dawn had just arrived on the little world.

He whirled from the lock and went to the door communicating with the stern of the ship. He'd have to look over the fuel tanks and other machinery, make sure that everything was all right. And he had to hurry. Johnny could imagine what was going on in the minds of the two he had left in the flame-lit valley. The speculation and apprehension, the pitting of hope against hope.

The door creaked open and Johnny stepped through into the living quarters.

The room looked lived in. After all these years it appeared as it must have that day nearly a thousand years before when the men who drove the ship had dared come into the Belt, had left their course to investigate the Flame in Space. They had been trapped, exactly as the crews of all those other ships had been trapped. Caught by radiations that turned them into something that didn't have human form, although human thoughts and aspirations and human hope might still remain. Adventurers all . . . men who felt within them the lure of the unknown, men who had dared to come and see and hadn't been able to get back again.

Broken dishes and crockery lay on the floor, where they had been swept off the table or hurled from the shelving by the rocking of the ship, by the shock of hammering debris. The bunks were unmade, exactly as they had been left when the men had tumbled out to rush forward and look out through the vision plate at the mystery which loomed ahead.

A strange tingle of fear rippled along Johnny's spine. He stopped and listened, looking around.

His hand slid down to the butt of his blaster.

Then he laughed, a throaty laugh. Getting jittery in an old ship. There wasn't anything here. There couldn't be anything here. Nothing except the ghosts of the men who had manned the craft ten centuries ago. He shuddered at the thought. Could it be possible that the ghosts of the old crew were still here? Was it possible that the things they had been turned into by the radiations still hovered in this room, keeping eternal watch?

He cursed at his fears and strode forward but fear still rode upon his shoulder, a little jeering fear that taunted him and yelped in hideous glee.

The fuel tanks were intact, the combustion chamber seemed undamaged. His inspection of the ship from the emergency boat had assured him that the tubes were unhurt. The ship could be navigated.

Back in the living quarters he stopped momentarily, his eyes lighting on a desk. The ship's log would be kept there. He had just time for a peek. Find out something about the ship. The name of its captain, the identity of the men who had served under him, its ports of call, its home port back on Earth.

He hesitated. The desk drew him like a magnet. He took a swift step forward and slammed into something. Something that yielded to the touch, but with a sense of terrible strength.

Heart in his throat, he backed away. He felt his legs and arms grow cold as ice, the muscles of his abdomen squeezing in, the sudden surge of fear hazing his brain. But his reflexes were at work. Like an automaton, he reacted to the spur of danger. His right hand swept the blaster free and he paced backward, on the alert, like a retreating cat, poised for instant action.

He felt his way through the door into the pilot cabin, backed warily for the open port. But there he stopped. Maybe he had imagined he ran into something back there in the living quarters. Maybe there wasn't anything at all. Space sometimes did queer things to a man. He needed this ship . . . Karen and George back on the asteroid needed it. He couldn't let himself be scared away by wild imaginings.

He swung slightly around to look out the valve. The valley of the pyramid was turned broadside to the ship. He strained his eyes trying to make out the wreckage that lay at the base of the pyramid, but the valley was full of shadows that flickered and would not be still and he could see no details.

Swinging around, he stepped forward and ran squarely into an invisible wall that yielded and tried to suck him in. Savagely, he fought free, threshing his arms, kicking with his heavy boots. Teetering on the edge of the valve, he brought the blaster up and pressed the firing button. The red tongue of flame lapped out and mushroomed. Inside the cabin something suddenly blazed into form. For a sickening instant he caught sight of a monstrous form, a nauseating mass of writhing shape.

A thread of sharp, red knowledge snaked through his brain. Some invisible monster of space had taken refuge in the ship, had laired within it, had made of it a home. Invisible until the breath of the gun had reached and scorched it and then the flaring flame had outlined its obscenity.

He tottered and fell backward into space. Floating away from the ship he saw the thing inside, a mass of blazing light, fighting to get through the open valve. With a curse between his teeth he trained the blaster on the port and pushed the button down full power. The kick of the gun hurled him backward, end over end.

Swinging slowly over he saw the portholes in the living quarters of the ship flare with light.

The thing, in its dying throes, was running madly through the ship.

He lost sight of the ship. Then invisible hands lifted him and flung him away. As he spun he caught a glimpse of a mighty flame blossoming in blackness . . . flame that leaped out and curled and reached for him with fiery fingers in all directions.

The ship had exploded! There must have been a tiny crack in one of the fuel tanks and the blazing monster had rushed into the engine room. In one shattering instant the fuel tanks had exploded. A soundless explosion that tore the ship to fragments, that sent blue and yellow flames tonguing out into the blackness of the void.

He was slowing down. By judicious use of the blaster he righted himself, stopped the spin into which the explosion had thrown him.

He shook his head to clear his thoughts.

The ship was gone. So was the emergency boat.

And he, himself, was trapped in empty space.

Chapter Five
Alone in Space

Looking down over the toes of his space-boots, he could see the asteroid, the valley a-glow with the shimmer of the flame. Down there waited two people, who had depended on him. Ones who had waited while he went out. Now he had failed them.

Bitterness rose in his throat and filled his mouth. His mind seethed with terrible thought.

The least he could do would be to go back and die with them. He might be able to do it.

He lifted the blaster and looked at it. He could use it as a rocket, force himself down into the valley.

Calculating carefully, he aimed the gun and pressed the button gently. He moved as the gun flared. Steadily he drove down toward the asteroid. He shifted the angle of the gun slightly to correct his flight and pressed the firing button again.

But there was no kick against the heel of his hand. The gun was dead! He had used up its charge. Feverishly he searched the belt for another charge, but there was none. Usually there were three emergency charge clips, but someone had been careless.

He was still gliding, but he would fall short of his mark. The gravity of the asteroid would grip him, but not enough to draw him to the surface. He would fall into an orbit. Like the derelicts that whirled around it, he would become a satellite of the rock that flamed in space.

He closed his eyes and tried to fight off the certain knowledge of his fate. He might throw away the gun and that would give him some forward motion. He might strip the belt of all equipment and fling it away as well, but he was still too far away. There was nothing else but to face inevitable death.

Life and death in space! He laughed, a short, hard laugh. There was life in space despite the scoffing of the skeptics. Life as expressed in the Space Beasts and in the invisible thing back in the ship. No one knew how many other forms of life. Life clinging close to the Asteroid Belt, making pilgrimages to a flame that flared in space, lairing in old derelicts.

Life that might be formed of silica, but probably wasn't, for that wouldn't explain the sudden flaring of their tissues before the hot breath of the blasters. Probably some weird chemistry of space as yet undiscovered and undreamed of by Earthly scientists.

Myths of space. Stories told by crazy asteroid miners home from lonely trips. But myths based on fact. A flame that burned blue atop a pyramid. A flame that gave new life and mutated the form of living things. Perhaps the silent sentinels of all life within the solar system. Perhaps the great, eternal life force that maintained all life . . . perhaps so long as that flame burned there would be life. But when it was black and dead life would disappear. Radiations lancing out to all parts of the solar system, carrying the attribute, the gift of life.

Johnny laughed again. Maybe he'd go crazy out here, make dying easier. Out here it was easier to understand, to take the evidence of one's eyes on faith alone, easier to believe. And now there'd be another myth. The Myth of Music. The instrument down there would play on and on . . . perhaps as long as the blue light shimmered. A Lorelei of space, as asteroid siren!

Music that charmed monsters. He sobered at the thought. There might be . . . there must be some connection between the curious instrument and the flame, some connection, too, with the grotesque Beasts. Establish the inter-relationship of the three, the Music Box, the Flame, the Beasts and one would have a story. But a story that he, Johnny Lodge, would never know. For Johnny Lodge was going to die in space. A story, perhaps, that no one would ever know.

A red light twinkled on the surface of the asteroid, just above the valley of the flame. Again the red light flashed, a long rippling flash that moved upward, away from the surface. He watched it fascinated, wondering. Up and up it moved, a thin red pencil of flame driving outward from the rock.

The explanation hit him like a blow. Someone was using a blaster for a rocket, was coming out in space to look for him!

George! Good old George!

Hysterically he shouted the name. "George! Hey, George!"

But that was foolish. George would never hear him. It was a crazy thing to do . . . a foolhardy thing to do. Space was dark and a man was small. George would never find him . . . never.

But the light was driving straight toward him. George knew where he was . . . was coming out to get him. Then, sheepishly, Johnny remembered. The helmet light! Of course, that was it.

Limp with the realization that he was saved, Johnny waited.

The pencil of red moved swiftly, blinked out and failed to go on for long minutes, then resumed again, much nearer. The charge had burned out and George had inserted another one.

A space suit glowed in the flare of the advancing blaster flame. The flame shifted slightly and the shit drove toward him. Then the flame blinked out and the bloated suit was bearing down upon him. Johnny waited with outspread arms. His clutching fingers seized the belt of the oncoming suit and hung on. He dragged it close against him. He heard the rasp of steel fingers clutching at his own suit.

"George," said Johnny, "you were a damn fool. But thanks, anyhow."

Then the visors of the two suits came together and Johnny saw, not the face of George, but the face of Karen Franklin!

"You!" said Johnny.

"I had to come," said Karen. "George wanted to, but I made him stay. If I hadn't reached you . . . if something had happened, he would have come out and got you anyhow. But I had to make the first try."

"But why did you bother about me?" Johnny demanded fiercely. "I bungled everything. I found a ship and blew it up. I lost the emergency boat. I threw away the only chance we had."

"Stop," yelled Karen. "Johnny Lodge, you stop talking that way. We aren't licked yet. I brought extra charges. We can use the guns to travel and there are lots of other derelicts."

They stared through the helmet plates straight into each other's face.

"Karen," said Johnny soberly, "you're all right!"

"Is that all?" she asked.

"No," he said, "That isn't all. I love you."

Johnny straightened from examination of the controls. The ship would run. Probably take a lot of coaxing and tinkering along the way but they would make it if a big meteor didn't come along. He looked out of the vision plate and shook his fist at space. And it seemed to him that Space stirred and chuckled at the challenge.

"Johnny," came Karen's voice, "look what I found!"

Johnny clumped out of the pilot cabin into the living quarters. Probably an old book or an antique piece of furniture. She already had found a bunch of old magazines, published 500 years before, and a camera with a roll of exposed film that might still be good.

But it wasn't a book or a piece of furniture. Karen was standing at the top of the steps that ran down into the cargo space. Johnny hurried to her side. The hold was filled with glinting ore. Ore that glittered and sparkled and shimmered in the light of their helmet lamps. Unfamiliar ore. Ore that Johnny didn't recognize and he had seen a lot of ore in years of wandering through space.

He went down the stairs and picked up a lump, studying it closely.

"Gold?" asked Karen. "Silver?"

The breath sobbed in Johnny's throat.

"Neither one," he said. "It's Metal Seven!"

"Metal Seven!" she gasped, with a tremor in her voice. "Enough for dozens of ships!"

The log book would tell where the discovery had been made. Perhaps on some lonely asteroid . . . perhaps on one of Jupiter's moons . . . perhaps clear out on the system's rim.

Jim Franklin hadn't been the first man to discover Metal Seven. Intrepid space-men, 500 years ago, had mined a curious new ore and were bringing it home when disaster struck. And now, through the discovery of this ship, Jim Franklin's daughter would give to the world again the long-lost secret of that mine.

"We'll build another ship," said Karen. "We'll go out again and find it."

Johnny tossed the chunk of ore away and scrambled to his feet.

"You better go to the lock," he said, "and signal to George to come on out. He'll be watching."

"What are you going to do?" she asked.

Johnny grinned. "Get this old tub ready to move. Soon as George gets here we blast off. We're heading for Earth with the richest cargo any ship ever hauled through space."

CONTRAPTION

"Contraption" first appeared in Star Science Fiction Stories No. 1, *an original anthology created by Frederik Pohl for Ballantine Books, which published the volume in February 1953. This story illustrates the fact that a Simak tale can have the feel of having been set in "Simak Country" without the author actually using any place names to confirm it. Indeed, "Contraption" could have taken place just down the road from "A Death in the House."*

—dww

He found the contraption in a blackberry patch when he was hunting cows. Darkness was sifting down through the tall stand of poplar trees and he couldn't make it out too well and he couldn't spend much time to look at it because Uncle Eb had been plenty sore about his missing the two heifers and if it took too long to find them Uncle Eb more than likely would take the strap to him again and he'd had about all he could stand for one day. Already he'd had to go without his supper because he'd forgotten to go down to the spring for a bucket of cold water. And Aunt Em had been after him all day because he was so no-good at weeding the garden.

"I never saw such a trifling young'un in all my life," she'd shrill at him and then she'd go on to say that she'd think he'd have some gratitude for the way she and Uncle Eb had taken him in and saved him from the orphanage, but no, he never felt no gratitude at all, but caused all the trouble that he could and was lazy to boot and she declared to goodness she didn't know what would become of him.

He found the two heifers down in the corner of the pasture by the grove of walnut trees and drove them home, plodding along behind them, thinking once again about running away, but knowing that he wouldn't, because he had no place to go. Although, he told himself, most any place would be better than staying here with Aunt Em and Uncle Eb, who really were not his uncle and aunt at all, but just a couple of people who had took him in.

Uncle Eb was just finishing milking when he came into the barn, driving the two heifers before him, and Uncle Eb still was plenty sore about the way he'd missed them when he'd brought in the other cows.

"Here," said Uncle Eb, "you've fixed it so I had to milk my share and yours, too, and all because you didn't count the cows, the way I always tell you to so you'll be sure you got them all. Just to teach you, you can finish up by milking them there heifers."

So Johnny got his three-legged milk stool and a pail and he milked the heifers and heifers are hard things to milk, and skittish, too, and the red one kicked and knocked Johnny into the gutter, spilling the milk he had in the pail.

Uncle Eb, seeing this, took the strap down from behind the door and let Johnny have a few to teach him to be more careful and that milk represented money and then made him finish with his milking.

They went up to the house after that, Uncle Eb grumbling all the way about kids being more trouble than they're worth, and Aunt Em met them at the door to tell Johnny to be sure he washed his feet good before he went to bed because she didn't want him getting her nice clean sheets all dirty.

"Aunt Em," he said, "I'm awful hungry."

"Not a bite," she said, grim-lipped in the lamplight of the kitchen. "Maybe if you get a little hungry you won't go forgetting all the time."

"Just a slice of bread," said Johnny. "Without no butter or nothing. Just a slice of bread."

"Young man," said Uncle Eb, "you heard your aunt. Get them feet washed and up to bed."

"And see you wash them good," said Aunt Em.

So he washed his feet and went to bed and lying there, he remembered what he had seen in the blackberry patch and remembered, too, that he hadn't said a word about it because he hadn't had a chance to, what with Uncle Eb and Aunt Em taking on at him all the blessed time.

And he decided right then and there he wouldn't tell them what he'd found, for if he did they'd take it away from him the way they always did everything he had. And if they didn't take it away from him, they'd spoil it so there'd be no fun or satisfaction in it.

The only thing he had that was really his was the old pocket knife with the point broken off the little blade. There was nothing in the world he'd rather have than another knife to replace the one he had, but he knew better than to ask for one. Once he had, and Uncle Eb and Aunt Em had carried on for days, saying what an ungrateful, grasping thing he was and here they'd gone and taken him in off the street and he still wasn't satisfied, but wanted them to spend good money from a pocket knife. Johnny worried a good deal about them saying he'd been taken in off the street, because so far as he knew he'd never been on any street.

Lying there, in his bed, looking out the window at the stars, he got to wondering what it was he'd seen in the blackberry patch and he couldn't remember it very well because he hadn't seen it too well and there'd been no time to stop and look. But there were some funny things about it and the more he thought about it, the more he wanted to have a good look at it.

Tomorrow, he thought, I'll have a good look at it. Soon as I get a chance, tomorrow. Then he realized there'd be no chance tomorrow, for Aunt Em would have him out, right after morning chores, to weed the garden and she'd keep an eye on him and there'd be no chance to slip away.

He lay in bed and thought about it some more and it became as clear as day that if he wanted a look at it he'd have to go tonight.

He could tell, by their snoring, that Uncle Eb and Aunt Em were asleep, so he got out of bed and slipped into his shirt and britches and sneaked down the stairs, being careful to miss the squeaky boards. In the kitchen he climbed up on a chair to reach the box of matches atop the warming oven of the old woodburning stove. He took a fistful of matches, then reconsidered and put back all but half a dozen because he was afraid Aunt Em would notice if he took too many.

Outside the grass was wet and cold with dew and he rolled up his britches so the cuffs wouldn't get all soaked, and set off across the pasture.

Going through the woods there were some spooky places, but he wasn't scared too badly, although no one could go through the woods at night without being scared a little.

Finally he got to the blackberry patch and stood there wondering how he could get through the patch in the dark without ripping his clothes and getting his bare feet full of thorns. And, standing there, he wondered if what he'd seen was still there and all at once he knew it was, for he felt a friendliness come from it, as if it might be telling him that it still was there and not to be afraid.

He was just a little unnerved, for he was not used to friendliness. The only friend he had was Benny Smith, who was about his age, and he only saw Benny during school and then not all the time, for Benny was sick a lot and had to stay home for days on end. And since Benny lived way over on the other side of the school district, he never saw him during vacation time at all.

By now his eyes were getting a little used to the darkness of the blackberry path and he thought that he could see the darker outline of the thing that lay in there and he tried to understand how it could *feel* friendly, for he was pretty sure that it was just a thing, like a wagon or a silo-filler, and nothing alive at all. If he'd thought that it was alive, he'd been really scared.

The thing kept right on feeling friendly toward him.

So he put out his hands and tried to push the bushes apart so he could squeeze in and see what it was. If he could get close to it, he thought, he could strike the matches in his pocket and get a better look at it.

"Stop," said the friendliness and at the word he stopped, although he wasn't sure at all that he had heard the word.

"Don't look too closely at us," said the friendliness, and Johnny was just a little flustered at that, for he hadn't been looking at anything at all—not too closely, that is.

"All right," he said. "I won't look at you." And he wondered if it was some sort of a game, like hide-and-seek that he played at school.

"After we get to be good friends," said the thing to Johnny, "we can look at one another and it won't matter then, for we'll know what one another is like inside and not pay attention to how we look outside."

And Johnny, standing there, thought how they must look awful, not to want him to see them, and the thing said to him, "We would look awful to you. You look awful to us."

"Maybe, then," said Johnny, "it's a good thing I can't see in the dark."

"You can't see in the dark?" it asked and Johnny said he couldn't and there was silence for a while, although Johnny could hear it puzzling over how come he couldn't see when it was dark.

Then it asked if he could do something else and he couldn't even understand what it tried to say and finally it seemed to figure out that he couldn't do whatever it had asked about.

"You are afraid," said the thing. "There is no need to fear us."

And Johnny explained that he wasn't afraid of them, whatever they might be, because they were friendly, but that he was afraid of what might happen if Uncle Eb and Aunt Em should find he had sneaked out. So they asked him a lot about Uncle Eb and Aunt Em and he tried to explain, but they didn't seem to understand, but seemed to think he was talking about government. He tried to explain how it really was, but he was pretty sure they didn't understand at all.

Finally, being polite about it so he wouldn't hurt their feelings, he said he had to leave and since he'd stayed much longer than he'd planned, he ran all the way home.

He got into the house and up to bed all right and everything was fine, but the next morning Aunt Em found the matches in his pocket and gave him a lecture about the danger of burning down the barn. To reinforce the lecture, she used a switch on his legs and try as hard as he could to be a man about it, she laid it on so hard that he jumped up and down and screamed.

He worked through the day weeding the garden and just before dark went to get the cows.

He didn't have to go out of his way to go past the blackberry patch, for the cows were in that direction, but he knew well enough that if they hadn't been, he'd gone out of his way, for he'd been remembering all day the friendliness he'd found there.

It was still daylight this time, just shading into night, and he could see that the thing, whatever it might be, was not alive, but simply a hunk of metal, like two sauce dishes stuck together, with a rim running around its middle just like there'd be a rim if you stuck two dishes together. It looked like old metal that had been laying around for a long time and you could see where it was pitted like a piece of machinery will get when it stands out in the weather.

It had crushed a path for quite a ways through the blackberry thicket and had plowed up the ground for twenty feet or so, and, sighting back along the way it had come, Johnny could see where it had hit and smashed the top of a tall poplar.

It spoke to him, without words, the way it had the night before, with friendliness and fellowship, although Johnny wouldn't know that last word, never having run across it in his school books.

It said, "You may look at us a little now. Look at us quick and then away. Don't look at us steadily. Just a quick look and then away. That way you get used to us. A little at a time."

"Where are you?" Johnny asked.

"Right here," they said.

"Inside of there?" asked Johnny.

"Inside of here," they said.

"I can't see you, then," said Johnny. "I can't see through metal."

"He can't see through metal," said one of them.

"He can't see when the star is gone," said the other.

"He can't see us, then," they said, the both of them.

"You might come out," said Johnny.

"We can't come out," they said. "We'd die if we came out."

"I can't ever see you, then."

"You can't ever see us, Johnny."

And he stood there, feeling terribly lonely because he could never see these friends of his.

"We don't understand who you are," they said. "Tell us who you are."

And because they were so kind and friendly, he told them who he was and how he was an orphan and had been taken in by his Uncle Eb and Aunt Em, who really weren't his aunt and uncle. He didn't tell them how Uncle Eb and Aunt Em treated him, whipping him and scolding him and sending him to bed without his supper, but this, too, was well as the things he told them, was there for them to sense and now there was more than friendliness, more than fellowship. Now there was compassion and something that was their equivalent of mother love.

"He's just a little one," they said, talking to one another.

They reached out to him and seemed to take him in their arms and hold him tight against them and Johnny went down on his knees without knowing it and held out his arms to the thing that lay there among the broken bushes and cried out to them, as if there was something there that he might grasp and hold—some comfort that he had always missed and longed for and now finally had found. His heart cried out the thing that he could not say, the pleading that would not pass his lips and they answered him.

"No, we'll not leave you, Johnny. We can't leave you, Johnny."

"You promise?" Johnny asked.

Their voice was a little grim. "We do not need to promise, Johnny. Our machine is broken and we cannot fix it. One of us is dying and the other soon will die."

Johnny knelt there, with the words sinking into him, with the realization sinking into him and it seemed more than he could bear that, having found two friends, they were about to die.

"Johnny," they said to him.

"Yes," said Johnny, trying not to cry.

"You will trade with us?"

"Trade?"

"A way of friendship with us. You give us something and we give you something."

"But," said Johnny. "But I haven't . . ."

Then he knew he had. He had the pocket knife. It wasn't much, with its broken blade, but it was all he had.

"That is fine," they said. "That is exactly right. Lay it on the ground, close to the machine."

He took the knife out of his pocket and laid it against the machine and even as he watched something happened, but it happened so fast he couldn't see how it worked, but, anyhow, the knife was gone and there was something in its place.

"Thank you, Johnny," they said. "It was nice of you to trade with us."

He reached out his hand and took the thing they'd traded him and even in the darkness it flashed with hidden fire. He turned it in the palm of his hand and saw that it was some sort of jewel, many-faceted, and that the glow came from inside of it and that it burned with many different colors.

It wasn't until he saw how much light came from it that he realized how long he'd stayed and how dark it was and when he saw that he jumped to his feet and ran, without waiting to say goodbye.

It was too dark now to look for the cows and he hoped they had started home alone and that he could catch up with them and bring them in. He'd tell Uncle Eb that he'd had a hard time rounding them up. He'd tell Uncle Eb that the two heifers had broken out of the fence and he had to get them back. He'd tell Uncle Eb—he'd tell—he'd tell—

His breath gasped with his running and his heart was thumping so it seemed to shake him and fear rode on his shoulders— fear of the awful thing he'd done—of this final unforgivable thing after all the others, after not going to the spring to get the water, after missing the two heifers the night before, after the matches in his pocket.

He did not find the cows going home alone—he found them in the barnyard and he knew that they'd been milked and he knew he'd stayed much longer and that it was far worse than he had imagined.

He walked up the rise to the house, shaking now with fear. There was a light in the kitchen and he knew that they were waiting.

He came into the kitchen and they sat at the table, facing him, waiting for him, with the lamplight on their faces and their faces were so hard that they looked like graven stone.

Uncle Eb stood up, towering toward the ceiling, and you could see the muscles stand out on his arms, with the sleeves rolled to the elbow.

He reached for Johnny and Johnny ducked away, but the hand closed on the back of his neck and the fingers wrapped around his throat and lifted him and shook him with a silent savagery.

"I'll teach you," Uncle Eb was saying through clenched teeth. "I'll teach you. I'll teach you . . ."

Something fell upon the floor and rolled toward the corner, leaving a trail of fire as it rolled along the floor.

Uncle Eb stopped shaking him and just stood there holding him for an instant, then dropped him to the floor.

"That fell out of your pocket," said Uncle Eb. "What is it?"

Johnny backed away, shaking his head.

He wouldn't tell what it was. He'd never tell. No matter what Uncle Eb might do to him, he'd never tell. Not even if he killed him.

Uncle Eb stalked the jewel, bent swiftly and picked it up. He carried it back to the table and dropped it there and bent over, looking at it, sparkling in the light.

Aunt Em leaned forward in her chair to look at it.

"What in the world!" she said.

They bent there for a moment, staring at the jewel, their eyes bright and shining, their bodies tense, their breath rasping in the silence. The world could have come to an end right then and there and they'd never noticed.

Then they straightened up and turned to look at Johnny, turning away from the jewel as if it didn't interest them any longer, as if it had had a job to do and had done that job and no longer was important. There was something wrong with them—no, not wrong, but different.

"You must be starved," Aunt Em said to Johnny. "I'll warm you up some supper. Would you like some eggs?"

Johnny gulped and nodded.

Uncle Eb sat down, not paying any attention to the jewel at all.

"You know," he said, "I saw a jackknife uptown the other day. Just the kind you want . . ."

Johnny scarcely heard him.

He just stood there, listening to the friendliness and love that hummed through all the house.

THE WHISTLING WELL

First published in 1980 in the original anthology Dark Forces, *edited by Kirby McCauley, who at the time was Clifford Simak's agent, this story is one that relies heavily on its author's boyhood. I suspect that as an intelligent and imaginative boy living in a countryside filled with mysterious hollows, cliffs, and caves, with extensive reaches of dark forest, and vistas from which one could see the Wisconsin River flowing from its deep-cut valley to the even larger Mississippi, Cliff developed the habit of looking at his own life, and at the people and places around him, and saying—as adventurous children do— "This is boring, but what if. . ." I think he wandered the forests and ridges and peopled them, in his mind, with Native Americans and goblins and soldiers and, as his world expanded, with aliens and, yes, dinosaurs.*

There actually was a whistling well on Cliff's grandfather's farm.

—dww

He walked the ridge, so high against the sky, so windswept, so clean, so open, so far-seeing. As if the very land itself, the soil, the stone, were reaching up, standing on tiptoe, to lift itself, stretching toward the sky. So high that one, looking down, could see the backs of hawks that swung in steady hunting circles above the river valley.

The highness was not all. There was, as well, the sense of ancientness and the smell of time. And the intimacy, as if this great high ridge might be transferring to him its personality. A personality, he admitted to himself, for which he had a liking, a thing that he could wrap, as a cloak, around himself.

And through it all, he heard the creaking of the rocker as it went back and forth, with the hunched and shriveled, but still energetic, old lady crouched upon it, rocking back and forth, so small, so dried up, so emaciated that she seemed to have shrunken into the very structure of the chair, her feet dangling, not reaching the floor. Like a child in a great-grandfather chair. Her feet not touching, not even reaching out a toe to make the rocker go. And, yet, the rocker kept on rocking, never stopping. How the hell, Thomas Parker asked himself, had she made the rocker go?

He had reached the ultimate point of the ridge where steep, high limestone cliffs plunged down toward the river. Cliffs that swung east and from this point continued along the river valley, a stony rampart that fenced in the ridge against the deepness of the valley.

He turned and looked back along the ridge and there, a mile or so away, stood the spidery structure of the windmill, the great wheel facing west, toward him, its blades a whir of silver movement in the light of the setting sun.

The windmill, he knew, was clattering and clanking, but from this distance, he could hear no sound of it, for the strong wind blowing from the west so filled his ears that he could pick up no sound but the blowing of the wind. The wind whipped at his loose jacket and made his pants legs ripple and he could feel its steady pressure at his back.

And, yet, within his mind, if not within his ears, he still could hear the creaking of the rocker, moving back and forth within that room where a bygone gentility warred against the brusqueness of present time. The fireplace was built of rosy brick, with white paneling placed around the brick, the mantel loaded with old figurines, with framed photographs from another time, with an ornate, squatty clock that chimed each quarter hour. There had been furniture of solid oak, a threadbare carpet on the floor. The drapes at the large bow windows, with deep window seats, were of some heavy material, faded over the years to a nondeterminate coloring. Paintings with heavy gilt frames hung on the walls, but the gloom within the room was so deep that there was no way of seeing what they were.

The woman-of-all-work, the companion, the housekeeper, the practical nurse, the cook, brought in the tea, with bread-and-butter sandwiches piled on one plate and delicate cakes ranged on another. She had set the tray on the table in front of the rocking old lady and then had gone away, back into the dark and mysterious depths of the ancient house.

The old lady spoke in her brittle voice, "Thomas," she said, "if you will pour. Two lumps for me, no cream."

Awkwardly, he had risen from the horsehair chair. Awkwardly he had poured. He had never poured before. There was a feeling that he should do it charmingly and delicately and with a certain genteel flair, but he did not have the flair. He had nothing that this house or this old lady had. His was another world.

He had been summoned here, imperatively summoned, in a crisp little note on paper that had a faint scent of lavender, the script of the writing more bold than he would have expected, the letters a flowing dignity in old copperplate.

I shall expect you, she had written, *on the afternoon of the 17th. We have matters to discuss.*

A summons from the past and from seven hundred miles away and he had responded, driving his beaten-up, weather-stained, lumbering camper through the flaming hills of a New England autumn.

The wind still tugged and pushed at him, the windmill blades still a swirl of movement and below him, above the river, the small, dark shape of the circling hawk. Autumn then, he told himself, and here another autumn, with the trees of the river valley, the trees of other far-off vistas, taking on the color of the season.

The ridge itself was bare of trees, except for a few that still clustered around the sites of homesteads, the homesteads now gone, burned down or weathered away or fallen with the passage of the years. In time long past, there might have been trees, but more than a hundred years ago, if there had been any, they had fallen to the ax to clear the land for fields. The fields were still here, but no longer fields; they had known no plow for decades.

He stood at the end of the ridge and looked back across it, seeing all the miles he had tramped that day, exploring it, getting to know it, although why he felt he should get to know it, he did not understand. But there was some sort of strange compulsion within him that, until this moment, he had not even questioned.

Ancestors of his had trod this land, had lived on it and slept on it, had procreated on it, had known it as he, in a few short days, would never know it. Had known it and had left. Fleeing from some undefinable thing. And that was wrong, he told himself, that was very wrong. The information he'd been given had been somehow garbled. There was nothing here to flee from. Rather, there was something here to live for, to stay for—the closeness to the sky, the cleansing action of the wind, the feeling of intimacy with the soil, the stone, the air, the storm, the very sky itself.

Here his ancestors had walked the land, the last of many who had walked it. For millions of years unknown, perhaps unsuspected, creatures had walked along this ridge. The land was unchanging, geologically ancient, a sentinel of land standing as a milepost amidst other lands that had been forever changing. No great mountain-building surges had distorted it, no glacial action had ground it down, no intercontinental seas had crept over it. For hundreds of millions of years, it had been a freestanding land. It had stayed as it was through all that time, with only the slow and subtle changes brought about by weathering.

He had sat in that room from out of the past and across the table from him had been the rocking woman, rocking even as she drank the tea and nibbled at the bread-and-butter sandwich.

"Thomas," she had said, speaking in her old brittle voice, "I have a job for you to do. It's a job that you must do, that only you can do. It's something that's important to me."

Important to her. Not to someone else, to no one else but her. It made no difference to whom else it might be important or unimportant. To her, it was important and that was all that counted.

He said, amused at her, at her rocking and her intensity, the amusement struggling up through the out-of-placeness of the room, the woman and the house, "Yes, Auntie, what kind of job? If it's one that I can do . . ."

"You can do it," she said, tartly. "Thomas, don't get cute with me. It's something you can do. I want you to write a history of our family, of our branch of the Parkers. I am aware there are many Parkers in the world, but it's our direct line in which my interest lies. You can ignore all collateral branches."

He had stuttered at the thought. "But, Auntie, that would take a long time. It might take years."

"I'll pay you for your time," she'd said. "You write books about other things. Why not about the family? You've just finished a book about paleontology. You spent three years or more on that. You've written books on archaeology, on the old Egyptians, on the ancient trade routes of the world. Even a book on old folklore and superstitions and, if you don't mind my saying so, that was the silliest book I ever read. Popular science, you call it, but it takes a lot of work. You talk to many different people, you dig into dusty records. You could do as much for me."

"But there'd be no market for such a book. No one would be interested."

"I would be interested," she said sharply, the brittle voice cracking. "And who said anything about publication? I simply want to know. I want to know, Thomas, where we came from and who we are and what kind of folks we are. I'll pay you for the job. I'll insist on paying you. I'll pay you . . ."

And she named a sum that quite took his breath away. He had never dreamed she had that kind of money.

"And expenses," she said. "You must keep a very close accounting of everything you spend."

He tried to be gentle with her, for quite obviously she was mad. "But, Auntie, you can get it at a much cheaper figure. There are genealogy people who make a business of tracing back old family histories."

She sniffed at him. "I've had them do the tracing. I'll give you what I have. That should make it easier for you."

"But if you have that—"

"I suspect what they have told me. The record is unclear. To my mind, it is. They try too hard to give you something for your money. They set out to please you. They gild the lily, Thomas. They tell about the manor house in Shropshire, but I'm not sure there ever was a manor house. It sounds just a bit too pat. I want to know if there ever was or not. There was a merchant in London. He dealt in cutlery, they say. That's not enough for me; I must know more of him. Even in our New England, the record is a fuzzy one. Another thing, Thomas. There are no horse thieves mentioned. There are no gallows birds. If there are horse thieves and gallows birds, I want to know of them."

"But, why, Auntie? Why go to all the bother? If it is written, it will never be published. No one but you and I will know. I hand you the manuscript and that is all that happens."

"Thomas," she had said, "I am a mad old woman, a senile old woman, with only a few years left of madness and senility. I should hate to have to beg you."

"You will not have to beg me," he had said. "My feet, my brain, my typewriter are for hire. But I don't understand."

"Don't try to understand," she'd told him. "I've had my way my entire life. Let me continue to."

And, now, it had finally come to this. The long trail of the Parkers had finally come down to this high and windswept ridge with its clattering windmill and the little clumps of trees that had stood around the farmsteads that were no longer there, to the fields that had long been fallow fields, to the little spring beside which he had parked the camper.

He stood there above the cliffs and looked down the slope to where a tangled mass of boulders, some of them barn-size or better, clustered on the hillside, with a few clumps of paper birch growing among them.

Strange, he thought. These were the only trees, other than the homestead trees, that grew upon the ridge, and the only boulder clump. Not, certainly, the residue of glaciation, for the many Ice Age glaciers that had come down across the Middle West had stopped north of here. This country, for many miles around, was known as the driftless area, a magic little pocket that, for some reason not yet known, had been bypassed by the glaciers while they crunched far south on each side of it.

Perhaps, at one time, he told himself, there had been an extrusive rock formation jutting from the ridge, now reduced by weathering to the boulder cluster.

Idly, with no reason to do so, without really intending to, he went down the slope to the cluster with its growth of paper birch.

Close up, the boulders were fully as large as they had appeared from the top of the ridge. Lying among the half dozen or so larger ones were many others, broken fragments that had been chipped off by frost or running water, perhaps aided by the spalling effect of sunlight.

Thomas grinned to himself as he climbed among them, working his way through the cracks and intervals that separated them. A great place for kids to play, he thought. A castle, a fort, a mountain to childish imagination. Blowing dust and fallen leaves through the centuries had found refuge among them and had formed a soil in which were rooted many plants, including an array of wild asters and goldenrod, now coming into bloom.

He found, toward the center of the cluster, a cave or what amounted to a cave. Two of the larger boulders, tipped together, formed a roofed tunnel that ran for a dozen feet or more, six feet wide, the sides of the boulders sloping inward to meet some eight feet above the tunnel's floor. In the center of the tunnel lay a heaped pile of stones. Some kid, perhaps, Thomas told himself, had gathered them many years ago and had hidden them here as an imagined treasure trove.

Walking forward, he stooped and picked up a fistful of the stones. As his fingers touched them, he knew there was something wrong. These were not ordinary stones. They felt polished and sleek beneath his fingertips, with an oily texture to them.

A year or more ago, in a museum somewhere in the west—perhaps Colorado, although he could not be sure—he had first seen and handled other stones like these.

"Gastroliths," the grey-bearded curator had told him. "Gizzard stones. We think they came from the stomachs of herbivorous dinosaurs—perhaps all dinosaurs. We can't be certain."

"Like the grit you find in a chicken's craw?" Thomas had asked.

"Exactly," the curator said. "Chickens pick up and swallow tiny stones, grains of sand, bits of shell to help in the digestion of their food. They simply swallow their food. They have no way to chew it. The grit in the gizzard does the chewing for them. There's a good possibility, one might even say, a high possibility, the dinosaurs did the same, ingesting pebbles to do the chewing for them. During their lifetime, they carried these stones, which became highly polished, and then when they died—"

"But the greasiness? The oily feeling?"

The curator shook his head. "We don't know. Dinosaur oil? Oil picked up from being so long in the body?"

"Hasn't anyone tried to extract it? To find out if there is really oil?"

"I don't believe anyone has," the curator said.

And here, in this tunnel, in this cave, whatever one might call it, a pile of gizzard stones.

Squatting, Thomas picked them over, gathering a half dozen of the larger ones, the size of small hen's eggs, or less, feeling the short hairs on his neck tingling with an ancient, atavistic fear that should have been too far in the distant past to have been felt at all.

Here, millions of years ago, perhaps a hundred million years ago, a sick, or injured, dinosaur had crept in to die. Since that time, the flesh was gone, the bones turned into dust, but remaining was the pile of pebbles the long-gone dinosaur had carried in its gizzard.

Clutching the stones in his hand, Thomas settled back on his heels and tried to re-create, within his mind, what had happened here. Here the creature had lain, crouched and quivering, forcing itself, for protection, as deeply into this rock-girt hole as had been possible. It had snorted in its sickness, whimpered with its pain. And it had died here, in this same spot he now occupied. Later had come the little scavenging mammals, tearing at its flesh . . .

This was not dinosaur land, he thought, not the kind of place the fossil hunters came to hunt the significant debris of the past. There had been dinosaurs here, of course, but there had not been the violent geological processes which would have resulted in the burying and preservation of their bones. Although, if there had been, they'd still be here, for this was ancient land, untouched by the grinding glaciers that must have destroyed, or deeply buried, so many fossil caches.

But here, in this cluster of shattered boulders, he had stumbled on the dying place of a thing that no longer walked on earth. He tried to imagine what form that now extinct creature might have taken, what it would have looked like when it still had life within it. But there was no way that he could know. There had been so many different shapes of them, some of them known by their fossils, perhaps many still unknown.

He fed the selected gizzard stones into the pocket of his jacket and when he crawled from the tunnel and walked out of the pile of boulders, the sun was bisected by the jagged hills far to the west. The wind had fallen with the coming of the evening hours and he walked in a hushed peace along the ridge. Ahead of him, the windmill clattered with subdued tone, clanking as the wheel went slowly round and round.

Short of the windmill, he went down the slope to the head of a deep ravine that plunged down toward the river. Here, beside the spring, parked beneath a massive cottonwood, his camper shone whitely in the creeping dusk. Well before he reached it, he could hear the sound of water gushing from the hillside. In the woods farther down the slope, he could hear the sound of birds settling for the coming night.

He rekindled the campfire and cooked his supper and later sat beside the fire, knowing that now it was time to leave. His job was finished. He had traced out the long line of Parkers to this final place, where shortly after the Civil War, Ned Parker had come to carve out a farm.

In Shropshire there had been, indeed, a manor house but, if one were to be truthful, not much of a manor house. And he had found, as well, that the London merchant had not dealt in cutlery, but in wool. There had been no horse thieves, no gallows birds, no traitors, no real scamps of any kind. The Parkers had been, in fact, a plodding sort of people, not given to greatness, nor to evil. They had existed nonspectacularly, as honest yeomen, honest merchants, farming their small acres, managing their small businesses. And finally crossing the water to New England, not as pioneers, but as settlers. A few of them had fought in the Revolutionary War, but were not distinguished warriors. Others had fought in the Civil War, but had been undistinguished there, as well.

There had, of course, been a few notable, but not spectacular exceptions. There had been Molly Parker, who had been sentenced to the ducking stool because she talked too freely about certain neighbors. There had been Jonathon, who had been sentenced to the colonies because he had the bad judgment of having fallen into debt. There had been a certain Teddy Parker, a churchman of some sort (the evidence was not entirely clear), who had fought a prolonged and bitter battle in the court with a parishioner over pasture rights held by the church which had been brought into question.

But these were minor matters. They scarcely caused a ripple on the placidity of the Parker tribe.

It was time to leave, he told himself. He had tracked the family, or this one branch of the family, down to this high ridge. He had found the old homestead, the house burned many years ago, now marked only by the cellar excavation, half filled with the litter of many years. He had seen the windmill and had stood beside the whistling well, which had not whistled for him.

Time to leave, but he did not want to leave. He felt a strange reluctance at stirring from this place. As if there were more to come, more that might be learned—although he knew there wasn't.

Was this reluctance because he had fallen in love with this high and windy hill, finding in it some of the undefinable charm that must have been felt by his great-great-grandfather? He had the feeling of being trapped and chained, of having found the one place he was meant to be. He had, he admitted to himself, the sense of belonging, drawn and bound by ancestral roots.

That was ridiculous, he told himself. By no matter what weird biochemistry within his body he had come to think so, he could have no real attachment to this place. He'd give himself another day or two and then he'd leave. He'd make that much concession to this feeling of attachment. Perhaps, by the end of another day or two, he'd have enough of it, the enchantment fallen from him.

He pushed the fire more closely together, heaped more wood upon it. The flames caught and flared up. He leaned back in his camp chair and stared out into the darkness, beyond the firelit circle. Out in the dark were darker humps, waiting, watching shapes, but they were, he knew, no more than clumps of bushes—a small plum tree or a patch of hazel. A glow in the eastern sky forecast a rising moon. A quickening breeze, risen after the sunset calm, rattled the leaves of the big cottonwood that stood above the camp.

He scrooched around to sit sidewise in the chair and when he did, the gizzard stones in his jacket pocket caught against the chair arm and pressed hard against his hip.

Reaching a hand into his pocket, he took them out. Flat upon his palm, he held them out so the firelight fell upon them. He rubbed a thumb against them. They had the feel and look of velvet. They glistened in the dancing firelight. The gloss on them was higher than was ever found in the polished pebbles that turned up in river gravel. Turning them, he saw that all the depressions, all the concave surfaces, were as highly polished as the rest of the stone.

The stones found in river gravel had obtained their polish by sand action, swirling or washed along the riverbed. The gizzard stones had been polished by being rubbed together by the tough contracting muscles of a gizzard. Perhaps some sand in the gizzard, as well, he thought, for in jerking up a plant from sandy soil, the dinosaur would not be too finicky. It would ingest the sand, the clinging bits of soil, along with the plant. For years, these stones had been subjected to continuous polishing action.

Slowly, he kept turning the stones with a thumb and finger of the other hand, fascinated by them. Suddenly, one of them flashed in the firelight. He turned it back and it flashed again. There was, he saw, some sort of an irregularity on its surface.

He dropped the other two into his pocket and leaned forward toward the fire with the one that had flashed lying in his palm. Turning it so that the firelight fell full upon it, he bent his head close above it, trying to puzzle out what might be there. It looked like a line of writing, but in characters he had never seen before. And that had to be wrong, of course, for at the time the dinosaur swallowed the stone, there had been no such thing as writing. Unless someone, later on, within the last century or so—He shook his head in puzzlement. That made no sense, either.

With the stone clutched in his hand, he went into the camper, rummaged in a desk drawer until he found a small magnifying glass. He lit a gas lantern and turned it up, placed it on the desk top. Pulling over a chair, he sat down, held the stone in the lantern light, and peered at it through the glass.

If not writing, there was something there, engraved into the stone—the engraving worn as smooth and sleek as all the rest of it. It was no recent work. There was no possibility, he told himself, that the line that resembled engraving could be due to natural causes. He tried to make out exactly what it was, but in the flicker of the lantern, it was difficult to do so. There seemed to be two triangles, apex pointing down in one, up in the other and the two of them connected midpoint by a squiggly line.

But there was as much as he could make of it. The engraving, if that was what it was, was so fine, so delicate, that it was hard to see the details, even with the glass. Perhaps a higher-power glass might show more, but this was the only magnifier he had.

He laid the stone and glass on the desk top and went outside. As he came down the steps, he felt the differentness. There had been blacker shapes out in the darkness and he had recognized them as clumps of hazel or small trees. But now the shapes were bigger and were moving.

He stopped at the foot of the steps and tried to make them out, to pinpoint the moving shapes, but his eyes failed to delineate the shapes, although at times they seemed to catch the movement.

You're insane, he told himself. There is nothing out there. A cow or steer, perhaps. He had been told, he remembered, that the present owners of the land, at times, ran cattle on it, pasturing them through the summer, penning them for finishing in the fall. But in his walks about the ridge, he'd not seen any cattle and if there were cattle out there, he thought that he would know it. If cattle moved about, there should be a crackling of their hocks, snuffling as they nosed at grass or leaves.

He went to the chair and sat down solidly in it. He reached for a stick and pushed the fire together, then settled back. He was too old a hand at camping, he assured himself, to allow himself to imagine things out in the dark. Yet, somehow, he had got the wind up.

Nothing moved beyond the reaches of the firelight and still, despite all his arguments with himself, he could feel them out there, sense them with a sense he had not known before, had never used before. What unsuspected abilities and capacities, he wondered, might lie within the human mind?

Great dark shapes that moved sluggishly, that hitched along by inches, always out of actual sight, but still circling in close to the edge of light, just beyond its reach.

He sat rigid in the chair, feeling his body tightening up, his nerves stretching to the tension of a violin string. Sitting there and listening for the sound that never came, for the movement that could only be sensed, not seen.

They were out there, said this strange sense he had never known before, while his mind, his logical human mind, cried out against it. There is no evidence, said his human mind. There need be no evidence, said this other part of him; we know.

They kept moving in. They were piling up, for there were a lot of them. They were deadly silent and deliberate in the way they moved. If he threw a chunk of wood out into the darkness, the chunk of wood would hit them.

He did not throw the wood.

He sat, unmoving, in the chair. I'll wear them out, he told himself. If they are really out there, I will wear them out. This is my fire, this is my ground. I have a right to be here.

He tried to analyze himself. Was he frightened? He wasn't sure. Perhaps not gibbering frightened, but probably frightened otherwise. And, despite what he said, did he have the right to be here? He had a right to build the fire, for it had been mankind, only mankind, who had made use of fire. None of the others did. But the land might be another thing; the land might not be his. There might be a long-term mortgage on it from another time.

The fire died down and the moon came up over the ridgetop. It was almost full, but its light was feeble-ghostly. The light showed nothing out beyond the campfire, although, watching closely, it seemed to Thomas that he could see massive movement farther down the slope, among the trees.

The wind had risen and from far off, he heard the faint clatter of the windmill. He craned his head to try to see the windmill, but the moonlight was too pale to see it.

By degrees, he relaxed. He asked himself, in something approaching fuzzy wonder, what the hell had happened? He was not a man given to great imagination. He did not conjure ghosts. That something incomprehensible had taken place, there could be little doubt—but his interpretation of it? That was the catch; he had made no interpretation. He had held fast to his life-long position as observer.

He went into the camper and found the bottle of whiskey and brought it out to the fire, not bothering with a glass. He sat sprawled in the chair, holding the bottle with one hand, resting the bottom of it on his gut. The bottom of the bottle was a small circle of coldness against his gut.

Sitting there, he remembered the old black man he had talked with one afternoon, deep in Alabama, sitting on the ramshackle porch of the neat, ramshackle house, with the shade of a china-berry tree shielding them from the heat of the late-afternoon sun. The old man sat easily in his chair, every now and then twirling the cane he held, its point against the porch floor, holding it easily

by the shaft, twirling it every now and then, so that the crook of
it went round and round.

"If you're going to write your book the way it should be written," the old black man had said, "you got to look deeper than
the Devil. I don't suppose I should be saying this, but since you
promise you will not use my name . . ."

"I won't use your name," Thomas had told him.

"I was a preacher for years," the old man said. "And in those
years, I learned plenty on the Devil. I held him up in scorn; I
threatened people with him. I said, 'If you don't behave your-
selves, Old Devil, he will drag you down them long, long stairs,
hauling you by your heels, with your head bumping on the steps,
while you scream and plead and cry. But Old Devil, he won't pay
no attention to your screaming and your pleading. He won't even
hear you. He'll just haul you down those stairs and cast you in the
pit.' The Devil, he was something those people could understand.
They'd heard of him for years. They knew what he looked like
and the kind of manners that he had . . ."

"Did it ever help?" Thomas had asked. "Threatening them
with the Devil, I mean."

"I can't be sure. I think sometimes it did. Not always, but
sometimes. It was worth the try."

"But you tell me I must go beyond the Devil."

"You white folks don't know. You don't feel it in your bones.
You're too far from the jungle. My people, we know. Or some of
us do. We're only a few lifetimes out of Africa."

"You mean—"

"I mean you must go way back. Back beyond the time when
there were any men at all. Back to the older eons. The Devil is a
Christian evil—a gentle evil, if you will, a watered-down version
of real evil, a shadow of what there was and maybe is. He came to
us by way of Babylon and Egypt and even the Babylonians and
Egyptians had forgotten, or had never known, what evil really
was. I tell you the Devil isn't a patch on the idea he is based on.

Only a faint glimmer of the evil that was sensed by early men—not seen, but sensed, in those days when men chipped the first flint tools, while he fumbled with the idea of the use of fire."

"You're saying that there was evil before man? That figures of evil are not man's imagining?"

The old man grinned, a bit lopsidely, at him, with still a serious grin. "Why should man," he asked, "take to himself the sole responsibility for the concept of evil?"

He'd spent, Thomas remembered, a pleasant afternoon on the porch, in the shade of the chinaberry tree, talking with the old man and drinking elderberry wine. And, at other times and in other places, he had talked with other men and from what they'd told him had been able to write a short and not too convincing chapter on the proposition that a primal evil may have been the basis for all the evil figures mankind had conjured up. The book had sold well, still was selling. It had been worth all the work he had put into it. And the best part of it was that he had escaped scot-free. He did not believe in the Devil or any of the rest of it. Although, reading his book, a lot of other people did.

The fire burned down, the bottle was appreciably less full than when he'd started on it. The landscape lay mellow in the faint moonlight. Tomorrow, he told himself, I'll spend tomorrow here, then I'll be off again. Aunt's Elsie's job is finished.

He got up from the chair and went in to bed. Just before he went to bed, it seemed to him that he could hear, again, the creaking and the scuffing of Auntie's rocking chair.

After breakfast, he climbed the ridge again to the site of the Parker homestead. He'd walked past it on his first quick tour of the ridge, only pausing long enough to identify it.

A massive maple tree stood at one corner of the cellar hole. Inside the hole, raspberry bushes had taken root. Squatting on the edge of the hole, he used a stick he had picked up to pry into the loam. Just beneath the surface lay flakes of charcoal, adding a blackness to the soil.

He found a bed of rosemary. Picking a few of the leaves, he crushed them in his fingers, releasing the sharp smell of mint. To the east of the cellar hole, a half dozen apple trees still survived, scraggly, branches broken by the winds, but still bearing small fruit. He picked one of the apples and when he bit into it, he sensed a taste out of another time, a flavor not to be found in an apple presently marketed. He found a still flourishing patch of rhubarb, a few scrawny rosebushes with red hips waiting for the winter birds, a patch of iris so crowded that corms had been pushed above the surface of the ground.

Standing beside the patch of iris, he looked around. Here, at one time, more than a century ago, his ancestor had built a homestead—a house, a barn, a chicken house, a stable, a granary, a corncrib, and perhaps other buildings, had settled down as a farmer, a soldier returned from the wars, had lived here for a term of years and then had left. Not only he but all the others who had lived on this ridge as well.

On this, his last trip to complete the charge that had been put upon him by that strange old lady hunched in her rocking chair, he had stopped at the little town of Patch Grove to ask his way. A couple of farmers sitting on a bench outside a barbershop had looked at him—reticent, disbelieving, perhaps somewhat uneasy.

"Parker's Ridge?" they'd asked. "You want to know the way to Parker's Ridge?"

"I have business there," he'd told them.

"There ain't no one to do business with on Parker's Ridge," they'd told him. "No one ever goes there."

But when he'd insisted, they'd finally told him. "There's only one ridge, really," they'd said, "but it's divided into two parts. You go north of town until you reach a cemetery. Just short of the cemetery, you take a left. That puts you on Military Ridge. You keep to the high ground. There are some roads turning off, but you stay on top the ridge."

"But that you say is Military Ridge. What I want is Parker's Ridge."

"One and the same," said one of the men. "When you reach the end of it, that's Parker's Ridge. It stands high above the river. Ask along the way."

So he'd gone north of town and taken a left before he reached the cemetery. The ridge road was a secondary route, a farm road, either unpaved or paved so long ago and so long neglected that it bore little trace of paving. Small farms were strung along it, little ridgetop farms, groups of falling-down buildings surrounded by scant and runty fields. Farm dogs raced out to bark at him as he passed the farms.

Five miles down the road a man was taking mail out of a mailbox. Thomas pulled up. "I'm looking for Parker's Ridge," he said. "Am I getting close?"

The man stuffed the three or four letters he'd taken from the box into the rear pocket of his overalls. He stepped down to the road and stood beside the car. He was a large man, rawboned. His face was creased and wrinkled and wore a week of beard.

"You're almost there," he said. "Another three miles or so. But would you tell me, stranger, why you want to go there?"

"Just to look around," said Thomas.

The man shook his head. "Nothing there to look at. No one there. Used to be people there. Half a dozen farms. People living on them, working the farms. But that was long ago. Sixty years ago—no, maybe more than that. Now they all are gone. Someone owns the land, but I don't know who. Someone runs cattle here. Goes out West in the spring to buy them, runs them on pasture until fall, then rounds them up and feeds them grain, finishing them for the market."

"You're sure there's no one there?"

"No one there now. Used to be. Buildings, too. Houses and old farm buildings. Not any longer. Some of them burned. Kids, most likely, setting a match to them. Kids probably thought they were doing right. The ridge has a bad reputation."

"What do you mean, a bad reputation? How come a bad—"

"There's a whistling well, for one thing. Although I don't know what the well has to do with it."

"I don't understand. I've never heard of a whistling well."

The man laughed. "That was old Ned Parker's well. He was one of the first settlers out there on the ridge. Come home from the Civil War and bought land out there. Got it cheap. Civil War veterans could buy government land at a dollar an acre and, at that time, this was all government land. Ned could have bought rich, level land out on Blake's Prairie, some twenty miles or so from here, for the same dollar an acre. But not him. He knew what he wanted. He wanted a place where timber would be handy, where there'd be a running spring for water, where he'd be close to hunting and fishing."

"I take it the place didn't work out too well."

"Worked out all right except for the water. There was one big spring he counted on, but a few dry years came along and the spring began running dry. It never did run dry, but Ned was afraid it would. It is still running. But Ned, he wasn't going to be caught without water, so, by God, he drilled a well. Right on top that ridge. Got in a well driller and put him to work. Hit a little water, but not much. Went deeper and deeper and still not enough. Until the well driller said, 'Ned, the only way to get water is to go down to the river level. But the rest of the way it is going to cost you a dollar and a quarter a foot.' Now, in those days, a dollar and a quarter was a lot of money, but Ned had so much money sunk in the well already that he said to go ahead. So the well driller went ahead. Deepest well anyone had ever heard of. People used to come and just stand there, watching the well being drilled. My grandfather told me this, having heard it from his father. When the hole reached river level, they did find water, a lot of water. A well that would never run dry. But pumping was a problem. That water had to be pumped straight up a long way. So Ned bought the biggest, heaviest, strongest windmill that was made and that windmill set him back a lot of cash. But Ned never complained. He wanted water and now he had it. The windmill never gave no trouble, like a lot of windmills did. It was built to last. It's still there and still running, although it's not pumping water anymore. The pump shaft broke years ago. So did the vane control, the lever to shut off the wheel. Now that mill runs all the time. There's no way to shut it off. Running without grease, it's gotten noisier and noisier. Some day, of course, it will stop, just break down."

"You told me a whistling well. You told me everything else, but nothing about a whistling well."

"Now that's a funny thing," the farmer said. "At times, the well whistled. Standing on the platform, over the bore, you can feel a rush of wind. When the rush gets strong enough, it is said to make a whistling sound. People say it still does, although I couldn't say. Some people used to say it only whistled when the wind was from the north, but I can't swear to that, either. You know how people are. They always have answers for everything whether they know anything about it or not. I understand that those who said it only whistled when the wind was from the north explained it by saying that a strong north wind would blow directly against the cliffs facing the river. There are caves and crevices in those cliffs and they said some of the crevices ran back into the ridge and that the well cut through some of them. So a north wind would blow straight back along the crevices until it hit the well and then come rushing up the bore."

"It sounds a bit far-fetched to me." said Thomas.

The farmer scratched his head. "Well, I don't know. I can't tell you. It's only what the old-time people said. And they're all gone now. Left their places many years ago. Just pulled up and left."

"All at once?"

"Can't tell you that, either. I don't think so. Not all in a bunch. First one family and then another, until they all were gone. That happened long ago. No one would remember now. No one knows why they left. There are strange stories—not stories, really, just things you hear. I don't know what went on. No one killed, so far as I know. No one hurt. Just strange things. I tell you, young man, unless I had urgent business there, I wouldn't venture out on Parker's Ridge. Neither would any of my neighbors. None of us could give you reasons, but we wouldn't go."

"I'll be careful," Thomas promised.

Although, as it turned out, there'd been no reason to be careful. Rather, once he'd reached the ridge, he'd felt that inexplicable sense of belonging, of being in a place where he was supposed to be. Walking the ridge, he'd felt this barren backbone of land had transferred, or was in the process of transferring, its personality to him and he'd taken it and made it fit him like a cloak, wrapping himself in it, asking himself: Can a land have a personality?

The road, once Military Ridge had ended beyond the last farmhouse and Parker's Ridge began, had dwindled to a track, only a grassy hint that a road once had existed there. Far down the ridge he had sighted the windmill, a spidery construction reared against the sky, its wheel clanking in the breeze. He had driven on past it and then had stopped the camper, walking down the slope until he had located the still-flowing spring at the head of the ravine. Going back to the camper, he had driven it off the track and down the sloping hillside, to park it beneath the cottonwood that stood above the spring. That had been the day before yesterday and he had one more day left before he had to leave.

Standing now, beside the iris bed, he looked around him and tried to imagine the kind of place this may have been—to see it with the eyes of his old ancestor, home from the wars and settled on acres of his own. There would still have been deer, for this old man had wanted hunting, and it had not been until the great blizzard of the early 1880s that the wild game of this country had been decimated. There would have been wolves to play havoc with the sheep, for in those days, everyone kept sheep. There would have been guinea fowls whistling in the hedgerows, for, in those days, as well, everyone kept guineas. And the chances were that there would have been peacocks, geese, ducks, chickens, wandering the yards. Good horses in the stable, for everyone in those days placed great emphasis on good horses. And, above all, the great pride in one's own acreage, in the well-kept barns, the herds of cattle, the wheat, the corn, the newly planted orchard. And the old man, himself, he wondered—what kind of man was old Ned Parker, walking the path from the house up to the windmill. A stout and stocky man, perhaps, for the Parkers ran to stocky. An erect old man, for he'd been four years a soldier in the Union Army. Walking, perhaps, with his hands clasped behind his back, and head thrown back to stare up at the windmill, his present pride and glory.

Grandfather, Thomas asked himself, what happened? What is this all about? Did you feel belonging as I feel belonging? Did you feel the openness of this high ridge, the windswept sense of intimacy, the personality of the land as I feel it now? Was it here then, as well as now? And if that should have been the case, as it certainly must have been, why did you leave?

There was no answer, of course. He knew there would not be. There was no one now to answer. But even as he asked the question, he knew that this was a land loaded with information, with answers if one could only dig them out. There is something worth knowing here, he told himself, if one could only find it. The land was ancient. It had stood and watched and waited as ages swept over it, like cloud shadows passing across the land. Since time immemorial, it had stood sentinel above the river and had noted all that had come to pass.

There had been amphibians floundering and bellowing in the river swamps, there had been herds of dinosaurs and those lonely ones that had preyed upon the herds, there had been rampaging titanotheres and the lordly mammoth and the mastodon. There had been much to see and note.

The old black man had said look back, look back beyond the time of man, to the forgotten primal days. To the day, Thomas wondered, when each worshipping dinosaur had swallowed one stone encised with a magic line of cryptic symbols as an earnest that it held faith in a primal god?

Thomas shook himself. You're mad, he told himself. Dinosaurs had no gods. Only men had the intelligence that enabled them to create their gods.

He left the iris patch and paced slowly up the hill, heading for the windmill, following the now nonexistent path that old Ned Parker must have followed more than a hundred years before.

He tilted back his head to look up at the spinning wheel, moving slowly in the gentle morning breeze. So high against the sky, he thought, so high above the world.

The platform of the well was built of hewn oak timbers, weathered by the years, but still as sound as the day they had been laid. The outer edge of them was powdery and crumbling, but the powdering and the crumbling did not go deep. Thomas stooped and flicked at the wood with a fingernail and a small fragment of the oak came free, but beneath it the wood was solid. The timbers would last, he knew, for another hundred years, perhaps several hundred years.

As he stood beside the platform, he became aware of the sound that came from the well. Nothing like a whistle, but a slight moaning, as if an animal somewhere near its bottom were moaning in its sleep. Something alive, he told himself, something moaning gently far beneath the surface, a great heart and a great brain beating somewhere far below in the solid rock.

The brains and hearts of olden dinosaurs, he thought, or the gods of dinosaurs. And brought himself up short. You're at it again, he told himself, unable to shake this nightmare fantasy of the dinosaur. The finding of the heap of gizzard stones must have left a greater mark upon him that he had thought at first.

It was ridiculous on the face of it. The dinosaurs had had dim intellects that had done no more than drive them to the preservation of their own lives and the procreation of their kind. But logic did not help; illogic surged within him. No brain capacity, of course, but some other organ—perhaps supplementary to the brain—that was concerned with faith?

He grew rigid with anger at himself, with disgust at such flabby thinking, at a thought that could be a little better than the thinking of the rankest cult enthusiast, laced with juvenility.

He left the well and walked up to the track he had followed coming in.

He walked along it rapidly, bemused at the paths his mind had taken. The place, he thought, for all its openness, all its reaching toward the sky, all its geographic personality, worked a strange effect upon one. As if it were not of a piece with the rest of the earth, as if it stood apart, wondering, as he thought this, if that could have been the reason all the families left.

He spent the day upon the ridge, covering the miles of it, poking in its corners, forgetting the bemusement and the anger, forgetting even the very strangeness of it, glorying, rather, in the strangeness and that fascinating sense of freedom and of oneness with the sky. The rising wind from the west tugged and pulled at him. The land was clean, not with a washed cleanness but with the clean of a thing that had never been dirty, that had stayed fresh and bright from the day of its creation, untouched by the greasy fingers of the world.

He found the gaping cellar-holes of other farmhouses and squatted near them almost worshipfully, seeking out the lilac clumps, the crumbling remains of vanished fences, the still remaining stretches of earlier paths, now not going anywhere, the flat limestone slabs that had formed doorsteps or patios. And, from these, he formed within his mind the profiles of the families that had lived here for a time, perhaps attracted to it even as he found himself attracted to it, and who, in the end, had fled. He tested the wind and the highness, the antiseptic ancientness and tried to find within them the element of horror that might have brought about their fleeing. But he found no horror; all he found was a rough sort of serenity.

He thought again of the old lady in the rocking chair that day he had sat with her at tea in an old New England house, eating thin-sliced bread and butter. She was touched, of course. She had to be. There was no earthly reason she should want to know so desperately the details of the family line.

He had told her nothing of his investigations. He had reported every now and then by very formal letters to let her know he was still working on the project. But she would not know the story of the Parkers until he had put the manuscript into her claw-like hands. She would find some surprises, he was sure. No horse thieves, no gallows birds, but there had been others she could not have guessed and in whom she could take no pride. If it was pride that she was seeking. He was not sure it was. There had been the medicine-show Parker of the early nineteenth century who had been run out of many towns because of his arrogance and the inferiority of his product. There had been a renegade slave trader in the middle of the century, the barber in an Ohio town who had run off with the wife of the Baptist minister, the desperado who had died in a hail of withering gunfire in a Western cattle town. Perhaps, he thought, Aunt Elsie might like the desperado. A strange tribe, this branch of the Parkers, ending with the man who had drilled a well that could have loosed upon the country-side the spawn of ancient evil. And stopped himself at that. You do not know it for a fact, he sternly told himself. You don't even have the smallest ground for the slightest speculation. You're letting this place get to you.

The sun was setting when he came back down the track, turning off to go down to the camper parked beside the spring. He had spent the day upon the ridge and he would not spend another. Tomorrow he would leave. There was no reason for staying longer. There might be something here that needed finding, but nothing he could find.

He was hungry, for he had not eaten since breakfast. The fire was dead and he rekindled it, cooked a meal and ate it as the early autumn dusk crept in. Tired from his day of tramping, he still felt no need of sleep. He sat in the camp chair and listened to the night close down. The eastern sky flushed with the rising moon and down in the hills that rose above the river valley a couple of owls chortled back and forth.

Finally, he rose from the chair and went into the camper to get the bottle. There was some whiskey left and he might as well finish it off. Tomorrow, if he wished, he could buy another. In the camper, he lit the lantern and placed it on the desk. In the light of the lantern, he saw the gizzard stone, where he had left it on the desk top the night before. He picked it up and turned it until he could see the faint inscription on it. He bent forward to try to study the faint line, wondering if he might have mistaken some small imperfection in the stone as writing, feeling a nagging doubt as to the validity of his examination of it the night before. But the cryptic symbols still were there. They were not the sort of tracery that could occur naturally. Was there anyone on earth, he wondered, who could decipher the message on the stone? And even asking it, he doubted it. Whatever the characters might be, they had been graven millions of years before the first thing even faintly resembling man had walked upon the earth. He dropped the stone in his jacket pocket, found the bottle, and went out to the fire.

There was an uneasiness in him, an uneasiness that seemed to hang in the very air. Which was strange, because he had not noted the uneasiness when he had left the fire to go into the camper. It was something that had come in that small space of time he'd spent inside the camper. He studied the darkening terrain carefully, and there was movement out beyond the campfire circle, but it was, he decided, only the movement of trees shaken by the wind. For in the short time since early evening, the wind had shifted to the north and was blowing up a gale.

The leaves of the huge cottonwood under which the camper sat were singing, that eerie kind of song that leaves sing in a heavy wind. From the ridge above came the banging clatter of the windmill—and something else as well. A whistle. The well was whistling. He heard the whistle only at intervals, but as he listened more attentively to catch the sound of it, it became louder and consistent, a high, unbroken whistling that had no break or rhythm, going on and on.

Now there was movement, he was certain, beyond the campfire light that could not be accounted for by the thrashing of the trees. There were heavy thumpings and bumpings, as if great ungainly bodies were moving in the dark. He leaped from the chair and stood rigid in the flickering firelight. The bottle slipped from his fingers and he did not stoop to pick it up. He felt the panic rising in him and even as he tried to brush it off, his nerves and muscles tightened involuntarily in an atavistic fear—fear of the unknown, of the bumping in the dark, of the uncanny whistling of the well. He yelled, not at what might be out beyond the campfire, but at himself, what remained of logic, what remained of mind raging at the terrible fear that had gripped his body. Then the logic and the mind succumbed to the fear and, in blind panic, he ran for the camper.

He leaped into the cab, slammed himself into the seat, reached out for the starting key. At the first turn of the key, the motor exploded into life. When he turned on the headlights, he seemed to see the bumping, humping shapes, although even in the light he could not be sure. They were, if they were there at all, no more than heavier shadows among all the other shadows.

Sobbing in haste, he put the engine into gear, backed the camper up the slope and in a semicircle. Then, with it headed up the slope, he pushed the gear to forward. The four-wheel drive responded and, slowly gathering speed, the camper went charging up the hill toward the track down which he had come, past the thumping windmill, only hours before.

The spidery structure of the windmill stood stark against the moon-washed sky. The blades of the rotating wheel were splashes of light, catching and shattering the feeble light of the newly risen moon. Over it all rose the shrieking whistle of the well. The farmer, Thomas remembered, had said that the well whistled only when the wind blew from the north.

The camper reached the track, barely visible in the flare of headlights and Thomas jerked the wheel to follow it. The windmill now was a quarter of a mile away, perhaps less than a quarter mile. In less than a minute, he would be past it, running down the ridge, heading for the safety of another world. For this ridge, he told himself, was not of this world. It was a place set apart, a small wedge of geography that did not quite belong. Perhaps, he thought, that had been a part of its special charm, then when one entered here, he shed the sorrows and the worries of the real world. But, to counterbalance that, he also found something more frightening than the real world would conjure up.

Peering through the windshield, it seemed to Thomas that the windmill had somehow altered, had lost some of its starkness, that it had blurred and changed—that, in fact, it had come alive and was engaging in a clumsy sort of dance, although there was a certain flowing smoothness to the clumsiness.

He had lost some of his fear, was marginally less paralyzed with fear than he had been before. For now he was in control, to a certain extent at least, and not hemmed in by horrors from which he could not escape. In a few more seconds, he would be past the windmill, fleeing downwind from the whistle, putting the nightmare all behind him. Putting, more than likely, his imagination all behind him, for the windmill could not be alive, there were no humping shapes . . .

Then he realized that he was wrong. It was not imagination. The windmill was alive. He could see its aliveness more clearly than imagination could have shown it. The structure was festooned and enwrapped by wriggling, climbing shapes, none of which he could see in their entirety, for they were so entangled in their climbing that no one of them could be seen in their entirety. There was about them a drippiness, a loathesomeness, a scaliness that left him gulping in abject terror. And there were, as well, he saw, others of them on the ground surrounding the well, great dark, humped figures that lurched along until they crossed the track.

Instinctively, without any thought at all, he pushed the accelerator to the floorboards and the camper leaped beneath him, heading for the massed bodies. He would crash into them, he thought, and it had been a silly thing to do. He should have tried to go around them. But now it was too late; panic had taken over and there was nothing he could do.

The engine spit and coughed, then slobbered to a halt. The camper rolled forward, came to a staggering stop. Thomas twisted the starter key. The motor turned and coughed. But it would not start. All the dark humps bumped themselves around to look at him. He could see no eyes, but he could feel them looking. Frantically, he cranked the engine. Now it didn't even cough. The damn thing's flooded, said one corner of his mind, the one corner of his mind not flooded by his fear.

He took his hand off the key and sat back. A terrible coldness came upon him—a coldness and a hardness. The fear was gone, the panic gone; all that remained was the coldness and the hardness. He unlatched the door and pushed it open. Deliberately, he stepped down to the ground and moved away from the camper. The windmill, freighted with its monsters, loomed directly overhead. The massed humped shapes blocked the track. Heads, if they were heads, moved back and forth. There was the sense of twitching tails, although he could see no tails. The whistling filled the universe, shrill, insistent, unending. The windmill blades, unhampered by the climbing shapes, clattered in the wind.

Thomas moved forward. "I'm coming through," he said, aloud. "Make way for me. I am coming through." And it seemed to him that as he walked slowly forward, he was walking to a certain beat, to a drum that only he could hear. Startled, he realized that the beat he was walking to was the creaking of that rocking chair in the old New England house.

Illogic said to him, *It's all that you can do. It's the only thing to do. You cannot run, to be pulled down squealing. It's the one thing a man can do.*

He walked slowly, but deliberately, marching to the slow, deliberate creaking of the rocking chair. "Make way," he said. "I am the thing that came after you."

And they seemed to say to him, through the shrill whistling of the well, the clatter of the windmill blades, the creaking of the chair, *Pass, strange one. For you carry with you the talisman we gave our people. You have with you the token of your faith.*

Not my faith, he thought. Not my talisman. That's not the reason you do not dare to touch me. I swallowed no gizzard stone.

But you are brother, they told him, to the one who did.

They parted, pulled aside to clear the track for him, to make way for him. He glanced to neither left nor right, pretending they were not there at all, although he knew they were. He could smell the rancid, swamp-smell of them. He could feel the presence of them. He could feel the reaching out, as if they meant to stroke him, to pet him as one might a dog or cat, but staying the touch before it came upon him.

He walked the track and left them behind, grouped in their humpiness all about the well. He left them deep in time. He left them in another world and headed for his own, striding, still slowly, slow enough so they would not think that he was running from them, but a bit faster than he had before, down the track that bisected Parker's Ridge.

He put his hand into the pocket of the jacket, his fingers gripping the greasy smoothness of the gizzard stone. The creaking of the chair still was in his mind and he still marched to it, although it was growing fainter now.

Brother, he thought, they said brother to me. And indeed I am. All life on earth is brother and sister and each of us can carry, if we wish, the token of our faith.

He said aloud, to that ancient dinosaur that had died so long ago among the tumbled boulders, "Brother, I am glad to know you. I am glad I found you. Glad to carry the token of your faith."

CLIFFORD D. SIMAK, during his fifty-five-year career, produced some of the most iconic science fiction stories ever written. Born in 1904 on a farm in southwestern Wisconsin, Simak got a job at a small-town newspaper in 1929 and eventually became news editor of the *Minneapolis Star-Tribune*, writing fiction in his spare time.

Simak was best known for the book *City*, a reaction to the horrors of World War II, and for his novel *Way Station*. In 1953 *City* was awarded the International Fantasy Award, and in following years, Simak won three Hugo Awards and a Nebula Award. In 1977 he became the third Grand Master of the Science Fiction and Fantasy Writers of America, and before his death in 1988, he was named one of three inaugural winners of the Horror Writers Association's Bram Stoker Award for Lifetime Achievement.

DAVID W. WIXON was a close friend of Clifford D. Simak's. As Simak's health declined, Wixon, already familiar with science fiction publishing, began more and more to handle such things as his friend's business correspondence and contract matters. Named literary executor of the estate after Simak's death, Wixon began a long-term project to secure the rights to all of Simak's stories and find a way to make them available to readers who, given the fifty-five-year span of Simak's writing career, might never have gotten the chance to enjoy all of his short fiction. Along the way, Wixon also read the author's surviving journals and rejected manuscripts, which made him uniquely able to provide Simak's readers with interesting and thought-provoking commentary that sheds new light on the work and thought of a great writer.

THE COMPLETE SHORT FICTION OF CLIFFORD D. SIMAK

FROM OPEN ROAD MEDIA

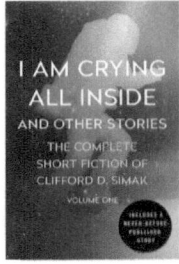

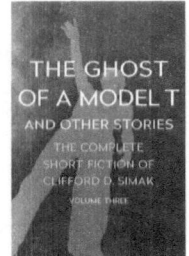

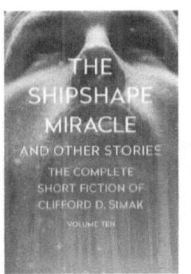

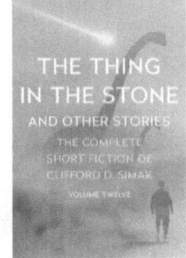

OPEN ROAD

INTEGRATED MEDIA

OPEN ROAD
INTEGRATED MEDIA

Find a full list of our authors and
titles at www.openroadmedia.com

FOLLOW US
@OpenRoadMedia

EARLY BIRD BOOKS

FRESH DEALS, DELIVERED DAILY

Love to read?
Love great sales?

Get fantastic deals on bestselling ebooks delivered to your inbox every day!

Sign up today at
earlybirdbooks.com/book

www.ingramcontent.com/pod-product-compliance
Lightning Source LLC
Chambersburg PA
CBHW030402030726
47497CB00002B/450